WHEN

SHE

WOKE

ALSO BY HILLARY JORDAN

Mudbound

WHEN
SHE
WOKE

A NOVEL BY

Hillary Jordan

ALGONQUIN BOOKS OF CHAPEL HILL   2011

Published by
ALGONQUIN BOOKS OF CHAPEL HILL
Post Office Box 2225
Chapel Hill, North Carolina 27515-2225

a division of
WORKMAN PUBLISHING
225 Varick Street
New York, New York 10014

This is a work of fiction. While, as in all fiction, the literary perceptions
and insights are based on experience, all names, characters, places,
and incidents either are products of the author's imagination or are
used fictitiously.

LIBRARY OF CONGRESS CATALOGING-IN-PUBLICATION DATA
Jordan, Hillary, [date]
    When she woke : a novel / by Hillary Jordan.—1st ed.
      p. cm.
    ISBN 978-1-56512-629-9
    1. Dystopias—Fiction. 2. Political fiction. I. Title.
    PS3610.O6556W47 2011
    813'.6—dc22   2011022799

10 9 8 7 6 5 4 3 2 1
First Edition

This book is for my father

"Truly, friend, and methinks it must gladden your heart, after your troubles and sojourn in the wilderness," said the townsman, "to find yourself, at length, in a land where iniquity is searched out, and punished in the sight of rulers and people."

—NATHANIEL HAWTHORNE, *The Scarlet Letter*

ONE

THE SCAFFOLD

WHEN SHE WOKE, SHE WAS RED. Not flushed, not sunburned, but the solid, declarative red of a stop sign.

She saw her hands first. She held them in front of her eyes, squinting up at them. For a few seconds, shadowed by her eyelashes and backlit by the hard white light emanating from the ceiling, they appeared black. Then her eyes adjusted, and the illusion faded. She examined the backs, the palms. They floated above her, as starkly alien as starfish. She'd known what to expect—she'd seen Reds many times before, of course, on the street and on the vid—but still, she wasn't prepared for the sight of her own changed flesh. For the twenty-six years she'd been alive, her hands had been a honey-toned pink, deepening to golden brown in the summertime. Now, they were the color of newly shed blood.

She felt panic rising, felt her throat constrict and her limbs begin to quiver. She shut her eyes and forced herself to lie still, slowing her breathing and focusing on the steady rise and fall of her belly. A short, sleeveless shift was all that covered her, but she wasn't cold. The temperature in the room was precisely calibrated to keep her comfortable. Punishment was meted out in other ways: in increments of solitude, monotony and, harshest of all, self-reflection, both figurative and literal. She hadn't yet seen the mirrors, but she could feel them shimmering at the edges of her awareness, waiting to show her what she'd become. She could sense the cameras behind the mirrors too, recording her every eyeblink and muscle twitch, and the watchers behind the cameras, the guards, doctors and technicians employed by the state and the millions watching at home, feet propped up on the coffee table, a beer or a soda in one hand, eyes fixed on the vidscreen. She told herself she would give them nothing: no proofs or exceptions for their case studies, no reactions to arouse their scorn or pity. She would sit up, open her eyes, see what was there to be seen and then wait calmly for them to release her. Thirty days was not such a long time.

She took a deep breath and sat up. Mirrors lined all four walls. They reflected back a white floor and ceiling, white sleeping platform and pallet, transparent shower unit, white sink and toilet. And in the midst of all that pristine white, a lurid red blotch that was herself, Hannah Payne. She saw a red face—hers. Red arms and legs—hers. Even the shift she wore was red, though of a less intense shade than her skin.

She wanted to curl into a ball and hide, wanted to scream and beat her fists against the glass until it shattered. But before she could act on any of these impulses, her stomach cramped and she felt a swell of nausea. She rushed to the toilet. She threw up until there was nothing left but bile and leaned weakly on the seat with her arm cushioning her sweaty face. After a few seconds the toilet flushed itself.

Time passed. A tone sounded three times, and a panel on the opposite wall opened, revealing a recess containing a tray of food. Hannah didn't move from her position on the floor; she was too ill to eat. The panel closed, and the tone sounded again, twice this time. There was a brief delay, then the room went dark. It was the most welcome darkness she had ever known. She crawled to the platform and lay down on the pallet. Eventually, she slept.

She dreamed she was at Mustang Island with Becca and their parents. Becca was nine, Hannah seven. They were building a sand castle. Becca shaped the castle while Hannah dug the moat. Her fingers furrowed the sand, moving round and round the rising structure in the center. The deeper she dug, the wetter and denser the sand and the harder it was for her fingers to penetrate it. "That's deep enough," Becca said, but Hannah ignored her sister and kept digging. There was something down there, something she urgently needed to find. Her motions grew frantic. The sand was very wet now and very dark, and her fingers were raw. The moat started to fill with water from below, welling up over her hands to her wrists. She smelled something fetid and realized it wasn't water but blood, dark and viscous with age. She tried to jerk her hands out of the moat, but they were caught on something—no, something was holding them, pulling them down. Her arms disappeared up to the elbows. She screamed for her parents, but the beach was empty apart from herself and Becca. Her face hit the sand castle, collapsing it. "Help me," she begged her sister, but Becca didn't move. She watched impassively as Hannah was pulled under. "Kiss the baby for me," Becca said. "Tell it—" Hannah couldn't hear the rest. Her ears were full of blood.

She started awake, heart tripping. The room was still dark, and her body was cold and wet. *It's just sweat,* she told herself. *Not blood, sweat.* As it dried she began to shiver, and she felt the air around her grow warmer to compensate. She was about to nod off again when the tone sounded twice. The lights came on, blindingly bright. Her second day as a Red had begun.

S HE TRIED TO GO BACK TO sleep, but the white light burned
through her closed lids, through her eyeballs and into her brain.
Even with an arm flung over her eyes, she could still see it, like a
harsh alien sun blazing inside her skull. This was by design, she
knew. The lights inhibited sleep in all but a small percentage of
inmates. Of these, something like ninety percent committed suicide within a month of their release. The message of the numbers
was unambiguous: if you were depressed enough to sleep despite the
lights, you were as good as dead. Hannah couldn't sleep. She didn't
know whether to be relieved or disappointed.

She shifted onto her side. She couldn't feel the microcomputers
embedded in the pallet, but she knew they were there, monitoring
her temperature, pulse rate, blood pressure, respiratory rate, white
blood cell count, serotonin levels. Private information—but there
was no privacy in a Chrome ward.

She needed to use the toilet but held it for as long as possible,
mindful of the cameras. While "acts of personal hygiene" were cen-
sored from public broadcast, she knew the guards and editors still
saw them. Finally, when she could wait no longer, she got up and
peed. The urine came out yellow. There was some comfort in that.

At the sink she found a cup and toothbrush. She opened her
mouth to clean her teeth and was startled by the sight of her tongue.
It was a livid reddish purple, the color of a raspberry popsicle. Only
her eyes were unchanged, still a deep black, surrounded by white.
The virus no longer mutated the pigment of the eyes as it had in the
early days of melachroming. There'd been too many cases of blind-
ness, and that, the courts had decided, constituted cruel and unusual

punishment. Hannah had seen vids of those early Chromes, with their flat neon gazes and disturbingly blank faces. At least she still had her eyes to remind her of who she was: Hannah Elizabeth Payne. Daughter of John and Samantha. Sister of Rebecca. Killer of a child, unnamed. Hannah wondered whether that child would have inherited its father's melancholy brown eyes and sensitive mouth, his high wide brow and translucent skin.

Her own skin felt clammy, and her body smelled sour. She went to the shower unit. A sign on the door read: WATER NONPOTABLE. DO NOT DRINK. Just beneath it was a hook for her shift. She started to take it off but then remembered the watchers and stepped inside still wearing it. She closed the door, and the water came on, blessedly hot. There was a dispenser of soap and she used it, scrubbing her skin hard with her hands. She waited until the walls of the shower steamed up and then lifted up her shift and quickly soaped and rinsed herself underneath. As always, the feel of hair under her arms surprised her, though she should have been used to it by now. She hadn't been allowed a lazor since her arrest. At first, when the hair there and on her legs had begun to grow out, going from stubbly to silky, it had horrified her. Now, the thought of such feminine vanity made her laugh, an ugly sound, loud in the enclosed space of the stall. She was a Red. Her femininity was irrelevant.

She remembered the first time she'd seen a female Chrome, when she was in kindergarten. Then as now, they were comparatively rare, and the vast majority were Yellows serving short sentences for misdemeanors. The woman Hannah had seen was a Blue—an even more uncommon sight, though she was too young then to know it. Child molesters tended not to survive long once they were released. Some committed suicide, but most simply disappeared. Their bodies turned up in dumpsters and rivers, stabbed or shot or strangled. That day, Hannah and her father had been crossing the street, and the woman, swathed in a long, hooded coat and gloves despite the sticky autumn heat, had been crossing in the opposite direction. As she approached, Hannah's father jerked Hannah toward him, and the sudden motion caused the woman to lift her lowered head. Her face was a startling cobalt blue, but it was her eyes that riveted Hannah. They were like shards of basalt, jagged with rage. Hannah shrank away from her, and the woman smiled, baring white teeth planted in ghastly purple gums.

Hannah hadn't quite finished rinsing herself when the water brake activated. The dryjets came on, and warm air whooshed over her. When they cut off, she stepped out of the shower, feeling a little better for being clean.

The tone sounded three times and the food panel opened. Hannah ignored it. But it seemed she wouldn't be allowed to skip another meal, because after a short delay a different tone sounded, this one a needle-sharp, intolerable shriek. She walked quickly to the opening in the wall and removed the tray. The sound stopped.

There were two nutribars, one a speckled brown, the other bright green, as well as a cup of water and a large beige pill. It looked like a vitamin, but she couldn't be sure. She ate the bars, leaving the pill, and returned the tray to the opening. But as she turned away, the shrieking started again. She picked up the pill and swallowed it. The sound stopped and the panel slid shut.

Now what? Hannah thought. She looked despairingly around the featureless cell, wishing for something, anything to distract her from the sight of herself. In the infirmary, just before they'd injected her with the virus, the warden had offered her a Bible, but his pompous, self-righteous manner and disdainful tone had kept her from taking it. That, and her own pride, which had prompted her to say, "I don't want anything from you."

He smirked. "You won't be so high and mighty after a week or two alone in that cell. You'll change your mind, just like they all do."

"You're wrong," she said, thinking, *I'm not like the others.*

"When you do," the warden went on, as if Hannah hadn't spoken, "just ask, and I'll see to it you get one."

"I told you, I won't be asking."

He eyed her speculatively. "I give you six days. Seven, tops. Don't forget to say please."

Now, Hannah kicked herself for not having accepted that Bible. Not because she would find any comfort in its pages—God had clearly abandoned her, and she couldn't blame Him—but because it would have given her something to contemplate besides the red ruin she'd made of her life. She leaned back against the wall and slid down it until her buttocks touched the floor. She hugged her knees and rested her head on top of them, but then saw the pitiful, little-match-girl picture she made in the mirror and straightened up, crossing her legs and folding her hands in her lap. There was no way to tell when she was on. Although the feed from each cell was continuous and the broadcasts were live, they didn't show every inmate all the time, but rather, shuffled among them at the discretion of the editors and producers. Hannah knew she was just one of thousands they had to choose from in the central time zone alone, but from the few times she'd watched the show she also knew that women, especially the attractive ones, tended to get more airtime than men, and Reds and other felons more than Yellows. And if you were one of the really entertaining ones—if you spoke in tongues or had conversations with imaginary people, if you screamed for mercy or had fits or scraped your skin raw trying to get the color off (which was allowed only to a point, and then the punishment tone would sound)—you could be bumped up to the national show. She vowed to present as calm and uninteresting

a picture as possible, if only for her family's sake. They could be watching her at this moment. *He* could be watching.

He hadn't come to the trial, but he'd appeared via vidlink at her sentencing hearing. A holo of his famous face had floated in front of her, larger than life, urging her to cooperate with the prosecutors. "Hannah, as your former pastor, I implore you to comply with the law and speak the name of the man who performed the abortion and any others who played a part."

Hannah couldn't bring herself to look at him. Instead, she watched the attorneys and court officials, spectators and jurors as they listened to him, leaning forward in their seats to catch his every word. She watched her father, who sat hunched in his Sunday suit and hadn't met her eyes since the bailiff had led her into the courtroom. Of course, her mother and sister weren't with him.

"Don't be swayed by mistaken loyalty or pity for your accomplices," the reverend went on. "What can your silence do for them, except encourage them to commit further crimes against the unborn?" His voice, low and rich and roughened by emotion, rolled through the room, commanding the absolute attention of everyone present. "By the grace of God," he said, on a rising note, "you've been granted an open shame, so that you may one day have an open triumph over the wickedness within you. Would you deny your fellow sinners the same bitter but cleansing cup you now drink from? Would you deny it to the father of this child, who lacked the courage to come forward? No, Hannah, better to name them now and take from them the intolerable burden of hiding their guilt for the rest of their lives!"

The judge, jury, and spectators turned to Hannah expectantly. It seemed impossible that she could resist the power of that impassioned appeal. It came, after all, from none other than the Reverend Aidan Dale, former pastor of the twenty-thousand-member

Plano Church of the Ignited Word, founder of the Way, Truth & Life Worldwide Ministry and now, at the unheard-of age of thirty-seven, newly appointed secretary of faith under President Morales. How could Hannah not speak the names? How could anyone?

"No," she said. "I won't."

The spectators let out a collective sigh. Reverend Dale placed his hand on his chest and lowered his head, as though in silent prayer.

"Miss Payne," said the judge, "has your counsel made you aware that by refusing to testify as to the identities of the abortionist and the child's father, you're adding six years to your sentence?"

"Yes," she replied.

"Will the prisoner please rise."

Hannah felt her attorney's hand on her elbow, helping her to stand. Her legs wobbled and her mouth was dry with dread, but she kept her face expressionless.

"Hannah Elizabeth Payne," began the judge.

"Before you sentence her," interrupted Reverend Dale, "may I address the court once more?"

"Go ahead, Reverend."

"I was this woman's pastor. Her soul was in my charge." She looked at him then, meeting his gaze. The pain in his eyes tore at her heart. "That she's sitting before this court today isn't just her fault, but mine as well, for failing to guide her toward righteousness. I've known Hannah Payne for two years. I've seen her devotion to her family, her kindness to those less fortunate, her true faith in God. Though her crime is grave, I believe that through His grace she can be redeemed, and I'll do everything in my power to help her, if you'll show her leniency."

Among the jury, heads nodded and eyes misted. Even the judge's stern countenance softened a bit. Hannah began to have hope. But then he shook his head sharply, as if he were dispelling an enchantment, and said, "I'm sorry, Reverend. The law is absolute in these cases."

The judge turned back to her. "Hannah Elizabeth Payne, having been found guilty of the crime of murder in the second degree, I hereby sentence you to undergo melachroming by the Texas Department of Criminal Justice, to spend thirty days in the Chrome ward of the Crawford State Prison and to remain a Red for a period of sixteen years."

When he banged the gavel she swayed on her feet but didn't fall. Nor did she look at Aidan Dale as the guards led her away.

THE SHOWER BECAME HANNAH'S one pleasure and a crucial intermission during the long, bleak hours between lunch and dinner. She'd learned that lesson on day two, when she'd showered first thing in the morning. The afternoon had crawled by while the silence beat against her eardrums and her thoughts careened between the past and the present. When, desperate for distraction, she tried to take a second shower, nothing came out of the nozzle. She cursed her keepers then, a savage "Damn you!" that would have shocked her younger, more innocent self, the Hannah of just two years ago whose life had revolved around the twin nuclei of her family and the church; who'd lived with her parents, worked as a seamstress for a local bridal salon, gone to services on Sunday mornings and Wednesday nights and Bible study classes twice a week, volunteered at the thrift shop and campaigned for Trinity Party candidates. That Hannah had been a good girl and a good Christian, obedient to her parents' wishes—in almost everything.

Her one secret vice was her dresses: dresses with keyhole necklines and mother-of-pearl buttons, sheer overlays and pencil skirts, made from sumptuous velvets and jewel-toned silks and voiles shot through with gold thread. She designed them herself and sewed them late at night, hiding them under the virginal white mounds of silk, lace and tulle that filled her workroom over the garage. When she finished one, she would double-check to make sure her parents and Becca were asleep and then creep back up to the workroom, lock the door and try it on, doing slow, dreamy pirouettes in front of the mirror. Though she knew it was vain and sinful, she couldn't help taking pleasure in the feel of the fabric and the way the colors warmed her skin. What a contrast to the dull clothing she had to wear outside that room, the demure dresses that her faith dictated, high-necked and calf-length, pastel or tastefully flowered. She wore these things dutifully, understanding their necessity in a world full of temptation, but she hated putting them on in the morning, and no amount of praying on the subject could make her feel differently.

Hannah was well aware of her own rebellious nature. Her parents had scolded her for it all her life while urging her to emulate her sister. Becca was a sunny, obedient child who swam through adolescence and into womanhood with an ease Hannah envied. Becca never struggled to follow God's plan or had any doubts about what it was, never yearned for something indefinably *more*. Hannah tried to be like her sister, but the more she suppressed her true nature, the stronger it burst forth when her resolve weakened, as it inevitably did. During her teens she was always getting into trouble over one thing or another: trying on lip gloss, doing forbidden searches on her port, reading books her parents considered corrupting. Most often though, it was for voicing the questions that cropped up so insistently in her mind: "Why is it immodest for girls not to wear shirts but not for boys?" "Why does God let innocent people suffer?" "If Jesus turned water into wine, why is it wrong for people to drink it?" These questions exasperated her parents, especially her mother, who would make her sit in silence for hours and reflect on her presumption. Good girls, Hannah came to understand, did not ask why. They did not even wonder it in their most private thoughts.

The dresses had saved her, at least temporarily. She'd always had a gift for needlework, and the walls of the Payne house were covered with her samplers, progressing from the simple cross-stitch of her early efforts—JESUS LOVES ME, HONOR THY FATHER AND MOTHER, GIVE SATAN AN INCH AND HE'LL BE A RULER—to elaborately embroidered verses illustrated with lambs, doves and crosses. She'd sewn clothes for her and Becca's dolls, embroidered flowers on her mother's aprons and JWPs on her father's handkerchiefs, using them as peace offerings when she fell from grace. But none of it had been enough to fill her or to silence the questions within her.

And then, when she was eighteen, she happened on the bolt of violet silk buried in the sale bin at the fabric store. From the moment she saw it she wanted to possess it. It shimmered with a deep, mysterious beauty that seemed to call out to her. She ran her fingers across it caressingly and, when her mother's back was turned, leaned down and rubbed its softness against her cheek. Becca hissed, warning her that their mother was coming, and Hannah dropped the fabric, but the voluptuous feel of it lingered on her skin. That night, a violet shape began to form in her mind, indistinct at first, growing sharper the more she imagined it: an evening gown with long sleeves and a high neckline, but with a low, scooped back—a dress with a secret side. From there it was just a short journey to imagining herself wearing it, not on a Paris runway or at a ball in the arms of a handsome prince, but alone, in a plain room with gleaming wood floors and one standing mirror where she could admire it without guilt, seeking to please no one but herself.

She waited a full week before riding her bike back to the shop, telling herself that if the fabric was gone, it was God's will, and she would obey. But not only was the bolt still there, it had been marked down another thirty percent. *So be it,* she thought, without a trace of irony. She was still eight years away from irony.

For six of them, the secret dresses had been enough. She'd made one or at most two a year, spending months on the designs before choosing the fabric and beginning the work. Creating them satisfied something within her that nothing else ever had, assuaging her restlessness and making it easier for her to fill her expected role. Her parents praised her for her newfound obedience and God for having shown her the way to it. Hannah, for her part, felt just as grateful to Him. God *had* shown her the way. With that bolt of violet silk, He'd given her a channel for her passions, one that harmed no one and would sustain her for years to come.

And so it had. Until she'd met Aidan Dale.

Now, sitting against the wall of her cell, waiting for the dinner tone to sound, Hannah thought back to their first meeting on that terrible Fourth of July two years ago. Her father managed a sporting goods store, and he'd had to work that day. He'd been coming home on the train when the suicide bomber blew up himself and seventeen other people. Her father had been at the far end of the car and was badly injured. He had a fractured skull, a perforated eardrum and multiple lacerations from the screws the terrorist had packed around the bomb, but the most worrisome injuries were to his eyes. The doctors said there was a fifty-fifty chance he wouldn't regain his sight.

The day after his surgery, Hannah had returned from the hospital cafeteria with a tray of drinks and sandwiches to find Aidan Dale kneeling with her mother and Becca beside her father's bed, beseeching God to heal his wounds. Hannah had heard him speak countless times before, but sitting in the sixtieth row listening to him on the loudspeakers was poor preparation for the effect of hearing him in person. His voice was so sonorous and compelling, imbued with such faith and passion that it seemed an instrument created for the sole purpose of reaching Him. It traveled through her like hot liquid, warming her and calming her fear. Surely God would not, could not ignore the pleas of that voice.

She set the food down and went to the bed. She'd never been this close to Reverend Dale before, and he looked younger than she'd expected. A curling lock of light brown hair fell onto his brow and nearly into his eye, and she found her fingers itching to smooth it back. Disconcerted—where had that come from?—she knelt across from him. When he looked up and saw her, his prayer faltered briefly, and then he closed his eyes and continued. Hannah bent her head, letting her hair fall forward to hide her confusion.

After he finished, he stood and came around to her side of the bed. For an anxious moment, all she could do was stare at his knees.

"You must be Hannah," he said.

She got to her feet, made herself look at him. Nodded. The compassion in his eyes made her own blur with tears. She mumbled a "Thank you" and looked down at her father, swathed in bandages and riddled by needles and tubes. The shape his body made beneath the sheet seemed too small to be his. All that was visible of him were the top of his head and one forearm, and as she reached down to stroke the patch of exposed skin, it occurred to her that she could be touching a perfect stranger and never even know it. A tear rolled down her cheek and fell onto his arm, and then she felt Reverend Dale's hand come down on her shoulder, a warm and reassuring weight. She had to fight the urge to lean into it, into him.

"I know you're frightened for him, Hannah," he said, and she thought how lovely her name sounded, shaped by his mouth: a poem of two syllables. "But he's not alone. His Father is within him, and Jesus is by his side."

As you are by mine. She was keenly aware of the mere inches that separated them. She could smell his scent, cedar and apples and a faint, sharp trace of raw onion, and feel the heat emanating from his body against her back. She closed her eyes, seized by an unknown sensation, a swoop of want and need and belonging. Was this what people meant, when they spoke of desire?

Her father moaned in his sleep, wrenching her back to reality. How could she be thinking such thoughts while he lay wounded and suffering before her? How could she be thinking them at all?

For Aidan Dale was a married man. He and his wife, Alyssa, had wed in their early twenties, and by all accounts and appearances their union was a happy one. His unfailing tenderness toward her and the rapt, adoring expression she wore when he preached were the cause of much sighing among the female members of the congregation—including Becca, who'd vowed at eighteen never to marry unless she were as deeply in love as the Dales. And yet, they were childless. No one knew why, but it was a subject of constant speculation and prayer at Ignited Word. All agreed there could be no two people better suited to parenthood, or more worthy of its joys, than Aidan and Alyssa Dale. That God had chosen to deny them this greatest of blessings was a mystery and a vivid illustration of His inexplicable will. If the Dales were saddened by it—and how could they not be? and why had they never adopted?—they bore it well, channeling their energies into the church. Still, it didn't go unnoticed that children, particularly those in need, were the special focus of Reverend Dale's ministry. He'd founded shelters and schools in every major city in Texas and funded countless others across the country. He was a regular visitor to the refugee camps in Africa, Indonesia and South America and had worked with the governments of many war-ravaged countries to enable adoption of orphans by American families.

The WTL Ministry brought in millions, but the Dales didn't live in a gated mansion or have an army of servants and bodyguards. Most of what came into the ministry went out again to those in need. Aidan Dale was known and admired the world over as a true man of God, and Hannah had always felt proud to be a member of his congregation. But what she was feeling at this moment—what his nearness and the simple touch of his hand were kindling in her—went far beyond pride and admiration. Sinfully far. *Forgive me, Lord,* she prayed.

Reverend Dale's hand lifted, leaving a cool, empty space on her shoulder, and he went back to stand before her mother. "Is there anything you need, Samantha? Any help at home?"

"No, thank you, Reverend. Between family and friends from church, we have more helping hands and casseroles than we know what to do with."

Gently, he said, "And you're all right for money?"

Hannah saw her mother's face color a little. "Yes, Reverend. We'll be fine."

"Please, call me Aidan." When she hesitated, he said, "I insist." Finally she gave a reluctant nod. Reverend Dale smiled, satisfied that he'd prevailed, and Hannah smiled too, knowing that her mother would sooner take up pot smoking or become a lingerie model than address a pastor, and especially this pastor, by his first name.

Aidan. Hannah tasted it in her mind and thought, *But I could.*

He gave them his private contact information and made them promise to call at any hour if they needed anything at all. When he extended his hand to Hannah's mother, she took it in both of hers, then bent and lay her forehead against it for a few seconds. "God bless you for coming, Reverend. It will mean the world to John to know you were here."

"Well, I—I'm just glad I was in town," he said, reclaiming his hand awkwardly. "I was supposed to be in Mexico this week, but my trip got postponed at the last minute."

"The Lord must love our father a great deal, to have kept you here," Becca said. Like their mother's—and, Hannah supposed, her own—her face was soft with reverence.

Aidan ducked his head like a teenaged boy being praised for how much he'd grown, and Hannah realized, with some astonishment, that he was not only genuinely embarrassed by their adulation but that he also felt himself to be unworthy of it. The swooping sensation came again, stronger this time. How many men in his position would be so humble?

"Yes," Hannah agreed. "He must."

Aidan's port chimed, and he glanced at it with evident relief. "I'd better get back," he said. "Alyssa and I will pray for John, and for all of you."

Alyssa and I. The words clanged in Hannah's head, reminding her that Aidan Dale was another woman's husband, a woman who had a name, Alyssa, and who worried about him the way Hannah's own mother worried about her father. By wanting him, Hannah wronged Aidan's wife as surely as if she lay with him. Shaken and ashamed, she shook his hand, thanked him and said goodbye. That night when she got home, she prayed for a long time, asking God's forgiveness for breaking His commandment and imploring Him to lead her away from temptation.

Instead, He sent Aidan Dale back to the hospital the following day, and the one after that and nearly every day for the next week. Hannah's mother and sister were in raptures over his continued attention to their family. Such an important man, with such a large flock to tend to, and yet here he was, praying with them daily! Hannah's own feelings were a tangle of elation and despair. She knew that God was testing her and that she was failing the test, but how could she not, when it was so cruelly rigged? Aidan (whom she was careful to call Reverend Dale, despite his protestations) brought them light and hope. He made Becca smile and took some of the fear from their mother's eyes. And once their father was off the pain-killers and clearheaded enough to remember what had happened to him, Aidan spoke quietly with him, once for almost two hours, lending him the strength to beat back the terror, rage and helplessness Hannah saw in his face when he thought she wasn't looking.

The morning the bandages were to come off, Aidan arrived early and waited with them for the surgeon. He said a prayer, but Hannah was too anxious to follow it. She stood by the bed and stroked her father's hand, knowing how desperately afraid he must feel at this moment. He'd always prided himself on being the kind of man who could be counted on, a man to whom others looked for advice and support. Dependence would wither his spirit, and the thought of that, of her father being diminished or broken, was almost as unbearable as the thought of losing him.

The surgeon arrived at last, and they all clustered around the bed while he cut off the bandages. The three women stood on one side, the doctor on the other, Aidan at the foot. Hannah's father opened his eyes. They seemed unfocused at first, and then they settled on her mother.

"You look beautiful," he said finally, "but you've gotten awfully skinny." They all erupted then, laughing through the tears as they kissed and hugged him.

"Thank God," Aidan said. The huskiness in his voice made Hannah glance up at him. His expression was grave, and he was looking not at her father but at her.

Then his eyes dropped, and he smiled and said, "Congratulations, John," leaving Hannah to wonder whether she'd imagined the thing she'd seen in them, the swoop of want and need and belonging.

S HE MADE IT TO THE NINTH day before she asked. She hated to do it, but it was either that or become one of the screamers.

"I'd like a Bible," she said, addressing the wall with the food compartment. Then she waited. Lunch came: two nutribars, one pill. No Bible. "Hey," she said to the wall, not quite shouting. "Is anybody listening? I want a Bible. The warden said I could have one if I asked." Reluctantly, she added, "Please."

It arrived with dinner. It was the original King James Version, not the New International Version that Hannah had grown up with. The leather cover was cracked, the pages dog-eared. The New Testament was more worn than the Old, except for Psalms, the pages of which were so tattered and smudged she could barely make out some of the passages. But the verse she sought was all too legible. "But I am a worm, and no man," she whispered. "A reproach of men, and despised of the people. All they that see me laugh me to scorn."

Her mother despised her now, she'd made that plain the one time she visited Hannah in jail, shortly before the trial began. By then Hannah had been incarcerated for three months. Her father had come every Saturday, and Becca whenever she could get away, but Hannah hadn't laid eyes on her mother since the day of her arrest. So when she walked into the visiting room and saw the familiar figure sitting on the other side of the grimy barrier, she started to cry, wrenching sobs of anguish and relief.

"Stop your sniveling," her mother said. "Stop it this instant or I'm walking right back out that door, do you hear?"

The words fell on Hannah like stones. She pushed back her

tears and drew herself up, returning her mother's wintry gaze—the eyes, the face so like her own—without flinching. It struck her that if an artist were to sketch their two silhouettes just then, they'd be mirror images of each other.

Even at fifty and even in a plain beige dress, Samantha Payne was a striking woman. She was tall and full-figured, with a dignified carriage that had led some to call her proud. Her large eyes were black, accented by bold slashes of brow, and her dark hair was no less luxuriant for being threaded with white. Hannah had inherited every bit of this bounty and then some. Over the years, she'd endured many a lecture from her mother on the folly of earthly vanity. She and Becca had sat through them together, but it had been apparent to them both that Hannah was the primary object of these admonishments.

"I'm not here to comfort you," Hannah's mother said now. "I have no more sympathy for you than you had for that innocent baby."

Hannah could hardly breathe against the weight of her mother's words. "Then why did you come?"

"I want to know his name. The name of the man who dishonored you and then sent you off to abort your child."

Hannah shook her head involuntarily, remembering the feel of Aidan's lips on her skin, kissing the inside of her elbow, the tender instep of her foot; of his hands lifting her hair off her neck, raising her arms, pushing her legs open so his mouth could claim every hidden part of her. It hadn't felt like dishonor. It had felt like worship.

"He didn't send me," she said. "It was my decision."

"But he gave you the money."

"No. I paid for it myself."

Her mother frowned. "Where would you get that kind of money?"

"I've been saving it for a while. I . . . I thought I might use it to start my own dress shop someday."

"Dress shop! A store for Jezebels and harlots is more like it. Oh yes, I found all the sinful things you made. I cut them to pieces, every last one of them."

Another brutal, unexpected hail of stones. They hit Hannah hard, rocking her back in her chair. All her creations, destroyed. Though she'd known she could never wear them openly, the mere fact of their existence, of their prodigal beauty, had buoyed her during the long, dreary days of her imprisonment. Now, she would leave nothing that mattered of herself behind.

"Did you make them for *him*?" her mother demanded.

"No. For myself."

"Why do you protect him? He doesn't love you, that much is plain. If he did, he would have married you."

Her mother must have seen something in her face, an unconscious flicker of pain. "He's already married, isn't he."

It wasn't a question, and Hannah made no answer to it.

Her mother held up a forefinger. "You shall not commit adultery." A second finger. "You shall not covet your neighbor's husband." A third. "You shall not murder." The little finger. "Honor your father and mother, so that you may—"

Her anger woke Hannah's own. "Careful, Mama," she said, "you'll run out of fingers." The remark shocked them both. Hannah had never spoken so derisively to her parents, or to anyone for that matter, and for a few seconds she felt better for having done so, stronger and less afraid. But then her mother's shoulders buckled and the flesh of her face seemed to wither, shrinking inward against the bones, and Hannah understood that her sarcasm had broken something in her mother, some fragile hope she'd clung to that the daughter she once knew and loved was not wholly lost to her.

"Sweet Jesus," her mother said, wrapping her arms around herself and rocking back and forth in her chair with her eyes closed. "Sweet Lord, help me now."

"I'm sorry, Mama," Hannah cried. She felt like she was breaking herself, into fragments so small they could never be found, much less pieced together again. "I'm so sorry."

Her mother looked up, her eyes bewildered. "Why did you do this thing, Hannah? Your father and I would have stood by you and the baby. Did you not know that?"

"I knew," Hannah said. Her mother would have stormed, and her father would have brooded. They would have rebuked and sermonized and interrogated and wept and prayed, but in the end, they would have accepted the child. Would have loved it.

"Then I don't understand. Help me to understand, Hannah."

"Because—" *Because I would have been compelled to name Aidan as the father or go to prison for contempt until I did. Because they would have notified the state paternity board, subpoenaed him, had him tested, ordered Ignited Word to garnish his wages for child support. Destroyed his life and his ministry. Because I loved him, more even than our child. And still do.*

Hannah would have done anything at that moment to erase the grief from her mother's face, but she knew that to tell the truth, to speak the syllables of his name, would only hurt her more, by stripping her of her faith in a man she revered. And if she blamed him and decided to reveal their secret . . . No. Hannah had aborted their child to protect him. She would not betray him now.

She shook her head, once. "I can't tell you. I'm sorry." Stones of her own, falling hard and heavy into the space between them. The wall rose in seconds. She watched it happen, watched her mother's face close against her. "Please, Mama—"

Samantha Payne stood. "I don't know you." She turned and walked to the door. Stopped. Looked back at Hannah. "I have one daughter, and her name is Rebecca."

ON THE FOURTEENTH DAY, Hannah was sitting against the wall thumbing listlessly through the New Testament when she felt wetness between her legs. She looked down and saw a bright smear of blood on the white floor. Its arrival unleashed a spate of emotions: Relief, because although the abortionist had assured her that her cycles would resume eventually, she hadn't been able to shake the idea that God would take away her fertility as punishment. Then, swiftly on the heels of that, bitterness. What difference did it make if she was fertile? No decent man would want to marry her now, and even if she found one who did, she couldn't have a child with him; the implant they gave all Chromes would prevent it. Then, despair. By the time she finished her sentence and the implant was removed, she'd be forty-two, assuming she survived that long. Her youth would be gone, her eggs old, her chances of attracting a man to give her children diminished. And finally, embarrassment, as she remembered the presence of the cameras. She felt herself blushing and just as quickly realized that no one could tell—a small blessing.

She stood up, ignoring the blood on the floor, and went to wash herself off. When she came out of the shower, the panel was open. Inside were a box of tampons, a packet of sterile wipes and a clean tunic. Looking at them, she felt a shame so profound she wanted to die rather than endure another moment of it. When she'd been lying on the table with her legs spread and a stranger's hand moving inside her womb, she'd thought that there could be nothing worse, nothing. Now, confronted with these everyday items that represented the absolute and irretrievable loss of her dignity, she knew she'd been wrong.

SHE ALMOST HADN'T gone through with it. She'd taken the pregnancy test at just over six weeks, after her second missed period, and then agonized for another month before screwing up the courage to act. She'd asked a girl she worked with, a salesperson at the bridal salon with whom she was friendly, though not friends. Gabrielle was a self-described wild child with a wicked sense of humor and a sailor's vocabulary that emerged whenever their boss and customers were out of earshot. She had an endless string of boyfriends, often overlapping, and was cheerfully matter-of-fact about her own promiscuity. Her manner had shocked and intimidated Hannah at first, but over time she'd come to appreciate Gabrielle's confidence and self-possession, how utterly comfortable she was in her own skin. Of everyone Hannah knew, Gabrielle was the only person she felt she could approach with this.

The next time she went to the shop for a fitting, Hannah asked Gabrielle if she would meet her for a coffee after work. They'd never socialized before, and the other girl appraised her with unconcealed surprise and curiosity.

"Sure," Gabrielle said finally, "but let's make it a drink."

They'd met at a bar a few blocks away. Gabrielle ordered a beer, Hannah a ginger ale. Her hand shook as she picked up her glass, and she set it back down again. What if Gabrielle decided to turn her in to the police? What if she told their employer? Hannah couldn't risk it. She was trying to think of a pretext for her invitation when Gabrielle said, "You in trouble?"

"Not me," Hannah said. "A friend of mine."

"What kind of trouble?"

Hannah didn't answer. She couldn't speak the words.

Gabrielle looked at the ginger ale, then back at Hannah. "This friend of yours knocked up?"

Hannah nodded, her heart in her mouth.

"And?" Gabrielle said. Watchful, waiting.

"She, she doesn't want to have it."

"Why are you telling me?"

"I thought you might . . . know somebody who could help her."

"And I thought that kind of thing was against your religion."

"My friend can't have this baby, Gabrielle. She *can't*." Hannah's voice broke on the word.

Gabrielle considered her for a long moment. "I might know somebody," she said. "If she's sure. She has to be really sure."

"She is." And Hannah was, at that moment, completely, agonizingly sure. She couldn't bring this baby into this situation, this world she and Aidan lived in. She started to cry.

Gabrielle reached across the table and squeezed Hannah's hand. "It's gonna be okay."

There were several somebodies, actually, each a small exercise in terror for Hannah, but eventually she spoke to a woman who gave her an address, careful instructions on what to do when she got there and the name of the man who would do it, Raphael. It was obviously a pseudonym, and Hannah was jarred by its dissonance. Why would an abortionist name himself after the archangel of healing? When she asked whether Raphael was a real doctor, the woman hung up.

The appointment was at seven in the evening in North Dallas. Hannah took the train to Royal Lane, then a bus to the apartment complex, and arrived early. She stood frozen in the parking lot, staring in dread at the door to number 122. The news vids were full of horror stories about women who'd been raped and robbed by charlatans posing as doctors; women who'd bled to death or died of infection, who'd been anesthetized and had their organs stolen. For the first time, Hannah wondered how much of that was true and how much was fiction disseminated by the state as a deterrent.

The windows of number 122 were dark, but the apartment next to it was lit from within. Hannah couldn't see the occupants, but she could hear them through the open window, a man, a woman and several children. They were having supper. She heard the clink of their glasses, the scrape of their silverware against their plates. The children started to quarrel, their voices rising, and the woman scolded them tiredly. The bickering continued unabated until the man boomed, "That's enough!" There was a brief silence, and then the conversation resumed. The ordinariness of this domestic scene was what made Hannah cross the lot in the end. This she knew she could never have, not with Aidan.

She entered the apartment without knocking and shut the door behind her, leaving it unlocked as she'd been instructed. "Hello?" she whispered. There was no answer. It was pitch black inside and stiflingly hot, but she'd been warned not to open a window or turn on the lights.

"Is anyone there?" No response. Maybe he wasn't coming, she thought, half hopeful and half despairing. She waited in the airless dark for long, anxious minutes, feeling the sweat gradually soak her blouse. She was turning to leave when the door opened and a large man slipped inside, closing it behind him too quickly for Hannah to get a look at his face. The loud crack of the deadbolt sent a surge of alarm through her. She made a wild movement toward the door and felt a hand grip her arm.

"Don't be frightened," he said softly. "I'm Raphael. I'm not going to hurt you."

It was an old man's voice, weary and kind, and the sound of

it reassured her. He let go of her arm, and she heard him move across the room toward the window. A sliver of light from outside appeared as he opened the curtain and peered out at the parking lot. He stood at the window for quite a while, watching. Finally he shut the curtain and said, "Come this way."

A beam of light appeared, and she followed it through the living room, down a short hallway and into a bedroom. She hesitated on the threshold.

"Come in," Raphael said. "It's all right." Hannah entered the room and heard him close the door behind her. "Lights on," he said.

Raphael, she saw then, didn't look like a Raphael. He was over-weight and unimposing, with stooped shoulders and an air of ab-sentminded dishevelment. She guessed him to be in his mid-sixties. His wide, fleshy face was red-cheeked and curiously flat, and his eyes were round and hooded. Tufts of frizzled gray hair poked out from either side of an otherwise bald head. He reminded Hannah of pictures she'd seen of owls.

He held out his hand, and she shook it automatically. Just as if, she thought, they were meeting after church. *Wonderful sermon, wasn't it, Hannah? Oh yes, Raphael, very inspiring.*

The room was empty except for two folding chairs, a large ta-ble and an ancient-looking box fan, which sputtered to life when Raphael turned it on. Heavy black fabric covered the one window. Hannah stood uncertainly while he opened a duffel bag on the floor, removed a bed sheet from it and spread it on the table. It was patterned incongruously with colorful cartoon dinosaurs. They jogged her back to her ninth birthday, when her parents had taken her to the Creation Museum in Waco. There'd been an exhibit de-picting dinosaurs in the Garden of Eden and another showing how Noah had fit them onto the ark along with the giraffes, penguins, cows and so forth. Hannah had asked why the Tyrannosaurus rexes hadn't eaten the other animals, or Adam and Eve, or Noah and his family.

"Well," said her mother, "before Adam and Eve were cast out of Paradise, there was no death, and humans and animals were all vegetarians."

"But Noah lived *after* the fall," Hannah pointed out.

Her mother looked at her father. "He was a smart guy," her father said. "He only took baby dinosaurs on the ark."

"Duh," Becca said, giving Hannah's arm a hard pinch. "Everybody knows that."

Becca was Hannah's barometer for her parents' displeasure; the pinch meant she was on dangerous ground. Still, it didn't add up, and she hated it when things didn't add up. "But how come—"

"Stop asking so many questions," her mother snapped.

Raphael interrupted Hannah's reverie. "Sorry about the sheets. I get them from the clearance bin, and this was all they had. They're clean, though. I washed them myself."

He opened a medicine bag, fished out a pair of rubber gloves and put them on, then began removing medical instruments from the bag and placing them on the table. Hannah looked away from their ominous silver glint, feeling suddenly woozy.

He gestured at one of the chairs. "Why don't you sit down."

She'd expected to have to get undressed right away, but when he'd finished his preparations, he drew up the other chair and started asking her questions: How old was she? Had she ever had children? Other abortions? When was her last period? When had her morning sickness started? Had she ever had any serious medical problems? Any sexually transmitted infections? Mortified, Hannah looked down at her hands and mumbled the answers.

"Have you done anything else to try to terminate this pregnancy?" Raphael asked.

She nodded. "I got some pills two weeks ago and, you know, inserted them. But they didn't work." She'd paid five hundred dollars for them and followed the instructions she was given carefully, but nothing had happened.

"They must have been counterfeits. About half the stuff out there is. No telling what you're getting." Raphael paused. Said, "Look at me, child."

Hannah met his gaze, expecting judgment and finding, to her surprise, compassion instead. "Are you sure you want to terminate this pregnancy?"

There was that phrase again: not *murder your unborn baby* or *destroy an innocent life,* but *terminate this pregnancy.* How straightforward that made it sound, how unremarkable. Raphael was studying her face. This close to him, she could see the network of tiny broken blood vessels radiating across his cheeks.

"Yes," she said. "I'm sure."

"Would you like me to explain the procedure?"

Part of her wanted to say no, but she'd decided before she came that she would not hide from herself the truth of what she was doing here today. She owed it that much, the small scrap of life that would never be her child. She hadn't dared research the procedure on the net; the Texas Internet Authority closely monitored searches of certain words and topics, and abortion was at the top of the list. "Yes, please."

Raphael pulled a small flask from his pocket, unscrewed the lid and took a drink—to steady his hands, he said—and then described what he was about to do. His matter-of-fact tone and the clinical terms he used, "speculum" and "dilators" and "pregnancy tissue," made it sound tidy and impersonal. Finally he asked Hannah if she had any questions. She had already asked and answered the most important ones in her own mind: whether this was murder (yes), whether she would go to hell for it (yes), whether she had any other choice (no). All but one, and it had tormented her ever since she'd decided to do this. She asked it now, her nails digging into the underside of the chair.

"Will it feel any pain?"

Raphael shook his head. "Based on what you've told me, you're only about twelve weeks pregnant. It's never been proven when fetal pain reception starts, but I can tell you for a fact that it's impossible before the twentieth week." Her shoulders slumped in relief, and Raphael added, "It'll be painful for you, though. The cramping can be severe."

"I don't care about that." Hannah wanted it to hurt. It seemed unconscionable to her, to take a life and not feel pain.

Raphael stood and had another swig from his flask. "Go ahead and undress now," he said. "Just from the waist down. Then lie on the table with your head at this end. You can use the extra sheet there to cover yourself."

He went into the adjoining bathroom, closing the door to give her privacy—this man who was about to peer between her spread legs. Hannah was grateful nonetheless for his discretion. She folded her skirt neatly, laid it on the chair and then tucked her panties beneath it, another gesture of decorum she knew to be ludicrous under the circumstances but couldn't help making. Being naked from the waist down made her feel dirtier somehow than if she were completely nude. Hurriedly, she got on the table and covered herself. Forced herself to say, "I'm ready."

THE PUNISHMENT TONE sounded, jerking her back into her cell, back into her bleeding body. *It all comes down to blood,* she thought, as she took the tampons and the wipes from the compartment and used them. *Blood that comes out of you and blood that doesn't.* Mechanically, she cleaned the floor, flushed the stained wipes, washed her hands and changed her tunic, making no attempt to shield her nakedness. *And when it doesn't, when you wait and pray and wait some more and still it doesn't come . . .* She lay down on her side on the sleeping pallet, wrapped her arms around her knees and wept.

H OW MANY DAYS HAD SHE been here? Twenty-two? Twenty-three? She didn't know, and her ignorance made her anxious. There were gaps of time she couldn't account for, moments when she seemed to wake from a sleep she suspected had never occurred. She came out of these spells sweaty and hoarse, with a mouth full of cotton. Had she been talking to herself out loud? Raving? Revealing something she shouldn't have?

She tried to stave off the spells with reading and pacing, but increasingly she felt too listless for either. Her reflection in the mirror had grown gaunt. She had no appetite, and she'd developed the ability to tune out the punishment tone to the point where it was just a distant, annoying whine, like a mosquito flying past her ear. She'd stopped taking her daily showers and her body smelled of stale sweat, but even this was a matter of indifference to her. Her usual fastidiousness had vanished along with her energy.

When she was lucid, the thing she feared most was that she'd said something to betray Raphael. The police had picked her up in the parking lot after a call from a suspicious neighbor, but Raphael had been long gone by that point, and as far as she knew they'd never caught him. She'd given them a false description, waiting until the third time they interrogated her before pretending to break and describing a slender, blond man in his thirties with an Earth First symbol tattooed on his right wrist. What Hannah didn't know was that the neighbors had seen a heavyset older man leave the apartment. Once the police caught her lying, they were merciless. They questioned her repeatedly, sometimes harshly, other times with an unctuous concern for her welfare that a first grader

could have seen through. She stuck to her story, against her lawyer's advice and despite her father's entreaties. She would not betray
Raphael, with his earnest handshake and sad eyes.

She could have, though. He'd certainly told her enough about
himself for the police to identify him. When he'd finished and
was cleaning up, and Hannah was still woozy from the painkillers,
she'd asked him why he did it. What she meant but didn't say was,
How can you bear to do it? By that point, Raphael had had more
sips from the flask and was in a talkative mood. He told her he'd
been an OB/GYN in Salt Lake City when the superclap pandemic
broke out (the crude slang term discomfited her; in her world, it
was always referred to as "the Great Scourge"), and Utah became
the nexus of the conservative backlash ("the Rectification") that
led to the overturning of *Roe v. Wade.* The decision had been cause
for celebration in the Payne household, but Raphael spoke of it
with anger, and of the Sanctity of Life laws Utah had passed soon
afterward, with outrage. Even more abhorrent to him than the lack
of exceptions for rape, incest or the mother's health was the abroga-
tion of doctor-patient privilege. Legally, he was bound to notify the
police if he found evidence that a patient had had a recent abortion; morally, he felt bound not to. Morality won. When he got
caught falsifying the results of pelvic examinations, the state took
away his medical license, and he left Salt Lake City for Dallas.

Hannah had been eleven when Texas passed its own version of
the SOL laws. Not many doctors had openly protested, but the
ones who had were vociferous. She could still remember their impassioned testimony before the legislature and their angry response
when the laws, which were almost identical to Utah's, inevitably
won passage. Most of the objectors had left Texas in protest, and
their like-minded colleagues in the other forty states that eventually passed similar statutes had followed suit. "Good riddance

to them. California and New York can have them," her mother had said, and Hannah had felt much the same. How could anyone sworn to preserve life condone the taking of it or seek to protect those who'd taken it, especially when the future of the human race was at stake? That was the third year of the scourge, and though no one close to Hannah had caught it, they were all infected by the fear and desperation that gripped the world as increasing numbers of women became sterile and birthrates plummeted. The prejudicial nature of the disease—men were carriers, but they had few if any symptoms or complications—hindered efforts to detect and contain it. In the fourth year of the pandemic, Hannah, along with every other American between the ages of twelve and sixty-five, went in for the first of many mandatory biannual screenings, and by the time the cure was found in the seventh year, there'd been talk of quarantining and compulsory harvesting of the eggs of healthy young women, measures that Congress almost certainly would have passed had the superbiotics come any later. As distressing as the prospect had been, Hannah was well aware that if she lived in a country like China or India, she would have already been forcibly inseminated. Humanity's survival demanded sacrifices of everyone, moral as well as physical. Not even her parents had objected when the president suspended melachroming for misdemeanor offenses and pardoned all Yellows under the age of forty, ordering that their chroming be reversed and their birth control implants removed. And when he'd authorized the death penalty for kidnapping a child, Hannah's parents had supported the decision, though it went against their faith. Child-snatching had become so endemic that wealthy and even middle-class families with young children traveled with bodyguards. Hannah and Becca were too old to be targets, but their mother still glared at any woman whose eyes rested on them too hungrily or for too long. "Remember this, girls," she'd say when they encountered one of the childless women who loitered like forlorn ghosts around playgrounds and parks, in toy stores and museums. "This is what comes of sex outside of marriage."

And this, Hannah thought now, studying her red reflection in the mirror. She'd been so certain of everything in those days: that she'd never have premarital sex, never be one of those sad women, never, ever have an abortion. She, Hannah, was incapable of such terrible wrongdoing.

It still surprised her that Raphael hadn't seen it as such. In his mind, it was the SOL laws that were wrong, and those who espoused them who were guilty of a crime. His deepest contempt was reserved for other doctors: not just those who'd supported and enforced the laws, but also those who'd remained mute out of fear. When Hannah asked him why he'd stayed in Texas instead of going to one of the pro-Roe states, he shook his head and took a swig from the flask. "I suppose I should have, but I was young and hotheaded, saw myself as a revolutionary. I let them talk me into staying here."

"Who?"

Raphael froze momentarily and then turned away from her, visibly agitated. "Her, I mean, my wife—that's what I meant to say. She's from here. She wanted to be near her sister, they're very close." He fumbled to close his bag, and Hannah didn't need to see the bare fourth finger of his left hand to know he was lying.

She felt a dull cramping sensation in her abdomen and clutched it involuntarily.

"You can expect quite a bit of cramping and bleeding for the next several days," Raphael said. "Take Tylenol for the pain, not ibuprofen or aspirin. And stay off your feet as much as you can."

He went to the door and paused with his hand on the knob. "The money. Did you bring it?"

"Oh. Yes. Sorry." Hannah looked in her purse, took out the cash card she'd bought that morning and handed it to him. He thrust it into his pocket without even checking the amount.

"Lights off," he said. The room went black. Hannah heard him open the door and exhale loudly, with what sounded like relief. "Wait ten minutes, then you can leave."

"Raphael?"

"What?" he said, impatient now.

"Is that how you think of yourself? As a healer?"

He didn't answer right away, and Hannah wondered if she'd offended him. "Yes, most of the time," he said finally. She heard his footsteps crossing the apartment, the bolt being turned, the front door closing behind him.

"Thank you," she said, into the empty dark.

THE CELL WENT suddenly dark, disorienting her. Had the tones sounded? She hadn't heard them. She groped her way to the platform and lay down on her back, lost in memory. Raphael had been so gentle with her, so compassionate. So different from the police doctor who'd examined her the night of her arrest. A woman only a little older than Hannah, with cold hands and colder eyes, who'd probed her body with brutal efficiency while she lay splayed open with her ankles cuffed to the stirrups. When she winced, the woman said, "Move again, and I'll call the guard to hold you down." Hannah went rigid. The guard was young and male, and he'd muttered something to her as the policeman led her past him into the examination room. She'd heard the word *cunt*; the rest was mercifully unintelligible. She clenched her teeth and lay unmoving for the rest of the exam, though the pain was fierce.

Pain. Something sharp jabbed her in the arm, and she cried out and opened her eyes. Two glowing white shapes hovered above her. *Angels,* she thought dreamily. *Raphael and one other, maybe Michael.* They spun around her, slowly at first and then faster, blurring together. Their immense white wings buffeted her up into heaven.

WHEN THE LIGHTS CAME ON, Hannah's lids opened with reluctance. She felt thick-headed, like her skull was stuffed with wadding. She pushed herself to a sitting position and noticed a slight soreness in her left wrist. There was a puncture mark on the underside, surrounded by a small purple circle. She studied herself in the mirror, seeing other subtle changes. Her face was a little fuller, the cheekbones less pronounced. She'd put on weight, maybe a couple of pounds, and although she was still groggy, her lethargy was gone. She dug through her memories, unearthed the two white figures she'd seen. They must have sedated her and fed her intravenously.

Something about the cell felt different too, but she couldn't put her finger on what. Everything looked exactly the same. And then she heard it: a high-pitched, droning buzz coming from behind her. She turned and spied a fly crawling up one of the mirrored walls. For the first time in twenty-some-odd days, she wasn't alone. She waved her arm and the fly buzzed off, zipping around the room. When it settled she waved her arm at it again, for the sheer pleasure of seeing it move.

Hannah paced the cell, feeling restless. How long had she been unconscious? And how much longer before they released her? She hadn't allowed herself to think beyond these thirty days. The future was a yawning blank, unimaginable. All she knew was that the mirrored wall would soon slide open, and she'd walk out of this cell and follow the waiting guard to a processing area where she'd be given her clothes and allowed to change. They'd take her picture and issue her a new National Identification Card sporting her new red likeness, transfer the princely sum of three hundred dollars to her bank account and go over the terms of her sentence, most of which she already knew: no leaving the state of Texas; no going anywhere without her NIC on her person; no purchasing of firearms; renewal shots every four months at a federal Chrome center. Then they'd escort her to the gate she came in by and open it to the outside world.

The prospect of crossing that threshold filled her with both longing and trepidation. She'd be free—but to go where and do what? She couldn't go home, that much was certain; her mother would never allow it. Would her father be there to pick her up? Where would she live? How would she survive the next week? The next sixteen years?

A plan, she thought, forcing down her growing panic, *I need a plan.* The most urgent question was where she'd live. It was notoriously difficult for Chromes to find housing outside the ghettos where they clustered. Dallas had three Chromevilles that Hannah knew of, one in West Dallas, one in South Dallas and a third, known as Chromewood, in what used to be the Lakewood area. The first two had already been ghettos when they were chromatized, but Lakewood had once been a respectable middle-class neighborhood. Like its counterparts in Houston, Chicago, New York and other cities, its transformation had begun with just a handful of Chromes who'd happened to own houses or apartments in the same immediate area. When their law-abiding neighbors tried to force them out, they banded together and resisted, holding out long enough that the neighbors decided to leave instead, first in ones and twos and then in droves as property values went into a free fall. Hannah's aunt Jo and uncle Doug had been among those who'd held out too long, and they'd ended up selling to a Chrome for a third of what the house had been worth. Uncle

Doug had died of a heart attack soon afterward. Aunt Jo always said the Chromes had killed him.

Hannah quailed at the thought of living in such a place, surrounded by drug dealers, thieves and rapists. But where else could she go? Becca's house was out too. Her husband, Cole, had forbidden her to see or speak to Hannah ever again (though Becca had violated this prohibition several times already, when she'd visited Hannah in jail).

As always, the thought of her brother-in-law made Hannah's mood darken. Cole Crenshaw was a swaggering bull of a man with an aw-shucks grin that turned flat and mean when he didn't get his way. He was a mortgage broker, originally from El Paso, partial to Western wear. Becca had met him at church two years ago, a few months before their father was injured. Their parents had approved of him—Becca wouldn't have continued seeing him if they hadn't—but Hannah had had misgivings from early on.

They surfaced the first time he came to supper. Hannah had met Cole on several occasions but had never spoken with him at length and was eager to get to know him better. Though he and Becca had only been dating about six weeks, she was already more infatuated than Hannah had ever seen her.

He was charming enough at first and full of compliments: for Becca's dress, Hannah's needlework, their mother's spinach dip, their father's good fortune in having three such lovely ladies to look after him. They were having hors d'oeuvres in the den. The vid was on in the background, and when breaking news footage of a shooting at a local community college came on, they turned up the volume to watch. The gunman, who'd been a student there, had shot his professor and eight of his classmates one at a time, posing questions to them about the Book of Mormon and executing the ones who answered incorrectly with a single shot to the head. When he'd finished quizzing every member of the class, he'd walked out of the building with his hands up and surrendered to the police. The expression on his face as they shoved him into the back of a squad car was eerily peaceful.

"Those poor people," Hannah's mother said. "What a way to die."

Cole shook his head in disgust. "Nine innocent people murdered, and that animal gets to live."

"Well," Hannah's father said, "he won't have much of a life in a federal prison."

"However much he has is too much, as far as I'm concerned," said Cole. "I'll never understand why we got rid of the death penalty."

Becca's eyes widened, reflecting Hannah's own dismay, and their parents exchanged a troubled glance. The Paynes were against capital punishment, as was Reverend Dale, but the issue was a divisive one within both the church and the Trinity Party. Soon after he'd been made senior pastor at Ignited Word, Reverend Dale had come out in support of the Trinitarian congressional caucus that cast the deciding votes to abolish the death penalty over the vehement objections of their fellow evangelicals. Hundreds of people had quit the church over it, and Hannah's best friend's parents had forbidden their daughter to associate with her anymore. The controversy had died down eventually, but Hannah's friend had never spoken to her again, and eight years later, the subject was still a sensitive one for many people.

The silence in the den grew awkward. Cole's eyes skimmed over their faces before settling on Becca's. "So, you agree with Reverend Dale," he said.

"'Vengeance is mine, saith the Lord,'" said Hannah's father.

"We believe that only God can give life, and only He has the right to take it."

"Innocent life, yes, but murder's different," Cole said. "It says so right in the Bible. 'Whoever sheds the blood of man, by man shall his blood be shed.'" He hadn't taken his eyes off Becca. Hannah could feel the force of his will pressing against her sister.

Becca hesitated, looking uncertainly from Cole to their father. "Genesis *does* say that," she said. "And so does Leviticus."

"Leviticus also says people should be stoned to death for cursing," Hannah said. "Do you believe that too?"

"Hannah!" her mother rebuked. "Do I have to remind you that Cole is a guest in our house?"

"I was speaking to Becca."

"That's no way to talk to your sister either," Hannah's father said, in his most disappointed tone. Cole's eyes and mouth were hard, but Becca's expression was more stricken than angry.

Hannah sighed. "You're right. I'm sorry, Becca, Cole."

Becca nodded acceptance and turned to Cole. The naked hopefulness with which she looked at him told Hannah this was no mere infatuation. Her sister couldn't bear conflict among those she loved.

"No, it's my fault," Cole said, addressing Hannah's parents. His face turned rueful, but his eyes, she noted, were a few beats behind. "I never should have brought the subject up in the first place. My mama always said, 'When in doubt, stick to the weather,' and Lord knows my daddy tried his best to beat it into me, but my tongue still gets the better of my manners sometimes. I apologize."

Becca beamed and shot Hannah a look: *See? Isn't he wonderful?*

Hannah made her lips curve in answer. She did see, and she could only hope that she was wrong. Or if she was right, that Becca would see it too.

But Becca's feelings for Cole only grew stronger, and Hannah's qualms deeper, especially after their father was injured. He was in the hospital for ten days and incapacitated for another month after that, and his absence left a void into which Cole stepped eagerly. He became the unofficial Man of the House, always there to fix the leaky sink, oil the rusty hinges, dispense advice and opinions. Becca was delighted and their mother grateful, but Cole's ever-presence in the house put Hannah's back up.

More than anything, she disliked his high-handedness with Becca. Their parents had a traditional marriage, following the Epistles: a woman looked to her husband as the church looked to God. John Payne was the unquestioned authority of the family and their spiritual shepherd. Even so, he consulted their mother's opinion in all things, and while he didn't always follow her counsel, he had a deep respect for her and for the role she played as helpmeet and mother.

Cole's attitude toward Becca was different, with troubling overtones of condescension. Becca had never been strong-willed, but the longer she was with him, the fewer opinions she had that weren't provided by him. "Cole says" became her constant refrain. She stopped wearing green, because "Cole says it makes my skin look sallow," and reading fiction, because "Cole says it pollutes the mind with nonsense." She gave up her part-time job as a teaching aide because "Cole says a woman's place is with her family."

Hannah kept her growing aversion to herself, hoping that Becca's ardor would cool once their father was well again, or failing that, that he would discern Cole's true character and dissuade her sister from marrying him. In the meantime, Hannah did her best to be cordial to him and was careful not to challenge him openly or express her doubts to Becca. Confrontation was not the way to defeat him; better to bide her time and let him defeat himself.

But she'd overestimated both her skill as an actress and her forbearance, as she discovered on Becca's birthday. Their father had been home for two weeks, but he still wasn't strong, so they kept the party to the immediate family—and Cole, of course. Hannah made Becca a dress out of soft lavender wool, and their parents bought her a small pair of opal earrings to match the cross they'd given her the year before.

"Oh, how beautiful!" she exclaimed when she opened the velvet box.

"Let's see them on you," their father said.

Becca froze, and her eyes darted guiltily to Cole.

"Go on, Becca," Hannah urged. "Try them on."

Looking trapped and miserable, Becca put on the earrings.

"They look lovely on you," their mother said.

"Yes, they do," Hannah agreed. "Don't you think so, Cole?"

He gazed at Becca for long seconds, his expression unreadable. "Personally I don't think Becca needs any adornment to look pretty," he said, with a tight smile. "But yeah, they're very nice."

After he left, Hannah cornered her sister in the kitchen. "What was that all about?"

Becca shrugged uncomfortably. "Cole says the only jewelry a woman should wear besides a cross is a wedding ring."

Hannah's antipathy toward him crystallized in that moment. Even more than his opinions, she disliked their absoluteness and the hypocrisy that underlay them. "But it's perfectly fine for him to wear all those big shiny belt buckles and turquoise bolo ties."

"It's different for men," Becca said. "You know that."

It *was* different, and Hannah had been well-schooled in the reasons why. Still, the double standard had always bothered her. And applied to Cole Crenshaw, it was infuriating. "No, I don't. But I'm sure Cole could give me a nice long lecture on the subject."

"I know why you don't like him," Becca said, her tone hard-edged. "You're jealous because I have a man in my life, and you don't."

"Is that what Cole says?"

Becca crossed her arms over her chest. "Don't think he hasn't noticed your coldness to him all these months. It hurts his feelings, and it hurts mine."

"I'm sorry, Becca. I've tried to like him, but—"

"I don't want to hear it," Becca said, turning away. "I love him, and I want to spend my life with him. Can't you just be happy for me?"

And that was that. Becca wed Cole as soon as their father was well enough to walk her down the aisle. Hannah made her sister's wedding dress and stood at her side holding a bouquet of calla lilies while she vowed to love, honor and obey Cole Crenshaw for all eternity. Then Becca was gone. She and Cole lived only a few miles away, but they might as well have moved to Maine. Hannah tried to make nice with him now that he was her brother-in-law, but he wasn't having it; the damage had been done. The sisters saw each other mostly on family occasions, and even then, Cole made sure they had little time alone together. Hannah felt Becca's absence keenly. As different as they were, they'd always been close. Now, Hannah had no one with whom she could share her inner life.

Part of it, she wouldn't have dared share. Though she hadn't seen Aidan Dale in over two months, he was still an insistent presence in her thoughts. As she sewed pearls onto veils and rosettes onto bodices, she remembered his many kindnesses to her family, the fervency of his prayers for her father, the comforting warmth of his hand on her shoulder. Again and again, she relived the moment when she'd looked into his eyes and seen her own feelings reflected there, or thought she had. Two things kept her from dismissing it as a wishful figment: He hadn't come back to the hospital after that day. And Alyssa Dale had.

She'd paid them a visit the very next morning. Hannah and Becca were alone with their father; their mother was home resting. The previous day's excitement and the long, tense buildup to it had left them all spent. Hannah was catnapping in the chair beside her father's bed. She was distantly aware of a murmured conversation taking place between Becca and another woman, but that wasn't what drew her up out of sleep. Rather, it was the prickling sense of being watched. She opened her eyes to find Alyssa Dale standing at the foot of the bed, exactly where Aidan had stood, staring down at her. Disconcerted, Hannah looked around the room, but Becca wasn't there.

"Your sister had a call, and she went outside to take it," Alyssa said softly. "She didn't want to wake your father."

"Oh," Hannah said. She felt slow and stupid. She knew she ought to get up and greet her visitor, but Alyssa's frank, assessing gaze seemed to pin her to the chair. In public Alyssa Dale was the quintessential minister's wife: demure and gracious, pretty without being beautiful enough to cause resentment, dignified without being aloof. Now, for the first time, Hannah perceived the intelligence that inhabited the other woman's mild hazel eyes. Had she missed it because she hadn't expected to see it there, or because Alyssa usually kept it hidden?

"Congratulations on your father's good news. You must be very relieved."

"We are, thank you." Hannah pushed herself to her feet, stretched out her hand. "I'm Hannah."

Alyssa nodded but didn't extend her own. "Yes, my husband has mentioned you. In his prayers."

Hannah let her hand fall to her side. "It's kind of you to have come."

"Aidan told me the Lord worked a miracle yesterday. I wanted to see it for myself."

Alyssa's eyes didn't leave Hannah's. The scrutiny made her want to squirm. "Well," Hannah said, "we're all incredibly grateful for his concern."

"The Lord's or my husband's? People do tend to confuse the two." Alyssa's tone was gently acerbic. "Of course, that's only because they haven't been around him before he's had his morning coffee."

Hannah said nothing, nonplussed by the image that popped into her mind of Aidan in his pajamas, his hair disheveled, his eyes heavy-lidded. Alyssa watched her with a knowing expression that held a hint of warning, and Hannah's cheeks burned as it occurred to her just how many women must have fancied themselves in love with Aidan Dale over the years. She must be one of dozens, hundreds even, who'd fantasized about him. Wished him unmarried to this astute, composed woman.

"Hannah," Becca said in a loud whisper. She stood in the doorway, holding up her port. "Mama wants to talk to you."

Hannah suppressed a sigh of relief. "Please excuse me, Mrs. Dale."

"No, I should be going," Alyssa said. "We're off to Mexico tonight, and South America and California after that, and I'm still not completely packed."

"A long trip, then," Hannah said.

"Three weeks. Long enough." She didn't need to add, *For him to forget you.*

For a while, it seemed he had. Summer gave way to fall, and the temperature finally dropped down into the double digits, and as the first holos of cavorting skeletons and witches on broomsticks began to appear on her neighbors' front lawns, Hannah's memories of Aidan started to lose their definition, taking on the hazy quality of images seen through tulle. If he'd ever had feelings for her—and she was becoming doubtful that he had—he must have since come to his senses, as she herself needed to do. Even to think of being with him, a married man, a man of God, was a grave sin. And so in Bible study, she made a point of sitting next to Will, a shy young man who'd been casting yearning looks her way for weeks, and when he finally got up the courage to ask her out, she accepted.

She'd had two serious boyfriends, one her senior year of high school and the other in her early twenties. They were nice young men, and she'd enjoyed their company and attention, but neither of them had stirred anything deeper in her than affection and a sporadic sexual curiosity she had no intention of exploring, not with them. That wasn't enough. *They* weren't enough.

Nor, she soon realized, was Will, though by every rational measure he ought to have been. He was a veterinarian, sweet, shy, funny in a self-deprecating way. They started dating in mid-October, and by mid-November, when the oak leaves began to drift to the ground in spiky brown curls, she knew that Will was falling along with them, and that she was not. "Please, Hannah, give him a chance," her mother urged, and so she continued to see him. He became ardent, spoke of love, hinted at marriage. She stilled his roving hands and deflected his near-proposals. Finally, when his frustration turned to anger, she cut him loose, bleeding and disoriented, her own heart perfectly intact.

Aidan wouldn't leave it intact, she'd known that from the first. Long before they became lovers, she could foresee that there would be an after, and that it would lay waste to them both.

Still. She hadn't envisioned this: herself a Red, an outcast, while

Aidan went on with his life and his ministry, moved with Alyssa to Washington to take up his new post as secretary of faith, continued to inspire millions by his words and example. Hannah knew he thought of her, missed her, grieved as she did for their lost child. Blamed himself and tormented himself with what-ifs. Probably hated himself for not coming forward.

Still.

She watched the fly buzz busily around the room. When it landed on the floor beside her, she killed it with a vicious smack of her hand.

I AM A RED NOW. It was her first thought of the day, every day, surfacing after a few seconds of fogged, blessed ignorance and sweeping through her like a wave, breaking in her breast with a soundless roar. Hard on its heels came the second wave, crashing into the wreckage left by the first: *He is gone.* The first subsided eventually, settling into a dull ache, but the second assailed her with relentless fury, rolling in every ten, twenty minutes, *gone, gone, gone,* swamping her with fresh grief. The sense of loss never diminished. If anything, it seemed to grow more raw as the day of her release neared. She wondered how her heart could hold so much pain and still continue its measured, insistent thumping.

If only he were here, I could go to him. The notion was absurd, a puerile fantasy, and though she dismissed it at once, its ghost lingered, flitting about at the edges of her thoughts and stirring up memories of the first time she'd gone to him, at the hotel in San Antonio. With them came the inevitable twinge of desire. Even now, after all that had happened, she still felt it.

It had started with a call, a couple of weeks before Christmas. The despondency that had weighed on her like a lead apron during the last weeks with Will had lifted, leaving her more determined than ever not to settle for anything less than a bone-deep love. She'd felt it once, or the beginnings of it; she could and would feel it again. Aidan Dale, she swept forcibly from her mind. She begged God's forgiveness for having desired him and swore to Him and herself that she'd never be so weak again.

Such was her state of mind when the church office called. A part-time coordinator's position had opened up with the First Corinthians ministry. Was Hannah still interested?

For a moment, she was too stunned to answer. She'd applied to work at Ignited Word several years before, but paying positions were rare and highly sought after, and nothing had ever come of it. The First Corinthians ministry, or the 1Cs as it was more familiarly known, was the church's charitable arm, charged with helping the community's neediest and most troubled members. It was also Reverend Dale's pet project. He could often be seen behind the wheel of one of its shiny white vans, delivering food to the poor, driving addicts to rehab and homosexuals to conversion therapy retreats. He'd named it for his favorite Bible verse, 1 Corinthians 13:2, which he often quoted in his sermons and interviews, always using the original King James scripture—"And though I have the gift of prophecy, and understand all mysteries, and all knowledge; and though I have all faith, so that I could remove mountains, but have not *charity,* I am nothing"—as opposed to the NIV version, which replaced the word *charity* with *love.* There are infinite kinds of love, Reverend Dale liked to say, but charity is the purest of them all, because it's the only one that doesn't ask, *What's in it for me?*

Had Aidan put Hannah's name forward for this position? And if he had—and why else would they be calling, after all this time— was it out of kindness, or something else?

"Miss Payne?" the woman said, drawing Hannah back to the conversation. "Would you like to come in for an interview?"

Kindness, Hannah told herself, as she scheduled the appointment. Kindness and nothing more.

She interviewed with the office manager, Mrs. Bunten, a middle-aged woman with a forbidding, deeply lined face that concealed a compassionate and motherly nature. Hannah later learned that the lines had been incised by grief; Mrs. Bunten had lost her husband and two sons in one of the scourge riots and been born again soon afterward. Now, ten years later, Ignited Word was her entire universe, and Reverend Dale was the glorious sun blazing at the center of it. That much was apparent to Hannah from the beginning. Mrs. Bunten spoke fondly enough of God and His Son, but it was when she talked about Aidan that her face took on the glow of true veneration.

The pivotal moment in the interview came when they were discussing Hannah's father's recovery. "A miracle," said Mrs. Bunten.

"Yes," agreed Hannah. "I thank God for it every day. God, and Reverend Dale."

Mrs. Bunten gave her a smile that was positively beatific. "I can see you're going to fit in perfectly here."

The job was twenty hours a week, most of it spent doing clerical work at the ICs office, although Hannah was sometimes asked to serve in the soup kitchen or make deliveries. Her first week, she didn't see Aidan once. But then on Monday of the following week, he walked into the office carrying an unwieldy tower of brightly colored boxes of children's toys. "Ho ho ho," he boomed, slightly out of breath.

Mrs. Bunten hurried to help him. Hannah followed more slowly, caught between eagerness and reluctance.

Mrs. Bunten took the top few boxes, revealing his face. "Thank you, Brenda," he said. Then he saw Hannah. "Oh, Hannah. Hello."

His smile was ingenuous, pleasantly surprised. Kind. Hannah plummeted. "Hello, Reverend Dale."

"Now, Reverend," said Mrs. Bunten, all but clucking as she handed Hannah the boxes and took the rest from him, "you know you shouldn't be carrying all that. Mrs. Dale will be mad at us both if you throw your back out again."

"Alyssa worries too much."

Mrs. Dale. Alyssa. Hannah turned away and set the boxes down. *His wife.*

"How's your father doing?" he asked.

"Daddy's well. He's back at work. His left eye's still a little fuzzy, but we're hopeful it'll heal in time." *Aidan doesn't feel it.*

"I pray it will. Please give my very best to him and your mother."

"I will." *He doesn't feel it, and that's for the best.*

He asked how Hannah was liking it here, and she said very much, thank you. He inquired after Becca and sent congratulations on her marriage. Mrs. Bunten interjected, marveling at how he never forgot a person's name once he'd prayed with them. He protested her tendency to exaggerate his virtues. Hannah made the appropriate responses. She felt numb and foolish.

Aidan's assistant interrupted them, calling to remind him about his four o'clock meeting with Congressman Drabyak. Aidan tapped his forehead ruefully, said he'd better be on his way, welcomed Hannah to the 1Cs and excused himself.

At the door, he turned back. "Brenda, I forgot to tell you, there are a bunch more toys out in the van. They need to be wrapped by tomorrow. I'm taking them to the shelter at three."

"We'll see to it, Reverend," Mrs. Bunten said.

Aidan turned to Hannah. "Would you like to come along? To the shelter? It's wonderful, watching the children's faces light up."

His own held nothing but friendly interest and eagerness—to see the children. Perhaps he hadn't put her name forward after all, not even out of kindness. Perhaps it was God's doing that she was here, a penance for her desire: to see his face and hear his voice and know that he could never be hers.

"I'd love to," she said.

And so it began, their long, tortured mating dance, though it was months before she recognized it as such. She existed in a state of silent longing, punctuated by bursts of guilt and fear that someone would notice. Aidan treated her as he treated everyone, with a pastor's professional warmth.

Hannah had been working at the church for six weeks when Alyssa came into the office with Aidan. She stopped short when she saw Hannah, and Hannah knew he hadn't told her. Because it was too unimportant to mention, or . . . ?

"Hello, Mrs. Dale."

"Hello," Alyssa said. "Becca, isn't it?"

Sensing the ignorance was feigned, Hannah said, "That's my sister. I'm Hannah."

"Hannah joined us just before Christmas," Aidan said. "She's doing a terrific job."

The remark sounded forced and awkward. Hannah smiled uncomfortably.

"Of course she is, darling," said Alyssa. She slipped her arm around Aidan's waist and gave Hannah a wintry smile. "My husband inspires hard work in others. People hate to disappoint him."

Aidan's unease was obvious, and Hannah was all but certain Alyssa had complimented him on purpose, because she knew how he hated being praised. Perhaps their marriage wasn't as idyllic as everyone believed.

"Oh, I'm sure Hannah would do a good job for anyone," he said.

"Well," said Alyssa, "let's not keep her from her work."

The Dales got what they'd come for—the keys to one of the vans—and left. Alyssa preceded Aidan out the door. At the last second he swiveled his head to look back at Hannah, and she had a queer sensation, as if she were pulling it with a string. Their eyes met, held, dropped away at the same time.

So, she thought. *So.*

AFTER THAT THE real torment began. Aidan's behavior toward Hannah was unchanged, but there was a charged quality to their interactions that had been missing before, and she knew she wasn't suffering alone. Their attraction grew slowly, haltingly, unacknowledged but unmistakable. To Hannah it often seemed like a pregnancy during which they were both waiting, with equal degrees of excitement and trepidation, for the inevitable emergence of the new thing they were creating between them. They were rarely alone together, and then, only briefly and by accident—a chance encounter on the stairs, a five-minute span when Mrs. Bunten was in the restroom. Aidan was constantly surrounded by people, all of them wanting something from him: his attention, his blessing, his opinion, the touch of his hand on their shoulders. Hannah grew to resent them all, even as she felt the echo of their hunger in herself.

Most of all, she resented and envied Alyssa Dale. Aidan's wife had become a frequent visitor to the ICs office, pitching in wherever help was needed. Mrs. Bunten commented on it one day, saying how nice it was that Mrs. Dale was taking such an interest in their work. With Hannah, Alyssa was coolly polite and, when Aidan was around, watchful. When it was just the women, she was more relaxed, though she always maintained a certain reserve, an air of apartness. Still, she worked as hard as any of them, was generous with praise and kept them amused with her wry sense of humor. Mrs. Bunten and the other women adored her, and even Hannah began to admire her. It occurred to her more than once that in different circumstances, she and Alyssa Dale might have been friends.

In the meantime, the tension between Hannah and Aidan continued to mount. At times it was so palpable she half expected it to materialize, sinuous and glistening, in the air between them. Every night before bed, she prayed for God's forgiveness. And every night, she lay sleepless and imagined Aidan lying beside her. She knew she should quit the 1Cs and remove herself from the temptation of being around him. She even composed a letter of resignation to Mrs. Bunten, but she couldn't bring herself to say "Send" any more than she could make herself ask God to help her stop loving Aidan.

In June, Hannah turned twenty-five. The morning of her birthday she walked into the office to discover a large potted orchid sitting on her desk. It looked as exotic and out of place in the spartan 1Cs office as a zebra pelt would have, or a Ming vase. The petals were yellow, with crimson splotches, and the plant was draped in a perfect *U*.

"Where did this come from?" she asked Mrs. Bunten. Alyssa, thankfully wasn't present; she'd accompanied Aidan on an extended mission to Africa.

"It was just delivered. Addressed to you."

Flustered, Hannah turned her back to the other woman and pretended to look for a card, knowing there wouldn't be one. When she touched one of the petals with her forefinger, it felt soft and vibrantly alive, like skin.

"You didn't tell us you had an admirer," Mrs. Bunten said in a coy, chiding tone.

"It's from my father," Hannah lied. "He always sends me an orchid on my birthday."

"Oh," said Mrs. Bunten, disappointed. "Well, happy birthday, dear. I'm sure you'll meet someone soon, as pretty as you are."

Hannah couldn't concentrate for the rest of the day. What did it mean, that Aidan had sent her this extravagant, sensual thing? For of course it had come from him; the absence of a card was the proof. Was he surrendering to his feelings at last? Should she? What would happen next?

She had three excruciating weeks to ponder the answers. It was the longest she'd gone without seeing him, and she was edgy and distracted. She comforted—and tormented—herself by watching vids of his preaching, often joined by her parents. At first she was nervous, afraid her face would give her away, but finally she realized that her expression mirrored theirs and those of every member of his audiences. The world loved Aidan Dale.

HE RETURNED ON a Friday, which was one of Hannah's days off, and then there was the weekend to get through. She went to church with her parents on Sunday as always. Aidan's sermon was unusually fervent that day, rousing the congregation to a near frenzy of exaltation. He concluded quietly, with a passage from 1 John: "Beloved, let us love one another, for love is of God; and everyone who loves is born of God and knows God." Though she was sitting too far back for him to see her, Hannah was sure he was speaking to her.

Monday, she wore her dark green dress, the one that always made her mother's brow crinkle because of the way its plain lines accentuated her figure. She spent the day in a state of twitchy anticipation and even stayed an extra half hour, but he didn't appear. She left feeling despondent and confused. He'd never uttered an inappropriate word to her. Never gone out of his way to be alone with her, never touched her. Had she imagined it all then?

The next morning she got a call from the church office: one of the volunteer chaperones for the True Love Waits jamboree in San Antonio this weekend had had to cancel due to a family emergency. Could Hannah take her place?

"Of course," she replied. She knew Aidan was attending; Mrs. Bunten had mentioned it yesterday. Had he suggested Hannah?

She spent a fretful week waiting, oscillating between certainties: he had, he hadn't, he had, he hadn't. Aidan himself was away again, overseeing the opening of a new shelter in Beaumont. Hannah could do nothing but wait: for Friday to arrive at last, for the caravan to reach San Antonio, for her teenaged charges to be checked into the hotel, welcome packets to be handed out, mixups and dramas—"I was supposed to be in *Emily's* room!"—to be sorted, the opening-night fellowship supper to be over. Aidan was supposed to be presiding, but there'd been thunderstorms in East Texas, and his flight had been delayed. The groans of disappointment this news elicited from the twenty-five hundred teens in the room drowned out Hannah's own small sound of frustration.

After supper she paced in her room, waiting for the vid to ring or not, combing over what few facts she had. Fact: the church office had hundreds of volunteers to draw from, but they'd called her, Hannah, just as they'd called her for the interview. Fact: Aidan was coming alone. Alyssa was away for a week, visiting her parents in Houston. Fact: the other volunteers were sleeping two to a room, but Hannah had one to herself. Could it be mere coincidence, that she was the odd woman out?

She was half expecting, half despairing of a call, so when she heard the knock just after eleven, it startled her. It came not from the door to the hallway, but from the one to the adjoining room: three soft raps. Hannah's heart leapt, but she didn't hurry. She proceeded to the door at the stately, measured pace of a bride walking down the aisle.

She took a deep breath, undid the latch and opened the door. Neither of them moved or spoke at first. They just looked at each other, absorbing the fact that they were here, together, alone.

Aidan's fine-boned face was etched with sorrow and longing. Hannah studied it, seeing for the first time that his features, while attractive, were unexceptional, and that what made it so arresting were the contradictions it held: boyishness and sensuality, self-assurance and humility, faith and apprehension, as if of some terrible blow yet to be struck which he alone could foresee.

"I'm not the man you think I am," he said. "I'm a sinner. Weak, faithless."

"You're the man I want," Hannah said. She felt oddly calm now that the moment was here, happening outside of her head. She had no misgivings, just a sense of absolute rightness that she knew could have come only from God.

"I'm the worst sort of hypocrite."

"No, not in this," Hannah said. "This is honest. This is *right*. Don't you feel it?"

"Yes, I feel it," he said, "like I've never felt anything in my life. But your honor, Hannah. Your soul."

She took his hand and brought it to her chest, laying it over her heart, then put her hand over his heart, which was beating in wild contrapuntal percussion to the hard steady cadence of her own. She waited, and finally he pulled her to him and kissed her.

He kept his eyes closed that first time, even when she cried out from the pain of it. At the sound, he grimaced as though he were the one being hurt. She hadn't told him she was a virgin, not out of any desire to hide the fact, but simply because it seemed self-evident. It was for him that she had waited.

"It's all right," she whispered.

He shook his head. "No, it's not." His hips moved faster. His body shuddered. And then he cried out himself, but not in pain.

Now, Hannah closed her own eyes and let herself imagine how it would be to see him again. To lie with her head cradled in the hollow of his shoulder while he stroked her hair and spoke of random things—a dream he'd had the night before, a sermon he was struggling with, an idea he hadn't shared with anyone else. But the fantasy stuttered and halted, just as their conversations all too often had when one of them inadvertently said the wrong word, puncturing the fragile membrane that sheltered them from the outside world. "Home" conjured Alyssa in the bed between them. "Church" raised the specter of discovery and scandal. "Tomorrow" or "next week" led to thoughts of a future together that they could never have.

For there was no question of Aidan's leaving his wife. He'd told Hannah so bluntly that first night, as he was getting dressed. "I can never offer you more than this," he said, waving his hand to encompass the rumpled bed, the generic room. "I love you, but I can never leave Alyssa. I can't bring that kind of shame on her. Do you understand? You and I will never be able to love each other openly."

"I understand."

"You deserve that, with someone," he said. "A husband, a family."

Lying in the damp bed with his scent on her skin and her body aching from their lovemaking, she couldn't imagine being with another man. Even the thought of it was repugnant.

"I don't want anyone else," she told him.

TWO

PENITENCE

SUNLIGHT BOUNCING OFF concrete, glinting on razor wire and steel, bathing her face in warmth. Cool wind buffeting her skin and stirring her hair, vivid blue of sky piercing her eyes. Sounds of cars whizzing past, a snatch of song from a radio, the tweeting of birds, the chirping of locusts, the crunch of two pairs of feet on gravel. The sensory input was dizzying, overwhelming. Hannah stumbled, and the guard walking beside her took hold of her upper arm to steady her. As he did so, his fingers brushed against the outside curve of her breast. Intentionally? She gave him a sidelong glance, but his wide brown face was impassive, and his eyes were staring straight ahead.

They approached a large, windowless building six stories tall: the prison. As they passed beneath its shadow, Hannah felt a chill that had nothing to do with the weather. Only the most violent felons were kept behind bars—first-degree murderers, serial rapists, abortionists and other offenders deemed incorrigible by the state. Most of them served life sentences. Once they went in, they almost never came out.

As they neared the gate, it began to move, sliding into the wall with a mechanical groan.

"You're free to go," the guard told Hannah. She paused on the threshold. "What's the matter, *pajarita,* you afraid to leave the nest?"

Giving no indication that she'd heard him, she squared her shoulders and stepped through the opening, into the world.

She stood in a short driveway leading to a parking lot. She walked to the edge of the drive and scanned the lot, one hand shielding her eyes against the morning sun. There was no movement, no sign of her parents' blue sedan. She fixed her eyes on the entrance, willing the car to appear, telling herself her father was just running late.

"Hey, gal." The voice, a man's, came from behind her. She turned and saw a small booth she hadn't noticed to one side of the gate. A guard was leaning against the doorjamb with his arms folded over his chest. "Guess your friend ain't coming," he said.

"It's my father," Hannah said. "And he'll be here."

"If I had a dollar for every time I heard that, I'd be rich as an A-rab." The guard was tall and skinny, with a smug, pimpled face and a protuberant Adam's apple that bobbed convulsively when he swallowed. He looked like he was about sixteen, though Hannah knew he had to be at least twenty-one to work at a state prison.

She heard the sound of a vehicle. She spun and saw a car pulling into the lot, but it was silver, not blue. Her shoulders slumped. The car stopped, backed up and exited.

"Looks like somebody taken a wrong turn," said the guard. Hannah glanced back at him, wondering if the irony was intended, then decided he was too stupid for that. "What you gonna do if your daddy don't show, huh? Where you gonna go?"

"He'll be here," Hannah said, a little too emphatically.

"You could bunk with me for a while, if you ain't got nowhere else to go. I got a real nice place. Plenty of room for two." His mouth twisted in a half-smile. Hannah felt her skin prickle with aversion as his eyes slithered down her body and back up again. How many other women had he propositioned like this, and how many had been desperate enough to take him up on it? Deliberately, she turned her back on him.

"I'm just trying to be friendly," said the guard. "I think you'll find the world ain't such a friendly place for a Chrome."

Out of the corner of her eye, Hannah saw him go back into the booth. She sat down on the curb to wait. She was chilly in her thin summer blouse and skirt, but she didn't care. The fresh air was divine. She breathed it in and lifted her face to the sun. From its position, it had to be close to noon. Why was her father so late?

She'd been waiting for perhaps twenty minutes when a yellow van pulled into the lot and headed toward the gate, stopping right in front of her. A sign painted on the door read: CRAWFORD TAXI SERVICE, WE'LL GITCHA THERE. The passenger-side window rolled down, and the driver, a middle-aged man with a greasy gray ponytail, leaned over and said, "You need a taxi?"

She stood up. "Maybe." In Crawford, she could get something to eat and find a netlet to call her father. "How far's town?"

"Fifteen minutes, give or take."

"What's the fare?"

"Well, let's see now," said the driver. "I reckon three hundred ought to just about cover it. Tip included."

"That's outrageous!"

He shrugged. "Ain't many cabs'll even pick up a Chrome."

"See what I'm talking 'bout, gal?" drawled the guard from behind her. "It's a tough ole world out there for a Red." He was standing in front of the booth now, grinning, and Hannah realized that he must have called the cab. He and his buddy the driver had no doubt played out this scenario many times, splitting their despicable proceeds after the fact.

"Well?" said the driver. "I ain't got all day."

How much money did she have left? There couldn't be much; almost all her savings had gone to pay for the abortion. Her checking account had had maybe a thousand dollars in it when she was arrested, but there would have been automatic deductions for her bills. The three hundred dollars she'd gotten from the state of Texas could very well be all she had to her name.

"I'll walk," she said.

"Suit yourself." He rolled up the window and pulled away.

"Changed your mind yet?" the guard said. He sauntered over to her. She tensed, but he merely handed her a scrap of paper. On it was scrawled a name, Billy Sikes, and a phone number. "That's my number," he said. "If I was you I'd hang on to it. You might decide you could use a friend one of these days."

Hannah crumpled it in her fist and let it fall to the ground. "I've got enough friends." She turned and started walking toward the road.

She was halfway to the entrance when a familiar blue sedan pulled in. She broke into a run. It stopped a few feet in front of her, and she saw her father behind the wheel, alone. She'd known better than to expect her mother or Becca, but still, their absence cut deep. For some time, neither he nor Hannah moved. They gazed at each other through the glass of the windshield, worlds apart. Her mouth was dry with fear. What if he couldn't stand the sight of her? What if he was so repulsed he drove away and left her here? She'd lost so much already, she didn't think she could bear to live without her father's love. For the first time since she'd entered the Chrome ward, she prayed. Not to God, but to His Son, who knew what it was to be trapped, alone, inside mortal flesh; who'd once known the terror of being forsaken. *Please, Jesus. Please don't take my father from me.*

The driver's door swung open, and John Payne got out, keeping the door between himself and Hannah. She approached him slowly, carefully, like a bird she was afraid of startling into flight. When she was still a few feet away, she stopped, uncertain. Her father stared at her without speaking. Tears were streaming down his face.

"Daddy?"

His chest heaved and he let out a choked sob. The sound lacerated her. Only once, at her grandmother's funeral, had Hannah ever seen her father cry. Her own eyes welled as he moved from behind the car door and held his arms out to her. She walked into them, felt them enfold her. She had never been more grateful for anything in her life than for this tenderness, this simple human warmth. She thought of the last few times she'd been touched: by the guard earlier, by the medic who'd strapped her down and injected her with the virus, by the bailiff in the courtroom, by the horrid police doctor. To be touched with love was a kind of miracle.

"My beautiful Hannah," her father said, stroking her hair. "Oh, my sweet, beautiful girl."

HE'D BROUGHT A cooler of food: turkey sandwiches, potato chips, an apple, a thermos of coffee. Plain fare, but after thirty days of nutribars, it tasted ambrosial. He was silent while she ate, his eyes fixed on the road. They were heading north on I-35, toward Dallas. *Toward home.* A tendril of hope unfurled in her mind. Maybe her mother had forgiven her, at least enough to let her move back in.

As if he were following her thoughts, her father said, "I can't take you home. You know that, don't you?"

The tendril turned brown, crumbled to powder. "I do now."

"If you would just talk to us, Hannah. Just tell us—"

She cut him off. "I can't. I won't." It came out shrill and defiant. In a milder tone, she said, "Telling you wouldn't help anything anyway."

Her father's grip tightened on the steering wheel, turning the knuckles white. "It would help me track the bastard down, so I could beat the living daylights out of him."

"Adjusting. You are out of your lane," said the pleasant voice of the computer. The steering wheel jerked slightly to the left under her father's hand, and he made a frustrated sound.

Hannah looked down at the half-eaten sandwich in her lap, her appetite gone. "I'm sorry, Daddy," she said. The apology was rote to her ear, a dying echo that had traveled too far from its original source, its meaning all but lost from overrepetition. She had said those words so many times—to him, to Becca, to her mother, to the ghost of her child, to God—knowing they weren't enough and never would be; knowing she'd feel compelled to keep saying them over and over again even so. Her life had become an apologetic conjugation: *I was sorry, I am sorry, I will be sorry,* with no hope of a future perfect, an *I will have been sorry.*

Her father let out a long breath, and his body relaxed a little. "I know."

"Where are you taking me?" she asked.

"There's a place in Richardson run by the Church of the Risen Lord. It's called the Straight Path Center." Hannah shook her head; she hadn't heard of either. "It's a kind of halfway house for women like you. If it works out, you can stay there for up to six months. That'll give us time to find you a job and a safe place to live."

The "us" reassured her, and the fact that the center was in Richardson, just south of Plano. "When you say 'women like me' . . ."

"Nonviolent Reds, as well as Yellows and Oranges. They don't accept Blues, Greens, or Purples. I wouldn't send you there if they did."

"Have you seen the place?"

"No, but I spoke with the director, Reverend Henley, and he seems like a sincere and compassionate man. I know he's helped many women find a path back to God."

Back to God. The words kindled a bright flare of longing within her, doused almost instantly by despair. She'd prayed to Him every day in the jail, before and during her trial, kneeling on the hard floor of the cell until her knees throbbed, begging for His forgiveness and mercy. But He'd remained silent, absent as He'd never been before. With every day that passed Hannah felt more desolate, like an abandoned house falling into ruin, cold wind whistling through the chinks. Finally, the day she was sentenced and taken to the Chrome ward, she acknowledged the inescapable truth: there would be no forgiveness or mercy for her, no going back to Him. How could there be, after what she'd done?

"But understand," her father continued, "this isn't vacation Bible school. They've got strict rules there. You break them and you're out. And then God help you, Hannah. We can't afford to get you a place of your own, even if your mother would let me pay for it."

"I know, Daddy. I wouldn't expect you to." They had no family money, and his salary was modest. It occurred to her now that without her income to supplement his, her parents would have to live much more frugally—one more thing for which she could reproach herself. "But who's paying for this center?"

"The ICs are sponsoring you. Reverend Dale himself appealed to the council."

Shame scalded her, and she saw it reflected in her father's face. Hannah, and by extension, the Payne family, was a charity case now. She remembered how she used to feel when she worked in the soup kitchen, putting trays of food into the hands of its ragged supplicants, people who stank of poverty and desperation, whose eyes avoided hers. How she'd pitied them, those poor people. How generous, how *virtuous* she'd felt helping them. *Them*—people totally unlike herself and her family, people who had fallen to a place she would never, ever go.

"He's also the reason you got in," her father said. "The center has a long waiting list." When Hannah didn't reply, he said, "We're lucky Reverend Dale has taken such an interest in your case."

She imagined how it must have felt for Aidan to make those calls. Had he pitied her? Felt benevolent? Thought of her as one of *them*?

"Yes," she said woodenly. "We're very lucky."

WHEN THEY MERGED onto Central the expressway was jammed as usual, and Hannah and her father proceeded the ten miles to Richardson at a crawl. He turned on the sat radio and navved to a news station. Hannah listened with half an ear. The Senate had passed the Freedom From Information Act eighty-eight to twelve. Right-wing militants had assassinated President Napoleón Cifuentes of Brazil, toppling the last democratic government in South America. Continued flooding in Indonesia had displaced more than two hundred thousand additional people in October. Syria, Lebanon and Jordan had withdrawn from the United Nations, citing anti-Islamic bias. The quarterback of the Miami Dolphins had been suspended for using nano-enhancers. Hannah tuned it out. What did any of it have to do with her now?

A family of three pulled up alongside them, pacing them. When the young boy in the backseat saw Hannah, his eyes went wide. She put her hand over the side of her face, but she could feel him staring at her with a child's unselfconscious directness. Finally, she turned and made a scary face at him, baring her teeth. His eyes and mouth went wide, and he said something to his parents. Their heads whipped around. They glared at her, and she felt a stab of remorse. Of course the boy was staring; she was a freak. How many times had she herself stared with morbid fascination at a Chrome, knowing it was impolite but unable to help herself? Though they were a common sight in the city, especially Yellows, they still drew the eye irresistibly. Hannah wondered how they endured it. How she would endure it.

Her father took the Belt Line exit, and they drove past the shopping mall where she and Becca used to go witnessing with the church youth group, past the Eisemann Center, where they'd seen *The Nutcracker* and *Swan Lake,* past the stadium where they'd gone to high school football games. These sights from her old life now seemed as quaint and unreal as models in a diorama.

They were stopped at a traffic light when out of nowhere, something thudded against Hannah's window. She started and cried out. A face was smashed against the glass. It pulled back, and she saw that it belonged to a young teenaged boy. A girl his age with rainbow-dyed hair and a ring through her lip stood behind him. The two of them were laughing, jeering at Hannah's fright.

"Hey, leave her alone!" Her father flung open his car door and got out, and the kids ran off down the street. "Punks! You ought to be ashamed of yourselves!" he called out after them. The boy shot him the finger. There was a loud honk from the car behind them, and Hannah jumped again—the light had turned green.

Her father got back in the car and drove on. His jaw was tight-clenched. He glanced at her. "You all right?"

"Yes, Daddy," she lied. Her heart was still racing. Was this how it was going to be from now on? Would she ever know a day without mockery or fear?

Her father pulled over in front of a nondescript four-story building on a commercial street. "This is it," he said. It looked like a medical park or an office building. A discreet sign above the door read, THE STRAIGHT PATH CENTER. A potted rosebush flanked the entrance. There were still a few late-fall blooms offering their fragile beauty to all those who passed by. They were red roses, once Hannah's favorite. Now, their vivid color seemed to taunt her.

She turned to her father, expecting him to shut off the engine, but he sat unmoving, looking straight ahead, his fingers still wrapped around the steering wheel.

"Aren't you coming in with me?" she asked.

"I can't. You have to enter alone, of your own free will, bringing nothing but yourself. It's one of the rules."

"I see." Her voice was tight and high-pitched. She swallowed, tried to sound less afraid. "How often can you visit?"

Her father shook his head, and the hollow feeling inside of her expanded. "Visitors aren't permitted, and neither are calls. Letters are the only communication they allow from the outside world."

Another prison then. Six more months without seeing him, without seeing Becca, without even hearing their voices—how would she bear it?

He turned to her, his face stricken. "I don't like it any more than you do, but for right now this is the best option we have. It's the only way I know to keep you safe until I can figure out some sort of living situation for you. I'll come for you as soon as I can."

"Does Mama know about this? Does she know you're here with me?"

"Of course. She's the one who found this place. It was her idea to send you here."

"To get me out of her sight," Hannah said bitterly.

"To help you, Hannah. She's angry right now, but she still loves you."

Hannah remembered her mother's face as she'd left the visiting room at the jail. How disgusted she'd looked, as if she'd smelled something foul. "Yeah, she loves me so much she's disowned me."

"She cried for days after they sentenced you. Wouldn't eat, wouldn't leave the house."

Hannah was unmoved. "It must be mortifying for her, having a convicted felon for a daughter. What would the neighbors say?"

Her father grabbed hold of her wrist. "You listen to me. It wasn't shame kept your mother at home, it was grief. Grief, Hannah." His fingers ground against her bones, but she didn't try to pull away. The pain was welcome; it kept the numbness at bay. "You can't imagine how hard this has been for her. For all of us."

Hard is loving a man you can never have, Hannah thought. *Hard is asking someone to kill your child and then holding still while they do it.* But she couldn't say those things to her father; she'd wounded him enough already. Instead, she asked after Becca.

With a sigh, he let go of her wrist. "She sends her love. She misses you." He paused, then said, "She's pregnant. It's twins, a boy and a girl."

"Oh! How wonderful!" And for a moment, it was, and Hannah was flooded with pure joy, just as Becca must have been when her hopes were confirmed. Hannah could picture her hugging herself, bursting with the wonder of it. She would have wanted to call their mother but waited until Cole got home from work so she could tell him first, her face glowing with shy pride. They would have gone together to the Paynes' house and shared the news, which would have been received with openmouthed delight by their father and a knowing smile by their mother, who would have suspected for some time. Hannah could see it all, could see her sister's hand cupped over her swelling belly, and later, around the baby's tender, downy head. Becca was made for motherhood. She'd dreamed of it ever since they were little girls, whispering their fantasies to each other in the dark. She wanted to have seven children, just like in

The Sound of Music. And her first daughter, she'd promised, would be named Hannah.

The memory was a cudgel, wielded with cruel indifference to the present. Hannah would have no namesake now. She wouldn't be a part of her niece's and nephew's lives, wouldn't be invited to their baptism, would never read stories to them or push them on a swing. "Aunt Hannah" would be words of disgrace to Becca's children, if they said them at all. Children who would have grown up alongside her own.

"She's due in April," her father said. "She and Cole are over the moon about it."

Hannah sifted through her emotions, searching for something unsullied to offer her sister, something she could wholly mean. She could find only one thing. "Give her my love," she said.

"I will. She sends you hers, and she said to tell you she'll write to you. When you write back, mail the letters to me, and I'll see that she gets them." He reached out and touched Hannah's cheek. "I know you're scared, but I'll figure out a plan, I promise. In the meantime, you'll be safe here and cared for. And maybe they can help you find some grace. I pray that they can, Hannah. I'll pray for you every day."

Her love for him rose up into her throat, forming a thick ball. "Thank you for everything you've done, Daddy. If it weren't for you—"

"You're my daughter," he said, before she could finish the thought. "That will never change."

She leaned over, hugged him hard, told him she loved him and then got out of the car. She walked past the rosebush to the entrance. There was an engraved brass plaque to the right of the door. It read:

AND I WILL BRING THE BLIND BY A WAY THEY
KNEW NOT; I WILL LEAD THEM IN PATHS THAT
THEY HAVE NOT KNOWN: I WILL MAKE DARKNESS
LIGHT BEFORE THEM, AND CROOKED THINGS
STRAIGHT. THESE THINGS I WILL DO UNTO THEM,
AND NOT FORSAKE THEM. —ISAIAH 42:16

She reread the last four words of the verse, whispering them aloud. *Not a prison,* she told herself, *a sanctuary.*

She could feel her father watching her from the idling car. She lifted a hand in farewell but didn't turn around. She drew herself up tall and tried the door. It was locked, but then a few seconds later she heard a click. She pulled the door open and stepped across the threshold.

MARY MAGDALENE HERSELF greeted Hannah. Three times larger than life, clad only in her long, rippling red hair, Mary gazed adoringly heavenward. One pale, plump arm was laid across her breasts, which peeked out, rosy-tipped, on either side. Hannah couldn't help but stare at them. She knew this painting—it hung in one of the chapels at Ignited Word—but in that version, she was certain, the Magdalene's hair covered her nakedness completely. The sight of so much lush pink flesh, so tenderly and sensually revealed, and in this of all places, was confusing, unsettling.

"That's Mary Magdalene," said a reedy voice, the vowels dipping in a thick twang.

Startled, Hannah dropped her eyes from the painting to the face of a young woman standing to her left. She was tall and rawboned, clad in a faded prairie-style dress that covered her from neck to feet. Her hair was done up in a bun and capped by a pleated white bonnet with long, trailing ties. She wore a small silver cross and held a straw broom in her hands. If it hadn't been for her lemon yellow skin, she could have walked straight out of the nineteenth century. Hannah stared at her in dismay. Clearly these people were extreme fundamentalists. Had her parents known that, when they'd decided to send her here? Had Aidan?

"She was a outcast, like us," the girl said. "Then Jesus made the demons inside of her cut and run. He sent 'em straight back to hell, just like that." She snapped her fingers. Her bony wrists stuck out several inches from the sleeves of her dress.

"I know who she is." Hannah wondered what the girl's crime was. Nothing too serious, or she wouldn't be a Yellow. Drug possession? Petty theft?

The girl cocked her head. "Oh yeah? You're so smart, tell me why she's nekked."

Hannah shrugged. "We're all naked before God."

"True," the girl said. "But wrong." She was plain-featured, with a weak chin and an unfortunate overbite. The kind of girl you'd dismiss, if it weren't for her eyes. They were a rich amber, and there was a mutinous spark in them that animated her face and made Hannah like her in spite of her churlishness.

"Why then?" Hannah asked, wishing she could let the girl's sleeves out for her. She was just a kid; seventeen, eighteen at the most.

"You'll find out." The girl gave her a sly smile and resumed her sweeping.

Hannah paced. Her eyes keep returning to the Magdalene, as they were plainly meant to; the painting and a simple wooden bench were the only objects in the otherwise austere room. The walls were white, the floors terra-cotta tile. Long horizontal windows near the ceiling let in thin shafts of light. There were three doors: the one she'd come in and two others, one near the girl and another directly beneath the painting. The latter was tall and narrow, made of dark, intricately carved wood rubbed to a high sheen. It looked old and foreign, like it belonged in some crumbling European castle. Hannah went over to it to examine it more closely.

"You can't go in there yet," the girl said.

"I wasn't going to open it. I just want to look at it." The carvings on the main panel, of a shepherd tending his flock, were very fine. Beneath were some words in Latin. Hannah ran her fingers lightly over the letters.

"It's from Luke," the girl said. "It says you gotta try to go in through the narrow door—"

"'Because many, I tell you, will try to enter and will not be able to,'" Hannah finished. "I know the passage."

The girl's face lit with hostility. "You don't know *nothing*. You think you do but you don't. Talk to me in three months, then we'll see what all you know." She bent and angrily brushed the collected debris into the dustpan, then went to the side door and pulled it open.

"Is that how long you've been here?" Hannah said, before she could leave. "Three months?"

"That's right," the girl said, stiff-backed and sullen.

"I'm Hannah. What's your name?"

"Eve." She said it warily, like she was waiting to be mocked.

"Is that your real name, or did they give it to you here?"

"It's mine."

"It's a lovely name," said Hannah.

Something flickered in the girl's eyes. "That's the only thing they let you keep here." She left, closing the door behind her.

A FEW MINUTES later, the door opened again and a couple entered the room, holding hands. The man was of medium height, trim and vigorous, with a head that was a little too large for his body. His clothes were plain: white button-down shirt, dark gray trousers, black suspenders. He was in his mid-forties, Hannah judged, handsome in an aging Ken-doll way, with a square jaw, a full head of dark blond hair and crinkles at the corners of his eyes. The woman resembled him strongly enough that they could be brother and sister, though she was considerably younger and more petite. She too was blonde and exuded robust good health and wholesomeness. A scattering of freckles across her pink cheeks added to the effect. Her attire was similar to Eve's, but the fabric was a rich blue and of much better quality. Both she and the man wore crosses like Eve's, only larger. Hannah felt reassured by their attractiveness and by their expressions, which were serious but not unfriendly. They came to stand before her, and the man spoke.

"I'm Reverend Ponder Henley, the director of the Straight Path Center, and this is Mrs. Henley." His round brown eyes had a surprised, slightly vacant look to them. Hers were a twinkling blue that matched her dress.

"How do you do," Hannah said, stifling an absurd impulse to curtsy. "I'm Hannah Payne."

"Why are you here, Hannah?" Mrs. Henley asked. Her voice was sweet and girlish and her tone mild, but Hannah knew the question was a test. She searched their faces, trying to discern what they wanted to hear. "To repent my sins," maybe, or, "To learn how to follow a straighter, godlier path."

In the end, though, she shrugged and said, "I have nowhere else to go."

Reverend and Mrs. Henley exchanged quick glances, their mouths stretching wide in approving smiles that revealed two sets of white, even teeth. Mrs. Henley's cheeks were adorably dimpled.

"That is the right answer, Hannah," said Reverend Henley. "Do you know why?" She shook her head, and he said, "Because it is the truthful answer. Without truth, there can be no salvation."

"Do you want to be saved, Hannah?" asked Mrs. Henley.

"Yes."

"And do you believe you *can* be saved?" asked Reverend Henley.

Again, Hannah considered lying. What if faith in God's forgiveness was required? What if they decided not to let her stay? She shook her head a second time. Their smiles broadened further.

"That is both the right and the wrong answer," said Reverend

Henley. "Right because you spoke honestly, but wrong because you *can* be saved. You're just too blind to see it now, but you *will* be saved, Hannah, if you walk the straight path. You've already taken the first steps toward salvation."

Maybe they can help you find some grace. Was it possible, Hannah wondered, that God was not lost to her after all? That the Henleys could shepherd her to a place where He would forgive her? Their serene, unblinking confidence said it was.

"'I will bring the blind by a way they did not know . . . and not forsake them.'" said Reverend Henley. "That is God's promise to us in Isaiah. And that is our promise to you, Hannah, on two conditions, that you obey our rules and that you never, ever lie to us. Will you swear to that?"

Hannah opened her mouth to say yes, but before she could speak, Mrs. Henley held up an admonishing forefinger and said, "Do not make this vow lightly, Hannah. 'He that worketh deceit shall not dwell within my house.'"

They waited, watching her with solemn faces. She tried to imagine a question they could ask her that she would want to lie about. Only one came to mind—"Was Aidan Dale the father of your child?"—and that, they would never think to ask. She had nothing else to hide, nothing else she cared enough about to want to hide.

"I swear it," she said.

The Henleys stepped close to her. Ponder Henley took her left hand and Mrs. Henley her right, forming a circle. Hannah's palms were damp, but theirs were warm and dry. She was several inches taller than the reverend and towered over Mrs. Henley, and she felt ungainly and red next to them. They bowed their heads. "Blessed Jesus," prayed Reverend Henley, "You have shown this walker the path to salvation. Guide her steps, Lord, and help her keep to the path when Satan tempts her to stray from it. Light her way, Lord, and open her eyes to Your will and her soul to true repentance. Amen."

The Henleys let go of Hannah's hands, leaving her feeling oddly bereft. Mrs. Henley took a cross identical to Eve's from her pocket and told Hannah to put it on.

"You must never take it off, even to sleep, until you're ready to leave us," said Reverend Henley. "The cross is the key that will allow you to enter the center and your assigned areas. You won't find much else in the way of technology here. We have no netlets, no servbots or smartrooms, nothing to come between us and God."

"Did you bring your NIC?" asked Mrs. Henley. Hannah nodded. "Give it to me. I'll keep it safe for you."

When she hesitated, Reverend Henley said, "No one is forced to stay here, Hannah. You're free to go at any time. All you have to do is ask, and we'll give you back your card. But once you leave and reenter the world, there's no returning, do you understand?"

"What about my renewal?" Hannah would have to leave the center for that, at the end of January. Renewals were mandatory every four months, and the consequences for tardiness were severe. If she didn't get her injection by her due date, the half-life of the virus would begin to deteriorate and the chroming gradually to fade until her skin color reverted to normal. Unfortunately, by that time she'd be too fragged out to care.

Fragmentation was the government's way of making sure Chromes stayed chromed. Melachroming, despite the best efforts of scientists, was impermanent; the compound that caused the skin mutation started to wear off after four months. So to guarantee that Chromes showed up for their renewals, the scientists had piggybacked a second compound onto the first, this one designed to remain dormant for four months before activating and beginning the fragmentation process. That was all Hannah, or anyone else other than the geneticists employed by the Federal Chroming Agency, knew; the exact science behind fragmentation was a closely guarded secret. But like every other American over the age of twelve, she'd been well-schooled in its effects.

It started with faint whispers, sporadic and indistinct. As your brain slipped further into fragmentation, they grew louder, giving way to full-blown auditory hallucinations. You became convinced that the world and everyone in it were malevolent. You didn't even notice that your skin was returning to normal, because the paranoia consumed you to the point where you disconnected from your physical self, forgetting to bathe, to brush your hair or change your clothes, to eat or drink. Your speech became nonsensical, as scrambled and incoherent as your thoughts. Eventually, the voices turned on you, and you mutilated or killed yourself. Only a renewal shot could stop the process.

Hundreds of Chromes had tried to beat it, to hold out long enough to get to the other side of it. None had succeeded. There was no other side.

"Of course, we'll take you when you're due," Mrs. Henley said. "We take all the girls. There's a Chrome center in Garland." She held out her hand for the card. Hannah pulled it from the pocket of her skirt and gave it to her.

"Thank you. And now," Mrs. Henley said, her blue eyes sparkling, "we'll leave you to get undressed."

"What?"

"You must set foot upon the path with nothing but yourself," Reverend Henley said. "Leave all your clothes on the bench, and when you're ready, go through the narrow door." He reached out and placed his hand on the crown of Hannah's head. "Be not afraid, for the Lord is with you."

The Henleys exited through the side door. When they were gone, Hannah lifted her eyes to Mary Magdalene's luminous face. She removed her blouse and skirt, her bra and panties, folding them and placing them on the bench one at a time, shivering in the cool air of the room. She felt numb and hollow, empty of everything except for a tiny spark of hope. She cupped her hands around it in her mind and followed Mary's gaze upward, beyond the bounds of the painting. *If this is what You ask of me, if this is the path back to You, I will take it.*

She slipped off her shoes and walked to the door, the tiles cold against the soles of her bare feet. There was no handle. She laid her palm against the wood and pushed, but it resisted her puny effort. She leaned her whole body against the door, pushing with all her strength. It swung inward with a groan, and she stumbled, falling in and down.

" 'NAKED CAME I out of my mother's womb, and naked shall I return thither.'" The women spoke in unison, their eyes fixed on Hannah.

There were about seventy of them, standing on what looked like a choir riser. They were grouped by color: Reds on the bottom rows, Oranges in the middle and Yellows, who outnumbered the others, on top. The effect was surreal, like a box of crayons missing the cool part of the spectrum. Half the Reds were holding dolls, and one of this group, Hannah was startled to see, was not a Chrome. The girl's white skin stood out starkly from that of the others.

Mrs. Henley stood in front of the riser, facing Hannah. To her relief, Reverend Henley wasn't in the room.

"What is this woman?" Mrs. Henley said, pointing at Hannah.

"A sinner," the women replied.

"How will she be saved?"

"By walking the straight path."

"Who will walk with her?"

"We will."

"Who will walk before her?"

"I will," said a lone voice from the front row. A Red about ten years older than Hannah stepped off the riser and approached her, holding out a folded brown dress. "Put this on." Hannah took it gratefully and pulled it over her head, fastening the buttons running up the bodice with clumsy fingers.

When Hannah was finished, Mrs. Henley said, "What does the path demand of us?"

"Penitence. Atonement. Truth. And humility," the women answered.

A door to Hannah's left was flung open and Reverend Henley strode into the room, pink-cheeked and ebullient. "Where does the path lead us?" he called out.

"To salvation."

He looked at Hannah, spreading his hands wide in benediction. " 'My soul shall be joyful in my God; for He hath clothed me with the garments of salvation, He hath covered me with the robe of righteousness.' " He turned and addressed the women. "Walkers, let us pray."

Hannah bowed her head along with the others, but she didn't hear his words or the women's rote responses. Her mind was fogged by weariness, her attention focused solely on keeping herself upright. The prayer continued for endless minutes. At last, Reverend Henley said amen and released them. Row by row, the women filed silently out of the room. Only Eve gave Hannah a parting glance. Whether it was one of sympathy or spite, she was too far away to tell.

The woman who'd given Hannah the dress stayed behind,

along with the Henleys. "Hannah, this is Bridget," Reverend Henley said. "Go with her, and she'll show you the path." He gestured at the door. Bridget turned obediently and walked toward it, but Hannah hung back, reluctant to leave the couple.

Mrs. Henley gave her a reassuring smile. "Go on, now."

Hannah obeyed, following Bridget from the room, toward salvation.

Unspeaking, Bridget led Hannah up two flights of stairs and down a featureless corridor to a set of swinging double doors. They entered a long room lit on one side by more of the high, slitted windows. Inscribed just beneath them, running in a continuous loop around all four walls, were the words PENITENCE, ATONEMENT, TRUTH AND HUMILITY. Only now did Hannah get the acronym. *They're missing OBEDIENCE, but I guess PATHO wouldn't be as catchy.*

"This is the Red dormitory," Bridget said, enunciating each word crisply. The room was lined with sixteen neatly made twin beds, each flanked by a small nightstand and a white, hospital-style curtain suspended from a track in the ceiling. A towel and a long white nightgown hung on pegs beside every bed except one. She conducted Hannah to it. "You will sleep here. You will make your bed every morning. You will draw the curtain while changing your clothes. At all other times, you will leave it open." Bridget pulled open the single drawer of the nightstand, revealing a comb, a box of hairpins, a nail file, a toothbrush and toothpaste. "You will store your personal items here."

"How long have you been here?" Hannah asked.

Bridget glanced with evident distaste at Hannah's fingernails, which were long and ragged from her imprisonment. "You will keep yourself neatly groomed."

Embarrassed but determined not to show it—why did the woman have to be so rude?—Hannah studied her with equal frankness. Noting the wrinkles across her forehead and the furrows bracketing her mouth, Hannah upped her initial estimate of Bridget's age by a decade. She was forty-five if she was a day.

With the ramrod carriage of a soldier, Bridget marched to the other end of the room and opened the doors to a large closet. Inside were communal supplies: stacks of white sheets and towels; long-sleeved white nightgowns and dresses in muted shades of brown, blue and gray, grouped by size; drawers containing white cotton underwear, brassieres and thick black tights; baskets of bonnets and sanitary napkins; and on the floor, a row of identical black flats, proceeding from small to large. "You will change your underthings daily and your dress every two days," Bridget said. "You will change your nightgown, bonnet, towel and sheets every Saturday."

Hannah followed her through a doorway into a large bathroom with multiple shower units, sinks and toilet stalls. A young woman was kneeling on the floor scrubbing the tile. She made a face when she saw Bridget and then quickly looked down to hide it. The scowl and the red skin notwithstanding, the girl was stunning, with Afrasian features: dark, almond-shaped eyes with uncreased lids, full lips, a flattened nose with rounded nostrils, a long, graceful neck. Hannah felt her beauty as a sweet pang in her heart, an inner *Oh!* of wonder. Beauty, whether of people or things, had always moved her in this way, and despite many stern lectures by her parents on the sinfulness of caring about temporal matters like a person's looks, a stubborn part of her had always refused to believe it was wrong. Wasn't beauty created by God, and so was her love of it not a love of Him?

"Good afternoon, Walker," Bridget said, in a considerably more civil tone than she'd used with Hannah. She even gave the girl something resembling a smile.

"Good afternoon," the girl replied, with a matching half-smile Hannah could tell was forced.

Bridget turned back to Hannah. "You will shower daily, before breakfast, for no more than three minutes. You will brush your teeth twice a day. You will wash your hands after using the toilet."

"I usually do," Hannah said tartly.

Bridget went on as if she hadn't spoken. "You will keep your hair pinned up and decently covered except when sleeping."

Fed up with the condescending litany, Hannah said, "Or what?"

"One step off the path and you'll be warned. Two and you'll be cast out." She strode from the room. Hannah heard a muttered *humph* and glanced down. The girl on the floor mouthed the word "bitch." For the first time in months, Hannah smiled.

Bridget was waiting by Hannah's bed with more instructions. "Worship is at six thirty in the morning and seven o'clock in the evening in the chapel. Mealtimes are at six, noon and six. If you arrive after the blessing has been said, you will not be served. You will spend weekday mornings in enlightenment and the afternoons doing useful work. You will have two hours of reflection time after evening worship. The lights go off at ten."

"What about weekends?"

"Saturday mornings you will devote to independent Bible study. The afternoons you may spend as you wish. Sundays are purely for worship." Bridget glanced up at a clock on the wall. "It's five thirty now. Get dressed, and I'll take you to supper."

Hannah looked longingly at the bed. "I'm not hungry," she said. "And I'm so tired."

"Meals and services may not be skipped unless you're ill."

"I *am* feeling a little unwell."

"'He that worketh deceit shall not dwell within my house,'" Bridget said.

Hannah had never hit anyone in her life nor wanted to, but at that moment her hand was twitching with the urge to slap the woman's smug red face.

"I'll be back to get you in twenty minutes," Bridget said. "Be ready, Walker."

When she was gone, Hannah took what she needed from the closet, drew the curtain around her bed and got dressed. The garments were strange and constricting and the fabric coarse, but she felt a little better once she had on underwear and shoes, a little less vulnerable.

She went to the bathroom to wash her face and hands and pin up her hair. The other girl was now on her feet, cleaning the large mirror behind the sinks. She gave Hannah a swift, friendly assessment. "Don't let Fridget get to you," she said. "She's just surged because her time's almost up, and they're booting her out of here in a month. Nut job actually likes it here." The girl's voice was low and mellifluous, with a roundness that suggested the Deep South. "I'm Kayla, by the way."

Relieved that everyone wasn't as unpleasant as Bridget, Hannah introduced herself. "Where are you from?" she asked Kayla.

"Savannah. We moved to Dallas when I was eight, but I've managed to hang on to the accent."

"How long have you been at the center?"

"Twenty-five days, and I mean to tell you it's been the longest three and a half weeks of my whole life. I'm out of here any day now, as soon as my boyfriend comes to fetch me. He's looking for a place for us."

The innocently spoken words were cruel reminders that Aidan

wouldn't be coming for Hannah. "So he doesn't mind . . . whatever you did?" she blurted out. She looked away then, mortified by her own rudeness. "I'm sorry. It's none of my business."

"No need to apologize," Kayla said, with a dismissive wave. "Anyway, it's no secret. I shot my stepfather." Her tone and expression were as remorseless as if she were talking about a mosquito she'd swatted. "My mama's not speaking to me, so I can't go home."

Alarmed, Hannah took a small, involuntary step back. If the center didn't admit violent Reds, then why had Kayla been allowed in here? And were there more like her?

"Don't worry," Kayla said drily, "I don't shoot scared little apples like you."

"Apples?"

"You know, red on the outside, white on the inside." She grinned. "I just made that up."

There was something about the girl, not innocence exactly—clearly Kayla was no innocent—but an openness and absence of guile that quieted Hannah's unease. "Mine isn't speaking to me either," she said.

"Yeah? What'd you do?"

Hannah pictured her mother at the jail, distraught and bewildered. *I betrayed every value she ever taught me. I committed adultery with a man of God. I murdered her unborn grandchild.*

"Hey," Kayla said, "whatever it is, you don't have to tell me."

The unexpected compassion brought a lump to Hannah's throat, and that stiffened her spine a bit. When had she become so pathetic, so grateful for any little scrap of kindness tossed her way?

She forced herself to look Kayla in the eye. "I had an abortion."

Hannah waited for the inevitable recoil—the reaction she herself would have had if someone had confessed that to her six months ago—but Kayla nodded matter-of-factly. "Sometimes you gotta do what you gotta do."

Hannah hesitated, then asked, "Is that how you felt about killing your stepfather? Like you had to do it?"

"Oh, I didn't kill him." She sounded regretful.

"So how come you're a Red instead of a Green?"

"My stepfather's rich and white. It's a winning combination." Hannah's brows drew together, and Kayla said, "Oh come on, don't tell me you buy all this crap about our so-called 'post-racial society.' Chromes may be the new niggers, but believe me, the old ones still get screwed good and regular."

At a loss, Hannah said nothing. Of course, she knew there was still racism—she wasn't that naive—but it wasn't a subject she'd ever given much thought to. Growing up, she'd almost never heard anyone make disparaging remarks about African Americans or people of any other ethnicity, and when someone had, her parents had been quick to denounce such statements as ignorant and unchristian. People of all races worshipped at Ignited Word, and the Paynes—and the church—were proud of that fact. Yes, Hannah reflected now, but how many nonwhite members did they actually have? And how many black, Hispanic or Asian families had ever been invited to her house for supper? The answers were troubling: relatively few, and none.

"Anyway, his fancy lawyer convinced the jury it was attempted murder," Kayla said. "Like I was after his fucking money, the lying cocksucker. I *wish* he was dead."

"Why? What did he do to you?"

Kayla's red hand rubbed the towel against the mirror in furious circles. "Son of a bitch was messing with my little sister. She's just thirteen."

Hannah shook her head, her mind shrinking away as it always

did from the incomprehensible but irrefutable fact that people did this to children, that they did it and somehow went on living with themselves. She'd met abused children at the shelter, kids as young as six who'd been molested by a parent, relative, family friend, priest, stranger. She'd looked into their eyes and known that no amount of kindness or love that she or anyone else gave them would ever completely heal them. These encounters had left her feeling heartsick, but they'd enraged Aidan. He didn't allow Blues to attend his services, even with an assigned chaperone (though all other Chromes were welcome, provided they sat in their designated area). Hannah had asked him once whether he thought God forgave child molesters. He was silent for a long time. "The Bible tells us He does, if they truly repent," he said finally. "But I don't believe even our Savior's blood is powerful enough to wash away that sin." It was the only time she'd ever heard Aidan blaspheme.

"I was aiming for his balls," Kayla said, "but I ended up shooting him in the gut. I should have used a knife is what I should have done."

"My cousin's a nurse," Hannah said, "She says stomach wounds are the most agonizing kind there are. It takes a long time to heal, and some people never do. They're literally poisoned by their own waste."

Kayla's hand went still and her lips quirked at the corners. "Is that a fact."

"Yep. It's supposed to be one of the worst deaths there is."

Her new friend smiled, a bright, fierce slash of teeth. "That's mighty good to know."

Hannah suddenly remembered the time. "I'd better get ready. Bridget will be back soon." She gathered her long hair, twisted it into a bun and tried to pin it up, but it was too heavy, and it defied her efforts, tumbling down her back.

Kayla moved behind Hannah. "Here, let me help you." With perfect ease, she took hold of Hannah's hair and started braiding it. "Most of the women here are all right, but you watch yourself around Fridget, hear? She not just a bitch, she's a snitch. You put one foot wrong, and she'll neg on you to the Henleys. She thinks if she's a good little rat, they'll let her stay past her six months, but it's not gonna happen. My uncle, he's the one who got me in here, he said they hardly ever make exceptions."

"They did for you," Hannah said. "Letting you come in the first place."

"Yeah, well, Uncle Walt's a big-time preacher in Savannah. He pulled some strings."

Kayla's hands were deft, and Hannah's hair was soon tamed and bound into a bun. "You're good at that," she said.

"I used to work at a salon. It's how I put myself through Baylor. Where'd you go?"

"College wasn't an option for me," Hannah said. There'd been no money for it, but even if she'd been able to get a scholarship, her parents would have opposed her going. They'd taught her that her highest purpose as a woman, the purpose for which she'd been created, was to get married, be a helpmeet to her husband and raise a family. She had grown up believing that, but sometimes she couldn't help thinking wistfully about what it would be like to have four years to do nothing but *learn*. One day the summer before her senior year of high school, she'd told her mother she was going to the mall and instead taken the train into Dallas. She'd gotten off at Mockingbird Station and walked the few blocks to the university, moving slowly in the 105-degree heat, taking shallow breaths through her mouth. The campus was mostly deserted, as she'd known it would be; like most universities in the hotter parts of the country, SMU had long ago closed its doors during the summer months. The cost of air-conditioning was prohibitive, and without it, the heat was too intense and the air quality too poor to hold classes.

Majestic oaks lined the empty walkways. Grateful for their shade, Hannah meandered through the campus, imagining the sidewalks thronged with students and herself among them. She saw a man emerge from a large building whose entrance was dwarfed by tall white columns. She mounted the stairs and went inside, stepping into quiet, and cool air that smelled deliciously of books: the library. Of course, it would have to be climate controlled year-round to protect the books from the heat and damp. She went through the scanner and past the security guard, then through a large set of double doors leading to the main reading room. Enormous as it was, it was crowded; most of the seats at the long wooden tables were filled. At least half of the people were elderly, seeking shelter from the heat. And oh, the books! Row upon row of them, more than she'd ever seen in one place.

"Hey there," said a young man behind the circulation desk. He was good-looking in an unkempt way, with artfully tousled hair and long sideburns—doubtless a student here. "Don't you have your student ID tab?"

Its absence must have set off an alert. Hannah looked down at her blouse and then pretended to search her purse, not wanting him to know she didn't belong here, in this beautiful, peaceful, book-filled space. "I guess I left it at home," she said.

Apologetically, he said, "I'm not supposed to let you in without one, unless you're over sixty-five. Which you're obviously not." He gave her an appreciative, lopsided grin. Flirting with her. "Though for you I believe I could make an exception."

Hannah looked back at him, this boy whom she might have dated if she'd gone to school here, and then she looked around the room at all the books, all the thousands and thousands of books containing so many answers to so many questions. Here, in this place, asking "Why?" would not be improper or sinful. Here, she could—

Her port buzzed: a message from her mother reminding her she had sewing circle at four. She pictured herself and the other women bent over their needles, chatting about a new gingerbread recipe they'd tried, a vid they'd seen the night before, the best place to find bargains on baby clothes, and mentally compared the image to the one in front of her: the students bent silently over their books, their lips moving as they memorized formulas and orders of mammals and the names of ancient kings, their minds grappling with philosophy, literature, quantum physics, international law. They were inhabitants of another country, one in which she was a foreigner and always would be.

"Thank you," she said, "but I don't belong here." She walked out of the room, out of the building, off the campus and back to the station, never once turning her head to look behind her.

"I was going to get my masters in education," Kayla said, bringing Hannah back to the present. "Had a scholarship to UT starting in September, and then this happened." She gestured at her red face.

"You lost a lot," Hannah said.

"Yeah. What about you?"

"I'm just a seamstress. Well, I used to be."

"And you still are," Kayla insisted. "Just because you're a Red doesn't mean that's all you are." She took Hannah's bonnet and set it on her head with a little flourish. "Ooh, girl, you're looking fine now. All you need is a scrub brush in your hand and you'll be almost as sexy as me."

Hannah tried to return Kayla's smile, but her own lips were

frozen. She stared at her reflection, stricken. An alien stared back at her.

"Come on," Kayla said. "Buck up, now. You'll make it through this."

"What if I can't?"

Kayla locked eyes with her. "You have to, or they win."

They heard footsteps approaching. "Here comes Fridget," Kayla said. "Remember what I told you."

Bridget appeared in the doorway. She surveyed Hannah with a cool, critical eye and finally gave her a grudging nod. "Follow me."

"I'm right behind you," Kayla murmured.

THEY ENCOUNTERED OTHER women along the way, emerging in color-coordinated groups from doorways and stairwells. Hannah heard a few low-voiced exchanges, but for the most part the women proceeded in silence. A cluster of the Reds with dolls stepped into the hallway. The pasty-faced girl was with them.

"Why isn't she a Chrome?" Hannah asked Bridget.

"She's with child."

"Ah." Because the virus mutated all skin cells in the body, including a fetus's, pregnant women were exempt from melachroming until after their babies were born. "And what are the dolls for?"

"You'll find out soon enough," Bridget said.

In the dining hall, Hannah attracted more than a few curious glances. The mortification she felt was acute—not an hour ago, these women had seen her naked—and she walked with her head bent and her shoulders slightly hunched, not meeting anyone's eyes. There were six long tables, each with twelve seats. Three of the tables were already full. Bridget took a seat at a fourth that was half full. Hannah sat down beside her, and Kayla seated herself on Hannah's other side.

"You will sit at the first available place," Bridget said. "You will not sit at an empty table unless all occupied tables are completely full. You will not save a seat for anyone."

Observing the other women enter the room, however, Hannah could see that the seating process was not nearly as arbitrary as Bridget would have had it be. There was subtle maneuvering taking place: the exchange of sidelong glances and small jerks of the head; deliberate pauses as women waited for a friend to catch up or avoided sitting next to someone they disliked. Hannah watched Eve stop to fiddle with her shoe until the group of Yellows she was with had passed her and then seat herself at the next table. Scant though it was, Hannah felt heartened by this evidence of rebellion and camaraderie.

A set of swinging doors opened, and chromed women emerged carrying pitchers of water and bowls and platters of food. "You will serve at table every fourth day and perform other assigned tasks in the afternoons," Bridget said. She pointed to a corkboard on the wall. "The work schedule for the week is posted every Monday morning."

"Are the assignments permanent, or do we rotate?"

"That depends. Do you have any useful skills?" Bridget's expression was skeptical.

"Yes, I'm a professional seamstress."

"How apt," Bridget said, with an unpleasant little smile. Before Hannah could ask what she meant, Bridget said, "Mrs. Henley will invite you to her parlor for tea on Saturday. You will inform her of your abilities at that time. You will refrain from exaggerating your skills."

"You will kiss my sweet red ass," Kayla said, under her breath.

Hannah's lips twitched in amusement. Bridget leaned forward, looking around Hannah at Kayla. "Were you saying something, Walker?"

"I was, Walker," Kayla replied, her face a picture of earnest piety. "I was asking Jesus to watch over us all as we travel the path."

Hannah clasped her hands before her and bowed her head. "Yes, Lord, please shepherd and watch over us, especially Walker Bridget, who will soon be leaving us and reentering the outside world."

"Amen," said Kayla. She was echoed by a soft chorus of other voices.

Hannah looked up to find Bridget regarding her suspiciously and several of the other women smirking. Bridget's eyes scoured the table. The pregnant girl, who was sitting at the far end with her doll in her lap, was slow to cover her smile with her hand, and Bridget fixed her with a murderous stare. The girl was saved—for the moment, at least—by the entrance of the Henleys. The room fell silent as they walked to the last two places at the last table. Reverend Henley held the chair for his wife, settling her comfortably before launching into a lengthy, meandering prayer of thanksgiving. Finally, he finished and took his seat, and the women began helping themselves to the food. A muted buzz of conversation arose. Hannah was relieved to hear it; she'd been afraid meals would be eaten in silence.

The food was plain and just as plainly economical—a tofu macaroni casserole and frozen green beans—but there were homemade rolls and real butter to go with them. The familiar yeasty smell was heavenly, and Hannah found that she was hungry after all. "You will not take more than your fair portion," Bridget said, and when the platter came round to Hannah, she saw why: there was barely enough for all twelve of them, and only if everyone was careful to take modest helpings. She served herself and passed the platter to

Kayla. When it reached the pregnant girl, she took twice as much as the rest of them. Hannah noticed a few resentful expressions, but no one objected.

"Pregnant women get double portions," Kayla said in a low voice. "Nobody likes to sit at Megan's table."

Kayla introduced Hannah to the women nearest them, but after the initial hellos, she didn't say much. She listened to the others speak quietly among themselves, mostly of news from home, which she gathered was a kind of currency here, with letters from husbands and boyfriends conferring the most status. To her surprise, Bridget not only joined in the conversation but was actually pleasant to everyone except Hannah and Megan. The other women were cordial in return, but as with Kayla earlier, Hannah could sense their wariness and dislike.

As she ate, she noticed an Orange at the other end of the table looking at her surreptitiously. Her face reminded Hannah of characters in an old 2-D vid she used to love when she was a child; silly, waddling creatures with tangerine skin and olive green hair. Becca had been scared of them, but they'd made Hannah laugh. They had a funny name—what was it? And why did the woman keep looking at her?

"I seen you on the news vids," the Orange said finally, in response to Hannah's questioning stare. The table fell silent, and she felt eleven pairs of eyes on her. "You must a loved him a whole lot, not to have told."

Pain, keen and unexpected, bloomed in her, and she knew it must be visible to the others.

"You must have snorted a whole lot of kite, not to have gotten off with a misdemeanor conviction," Kayla said to the woman. "Kite or amp. Which was it, Walker?"

Stung, the woman looked down at her plate, but not before Hannah saw the hunger in her eyes, the sick, helpless yearning of an addict for the thing she knew would destroy her.

"It's all right," Hannah told Kayla. Addressing the woman, she said, "Yes, I loved him. I couldn't help but love him."

The woman looked up, and Hannah remembered the name of the creatures from the vid: Oompa Loompas. Preposterous, capering objects of ridicule, barely recognizable as human beings.

THE EVENING SERVICE was long and the sermon dull— Reverend Henley, Hannah was beginning to see, was not the sharpest knife in the drawer, and he liked to hear himself talk— but she found comfort in the fellowship, and when it came time to pray, she did so earnestly, thanking God for this place of refuge and asking His help in keeping to the path. Though she didn't feel His answering presence within her, it was good to be in communication with Him again, after a month of shamed silence.

Afterward, Bridget showed Hannah the rest of the center: the reading room with its shelves of Christian books and printed periodicals; the laundry room and cleaning supply closet; the kitchen; the sewing room ("Most likely you will work here—*if* you are as good as you say"); the closed doorways to Mrs. Henley's parlor and Reverend Henley's study ("You will not disturb the reverend while he's working or seek to have a private meeting with him for any reason; if you have a problem, you will go to Mrs. Henley"). Hannah trailed after her guide wearily, buoying herself with the thought of the bed waiting at the end of the tour.

Bridget opened the door to a windowless room containing ten straight-backed wooden chairs arranged in a circle. One entire wall was a vidscreen. So, some technology was allowed. "This is your place of enlightenment," Bridget said. "You will come here tomorrow, immediately after the morning service."

"You won't be with me?"

"No. My place is elsewhere." The brief cheer Hannah felt at this news was dashed when Bridget added, "I'll come for you afterward and accompany you to lunch."

"Where's your place?"

"Upstairs, with others like myself."

Again, that contemptuous tone. It rankled Hannah, breaking through her fatigue. "Why are you doing this?"

"Doing what?"

"Being my guide or whatever."

"Pathfinder," Bridget corrected. "It's my duty, as the Red who has been here the longest."

"I think you enjoy it," Hannah said. "Being the authority, telling people what to do. I bet you volunteered."

The other woman's nostrils flared. "You are mistaken," Bridget said, spitting out the words, "if you think that I would want to spend a single minute with one of *you*."

The day's indignities, large and small, coalesced in Hannah's breast, forming a hot ball of fury. As Bridget started to turn away, Hannah grabbed her hand, holding it up at eye level with her own: red on red. "I don't see any difference between us," she said. "We're both killers, aren't we? Who'd you kill, Bridget?"

Bridget yanked her hand out of Hannah's, drawing it back as though she were going to strike her. Hannah stood unmoving, marking the naked emotions that chased across Bridget's face and seeing, as manifestly as if the other woman had confided in her, the terrible pain beneath her outrage. Suddenly Hannah felt sorry for her, this bristling, anguished, middle-aged woman. She recalled how frightened she herself had been just a few hours ago, in the safety of her father's car, when the boy had taunted her, and she thought of how much more so she'd be when she had to go into the world as a Chrome.

But just as she was about to apologize, Bridget seemed to collect herself, lowering her hand to her side and her mask of chilly indifference back in place. "You have just stepped off the path, Walker. How unfortunate."

"What are you talking about?" Hannah asked.

"You will not intentionally lay hands on another walker. It's one of the rules."

"You didn't tell me that."

Bridget's eyebrows shot up in mock consternation. "Oh, I'm certain I did. I'm afraid I'll have to report you to Mrs. Henley."

Which would *not* be a good way to begin here. "Look," Hannah said, in a conciliatory tone, "I'm sorry I snapped at you. It's been a rough day."

"You think this is rough? This is nothing compared to what it's like out there, on your own. *Nothing.*" Bridget's voice broke on the word. Abruptly, she turned away from Hannah and started walking down the hall.

"What happened to you?" Hannah called softly after her.

Without stopping or turning around, Bridget said, "You'll find out what rough really is, when they kick you out of here." She went down the stairs that led to the dormitory. Hannah stood looking after her, knowing she had no choice but to follow.

EXHAUSTION TRUMPED THE strangeness of her surroundings, and Hannah slept deeply that first night, waking when the lights went on at five thirty. Dazed, she blinked against their glare. For a few awful seconds, she thought she was back in the Chrome ward, but then she heard movement on either side of her, the squeak of bedsprings and the little sighs and groans of other women pulled reluctantly from sleep, and memory returned. She knew she should get up, but her limbs were heavy. The hiss of running water and the soft drone of the women's voices were pleasant, soothing. Her eyes were just starting to flutter closed again when she felt the bed shake.

"Wake up," someone said in a loud whisper. Hannah opened her eyes and saw Kayla standing at the foot of the bed. "Fridget's watching. Come on." She turned and headed for the bathroom.

Hannah forced herself to a vertical position, got out of bed and collected her meager toiletries.

The bathroom was crowded. The women's red faces were thrown into vivid relief by the white of the walls and their nightgowns. A couple of women acknowledged her with little dips of their heads, and Megan gave her a shy smile, but most of them ignored her, intent on their own toilettes. Hannah brushed her teeth and coiled her braid into a bun, pinning it up as best she could. There was a line for the toilets and then for the showers. By the time it was her turn, the water was tepid, and she had to rush to finish in time for breakfast. Still, it felt good to be clean, to have washed away the residue of the Chrome ward.

Hannah dressed and made her bed. Bridget was waiting for her by the door. She was about to follow her from the room when she heard a loud cough from behind her. She turned and saw Kayla looking at her with a wrinkled brow, patting the top of her head. Hannah was momentarily baffled, but then she remembered: *You will keep your hair decently covered except when sleeping.* She fetched her bonnet from the peg and put it on, taking some satisfaction in Bridget's moue of disappointment.

They proceeded to the dining hall, with Kayla close behind them. Hannah hadn't had a chance to speak with her new friend since the afternoon before, and she was hoping they'd sit next to one another again. But when they got there, Bridget moved quickly to take the last two seats at the open table, forcing Kayla to sit elsewhere.

Once everyone was assembled, Mrs. Henley entered alone and said a considerably less long-winded grace than her husband's. Breakfast was scant: a small bowl of oatmeal, a glass of milk and an apple. Afterward, still hungry, Hannah went with Bridget to consult the work schedule. They found their names under kitchen service for tomorrow's lunch and Friday's breakfast. Bridget also had chapel service all week. Hannah scanned the roster, which also included bathroom service, laundry service, floor service and sewing service, but her own name was missing.

"I don't seem to be on here," she said.

"You'll have other work to do in the afternoons this week."

There was also, Hannah saw, a heading called Zilpah, with one name listed beneath it. She wanted to ask what it meant but swallowed the question. To show ignorance was to show weakness. She would not bare her throat to Bridget.

"Hannah?" called a sweet, lilting voice. Mrs. Henley was beckoning her over to her table.

Bridget smirked. "It seems she wants a word with you."

Bitch. Bracing herself for a reprimand, Hannah went to Mrs. Henley.

"Good morning, Walker," she said, with a dimpled smile. "How are you settling in?"

"Fine, thank you."

"I'm glad to hear it." Mrs. Henley's cheeks were a little flushed, as though she'd just come from the bath. Wisps of blond hair peeked out from the edges of her bonnet. "It's my custom to invite every new walker for tea in my parlor. Did Bridget show you where my parlor is?"

"Yes, ma'am."

"Come on Saturday, at three o'clock. We'll have some chamomile and a nice cozy chat." Hearing dismissal, Hannah turned to go.

"One more thing," Mrs. Henley added. "Walker Bridget told me you stepped off the path last night."

Hannah turned back. "Yes, ma'am. But I didn't mean to."

"So you touched her by accident?"

"No, ma'am."

Little corrugations appeared in Mrs. Henley's brow. "I don't understand. Either it was deliberate or it wasn't."

"I didn't know it was against the rules," Hannah said. "Bridget didn't tell me until afterward."

"That's odd, because she told me she did."

"She didn't."

"Well, then you're not to blame. If Bridget lied about telling you the no-touching rule, it would be she who stepped off the path, not you." Mrs. Henley's tone was sympathetic. Hannah relaxed a little. "Of course, Bridget's already strayed once. This would be her second misstep, which would mean we'd have to cast her out. Poor thing, she's had such a difficult time." Mrs. Henley leaned forward, lowering her voice confidingly. "She had the scourge, you know. She wanted children badly, but the superbiotics came too late for her. After the cure was found, her husband left her for a younger woman who was fertile."

Hannah said nothing, stunned and unnerved that Mrs. Henley would divulge such intimate secrets about another walker. What would she reveal to Bridget or the others about Hannah?

"And after going through all that," Mrs. Henley continued, "to end up killing another woman's baby . . ."

"On purpose?"

"No, it was an accident. But she did bring it on herself."

So *that's why Bridget hates Megan and me,* Hannah thought. *Because we meant to do it.*

"So, are you sure she didn't mention the rule?" Mrs. Henley's mouth parted, revealing her pink tongue and the white tips of her incisors.

Hannah told herself that Bridget had it coming; that if she stayed, she'd just make Hannah's life miserable; that she was due to leave in a month anyway. And then Hannah remembered the phrase Bridget had used—"out there, on your own"—and the terror in her eyes when she'd said it. At least Hannah had her father to help her. When she left here, she wouldn't be alone in the world.

"It's possible I forgot," she said, with downcast eyes. "I was so exhausted last night."

Mrs. Henley was all kindness. "Of course you were. It must have been a long day. But tiredness and forgetfulness aren't excuses for disobedience. I'm sure Moses was tired when he came down from Mount Sinai, but he didn't forget one of God's commandments, did he?"

"No, ma'am."

Mrs. Henley shook her head sadly. "And on your first day too.

Just a few hours after you gave us your solemn word that you'd obey our rules."

"I'm sorry, Mrs. Henley."

"I'm very disappointed in you, Hannah, and I know Reverend Henley will be too. He takes these things so hard."

Looking into Mrs. Henley's sorrowful blue eyes, Hannah felt that she *was* guilty, if not of breaking the rule she was accused of, then of a weakness of purpose, an essential failure of spirit. She'd let down so many people: her family and friends, her employers, Aidan. And now, the Henleys, who'd been kind enough to take her in and offer her this chance at redemption. A chance she was proving unworthy of.

"And of course, your parents and Secretary Dale will have to be told," Mrs. Henley said.

Hannah felt an upwelling of panic. They mustn't know, she mustn't shame them any more than she already had. She found herself babbling, pleading, "I'm sorry, Mrs. Henley, please don't tell them, I'll do better, I promise, I'll—"

Mrs. Henley stopped her, saying, "It's good that you're sorry, Hannah. Penitence is the first thing the path demands of us. I want you to reflect and pray on what you've done, and we'll speak more about it on Saturday, when we have our chat." Hannah wanted to say more, but Mrs. Henley held up one small, pale hand.

"Go now, and begin your enlightenment."

HANNAH STOPPED JUST outside the dining hall and sagged against the wall, giving her heart time to slow its wild thudding. Her thoughts were scattered, bewildered. What in the world had just happened to her? Who was that groveling creature? Reason returned as she calmed down, and with it, anger. Mrs. Henley had enjoyed their encounter; Hannah was sure of it. The woman had played her like a harp, and Hannah had obligingly sounded every note she wanted to hear. Reverend Henley might be a kind man, genuinely interested in helping others find a path to God, but his wife was something else.

The quietness of the hallway made Hannah aware that she was late for enlightenment. She walked hurriedly to the room Bridget had shown her the night before. The door was open, and she paused at the threshold. Eight women, all Reds except for Megan, all holding dolls, sat in the circle of chairs, along with a tall, angular man in his forties with a glossy, shaven head and an air of authority—the enlightener, presumably. A stool, conspicuously empty, was in the center of the circle. When she saw it, Hannah felt a ripple of disquiet, which intensified as she took in the bizarre scene before her. One woman was rocking her doll in her arms, crooning to it; another was bouncing hers on her knee; a third was holding hers facedown on her shoulder and patting its back as though burping it.

Hannah gripped the door jamb. *Dear God. Help me.*

"Come in, Walker," the enlightener said in a stern, commanding voice, "and close the door." Fighting the urge to flee, Hannah obeyed him.

The enlightener pointed to the stool. "Be seated." Somehow, her legs carried her to it. It swiveled as she sat down. Sketching an arc in the air with his finger, he said, "Look upon them, Walker. For to look upon them is to look upon your own sin."

Hannah revolved in a slow, clockwise circle, her eyes drawn to the dolls. They were all life-sized—infant-sized—but otherwise they were varied. Some were crude, with buttons for eyes, yarn for hair and hideous, cross-stitched red mouths, while others were better crafted. Two were brown; the rest were a pale apricot.

The only sound in the room was the eerie, high-pitched crooning of the woman rocking the doll. She began to sing to it, touching various parts of it: *"Here is my HEAD, and here is my NOSE. Here are my FINGERS and here are my TOES. Here is my TUMMY and here is my KNEE. Thank you, God, for making ME. Here is my—"* The woman broke off her song abruptly and jiggled the doll, saying, "Shh, shh. Don't cry, baby, please don't cry. Mama's here."

Hannah swiveled so she didn't have to watch, but the mad baby talk continued, on and on. The enlightener ignored it, his attention fixed on Hannah, his eyes ablaze with some emotion she couldn't name. Whatever it was, it made her skin crawl. She turned to the woman sitting to his right, who was considerably older than the rest of them—almost too old to get pregnant. The woman looked at her with weary compassion.

"Sonia, why don't you begin," the enlightener said to her. He leaned forward in his chair, steepling his fingers.

The older woman held up her doll, showing it to Hannah and the others. "This is my son, Octavio," she said, with a Spanish accent. "He would have been my eighth child, but I murdered him, against God's commandment and the wishes of my husband." She turned the doll toward herself and addressed it. "Forgive me, Octavio, for taking your precious life."

The woman next to her spoke. "This here's my little boy, Matthew. I murdered him 'cause I didn't trust in the Lord to provide for him after his daddy left us. Forgive me, Matthew, for taking your precious life."

"This is my baby girl, Aisha. Her father raped me, but it wasn't her fault. She was innocent, and I murdered her. Forgive me, Aisha."

Megan held up her crude doll. "This is my unborn baby, John Wyatt or Gemma Dawn, depending on if it's a boy or a girl. I tried to kill it, but God stopped the pill from working." Her tone was sullen. *No penitence there,* Hannah thought.

"*Him* or *her,* Megan, not *it,*" the enlightener said reprovingly.

"I tried to kill *him,*" Megan said, "but God saved him. I'm sorry, baby." She addressed this last to her slightly rounded stomach.

The wretched circuit continued, with Hannah as its fulcrum, until all the women except the mad one—who seemed completely unaware of what was happening around her—had confessed and apologized. Finally, the enlightener turned to Hannah.

"And you, Walker? Why are you here?"

She replied without equivocation. "I killed my unborn child."

"Why did you do it?"

"Because I was afraid," she said. And not, Hannah realized suddenly, just for Aidan, but also for herself. He wouldn't have left his wife for her; he'd made that clear. And the thought of bearing and raising a child alone had terrified her. The truth, buried for months, hit Hannah hard: she'd acted as much out of selfishness as out of love.

"Afraid? Of what? The shame of being an unwed mother?" The enlightener stood and approached her, looming over her. His face was an angry, mottled pink. "Where was your fear of God's wrath, woman? It was Him you transgressed against. When you defiled your body with fornication and then abortion, you defiled God. When you stole the life of your innocent child, you stole what was God's." He was almost shouting now, sprinkling Hannah's upturned face with little flecks of spittle. "Every time a woman's weakness leads her to defy God's commandments, Satan laughs. He was laughing when Eve took the forbidden fruit from the tree. He was laughing during the Great Scourge, when the fornication of women spread the foul pestilence that made their wombs barren. He was laughing when they begged God for children but could not conceive, oh yes, he was drinking their tears of despair like wine. Could you hear him laughing, Walker, when you spread your legs for the man who impregnated you, and when you spread them again for the butcher who scraped your precious child from your womb? Could you feel God's wrath raining down on you?" He thrust his hand up toward the ceiling, fingers spread wide, and held it there for several seconds before lowering it to his side. His voice softened. "But God is merciful. He sent His only Son, Jesus Christ, to redeem your sins and offer you a path to salvation, through penitence, atonement, truth and humility. Do you humbly repent your sin against God, Hannah Payne? Are you ready to atone with all your soul for the murder of your child?"

Hannah bowed her head. "I'm ready." She felt her arms break out in goosebumps as she said the words—the same ones she'd said to Raphael just before he performed the abortion.

"Go, then, to the sewing room, and make a doll in your child's image. Shape it not just from cloth and thread, but from all the anguish and repentance in your soul. With each stitch, imagine the precious life that you have extinguished: the eyes that will never see the wonder of God's creation, the mouth that will never suckle your breast or sing God's praises, the hands that will never clasp your finger or wear a wedding ring. Take as much time as you need, and when you've finished, rejoin us here in the circle."

Hannah stood and went to the door. As she was about to leave, the enlightener said, "Don't forget to give the baby a name."

SHE SPENT FOUR days making it, working on it every morning and afternoon as well as during her two nightly hours of free time. There was a sewing machine, but she didn't use it. She wanted the doll to come wholly from her hands. She worked in a state of rapt concentration, bordering on trance. The doll was a prayer, pulled stitch by stitch from her soul, and she sewed it slowly and painstakingly. By the time she stumbled to bed each night, her fingers were so cramped she could barely button her nightgown.

In the mornings she was alone in the sewing room, but after lunch she was joined by two Yellows, who spent the afternoons making dresses and bonnets, stitching quilts and mending used clothes for the poor. The women spoke quietly to each other, leaving Hannah to herself. Mrs. Henley stopped by occasionally to check their work and add new garments to the to-do pile. Hannah she mostly ignored; at least, until the third day.

"You certainly are taking your time with that," Mrs. Henley said, peering down at Hannah's doll. "How much longer will you need?"

"I'm hoping to finish by tomorrow afternoon," Hannah said, then added, "The enlightener said to take as much time as necessary."

Mrs. Henley's blue eyes narrowed. "You're not trying to avoid enlightenment, are you? Because that would be a very serious step off the path."

"No, ma'am."

"Let me see." Mrs. Henley held out a peremptory hand.

With a strange reluctance, Hannah handed the other woman the doll. She studied it in silence. "Well, Hannah," she said finally, "this is exceptionally fine work. You must be very proud of it."

Recognizing the trap, Hannah bent her head. "No, ma'am. I just want to make it as good as I can. To . . . do justice to the baby."

Mrs. Henley handed the doll back. "Take care, Walker, that you don't enjoy your penance too much."

Hannah finished late Friday afternoon, just before supper. She examined the doll one last time, scrutinizing it for flaws, but could find none. It was a perfect offering. She left the sewing room, carrying the doll before her with her head held high, meeting the astonished eyes of every woman she passed on the way. A collective murmur of wonderment arose when she entered the dining hall, rippling across the room in her wake, dropping into a profound silence when she sat down. The doll was so lavishly and exquisitely wrought—the eyes with their impossibly delicate lashes so lambent, the pink rosebud of the mouth so tender, the fingers and toes with their tiny half-moon nails so plump and sweet—that it seemed merely asleep rather than inert. But it wasn't just the object she held that commanded the attention of every woman in the room, it was Hannah herself. Her creation had transformed her, dispelling her despair. She felt vibrant again, alive as she hadn't since her arrest, and she could see it reflected in their eyes.

The women were so riveted that when the Henleys made their usual majestic entrance, no one except Hannah noticed. Ponder Henley had the flummoxed look of a leading man who'd come onstage to discover the entire audience facing the other way. Mrs. Henley, however, was unmistakably irked, especially when she discerned the focus of the women's attention. The look she flashed Hannah was venomous.

Hannah lifted her chin and calmly returned Mrs. Henley's gaze. She would not be cowed by her again.

Later, after the evening service, Hannah sought out Kayla. They went to the sewing room, which Hannah knew would be empty this time of night. When the door closed behind them, Kayla gestured at Hannah's doll and said, "Just a seamstress, huh? Like Jesus was just a carpenter."

Hannah shrugged, a little abashed. Her defiance had drained away, leaving only fatigue and anxiety about her meeting with Mrs. Henley tomorrow.

"I thought the Mrs. was going to have a hissy fit," Kayla went on. "And did you see Fridget's face? Looked like she'd swallowed a gallon of sour milk."

Hannah made an unpleasant face of her own, and Kayla said, "How's it going with her, anyway?"

"Not well. We had an argument the other night, and I lost my temper. Afterward she told Mrs. Henley I'd touched her on purpose."

"Did you?"

"All I did was grab hold of her hand. I didn't know it was against the rules."

"Let me guess, she didn't tell you."

"No. Why's it forbidden, anyway?"

"They say it's to keep us focused on the spiritual as opposed to the physical, but I think they do it to make us feel as much like pariahs as possible. That, and they're probably afraid of winding up with a center full of baby dykes."

Hannah stared at Kayla. Surely she didn't mean . . .

"You know, budding lesbians."

Flustered, Hannah said, "I'm sure no one here would do anything like that."

"You say that now, but talk to me in five weeks. Sometimes I miss TJ so bad, even Fridget starts to look sexy." Hannah's unease must have shown, because Kayla laughed and said, "Relax, you're not my type."

Hannah changed the subject. "Mrs. Henley told me Bridget killed a child. Do you know how it happened?

"Drunk driving. She hit a pregnant woman who was crossing the street. The woman survived, but she was paralyzed from the waist down, and she lost the baby. It was all over the vids."

"Mercy. How could you live with that every day?" The response was reflexive. As soon as Hannah had said it she thought, *But I live with it, somehow.*

"Oh, Fridget manages just fine," Kayla said. "We're in enlightenment together, you know. She acts all humble and sorry, but that's all it is, an act. The woman's an iceberg."

But Hannah knew that Kayla was wrong, that it was the iceberg that was the act, a barricade Bridget had built against the horrific truth of what she'd done. Because if she let herself fully acknowledge it, it would destroy her. This wasn't intuition on Hannah's part, but something surer than that, something she knew in her bones, just as she'd known that Mrs. Henley had taken pleasure in her distress. She'd always been a fairly good judge of character, but never to this extent. Where was this newfound insight of hers coming from? Hannah shook her head as a second, more unsettling question occurred to her: What did it mean that she, unlike Bridget, could live with what she'd done? Perhaps Bridget was actually a better person than she was.

"Anyway," Kayla said, "you should be rid of her in a few days. Usually they turn you loose after a week, though not always. It's up to the Mrs."

"Why her and not Reverend Henley?"

A snort of laughter. "He may have the title of director, but make no mistake, she's the ruler of this roost. Man hardly ever comes out of his study except to eat and preach. Just holes up in there all day long, working on his interminable sermons. I think Mrs. Henley likes having him out of the way."

"I'm supposed to have tea with her tomorrow. I wanted to ask you about that."

Kayla stiffened, and her eyes slid away from Hannah's. "What about it?"

"What should I expect? What did she talk to you about?"

"We're not supposed to discuss it."

"I won't say anything, I promise," Hannah said.

"Look, I can't. If she found out . . ."

"How would she find out? I'm certainly not going to tell her."

"I can't, Hannah," Kayla said curtly. "I'm sorry. We'd better get back."

They walked to the dormitory in awkward silence. When they passed the door to Mrs. Henley's parlor, Hannah sensed rather than saw Kayla flinch.

Hannah was restless and unable to concentrate during Bible study the next morning. After lunch, she went to the reading room and browsed through the material there to pass the time until three o'clock. In addition to titles like *Darwin the Deceiver* and *A Crown to Her Husband: 365 Devotions for the Virtuous Wife,* she found an old book of Aidan's, *A Life of Purpose, A Life in Christ,* published when he was still a junior pastor at Ignited Word. The photo on the back was of him on the day he graduated from seminary, his face alight with happiness and hope. Hannah stared at it, seared by the image, thinking of the few times she'd seen him look like that. Most all of them, he'd been among the children at the shelter. Only once had he ever been so wholly joyous and abandoned with her.

He'd asked her to meet him on a Saturday at one of their usual hotels, but at the unprecedented hour of seven in the morning. It was late October. A rare cool front had come through the night before, and the temperature had dropped to the mid-seventies. Hannah rode her bike to the hotel. When she arrived, she found Aidan waiting for her in his car.

"Get in," he said, surprising her; they'd never gone anywhere together, just the two of them.

"Where are we going?"

"It's a secret."

They headed downtown and then took I-20 east. Aidan held her hand and stroked the back of it with his thumb, and after half an hour, Hannah began to drowse off. Her last thought before she surrendered to sleep was how delicious it felt, and how paradoxically liberating, to give herself over so completely to his will.

She woke sometime later, when the road changed from asphalt to rutted dirt, and found herself in the middle of a forest of towering pines. The sharp, heady scent of them filled the car. She inhaled deeply, thinking that she'd never smelled air so wondrously fresh in all her life. "Where are we?"

"In the enchanted forest," Aidan said. "You forgot to drop your bread crumbs, so you're doomed to wander here until a prince comes along and breaks the spell with a kiss."

Surprised by his mood—Aidan was many things, but whimsical had never been one of them—Hannah said, "What if I don't want him to break it? Will he wander here with me forever?"

"Yes, but then he could never kiss you. You'd be stuck with a frustrated grouch for all eternity."

She smiled. "And the poor prince would be stuck with a foul-tempered shrew."

They pulled up in front of a rustic wooden cabin. Beyond it, through the trees, Hannah could see a tantalizing shimmer of blue. "And that," Aidan said, "is the magic lake. They say if you dive into it at the exact instant the setting sun touches the horizon, you'll be granted your heart's desire."

He'd brought everything they needed: a cooler of food, swimsuits, sunscreen, inner tubes. Hannah wasn't a practiced swimmer—they'd closed all the pools when she was a child because of the drought, and she'd been to the beach only a handful of times since—but it came back to her quickly. They spent the day like teenagers, splashing around, lazing on the porch, feeding each other pickles and orange slices, laughing, kissing. Aidan stroked her hair and face, but his caresses never strayed lower, and when Hannah's hand started to slip under the waistband of his bathing trunks, he took hold of it and shook his head. "Let's not," he said.

She didn't question him. She didn't ask what time they would have to leave, or whose cabin it was, or what excuse Aidan had given his wife to explain his absence. She lived with him in the fugitive joy of each moment. As the sun got low in the sky, he took hold of her hand and led her to the dock. The sun was a molten red orb, like a great burning heart. They stood and watched it sink until it was almost touching the horizon.

"Now!" Aidan cried, and started to run. Hannah ran beside him, bare feet pounding the boards of the dock, and hurtled her body off the end of it into the air. They hung suspended together above the water for an eyeblink before their hands separated and they plunged in. She came up before he did. Breathless, she treaded water, waiting for him to appear. Just when she was beginning to worry, he erupted from the lake right in front of her, making her shriek. He laughed, his own face incandescent with happiness, and she glimpsed what he must have looked like as a little boy. His beauty and innocence snatched her heart and squeezed it like an implacable fist.

Thirteen months ago, she thought now. *A lifetime ago.* She shoved the book back into its place on the shelf.

AT PRECISELY THREE o'clock, she rapped on Mrs. Henley's door.

"Come in," Mrs. Henley called. Hannah opened the door and stepped into the parlor. It was an intimate, feminine space, decorated in cheerful shades of yellow and blue. Unlike every other room Hannah had seen at the center, the parlor had two eye-level windows, covered by embroidered white curtains sheer enough to let light in but too opaque to see through. She longed to reach out her hand and part them, to get a glimpse of the world beyond these walls.

"Do you like my new curtains?" Mrs. Henley asked. "I made them myself." She was sitting in a comfortable armchair facing away from the windows. On a table in front of her was a tray with a teapot, two china cups and a plate of cookies.

"They're lovely."

"Thank you. That's quite a compliment, coming from a seamstress of your talents." Mrs. Henley's forehead crinkled. "But where is your beautiful doll? You know you're supposed to carry it with you at all times."

A spike of alarm shot through Hannah; in her distracted state, she'd left the doll in the reading room. "I forgot it. I can go back and fetch it if you like."

Mrs. Henley considered her for a moment, and then her face relaxed. "Well," she said, "I suppose we can overlook it this once."

Hannah's breath left her with an audible *whoosh,* and Mrs. Henley smiled. "Goodness, where are my manners!" She gestured at the sofa opposite her. "Please, sit down. Would you like a cup of tea?"

"Yes, thank you."

The wall opposite Hannah was covered with a large collection of mostly amateurish art. In addition to needlepointed, stitched, carved, painted and quilted versions of the ubiquitous PENITENCE, ATONEMENT, TRUTH AND HUMILITY, there were several sketches of Jesus, watercolors of Bible scenes, wreaths made out of twigs and dried roses, carved wooden crosses and other homespun efforts.

"Aren't they sweet?" Mrs. Henley said. "They're all gifts the girls have given me and Reverend Henley over the years. It never fails to humble us, to know we've touched a walker's life so deeply."

She poured the tea. Hannah's hand trembled as she took her

cup, and it made a little rattling noise against the saucer. "There's no need to be nervous, Hannah," Mrs. Henley said. "This is just an informal chat, so we can get to know one another better. Would you like a cookie? I baked them this morning."

Hannah took one. Her mouth was so dry she choked on it and started coughing. She washed it down with tea.

When she'd recovered, Mrs. Henley asked, "So, were you a professional seamstress?"

"Yes, ma'am."

"What kind of work did you do?"

"Bridal clothes, mostly. I sewed for a salon in Plano."

"Ah, pity. I don't suppose they'll want you back now. After all, what bride would want her wedding dress handled by . . ." Mrs. Henley stopped, as if suddenly aware she'd been impolitic, then said, with artificial brightness, "Well, perhaps you can get work at a factory or some other place where they won't care."

"Yes, perhaps I can." Hannah gave the other woman a bland, polite half-smile and stilled her mind, marshaling her defenses.

Mrs. Henley set her teacup down and leaned forward, crossing her legs at the ankles. *Here we go,* Hannah thought.

"When was it you had the abortion?"

"June."

"And how far along were you?

"Three months."

"So, that would mean you got pregnant sometime in March. Were you able to pinpoint the exact . . . occasion when it occurred?"

Hannah closed her eyes, remembering: the hotel in Grand Prairie. They hadn't been together in six weeks, and they'd been frantic, desperate.

"Hannah? You haven't answered my question."

"Yes."

"Did he know you were going to have an abortion?"

"No."

"Did he even know you were pregnant?"

"No."

"That's quite a violation of his paternal rights. You're lucky he didn't file charges against you."

Hannah nodded, not trusting herself to speak. She could feel her pulse quickening, becoming erratic.

"Of course," Mrs. Henley said, "if he had, his identity would have been made public. And if you'd had the baby, you would have been compelled to name him." She squinted a little, studying Hannah's face like a particularly intriguing museum exhibit. "I understand you also refused to name the abortionist."

"I never knew his name," Hannah said.

With a little wave of her hand, Mrs. Henley said, "Well, I won't ask you to reveal that, nor will I ask the name of the baby's father. Their identities are none of my concern. But I *will* need to know the details of your transgression, as unpleasant as it might be for you to recount them and for me to hear them. Let's begin with the moment you got undressed and lay down on the table—was it a table?"

Hannah stared at her, uncomprehending.

"Truth is the third thing the path demands of us," Mrs. Henley said, in a voice like honey poured thinly over granite. "As the reverend and I told you when you came to us, truth is not optional here, and a lie of omission is still a lie. So I ask you again, was it a table?"

"Yes."

"Show me how it was, how you were positioned. You can use the sofa or the floor, whichever you prefer."

Rooted by horror, Hannah could neither move nor look away. Mrs. Henley's avid eyes were locked on hers, siphoning her shame, and she saw that there was no bottom in their blue depths, no ter-minus, just limitless, insatiable hunger.

"I was prepared to forgive your first step off the path with Bridget," Mrs. Henley said, "since you were new here and un-used to our ways. But if you can't be truthful with me, Hannah, I'll be forced to conclude that this is a pattern of defiance and deceitfulness."

Hannah closed her eyes. Where else could she go? There was nowhere. Slowly, mechanically, she lay down on her back and brought her knees up.

"The *exact* position, Hannah," Mrs. Henley said, in an exasper-ated tone.

Hannah parted her legs, and it all came flooding back: the hot room, the feel of cold metal entering her, the pain. She heard her-self whimper—then, now.

"Look at me, Hannah." She turned her head. Mrs. Henley leaned forward, cocking her own head sideways. "How did you feel as you lay there, waiting for the abortionist to begin?"

"I wanted to die," Hannah said. Falling, falling into that hun-gry blue.

THE INTERROGATION WENT on and on: "How long did it take?" "Was there a great deal of pain?" "Did you see the aborted fetus afterward?" "How did your parents react?" "What was it like to wake up in the Chrome ward and see yourself for the first time?" "Did you imagine people you knew sitting at home watching you?" And over and over again, the question, "How did that make you feel?" After ten minutes, Hannah felt close to the end of her reserves; after an hour, she felt scraped as raw as she had after the abortion. The room was stuffy and warm, and she could smell the sharp odor of her own body. Mrs. Henley's complexion was rosy and there was a slight sheen on her upper lip, but apart from that she seemed perfectly comfortable. *In her element,* Hannah thought, *like a rattlesnake basking on a rock in the sun.*

Finally, Mrs. Henley said, "You can sit up now, Hannah."

Hannah righted herself, feeling a little dizzy.

"Would you like some more chamomile, dear?"

"No, thank you." She would rather have drunk arsenic.

"I have to say, one thing that surprised me was the degree of interest Secretary Dale showed in your case. Do you know, he personally called Reverend Henley to speak with him about you? And of course, there was his appeal at your trial. So eloquent, so . . . impassioned." Mrs. Henley took a sip of tea, her blue eyes dancing merrily over the rim of the cup.

Striving to keep her voice even, Hannah said, "Yes, we're all very thankful, my family and I, for his kindness. But that's the kind of pastor Reverend Dale is. He feels personally responsible for every member of his congregation."

Mrs. Henley's pale eyebrows formed two incredulous arches. "Surely not to the extent of calling in from Washington DC every time one of his former flock goes astray?"

"I really can't say." Hannah felt sweat dripping down her torso under her dress and hoped it wasn't visible.

"Of course, you were also his employee, weren't you. Did you see Reverend Dale often?"

Just then, a side door opened and Ponder Henley came in. He had a notepad in his hand, and his eyes were lit with boyish eagerness. He didn't seem to see Hannah; his attention was all for his wife, who quickly hid her irritation at being interrupted behind a delighted smile.

"You were right," he exclaimed. "Those passages from Leviticus make all the difference. Listen to this—"

"I have company, Ponder. Hannah's come for tea."

Reverend Henley looked startled and then crestfallen to find his wife occupied. "Oh! Well, don't let me interrupt you. I know how you girls enjoy your little chats."

"It's true, we do," Mrs. Henley agreed. "But of course your sermon is *much* more important, and you know how I love hearing you practice." Reverend Henley practically glowed under his wife's adoring gaze. "Hannah and I can continue our talk another time. Just let me see her out, and I'll be right there."

As the door shut behind him, Mrs. Henley glanced at the wooden clock on the wall. "Good heavens, it's already four thirty." She looked back at Hannah, and her nose wrinkled ever so slightly. "I bet you'd like to shower and change your dress before supper. You go right ahead, and if Bridget or anyone else questions you, tell them I gave you special permission."

Hannah got unsteadily to her feet, and Mrs. Henley escorted her to the door. "I'm so glad we had this talk, Hannah. I must ask that you keep it strictly between us. I'd be very dismayed if I found out you'd been discussing it with any of the other walkers."

"I won't," Hannah said, understanding now Kayla's reticence and discomfiture. Who would want to share such humiliation with anyone?

On the way back to the dormitory, she passed several other women in the hallway. When they caught sight of her face, they looked at her with pity, giving her a wide berth.

HANNAH SPENT THE WEEKEND brooding about her talk with Mrs. Henley. Her shame eventually gave way to indignation and then full-fledged anger, both at the woman's cruelty and at her own paralysis and complicity in the face of it. Why hadn't she lied, as she had with the police interrogators? Why hadn't she walked out of the room, out of the center? Could the outside world possibly be any worse than this?

Hannah wondered too how much her mother had known about this place when she proposed sending her here. Had her mother been aware of the Henleys' methods of enlightenment? And what about Aidan, had he known? Hannah told herself he couldn't possibly have, but doubt festered in her mind.

Monday at breakfast, Bridget informed Hannah that she was no longer her pathfinder. "There's a new walker coming on Wednesday, and Mrs. Henley has asked me to show her the path. As of today, you're on your own."

"I'm crushed," Hannah said. "After all the good times we've had."

Kayla, sitting across from them, choked on her oatmeal.

After breakfast, the two of them joined the other women clustered in front of the work roster. Kayla was pleased; she'd been allotted chapel service—easy duty. Hannah expected to see her own name under sewing service but discovered instead that she'd be taking over her friend's job cleaning the bathrooms.

"Tough luck," Kayla said. "Still, Bathroom Slave's not so bad. At least you get to be alone. Beats the hell out of Laundry Wench—being stuck in a sauna with three other cranky, stinky women."

Bridget's name was written under the mysterious Zilpah heading. Hannah pointed to it and asked, "What's that?"

"Personal lackey to Mrs. Henley. I've never done it—she only assigns it to her pets—but from what I've heard it's mostly writing letters, tidying the parlor and the study and chauffeuring her around town."

"They get to leave the center?"

"Yeah, and you should hear them lording it over the rest of us." Kayla humphed. "As far as I'm concerned, they're welcome to it. The farther I stay away from that woman, the better."

"You and me both," Hannah said, with more feeling than she'd intended.

"You all right, after Saturday?" Kayla asked. "You looked kinda… wrung out. Everybody does, though," she added quickly.

"I'm fine." The words were rote and, from the look on Kayla's face, unconvincing. Hannah wondered if she'd ever be able to mean them again.

When she walked into enlightenment a few minutes later, she was relieved to see that the stool was gone, and there were now ten chairs in the circle. The enlightener's eyes widened a fraction when he caught sight of her doll, but he said nothing. When everyone was seated, he turned to the woman on his left.

"Monica, why don't you begin," he said.

"This is my daughter, Shiloh. Her father threatened to leave me if I didn't have the abortion, but I should've cared more about her than him. Forgive me, Shiloh, for taking your precious life."

"This is my little boy, Christopher. I was afraid my parents would kick me out if they found out I was pregnant. Forgive me, Christopher, for taking your precious life."

"This is my daughter, Aisha…"

"This is my sweet Octavio…"

At last, it was Hannah's turn. She didn't hesitate. She'd known what she would have named her child since soon after she discovered she was pregnant. Her child and Aidan's, begun from a tiny mote of matter and nurtured within the sea of her womb. Hidden, wondrous, unknowable. Unwelcome.

"This is my daughter, Pearl," she said.

WEDNESDAY AFTERNOON, HANNAH took her place on the choir riser with the others to "welcome" the new walker. A current of unmistakable excitement pulsed through the room as they awaited her arrival. They were a pack, scenting prey, and Hannah was one of them. But when the woman—a middle-aged Red with graying hair and sagging breasts—opened the narrow door and stepped inside, starting in fright at the sound of their voices, cowering and covering herself at the sight of them, Hannah's excitement evaporated, and compunction and pity took its place.

Later, she realized that their reaction owed more to boredom than to prurience or cruelty. The days at the center passed with intolerable slowness, running together like the colors in a jar of used paintbrushes, merging into a uniform, leaden gray. Sermons, meals, enlightenment, work, repeat. She and every other woman here were starved for variation.

She lived for Saturday afternoons, when her time was her own, and for letters from her father and Becca, bittersweet as they were to read. They arrived already opened, presumably by Mrs. Henley. Her father's were awkward, relentlessly chipper briefings on the weather, local news and the family:

Dear Hannah,

I hope you're doing well and making some friends there. We're all fine, bracing for an ice storm tomorrow, though it's 65° and sunny today. Typical Texas weather in other words!

Reverend Maynard is settling in as head pastor, but he's got some mighty big shoes to fill. Attendance has fallen off quite a bit since Reverend Dale left. As much as we miss him, we're all proud of the job he's doing in Washington. I guess we were lucky to have had him to ourselves for as long as we did. He and Alyssa are coming home for Thanksgiving, and the rumor is he's going to lead the Wednesday night service. I'm hoping he'll put in a good word Upstairs for the Boys while he's at it. They're playing the Giants on Thanksgiving Day, and they'll need every prayer they can get to win. Walton sprained his wrist two weeks ago, and the offense has been paralyzed without him. It'll be a miracle if we make the playoffs this year.

Becca's finally over the worst of her morning sickness, and she's starting to show. I'm building cribs for the babies and your mother's knitting up a storm—you should see all the pink and blue yarn scattered all over the house.

With the holidays coming I've had to put in a lot of extra hours at the store, so I haven't had much time to look for a job or an apartment for you. But I'll get on it right after New Year's, I promise. In the meantime know that my thoughts and prayers are with you. I miss you. We all do.

Love,
Dad

Becca managed better. She wrote humorously of her pregnancy, her day-to-day life, people they knew from church. Every once in a while, when she spoke of Cole, Hannah detected an undertone of disquiet in her words:

Dear Hannah,

How I wish you were here! I've had to let the waistlines of all my skirts out AGAIN, and you know how much I love sewing. My fingers look like pincushions.

Now that I'm starting to show, Cole's getting more protective than ever. I swear, he hardly lets me leave the house except to go to church! He's joined this new Christian men's group, and they have meetings a couple of nights a week. He won't tell me the name of it or where they meet—all I know is it's not part of Ignited Word—but he says it's similar to the Promise Keepers.

I hope you're doing okay and have made some friends there. I know they keep you busy but please write more often if you can. I miss you so much. Mama's still mad, but I'll keep working on her.

Off now in search of cheesecake. And olives. Last week it was BLC sandwiches (bacon, lettuce & maraschino cherries).

All my love,

Becca

Hannah worried about her sister and father but was powerless to help them. No doubt they felt the same. It didn't escape her that although they both expressed hope that she was well, neither of them ever actually asked how she was. Perhaps, she thought, they couldn't bear to hear the answer. She kept her replies short and light, sparing them the truth: that she felt increasingly as though she'd wandered into hell.

Enlightenment was the worst, and she came to dread it more with every passing day. She never knew what to expect: a lecture from a visiting doctor on the gory specifics of the procedure, complete with jars of fetuses in formaldehyde; an "ideation session" where they had to imagine alternate futures for their aborted children; a holovid showing bloody, half-aborted babies trying to crawl out of their mothers' wombs. But the worst were the survivors who came in person: a teenaged girl whose arm had been ripped off when her mother tried to abort her at twenty-six weeks; a man who'd suffered from cerebral palsy and crippling depression all his life, only to learn in his forties that his twin brother had been aborted, and that his own brain had been perforated during the procedure. These sessions left Hannah feeling so scalded and depressed that even Kayla couldn't reach her. The hope she'd felt when she first arrived at the center gradually slipped away, and she found herself struggling to maintain her faith. Her conversations with God began to take on a doubtful, then an accusatory note. How could He approve of what the Henleys were doing here? Could this really be the path to Him?

What little sanity Hannah retained she owed to Kayla, whose spirits were less wilted by the grim climate of the center. She joked about everything: the food, their clothing, their red skin, Bridget and especially the Henleys, whom she'd nicknamed Moral and Harpy. Kayla made up bawdy limericks about them, saving them up for when Hannah was feeling low and delivering them in an atrocious Irish accent:

> There once was a reverend called Moral.
> With his wife he had only one quarrel.
> Though he'd nightly beseech her,
> His pleas could not reach her;
> This Harpy refused to go oral.

Hannah was unused to such obscenities, but once her initial discomfiture wore off, she found herself laughing every bit as hard as Kayla. Where the Henleys were concerned, the nastier the better.

But toward the end of Hannah's first month at the center, Kayla's mood darkened, and she turned restless and short-tempered. Hannah asked her several times what was the matter, but she wouldn't say. Finally, she confessed that she hadn't heard from her boyfriend in some time.

"The first month I was here, TJ sent me letters every few days.

And now, nothing for two weeks. I'm worried something's happened to him."

"What did his last letter say?" Hannah asked.

"Just that he hadn't found us an apartment yet, but he was looking hard."

"I'm sure you'll hear from him soon."

But Kayla heard nothing, and she became more and more agitated. A week later, on a Monday, she took Hannah aside after breakfast.

"I've decided," Kayla said. "If I haven't heard from him by Friday, I'm leaving. This just isn't like him. Something must be wrong."

A wave of despair swelled and broke inside of Hannah. How could she endure it here, without a friend? "There could be other reasons he hasn't written," she said.

"Like what?"

Hating herself a little but unable to stop herself, Hannah said, "What if he's just . . . changed his mind and doesn't have the guts to tell you?"

"He wouldn't do that," Kayla said, with an emphatic shake of her head. "If he hasn't written, it's because he can't."

"What if you're wrong? Where will you go?"

"I'm not wrong," Kayla said. But she no longer sounded quite so certain.

There was no letter from TJ that day or the next. Hannah's anxiety, both for her friend and for herself, was acute, and she slept poorly both nights. Wednesday crawled by. Reverend Henley was the featured guest at enlightenment that day, and for three stultifying hours he led a "discussion" of God's view of abortion, during which not even the enlightener could get a word in edgewise. By suppertime Hannah felt glazed with fatigue. She and Kayla were at different tables, but they managed to sit next to each other during chapel. Kayla was so fidgety, she earned a glare from Reverend Henley, and Hannah knew she was impatient to get back to the dormitory and see whether TJ had written. They walked there together in silence. There was no letter waiting on Kayla's nightstand. Her shoulders drooped.

"There's still one more day," Hannah said.

"No." Kayla's head came up, and she jerked it in the direction of the hallway. Her mouth was a flat, determined line. Hannah followed her to the sewing room and closed the door behind them.

"I'm not waiting till Friday," Kayla said. "First thing tomorrow, I'm going." Hannah couldn't speak; it felt like there was a stone lodged in her throat.

Kayla took Hannah's hand. "Look, why don't you come with me? We could help each other."

Hannah considered it; in fact, she'd been mulling it over all week. But how would she live? And what would she tell her father? He'd be so disappointed in her for squandering this gift of a sanctuary, this chance at redemption. And her mother, what would she think? For the first time Hannah acknowledged the hope she'd held on to, that if she spent six months in this place—if she proved how truly penitent she was—she'd be forgiven, not just by God, but also by her mother. Slender as that hope was, she knew that if she left now, it would vanish.

"I can't," she said. "I'm sorry."

"I understand. You're just having too much fun here." Kayla's smile was strained and her eyes anxious.

"You'll find him."

"What if I don't? I don't think I can make it on my own."

"You have to, or they win, remember?"

Kayla nodded, and Hannah gave her a quick, hard hug.

"Here, before I forget." Kayla pulled a piece of paper from her pocket. "This is my number."

As Hannah took it, she thought of Billy Sikes and his hideous offer, and her eyes welled with tears. Who could have predicted, on that day six weeks ago, that she would have a real friend, someone who could look at her and see something besides a contemptible criminal?

"Don't you start now, you'll get me going too," Kayla said. "You'll have to memorize it before you leave or write it somewhere on yourself, because they won't let you take anything with you. I want you to promise me you'll call me as soon as you get out."

"I will." Hannah put the number in her pocket, and they hugged again, longer this time. The physical contact was almost unbearably sweet. Hannah's parents had always been unsparing with hugs and kisses, and she and Becca had often crawled into one another's beds for comfort. And then there'd been Aidan, whose touch had felt like a homecoming. How she missed it, missed all of them.

Kayla pulled away first. "You take care of yourself, hear? Don't let this place get to you."

The door opened suddenly, startling them, and Mrs. Henley stuck her head in. "Oh, here you are, Hannah," she said, with unconvincing surprise. She fingered her cross, and Hannah suddenly apprehended that the walkers' crosses must be transmitters. She wondered uneasily if they were also microphones and then decided not. If they were, she and Kayla would have been kicked out a long time ago.

"We just got a large donation of fabric," Mrs. Henley said. "I'm moving you to sewing service beginning tomorrow. You'll be making dresses for the center."

"Yes, ma'am."

"Reflection time is not for idle gossip," Mrs. Henley said, with a reproving frown. "I'd suggest you both go and study your Bible."

THAT NIGHT HANNAH dreamed of falling, lurching awake again and again. When she got up in the morning, groggy and late, Kayla was already gone, her bed left unmade in a last, small act of defiance. The sight of the empty bed suffused Hannah with despair. She washed up hurriedly, distracted. Her fingers were clumsy, and by the time she got her hair to stay up, she was the only one left in the bathroom. She arrived in the dining hall just as Mrs. Henley was finishing the prayer of thanksgiving. Wonderful. Now, not only would Hannah get no breakfast, but she'd also have to sit at the woman's table.

"I have an announcement to make," said Mrs. Henley, when Hannah was seated. "Walker Kayla willfully stepped off the path this morning, and Reverend Henley had to cast her out."

The petty lie ignited a sudden, disproportionate fury in Hannah. She couldn't, wouldn't let the slur against her friend's character stand. "That's odd," she said.

Mrs. Henley paused with her fork halfway to her mouth. "And why is that?"

Hannah looked away, pretending to be chagrined. "Oh, I must be mistaken."

"About what?"

Hannah answered with a small shake of her head.

"About what are you mistaken, Walker?"

"Well, it's just, I could have sworn I heard Kayla say last night that she was *planning* on leaving this morning."

The table went still. Hannah's eyes swept around it, saw ten dumbfounded faces and one livid one. Mrs. Henley set her fork down.

"Are you questioning my word?"

Her words were like rocks dropped into water. Within seconds, the silence that rippled out from them had encompassed the entire dining hall.

"Oh, no, ma'am," Hannah said, wide-eyed. "I know that you of all people would *never* say something that wasn't true. Obviously I misheard Walker Kayla."

"Obviously you did," said Mrs. Henley. "If I were you, I'd listen with more care in the future. Spreading false rumors is a grave step off the path."

Hannah bowed her head, hiding a small, satisfied smile. "Yes, ma'am."

She went to the morning service hungry and exhausted. The sermon was even duller than usual, and she nodded off, waking to the thunderous voice of Reverend Henley.

"Hannah Payne! Wake up!" He scowled down at her from the pulpit, his face crimson with outrage. "On your knees, Walker!" She slid to the floor. "You have followed Satan's way instead of God's, just as Jezebel did when she cut off the prophets of the Lord. You have disrespected me, and you have disrespected and insulted God in His very own house. You should be ashamed of yourself."

At some point, Hannah stopped listening to his ranting. She was thinking about shame, her constant companion since the abortion. What had carrying all that guilt and self-loathing accomplished? Nothing, except to sap her confidence and enfeeble her. And she couldn't afford to be weak, not if she wanted to survive. *No more,* she resolved. She was done with shame.

She remained kneeling until Reverend Henley finally ran out of steam, concluded the service and made a huffy exit from the chapel. As the women began to file out, Mrs. Henley came over to her.

"I don't know what to think, Hannah," she said. "First the

business at breakfast, and now here you are falling asleep during
services. Do you have anything to say for yourself?"

"No, ma'am."

"Reverend Henley thinks this is your first step off the path, but
you and I know better, don't we?"

"Yes, ma'am." *That's it then. I'm out.*

"I think we need to have another chat. Shall we say Saturday at
three in my parlor?" Mrs. Henley's eyes mined Hannah's. Plucking, plucking. Dining on her fear.

Hannah made herself nod her head.

"Excellent!" Mrs. Henley said. "I'll make us some lemon bars."

WHEN HANNAH ENTERED the enlightenment room
a few minutes later, the stool was back in the center of the circle,
and poor, mad Anne-Marie was sitting on it, fixated as usual on
her doll. Today she was pretending to feed it, making airplane
approach sounds as she swooped an imaginary spoon toward its
mouth. "*That's* my good boy!" she exclaimed after each bite.

The enlightener stood and joined her in the center. "This is
Walker Cafferty's last day among us," he announced. "Today she'll
be leaving and going out into the world."

Hannah couldn't help but feel relief. Looking around the room
at the other women's faces, she could tell she wasn't the only one.

"Anne-Marie Cafferty," the enlightener said, "for six months
you have walked the path of penitence, atonement, truth and humility. You have been enlightened as to the evil of the sin you committed, and you have repented. Walkers, let us now pray in silence
for this woman, that she may continue on the path and one day
find salvation."

Hannah hadn't prayed in days, but she did so now: *Please God,
if You're there, if You're listening, look out for her.*

"Mmm! Yummy carrots!" Anne-Marie said. "Just one more bite and Mama will give you some applesauce."

"Like all walkers," the enlightener said to Anne-Marie, "you must leave this place the same way you came in, with nothing but yourself." Hannah's head jerked up, in time to see Anne-Marie's hand pause in mid-swoop.

The enlightener extended his hand. "Give me the doll."

She ignored him, putting it facedown against her shoulder. "Burp for Mama now."

"Give me the doll, Walker," he repeated.

Anne-Marie's face puckered. "No," she said. "No, no, no. You're scaring the baby. Don't cry, sweetheart, Mama's here, and she's not going to let anything happen to you."

The enlightener took hold of the doll's arm and pulled. Anne-Marie's expression turned feral. Wresting it away from him, she leapt up from her chair and ran for the door. He headed her off, grabbing the doll again. She fought him like a wild thing, pulling in the opposite direction.

"Nooooo!" she screamed. "You can't have him!"

There was a tearing sound, and the doll's legs came off in the enlightener's hand. White wads of stuffing hung from the leg holes. Anne-Marie stared at it in horror, then crumpled to the floor and began to keen—strangled, guttural cries like the mewling of a dying animal. They were the most terrible sounds Hannah had ever heard. Helplessly, she started to cry. They were all crying now, all except the enlightener, who was looking down, grimly triumphant, at Anne-Marie.

He pointed an accusing finger at her. His eyes swept around the circle. "*That* is how God feels when you abort one of His beloved children."

Graphic, murderous fantasies such as Hannah had never had

in her life rioted in her head. She pictured him being tortured, dismembered like Anne-Marie's doll by a frenzied mob of female Chromes; drowning in a giant vat of formaldehyde; being burned alive, crucified, stabbed, shot. Suddenly she was on her feet.

"What kind of monster are you, to treat her like that?" she cried. "Do you honestly think God would approve of what you just did, do you think He's up in Heaven right now saying 'Good job, way to torture that poor woman'?"

His long legs carried him across the room so swiftly Hannah didn't even have time to flinch. He grabbed hold of her shoulders and shook her so hard her head snapped back. "Brazen harlot! How dare you speak to me that way?"

She looked into his eyes. "I hope you burn in your own idea of hell, you sick, sadistic son of a bitch."

The back of his hand crashed into the side of her face, knocking her to the floor. Someone screamed. The room spun crazily. The enlightener was roaring at her, but it was just noise. What Hannah heard most distinctly was the loud, stubborn thumping of her own heart. It reminded her that she was alive, that she was herself. She got to all fours and rested there until the room steadied a little, then lurched to her feet and out the door.

The enlightener followed her into the corridor, shouting, "'And I will make thy tongue cleave to the roof of thy mouth, that thou shalt be dumb'!"

Doors opened, and the pink male faces of other enlighteners peered out curiously. Hannah staggered down the hall, down the stairs toward Reverend Henley's office, with the raving enlightener on her heels.

"'The Lord shall smite thee with a consumption, and with a fever, and with an inflammation, and with an extreme burning, and with the sword, and with blasting, and with mildew'!"

Reverend Henley's door flew open just before Hannah reached it, and he stepped into the hallway with Mrs. Henley just behind him. Their faces were almost comically shocked.

"What is going on here?" demanded Reverend Henley.

He looked in confusion from Hannah to the enlightener, who was vowing, "'And they shall pursue thee until thou perish'!"

An odd calm descended on Hannah. "I'm leaving now," she said quietly to the Henleys.

The reverend held his hand up for silence, and the enlightener sputtered to a stop. "What did you say, Walker?"

"I said I'm leaving." Hannah pulled the cross from around her neck and held it out to him. "I'd like my NIC back now. And my clothes."

Reverend Henley's face filled with consternation. "If you deliberately step off the path, you'll be consigning your soul to perdition."

"This woman is already damned," declared the enlightener. "She's a witch who has willfully turned her face from God and embraced Satan."

"'Thou shalt not suffer a witch to live,'" said Mrs. Henley. Her eyes were blades. They darted from Hannah to something behind her.

Hannah looked over her shoulder and saw that a large crowd had gathered in the hallway. The faces of the enlighteners looked pallid and sickly surrounded by the rainbow faces of the women.

Hannah turned back to Reverend Henley and said, in a carrying voice, "You promised I could leave whenever I wanted and that you would give me back my belongings. Are you going to keep your word?"

His face darkened. "How dare you question my integrity?" he said, snatching the cross from Hannah's hand. "I cast you out! Go and wait in the foyer. Someone will bring you your things."

But the malicious gleam in Mrs. Henley's eyes said otherwise. Without her NIC, Hannah wouldn't have access to her bank account, health insurance, medical records, anything. And if she were stopped by the police and didn't have it on her person, they could add as much as a year to her sentence. "I'll wait here," she said, thankful for the watching crowd.

"Shameless whore! We should cast you out naked," Mrs. Henley said.

"'Yea, let thy nakedness be uncovered, let thy shame be seen'!" said the enlightener. His eyes dropped from Hannah's face to her breasts.

Reverend Henley shook his head. "No, Bob."

Bob? Hannah thought, with a kind of surreal incredulity. *This monster's name is Bob?*

"And why not?" said the enlightener. "She deserves that and worse."

"Because," said Reverend Henley, "I gave my word." To his wife, he said, "Fetch her belongings."

For a moment Hannah thought Mrs. Henley might actually defy him, but finally she gave a stiff nod and went into her parlor. Hannah waited in the charged quiet of the hallway. A few minutes later Mrs. Henley reappeared, holding her clothes. Her NIC, she was relieved to see, was on top. She took the bundle, half expecting the Henleys to order her to strip and change right there.

"'Cast out the scorner'!" Reverend Henley said, in a stern, ringing voice. "Go now, Hannah Payne, into the cruel and savage world, and reap the wages of your sins."

As she turned to leave, the enlightener—*Bob,* she thought again, suppressing a hysterical urge to laugh—hissed, "Jezebel. Witch." Some of the women echoed his words, jostling her aggressively as she walked through their ranks, but most moved silently out of her path. Eve was one of the latter. The admiration on the girl's yellow face made Hannah stand taller.

And then the women were behind her, and she was opening the door to the foyer, and she was through it and blessedly alone. The air was refreshing after the oppressive closeness of the hallway, and for a moment Hannah merely leaned with her back against the door, drawing deep breaths into her lungs. Suddenly the high neck of her dress felt unbearable, a noose choking her. She stripped it off, and then the rest of it—the cheap, ugly underwear, the black shoes, the thick tights, the hated bonnet—letting everything fall to the floor in an untidy heap. She put on her own clothes. The formerly high-waisted skirt fell to her hips, and her blouse, which had been loose when she'd left the Chrome ward, now hung on her. Finally, she unpinned her hair. It cascaded across her shoulders and down her back, and she realized how much she'd missed the comfort of its weight, how exposed she'd felt without its protection. The thought made her lift her eyes to the painting of Mary Magdalene, her sister in sin, clad only in her own hair.

"Wish me luck," Hannah whispered.

She stepped out into a cold, drizzly December day. The door closed behind her, and she heard the bolt click shut—a sound of exquisite finality. She lifted her face to the sky, relishing the bracing air and the feel of the rain misting her skin. *I'm free,* she thought, though she knew the notion was absurd; she was anything but. She was trapped in this hideous red body, forbidden to leave the state. Wherever she went, she'd be a target. Even so, she felt a rush of exhilaration. She wondered if Kayla had stood here this morning and felt this way, if she'd had this same irrational sense of liberation and possibility. The thought of her reassured Hannah. She'd walk to Becca's—Cole would be at work for several hours still—and call Kayla from there. If she'd found TJ, the two of them would help her. If not, she and Kayla would figure out some sort of plan.

Hannah reached into the pocket of her dress for the scrap of paper with Kayla's number on it. Only when her fingers found no pocket did she register that she wasn't wearing the dress, that it was lying on the floor of the foyer. She hadn't memorized the number; she hadn't had time. She didn't even know Kayla's last name.

Hannah whirled and reached for the handle of the door, knowing before she pulled on it that it was locked against her.

THREE

THE MAGIC CIRCLE

Hannah's ebullience dwindled and eventually disappeared during the long, wet walk to Becca's. Female Reds were rare enough that she was a target of curiosity. People ogled her from cars and shops. An elderly couple crossed to the other side of the street when they saw her coming. A guy on a bicycle was staring at her so intently he nearly got hit by a bus. "Watch out," she cried, but the sound was swallowed by the simultaneous blast of the bus driver's horn. The biker swerved, and the bus just missed him. He slammed into a parked car and was thrown to the pavement.

"Fucking red bitch!" he yelled. Pulse racing, Hannah quickened her stride. The drizzle turned into a steady rain. Before long, her blouse and skirt were drenched, and her hair was a cold, sodden mass against her back. Her feet in their thin flats made squishing sounds with each step.

Somebody whistled loudly. "Hey, Scarlet, want a ride?" Hannah looked and saw a car pacing her. A kid in his late teens was leaning out of the passenger-side window, leering at her. She crossed her arms over her breasts, aware of how her wet clothes adhered to her body. "Bet you ain't been ridden in a while," he said.

"Juicy thing like you needs regular squeezing," called out his buddy in the driver's seat.

"I'll make the juice run out of you, sweet thing."

Hannah ignored them, staring straight ahead, trying not to let her fear show. She was well aware that if they pulled her into the car, no one would stop them. They could take her anywhere, do anything to her.

"Come on Scarlet, I never had a Red before, but I always did like my meat rare."

"Yeah, baby, with you in the middle and us on either side, we'd make us a nice roast beef sandwich."

She wanted to run but knew instinctively it would turn her into prey, so she kept herself to a purposeful walk. Finally, they tired of their sport and drove on.

Halfway to Becca's, the skies darkened and then opened, loosing a torrent of water. Hannah took shelter under the awning of a pawnshop, shivering from cold. The window was filled with the sad and obsolete detritus of people's lives: gold wedding bands and watches, old corded appliances and 2-D vidscreens. She felt a forlorn kinship with these dusty former objects of desire, abandoned by the people who'd once possessed them.

The door to the shop opened and a middle-aged woman stuck her head out. "You got something to pawn, honey?" She had a shellacked quality: dyed maroon hair sculpted into a rigid beehive, face coated with thick, shiny makeup.

"No, I'm just trying to get out of the rain for a few minutes."

With a jerk of her chin, the woman said, "Stay dry someplace else. Chromes are bad for business."

"Do you have any raincoats for sale?" Hannah said. "Or umbrellas? I can pay." Even more than the quaver she heard in her voice, she hated the glimmer of pity that briefly softened the woman's shrewd eyes.

"Wait there a sec." The woman went back inside and reappeared shortly holding a cheap plastic poncho, which she thrust at Hannah. "Here, take this."

"How much do I owe you?" She fumbled for her NIC.

"Forget it," the woman said, with a dismissive wave of one

ring-encrusted hand. Her fingernails flashed miniature holograms of Elvis. "Now move along, before I call the cops."

The poncho swallowed Hannah and had an unpleasantly musky odor, like it had been used as a bed by an unwashed dog. But it covered her from head to toe and, mercifully, had a hood. She drew it up before moving on, into the indifferent fury of the storm.

THE PONCHO RENDERED her unremarkable, just another figure hurrying home through the rain, and she made it to Becca's without further incident. She paused on the sidewalk in front of the house, a cookie-cutter three-bedroom ranch thrown up quickly and cheaply in the boom days of the 1990s, renovated after the Second Great Depression, and now, like most of its neighbors, sorely in need of another makeover. A pinecone wreath with a bright red bow hung on the door. Hannah had totally forgotten about Christmas, and its existence in light of her current circumstances seemed preposterous, a bad joke. She imagined her red self wrapping presents, singing carols, decorating gingerbread men. What a festive spectacle she would present.

Her feet dragged as she went up the walk, and she stopped at the foot of the steps leading to the porch. What if Cole was home, or Becca had company? Maybe Hannah should find a netlet and call first. But it was too late; the house sensors had detected her. Hannah heard footsteps approaching, and now the door was opening, and in the instant before she bowed her head to hide her face, she had a brief glimpse of her sister behind the screen.

"May I help you?" Becca said, with the characteristic sweetness she showed to everyone, even a bedraggled stranger on her doorstep.

Hannah was paralyzed. She couldn't make herself lift her head, couldn't bear to see the inevitable shock, revulsion and, worst of all, pity on her sister's face. But then she heard a hissed intake of breath, followed by the creak of the screen door opening and the scrape of Becca's feet on the steps. And then hands were gently pushing back the hood of the poncho, and Hannah felt the rain drumming against her bare head.

"Hannah," Becca said. Just that, just her name, infused with sorrow but also with such love and faith that she knew it would be all right, Becca wouldn't despise or repudiate her.

Hannah looked up, and then it was she who was gasping in shock, because her sister's eyes were swollen from crying, and one of them was encircled by a livid purple bruise. She opened her mouth to spew her rage at Cole, that despicable, cowardly, pathetic—

Becca forestalled her with an upraised hand. "Please, Hannah, don't." *Don't judge me. Don't pity me.*

That, Hannah understood all too well, and so she swallowed her words, if not her anger, and bowed her head slightly, leaning forward in invitation. After a few seconds she felt the soft touch of her sister's forehead against hers—their childhood ritual, performed after they'd had a fight or one of them had been bullied at school (usually Becca) or grounded by their parents (usually Hannah). They stayed like that for some time, comforting each other silently, and as always, pulled away at the same moment.

"Come on," Becca said, taking Hannah's arm and leading her up the steps. "Let's get you dry."

Inside, Becca clucked over her pitiful condition and shooed her off to the shower. Hannah was chilled through, and the hot water was bliss. When the brake cut it off, she stood under the warm air of the dryjets until long after her hair and skin were dry.

Afterward she examined herself in the mirror. Her body was gaunt. She could count her ribs and see the sharp jut of her hipbones. A lump had formed on the side of her head, and her right ear was bruised and tender, but the skin wasn't broken. Nor, she thought, with a flicker of satisfaction, was she. Bob and the Henleys had done their worst, and she had survived—if not unscathed, then at least intact.

She borrowed a soft wool sweater and an old skirt she'd made for Becca's eighteenth birthday, which their mother had insisted Hannah let down because it was too short. She could still picture her fingers angrily ripping out the thread, and Becca telling her it didn't matter, the skirt was still lovely, and herself trying in vain to explain to Becca why she was wrong, why two inches made all the difference between lovely and not. Now, her teenaged indignation over such a small thing seemed impossibly distant, a far green shore of irretrievable innocence.

Hannah joined Becca in the kitchen, where she was greeted by the homey smells of coffee and beef stew, overlaid by the crisp aroma of pine from the Christmas tree in the living room. She was famished, and she quickly downed a bowl of the stew, scalding her mouth in her haste. Becca took the bowl and went to the stove to refill it.

"What happened at the center, Hannah? Daddy said they kicked you out."

"Actually I left before they had the chance to."

"Was it awful?"

"It was unspeakable."

Becca put the bowl down in front of Hannah and sat across from her, studying her with a worried expression. "I wondered. Your letters didn't sound like you." She reached across the table and gave Hannah's hand a squeeze. "You've gotten so thin."

Hannah studied their two hands, so alike in shape, and now so blatantly mismatched. "And red, don't forget red," she said.

"Can you bear it?" Becca asked softly.

Hannah pulled her hand from her sister's and gestured toward her eye. "Can you? And don't tell me you tripped and fell."

"It isn't like you think," Becca said. "Cole's never hit me before, he's not like that." She shook her head. "It's this men's group he belongs to, it's changed him. He's angry all the time, and he's always going out late at night. Twice I've found blood on his clothes the next day."

Hannah felt the hairs on the back of her neck rising. "What does he say about it?"

"Nothing. He doesn't talk about it, and I don't dare ask him." Becca paused, bit her lip.

"Tell me, Becca."

"A few days ago I found something, in his jacket pocket."

"What?"

"A ring. I've never seen him wear it, he must put it on after he goes out."

"What is it? What's on this ring?"

Becca's eyes, frightened and despairing, lifted to Hannah's. "A clenched hand, pierced by a bloody spike," she whispered. "I think Cole's joined the Fist."

Hannah's body went cold. The Fist of Christ was the most brutal and feared vigilante group in Texas, known to be responsible for the deaths of dozens of Chromes and the beating and torture of hundreds more. The Fist was made up of independent cells of five called Hands. The members wore flesh-colored rubber masks. Each struck a single blow with whatever weapon he chose to use: a boot or a brass-knuckled fist, a club, a knife, a gun. Each had the power when his turn came to maim, kill or let live, at his sole discretion. The only evidence they left behind was that symbol, branded or lasered into the flesh of their victims. Few of the Fist's members had ever been caught and even fewer convicted. The leaders had eluded capture, protected by the autonomy of the Hands and the fanatical loyalty of their members.

Hannah's parents considered the Fist blasphemous thugs, as did Aidan; he'd spoken against them from the pulpit on more than one occasion. But she'd heard plenty of other people at church defend and even champion their activities, saying, "Somebody needs to take out the garbage."

"You have to leave him," Hannah said, knowing even as she spoke that Becca would refuse, and that even if she agreed, Cole would never let her go.

"I can't." Becca's hand cupped the mound of her belly. "He's the father of my children, Hannah. And I still love him."

"How can you, knowing what he's out there doing? How long are you going to keep washing the blood from his shirts?"

"He's only been in it a couple of months. If I leave him, he'll never stop."

"The Fist tortures and kills people, Becca. People like me."

"Cole hasn't killed anyone."

"You can't know that."

"I can and I do." Becca's expression turned defiant. "My husband's no murderer. Cole believes in the sanctity of life. If I stay with him, I can help him stop. I *do* help him. Some nights, he says he's going out, and I . . . I change his mind." Her face colored, and Hannah thought, *Yeah, I bet I know how,* and then was immediately contrite. When had she become so crude and cynical, and toward her sister of all people?

"And when little Cole and his sister come," Becca went on, "Cole won't want to be part of that ugliness anymore. He won't need it anymore, not with his baby son and daughter at home."

Knowing she'd never convince Becca otherwise, Hannah changed tacks. "Have you told Mama and Daddy?"

"No. You know Daddy, he'd be bound to say something, and I'm afraid of what might happen. Cole would never hurt him, but if the others found out he knew . . ." Becca trailed off and looked down at the table.

"Cole hurt *you*. What's to keep him from doing it again?"

"He swore to me he wouldn't."

"Gee, that makes me feel so much better."

"Hannah, he cried afterward, and I've never seen him cry before. And we've prayed on it together, every night since."

"Praying on it? *That's* your solution?" Hannah said.

The scornful remark shocked them both. Becca was staring at her as if she were an alien with a few too many tentacles, which, Hannah supposed, wasn't that far from the truth. Not so long ago, she too would have turned to God for help as a matter of course, would have believed without question that He was interested enough in her one small life to intervene in it. She probed the place within herself where He used to reside and found an empty, ragged socket. Her faith—not just in His love, but in His existence—was gone.

"Oh Hannah, what's happened to you?" Becca's face was wet, but Hannah could muster no tears of her own, nor could she offer her sister any explanation. Not for this, not for any of it.

The pleasant baritone of the house computer spoke, startling them. "Cole is home," it announced. They heard the sound of a car door slamming.

Becca jumped up, hands fluttering around her like swallows. "You have to leave. If he finds out you've been here I don't know what he'll do. Go out the back way and hide in the toolshed, and I'll come to you when I can."

Hannah was halfway down the hall when she heard the front

door bang open. "Where is she?" Cole yelled. "I know she's here."
A brief silence. "Answer me, Becca!"

Hannah halted. "I'm right here, Cole," she said. The surprisingly calm sound of her voice bolstered her courage. She went to the threshold of the living room and met his furious glare. He was dressed for a cattle drive or a shootout, in a black felt cowboy hat, lizard boots and a belt buckle the size of a hubcap.

His eyes raked over her contemptuously, and then he turned his attention to Becca. "What'd I say to you about your sister, huh? What'd I say?"

"That, that she wasn't welcome here," Becca stammered.

"Was there any part of that you didn't understand?"

"No, Cole."

"Then why'd you let her in? Why'd you disobey me?"

"I let myself in," Hannah said. "The back door was open."

"You must both think I'm pretty stupid."

"No, honey, of course not," Becca said, in a splintered, desperate voice Hannah had never heard before. It filled her with rage. A person's voice didn't come to sound like that overnight, she thought. No, someone had to work on them for a while, with real persistence, to make them skip over unease, dismay and distress and leap so quickly to abject fear. Looking at the man who'd made her sister's voice unrecognizable, Hannah felt the urge to do violence for the second time in a span of a few hours.

"I figured she'd come here," Cole said. "And I figured you'd let her waltz right in. I put a sat alert on her the day she got out of the Chrome ward."

Hannah kicked herself mentally. She'd forgotten about the nanotransmitters. All Chromes were implanted with them as a public safety measure. Anyone who did a simple search on her name could pinpoint her location and observe her movements via geosat. But it simply hadn't occurred to her that Cole or anyone else she knew would be tracking her, much less that he would have put an alert on her. And it should have. By coming here, she'd put Becca in danger.

With effort, Hannah made her tone mild and earnest. "I just came to apologize to my sister. To ask her forgiveness for shaming her and the family. I thought I owed her that."

"You haven't asked for *my* forgiveness," Cole said. He set his hat carefully on the coffee table, brim up, then moved behind Becca and pulled her to him, her back against his chest, his arm crossed protectively over her abdomen.

Hannah forced the words out. "I'm sorry for the shame my actions brought on you, Cole. Please forgive me."

Without taking his eyes off Hannah, Cole put his mouth up against his wife's ear. "Did you forgive her, Becca?"

Becca's eyes were wide and uncertain: what was the right answer, the one that would defuse him? Finally, she said, "Yes, Cole, I did."

His expression turned tender, and he kissed the top of her head. "Of course you did, baby," he said, stroking her hair with his thick fingers. "I wouldn't expect anything different from you." Her eyes closed in relief, and she sagged slightly against him.

"My wife's the most forgiving person I've ever known," Cole said. His voice was thick with emotion, part of which, Hannah realized, was self-reproach. "It's why I fell in love with her." His hand traveled down to Becca's bruised eye. He caressed the area beneath it gently with his thumb and then let his hand drop to his side.

He stepped out from behind her. His face hardened. "But me, I'm the opposite. There are just some things I can't forgive. Some things don't deserve to be forgiven."

Becca's eyes flew open. "Please, Cole—"

"Go wait in the other room, Becca. I want to speak with your sister alone." When she didn't move, he said, "Do as I say."

With an anguished glance at Hannah, Becca left. Hannah released a long breath and felt the bulk of her fear go with it. As long as Cole's anger was directed at her, Becca was safe. As for Hannah herself, there was nothing this man could do to her that mattered.

"What is it you want to say to me, Cole? That if I ever come near Becca again, you'll make me sorry? That you'll kill me if you have to?"

He furrowed his forehead like a child trying to figure out a magic trick. "That's right. I'll do whatever it takes to protect my wife."

"I'm glad to hear you say that. When are you planning to move out?"

"What the hell are you talking about?"

"Becca's black eye. She told me she fell, but you and I both know that's a lie."

And there was the remorse again, flaring in Cole's eyes before he covered it over with anger. A chink, and not an inconsiderable one. *Well,* Hannah thought, *let's see how wide we can make it.*

"Do you really want to be that guy, Cole? The guy who beats up his pregnant wife?"

Cole's face was turning a dark, ugly red. "You listen to me—"

"At the shelter where I used to volunteer, they taught us that if a man hits a woman once, there's a strong chance he'll do it again. And after the second time, he almost never stops. He gets a taste for it, beats whoever he can—his wife, his kids. You going to knock Cole Jr. and his sister around too?"

"Shut your filthy red mouth," he said, but Hannah could see

that she'd shaken him, that his bluster was nothing but a cloak for his shame. "Who the hell are you to talk to me like that?"

"I'm a woman who's destroyed two lives, one of them my own. And I'm telling you, it's not a road you want to go down."

A mistake—she knew it as soon as she'd said it. He closed the distance between them, looming over her. "Let me get this straight. You're comparing me to you, a murdering slut who defiled God's commandments and dishonored her family name. You're saying you and I are alike. Well keep talking, and you'll find out just how different we are. You've got no idea who you're dealing with."

"You're right, I don't," Hannah said. "Who *am* I dealing with? Cole the loving husband and protector or Cole the wife-beater?"

"Shut up."

He was a hair's breadth away from hitting her; she could feel it in the tautness of his body, could smell it in the pungency of his sweat. But she could smell the fear in him too, not of her, but of himself, the man who'd hurt the woman he loved and might again.

Softly, Hannah said, "The real question, the one you need to ask yourself, is which Cole's going to win out in the end?"

"Get out of my house," he said, in a choked voice. "And don't ever come near my wife again."

Hannah went to the entryway, took her smelly poncho from the hook and put it on. As she opened the door, Cole said, "I'll be watching."

She locked eyes with him. "So will I. And I won't hesitate to go to the police if you don't keep your *fist,*" she said, with deliberate emphasis, "away from my sister."

SHE WALKED AIMLESSLY FOR CLOSE to an hour, heedless of the rain. Her mind was racing, replaying the scene with Cole and wondering if she'd handled him right, if her gamble would pay off. Knowing that if it didn't, Becca would suffer the consequences. She'd asked if Hannah could bear it, and she could, she could bear all of it—being a Red, losing Aidan, losing her faith—as long as she knew that her sister was alive and well. She could even endure never seeing Becca again, if that's what it took to keep her safe. But if anything should happen to her...

Hannah stumbled on a rough patch of pavement and was jolted out of her head and back into her body. Her legs ached, and Becca's loafers, which were too narrow, had rubbed blisters in half a dozen places. She was cold, thirsty, bone-tired. She needed a place to rest and gather her thoughts. More urgently, she needed a place to sleep tonight. But where could she go? Not home. Not to the ıCs shelter; even if her pride allowed it, the Henleys must have already called the office to report her disgrace. Not to Gabrielle, tempting as the idea was. The police knew nothing of her involvement, and Hannah wouldn't repay her kindness by endangering her through association. Hannah had a few girlfriends from high school, a few others from work and church. She pictured them opening their front doors to find her standing on their doorsteps: Rachel stiff and formal, mouth pursed in disapproval; Melody uncomfortable, nervous someone would see them together; Deb awkward and so, so sorry. No, the only friend who would truly welcome her was Kayla. But first, she had to find her.

Fortunately, Cole had given her the key: the Chrome tracking system. She wouldn't even need a last name; a search would pull up the photos and criminal records of every Chrome named Kayla in the state of Texas. Geosat would do the rest. If Kayla was out of doors, Hannah would be able to see her walking down the street.

She needed her port, but her father had it, and after all that she'd borne today, the thought of calling him, of weathering his dismay and frustration and worry over her departure from the center, was overwhelming. Of her parents, he was the one she most dreaded disappointing. Hannah's mother had always, on some level, expected to be disappointed by her, whereas her father had an almost childlike faith in her. Her failings bewildered him, and her rebellions left him crestfallen rather than angry. When she was twelve, she'd snuck out of the house on Angeles Day for an illicit bike ride. She'd been restless and tired of the day's solemnity, of kneeling all morning with her parents and praying for the souls of the innocent dead, of waiting for the clock's hands to reach the fateful moment of 11:37 and the bells of the neighborhood churches to begin their mournful tolling; and then afterward, of watching the familiar montage of images on the vid: the mushroom cloud rising over the Pacific, the miles of rubble strewn with the charred bodies of the victims, the mass burials and funerals, the bombs falling on Tehran. And so, in the afternoon, she'd climbed out her bedroom window and ridden her bike around the neighborhood for a glorious half hour. When she'd returned home, breathless and invigorated, her father had been waiting for her on the porch steps.

"Come and sit with me a minute," he said quietly. His expression was pained, and Hannah wished it were her mother sitting there instead, angry and accusatory. "Did you have a good time on your bike ride?"

She considered saying no, but she hated to lie to him. "Yes."

"What did you enjoy about it?" She shrugged, at a loss, and picked at some peeling paint on the step. "What did you enjoy?" he pressed.

"Being outside, I guess," she said, in a voice made small and strained by the lump in her throat.

"What else?"

"Getting chased by the McSherrys' dog. Going really fast down the hill on Maple."

"What were you thinking about?" Hannah shook her head, staring unseeing at the step, her eyes burning. "Tell me," her father said.

"The wind was whooshing against my face, and I thought how . . . how good it felt." She started to cry, and he sat with her in silence as the sobs ripped through her; as she pictured a carefree twelve-year-old girl much like herself, coasting down a hill on her bike in Los Angeles on a day much like this, her face lifted to the wind, to the sudden searing blast of air from the bomb that would incinerate her and her family and seven hundred thousand others.

When Hannah had cried herself out, she felt her father's arm go around her. "I'm sorry, Daddy," she said, leaning into him.

"I know."

A SIREN WAILED nearby, startling her. Hannah looked around her and realized she was near the Harrington Library. She headed toward it, feeling her spirits lift a little when she saw the familiar cream-colored stone building with the American and Texas flags waving proudly in front. Even as a child, when Plano had still had several public libraries to choose from, the Harrington had been her favorite, because it had the most books and the best librarians, the kind who never raised a reproving eyebrow over her selections. Until she was sixteen, she hadn't been allowed to go to the library without one of her parents, a prohibition she'd broken every chance she got. She hid the books she checked out under her mattress and then, after her mother discovered that hideaway, inside her old stuffed lion. Even if her parents hadn't monitored her port for forbidden downloads, she would still have preferred to read real books. She liked the smell of them and the weight of them in her hands, liked turning the pages that other hands had turned before her and imagining the faces that went with them.

Unlike the library at her Christian high school, whose collection was limited to books and vids considered wholesome influences on young minds, the Harrington had a wealth of enticingly inappropriate material. The Satan's Pen list distributed by her school became Hannah's reading list. She discovered Hogwarts and Lyra's Oxford, met Holden Caulfield and Beloved and Lady Chatterley, whose amorous encounters made Hannah's body ache in unaccustomed ways. And of course, there were the fashion magazines: *Vogue* and *Avant* and dozens more, which excited her imagination so much at times that she had to get up and pace. No one even noticed, much less reproached her. No one cared what she was reading or thinking about; they had their own passions to explore.

More than anything, the Harrington had always been a place where Hannah felt safe and welcome, so it was with some trepidation that she opened the door and stepped inside. Ostensibly, they couldn't deny her entry; discrimination against Chromes was illegal in municipal buildings. In fact, it was illegal in any building open to the public, but the law was rarely enforced in privately owned businesses, and NO CHROMES ALLOWED signs were commonplace.

The guard was a young, tough-looking Latina, and her expression turned wary when she saw Hannah. But it was a professional wariness, cool and assessing rather than hostile. She scanned Hannah's NIC without comment and read the information that came up on her vid. When her eyes lifted, the watchfulness had been replaced by compassion. Mortified, Hannah realized the guard knew she'd had an abortion; that every person who scanned her card from now on would know it. *Stupid, stupid.* Of course they would. Why hadn't she anticipated that?

"There's a room with private carrels in the back," the guard said.

The kindness was intolerable. "I'm familiar with the library," Hannah replied curtly.

The main reading room was perfectly quiet, or so Hannah thought until its occupants caught sight of her. As awareness of her presence traveled across the room, the silence deepened and congealed with animosity so oppressive she could hardly breathe. She hurried through and slipped gratefully into an empty vid carrel in the back room. She activated the privacy mode, scanned her NIC and said her PIP: "I can do all things through Christ who gives me strength." Once, this had been a guiding credo of her life; now, it was just a hollow string of words.

When she opened her mail, the computer informed her that she had 1,963 messages. The number startled her. Even for a five-month absence, that was a lot. She flicked through them. There was the usual marketing spam, but there were also a large number of messages from individuals with unfamiliar names. She touched the screen, opening a vidmail at random. BURN IN HELL, MURDERER! it said, the flaming red letters hurtling toward her face. Just a holo, but she recoiled as if she'd been struck. She opened another and heard an infant wailing. Over it, a woman's voice said, "I hope you hear the cries of the baby you killed every night for the rest of your life."

"Delete all mail from all unknown contacts," Hannah said.

"Deleting."

She was left with a paltry half a dozen messages. But one was from Edward Ferrars. Hannah's heart contracted painfully as she stared at it. Ferrars was the name under which she and Aidan had registered at hotels. Hannah had chosen it; of all Jane Austen's amiable clergymen, Edward Ferrars had always been her favorite. *But I'm no Elinor,* Hannah thought. Alyssa was his Elinor: mild, virtuous, sensible.

It was a vidmail, which surprised Hannah. There was no such thing as truly secure netspeak, and so she and Aidan had messaged each other rarely, and only in text. The vidmail was dated August 20—prior to the trial, when she'd still been in jail. She hadn't been in communication with him since before she was arrested, hadn't seen him until he'd spoken on her behalf at the sentencing hearing. He'd been stern and mournful that day, but whatever else he'd been feeling, he'd concealed it well. Had he been outraged by what she'd done? Disillusioned? Sickened to the point where he no longer loved her? Had he testified out of compassion only, as her pastor?

She had to know. She couldn't bear to know. And so she went through the other five messages first: Two tearful vidmails, one from her aunt Jo and the other from Mrs. Bunten, saying they'd pray for her. A brusque note from her employer at the salon, informing her that her services were no longer required. A distinctly wistful vidmail from her former boyfriend Will, who evidently hadn't heard about her disgrace, saying he'd moved to Florida and was engaged to be married and thought she'd want to know. A note from Deb saying how sorry she was that this had happened, it was just awful, if there was anything she could do, anything at all.

There was no more putting it off. Hannah swallowed hard and said, "Play message from Edward Ferrars."

And there floating in 3-D before her was her beloved. He was sitting in a darkened office she didn't recognize, illuminated by a single lamp. He looked melancholy, and as always, it became him, lending him a poignant beauty.

"I pray you get this, Hannah. I can't imagine what you're enduring at this moment, in that jail. I hate that you're alone in this, that you're bearing the brunt of our sin all by yourself. I hate that you did this thing for me. That our child—" His voice broke. He closed his eyes and rubbed them with one pale, long-fingered hand. Hannah's arms ached to pull his head into her lap, her fingers to smooth the care from his brow.

"By the time you watch this, the trial will be over. I hope you were honest. I hope you cooperated with the police and named the abortionist. And I hope you named me as the father and revealed me for the hypocrite I am. God help me, I know I should come forward. I tell myself I keep silent for Alyssa's sake, but maybe I just don't have the will and the courage to speak the truth. And how can I shepherd the nation to God if I can't go through the narrow door myself?" A ripple of revulsion ran through Hannah as she remembered her initiation at the Straight Path Center.

"If you'd told me you were pregnant, I would have acknowledged the baby. I hope you know that, Hannah. I think you must, or you wouldn't have done this thing. What a perfect irony, to have lost the only child I might ever have fathered. What a divine jest! God is truly a brilliant teacher." His mouth twisted in a bitter smile.

"I know you must have wondered why Alyssa and I don't have children. Everyone does, though they don't ask. It's because of me, because of my weakness and arrogance and selfishness. Just before I met Alyssa, I went on a mission to Colombia, and I slept with a woman I met there. Only once, but it was enough to give me the scourge. This was in the early days, before they started the testing, and I had no symptoms. It didn't even occur to me that I might be infected; how could something like that possibly happen to *me*? And then I met Alyssa and we fell in love and got engaged, and I didn't want to wait. And I cajoled and begged and pushed her and finally, about a month before the wedding, she relented and let me make love to her. For which I handsomely rewarded her." Aidan let out an ugly bark of laughter. "We found out when we got the results of the blood test for the marriage license. If I'd just been patient and respected her wishes, if I'd respected *God's* wishes, I wouldn't have infected her. As it was, she went through almost five years of hell before they found the cure. By that time she was sterile, of course."

So much that Hannah had never understood about Aidan now made terrible sense: his bouts of darkness, his devotion to children, his stoic attitude toward his wife. *I can never leave Alyssa. I won't bring that kind of shame on her.* The unspoken word being *again*.

"She forgave me somehow, and we went on with our lives and our ministry. Our ministry became our life. I've tried many times to talk her into adopting, but she's always refused. I think it's her way of avenging what I did to her. God knows she's entitled to some form of retribution." He bowed his head. "So now you know what kind of man you once loved."

Stung by his use of the past tense, Hannah said, "And still do."

As if he'd heard her, Aidan said, "How could you love me, after everything I've brought on you? You'd have to hate yourself to love me. And I don't want you to hate yourself, Hannah. This isn't your fault, it's mine. Do you remember when you told me that our love had to have come from God, that He'd brought us together for a purpose? At the time I thought you were just rationalizing our sin, but now I know you were right. *This* was His purpose: to punish me for what I did to Alyssa."

Hannah felt a hot pulse of anger. So this was how he saw her: as a mere instrument of his punishment, a flail or a cudgel lacking any volition of her own?

"I deserve to suffer, but I can't bear it that you've had to. And if they convict you . . ." He broke off, swallowed. "I'll do everything in my power to help you. I doubt the governor would pardon you, but perhaps I can persuade President Morales to, when I've known him longer. In the meantime, I've transferred some money to your account to help give you a start once they release you. I know how proud you are, but you mustn't be reluctant to use it. Your safety could depend on it. If you need more, if you need anything at all, send a message to this address.

"I'll pray for you, my love," he said. "I won't ask you to forgive me, but I'm truly sorry for everything." His hand reached out as if to touch her, and then the holo collapsed, and the vid returned to the first frame.

Hannah stared at Aidan's face, frozen in rue, and felt her anger intensifying. In all the time she'd loved him, she'd never once felt sorry about it. Not when she was lying on the abortionist's table. Not when she was examined, interrogated, incarcerated. Not when she was disowned by her own mother, convicted of murder, injected with the virus that would make her a pariah. Not when she saw her red self for the first time. Not when she sat in her father's car or Mrs. Henley's parlor or Becca's kitchen. All of this she had endured, without ever regretting her love for him. The rage that had been building in her erupted.

"How *dare* you be sorry?" she shouted at the screen. She wanted to hit it, to hit him, to make his features contort in pain or rage to match her own—anything but regret.

She navved to her bank account, saw the number on the screen: $100,465.75. "Damn you," she said. As unpalatable as the thought of taking his money was, she knew he was right: she'd need it to survive. Even with it, life would be precarious, especially if she were alone. The fact of her solitude struck her then, bludgeoning her with its absoluteness. She was lost to everyone who'd ever loved her, and they to her.

Except Kayla. The thought of her friend was a spar, and Hannah grasped it.

"Search for all Reds in the state of Texas named K-A-Y-L-A." There was only one: Kayla Mariko Ray, serving five years for attempted murder. Her photo had the telltale look of the Chrome ward: haggard red face, glassy eyes.

"Locate," Hannah said. A satellite image of East Dallas appeared, zoomed in on the intersection of Skillman and Mockingbird, then on a figure crossing the street. As the overhead image sharpened, Hannah recognized Kayla. She was running, Hannah saw, and there was someone else running behind her.

A man, chasing her.

KAYLA WAS FAST, but her pursuer was faster. Hannah could do nothing but watch with mounting dread as he narrowed the gap between them and finally caught her. She flailed out, hitting him in the face. He gripped her by both arms. The two of them struggled. He said something to her, and she stopped resisting him, her arms falling to her sides. Still holding on to one of them, he led her back down the street in the direction they'd come from. It was clear that she went unhappily; whether she went willingly or not, Hannah couldn't tell. They walked for several blocks and then went inside a house on Kenwood Avenue.

Hannah watched for another ten minutes, but no one emerged. She memorized the address and hurriedly logged herself out. She'd take the train to Mockingbird and walk from there, which would take her a couple of hours. She didn't allow herself to think about what she'd do if Kayla was gone when she got there.

It was dusk when she left the library, and the rain had stopped. Darkness fell quickly, which she was glad of; it made her less conspicuous. The train station was a couple of miles away, and by the time Hannah reached it she felt weak from hunger and thirst. There was a McDonald's across the street. She went to the entrance and was about to open the door when she saw the sign: CHROMES MUST USE DRIVE-THRU. She followed the driveway around to the back and entered her order onto the touchscreen, then paid with her NIC. *One Happy Meal, hold the happiness,* she thought. The pimply teenager at the pickup counter handed her the bag gingerly, careful not to touch her. He did, however, remember to thank her and wish her a McWonderful day.

She carried the bag to the train station and ate sitting on one of the benches on the platform. The salty, greasy food tasted as good as anything she'd ever eaten in her life. She heard footsteps and saw another Chrome—a young male Yellow—walking toward her with an ostentatious outlaw strut. Not a threat, she decided. As he passed her he gave her a slow, insolent appraisal, followed by a wink. There was a loud bang from the street below. Hannah was a little startled, but the Yellow jumped as if he'd been shot and whirled toward the entrance, dropping into a fearful crouch, muscles tensed for fight or flight. It took him a few seconds to register his mistake. He stood up, scowled at Hannah as if it were her fault, then reassumed his mask of insouciance and sauntered down the platform. The cheap food roiled in her stomach, pushing up into the back of her throat. Was this her future then, to sit on public benches, shoveling food in her mouth like a starved animal and waiting for some violence to befall her?

The train arrived. It was the end of rush hour, and most people were leaving rather than entering the city, so Hannah's car was only a third full. She took a seat apart from the other passengers, but even so, the ones nearest her moved away, scooting farther down the bench and, in the case of a mother with a toddler in her arms, getting up and going to the next car. Hannah found herself in a kind of magic circle of ignominy. Her first instinct was to try to make herself invisible, but then a sudden defiance rose in her, and she looked directly into the faces of her fellow passengers, these people who felt so repelled by and morally superior to her. Most avoided her gaze, but a few glared back at her, affronted that she'd dared to rest her eyes on them. She wondered how many of them were liars, their outer purity masking crimes as dark or darker than her own. How many would be Chromes themselves, if the truth in their hearts were revealed?

She got off at Mockingbird Station and descended the steps, recalling with a pang her long-ago visit to the SMU library. She shoved the memory aside and headed in the opposite direction, toward Greenville. When she reached it she turned right, following the path Kayla and her abductor—if that's what he was—had taken, then left onto Kenwood.

Hannah stopped on the sidewalk in front of the small brick house she'd seen on the vid. Old-fashioned iron sconces flanked the steps that led to the porch, casting a friendly glow over the neatly tended yard. Chrysanthemums bloomed in pots on either side of the front door. The windows were shuttered, but she found it almost impossible to imagine anything sinister happening behind them. Still. She thought of Mrs. Henley's sweet, dimpled smile and told herself to stay on her guard.

The door was opened by a young man in his early twenties wearing a Dallas Cowboys sweatshirt. He put Hannah in mind of a cherub, if cherubs could be six and a half feet tall: tousled light brown curls, long-lashed blue eyes, a heart-shaped face that registered something between surprise and shock when he saw her.

"I'm here to see Kayla," Hannah said, without preamble.

"Oh." He looked over his shoulder, a quick, furtive movement. "Are you a . . . friend of hers?"

His transparent unease deepened Hannah's own. "Yes. Is she here?" She tried to peer into the room behind him, but his body blocked her view.

He considered her for a moment, then yelled, "Kayla!" There was no answer. "Kayla, there's someone to see you." To Hannah he said, "Come in. I'm TJ."

She relaxed a little and stepped inside. "I'm Hannah. Nice to meet you."

"Who is it?" Kayla called out from another room. She sounded quavery and congested, like she'd been crying.

"Is she all right?" Hannah asked TJ. He shrugged his shoulders and looked at his feet. She was about to barge down the hall and find out for herself when Kayla appeared. Her eyes were puffy, and she was holding a wad of tissue in one hand. When she saw Hannah she burst into tears. Hannah went to her, shooting a look at TJ.

"Uh, I'm gonna run and pick us up some supper," he said. He grabbed his jacket from the front closet and made a hasty exit.

Kayla sobbed inconsolably, her slender body jerking against Hannah's, threatening to pull away like a kite string in a high wind. She held her until she calmed down enough to confirm what Hannah had already guessed: "You were right about him. Bastard's leaving me, moving to Chicago in three days. He started job-hunting a month ago, didn't even have the balls to write and tell me."

Hannah led her to the couch. Haltingly, between outbursts of fresh tears, Kayla related the events of the last twelve hours. She'd come to TJ's directly from the center, but no one was home, so she'd waited on the back porch. He showed up a few hours later carrying an armload of moving boxes, which he promptly dropped when he saw her appear from behind the house.

"Is this his place?" Hannah asked. The house had a feminine sophistication that was at odds with her idea of a bachelor pad.

"No, his mom's. He lives with her. She's a flight attendant, she's gone a lot."

"She's away now?"

"Yeah, but she's coming home day after tomorrow. To see him off." More tears. "TJ works for a biotech company, supposedly he's being transferred. I know jobs are scarce, but I feel like if he really loved me, he'd look for something here in Texas."

Hannah couldn't disagree, but Kayla was so forlorn. "Maybe he did, and he couldn't find anything," she offered.

"Don't," Kayla said, with a hint of her old spirit. "I don't need any more false hope."

"Well, he must care something about you, or he wouldn't have chased after you the way he did."

"How do you know that?"

Hannah explained how she'd found Kayla on geosat. "I almost had a stroke. I thought you were being kidnapped."

"When he told me he was leaving, I was so upset I just took off running. He talked me into staying, at least for tonight and to-morrow." Kayla blew her nose loudly. "Why'd you leave the center, anyway? I thought you were gonna tough it out."

The anger and determination that had carried Hannah through the day vacated her all at once. She felt like her bones had been extracted, leaving only a sac of shapeless, inert flesh. "Can I tell you later? I just can't go back there right now."

"You all right?"

"Not really, no. But I'm alive. I'm beginning to think that's as good as it gets for people like us."

"Oh, Hannah. What are we gonna do?"

Hannah heard the fear in Kayla's voice as from a great distance. She knew her friend needed reassurance, but she was too tired to give it, too tired even to feel afraid herself, though she knew she would later. She shook her head. "I don't know. Eat and then sleep. I can't think any further ahead than that."

TJ returned with a twelve-pack of beer and a pizza and salad from Campisi's. Hannah declined the beer, but Kayla knocked back several over the course of the meal, which they ate in strained silence. A few times Hannah caught TJ looking at Kayla the way Becca had looked at her earlier: like he was trying, and failing, to find the woman he once loved in the woman she'd become. Would Aidan's face look like that if he saw Hannah? Would he even recognize her? She shut down that train of thought. Even if she could bear to find out the answers, there was no point in speculating on something that would never happen.

As they were finishing, Kayla stood abruptly. "Hannah's staying here tonight," she said.

"Uh, sure," TJ replied. He looked at Hannah. "You're welcome to stay tomorrow night too if you want."

"Thank you," Hannah said, relieved.

"She can sleep with me in your mom's room," Kayla said.

"Okay. Whatever you want."

Kayla's eyes ignited. "Really, TJ? *Whatever* I want?"

"Kayla—"

Hannah got to her feet. She'd had all the confrontation she could handle today. "I'm beat. I think I'll hit the sack."

"Good idea," Kayla said. She stalked from the room.

"Thank you for letting me stay," Hannah said to TJ.

"I'm glad you came. She needs someone."

"She needs *you*. She was counting on you."

He shook his head. The unhappiness on his sweet face was incongruous. "I can't," he said. And she could see it: that he'd tried, truly tried, to rise to this situation, and failed. She could see the little cracks in his character that had made his failure inevitable; could see that though it would haunt him for a while, he would get past it eventually, would shrug off his guilt and, except for the occasional unbidden and quickly suppressed memory, put Kayla from his mind. Not because he was a bad person, but because that was his essential nature. Cherubs weren't meant to be unhappy.

In the bedroom Hannah found Kayla rummaging through a bureau for sleepwear. TJ's mother's tastes ran to the sensual; the search yielded half a dozen scanty silk nightgowns in assorted colors and a black lace teddy that made Hannah's face hot just to look at it. Kayla held it up and wiggled it suggestively. "Wouldn't you love to walk into breakfast at the center wearing this? Reverend Henley's eyes would pop right out of his big fat head." They laughed, an unfettered sound that dispelled some of the ugliness of the day.

Hannah chose the least revealing of the nightgowns and took it into the bathroom to change. She slid it over her head, enjoying the feel of the silk against her skin after months of coarse cotton. Remembering, inevitably, the time she'd worn the violet silk for Aidan: the feel of his fingers digging into her hips, of the wall against her back, hard and unyielding, as he had been. It was the only time he was ever rough with her. Afterward he was contrite:

Had he hurt her? Frightened her? She lied and said no. There *had* been pain, but it had been threaded with a dark pleasure she'd never experienced before. Her last thought before she'd fallen into a dead sleep was how strange it was, and how unsettling, that the one could coexist with and even intensify the other.

She'd awoken later to find Aidan staring down at her pensively.

"What?" she asked.

"Did you make that?" He nodded his head in the direction of the dress lying crumpled on the floor.

"Yes."

"For me?"

"No. For myself. It's something I've been doing for years. No one knows about it."

"Are they all . . . like that?"

Hannah hesitated. Would he think ill of her for creating things so sensual, so at odds with their faith? "Yes," she admitted.

"Why do you do it?"

She shrugged uncomfortably. "I'm not sure you'd understand."

"Try me," he said, with an odd intensity.

"It's like I have to make them, or I'll explode. Like they're . . ." She put her hand to her chest and tapped it.

"Like they're an essential part of you. A part you can't express any other way."

"Exactly," she said, surprised.

"For me it's murder weapons and red herrings."

"What?"

"I've been writing mystery stories since I was a kid," Aidan said. "I tried to stop when I was in seminary, but I missed it too much." His expression was bashful, almost childlike. She felt a welling of tenderness for him.

"Have you ever had one published?"

"No. I've never shown them to anyone."

Not even Alyssa? Hannah didn't voice the question, but she hoped the answer was no. She wanted to have something of him no one else had. "Why not?"

"They're not that good."

"I bet they are. You're wonderful with words."

"Besides, it's hardly appropriate for a clergyman to be writing about murder."

Or having an adulterous love affair with a member of your congregation. "Will you let me read one?" Hannah asked. Aidan hesitated. "C'mon," she said, "I showed you mine."

His eyes slitted, and his lips curved in a lazy, intimate smile. His hand lifted to her breast. "So you did," he said, circling her nipple with his forefinger. "But I like you better without it."

The memory was so vivid she could almost feel his hands on her. She let her lids fall closed, circled her nipples lightly, tugged on them as he'd done. Felt a twinge of arousal, a hollow, mechanical echo of what she'd felt with Aidan. She opened her eyes. Her hideous red self stared back at her.

"Lights out," she said.

She returned to the bedroom and slipped under the covers. Kayla didn't respond to her murmured, "Good night," and Hannah assumed she was asleep. She closed her eyes, feeling bone-tired but safe for the first time in months. And yet, despite her exhaustion, sleep eluded her. Images of the faces she'd seen today paraded before her mind's eye: the enlightener, the Henleys, the two boys in the car, the woman at the pawnshop, Becca, Cole, the guard at the library, Aunt Jo, Mrs. Bunten, Aidan, the teenager at McDonald's, TJ. A grim pageant of fury and malice, shock and disgust, pity and grief. These were the emotions Hannah elicited in other people now.

Beside her Kayla sighed and sat up. The floorboards creaked under her weight. Hannah heard a whisper of sound, the soft whoosh of fabric falling to the floor. The brush of bare feet against wood. A squeak of bedsprings. Murmurs, which faded to silence, which was broken by moans, sporadic at first and then rhythmic and urgent. A woman's cry, a man's gasp. Silence. Finally, the sound of weeping: first one woman, and then two.

H ANNAH SLEPT UNTIL WELL PAST noon, waking to the heavenly smell of frying bacon. It told her immediately that she was no longer at the center; that she wouldn't have to endure another hasty, tepid shower and meager breakfast, another soporific sermon by Reverend Henley, another gruesome enlightenment session with Bob. She showered and put on the clothes Kayla had left for her: jeans, a cotton sweater, underwear, socks, sneakers. Hannah had never worn pants before, and the snug feel of them was discomfiting. She'd been taught that pants were inappropriate for girls because they were immodest, an explanation that had never made sense to her, given that pants, unlike all but floor-length skirts, covered a hundred percent of a woman's legs. Once, just after she turned sixteen, she pressed her mother as to exactly why they were immodest. "Because they remind men of your legs and what's between them," her mother replied. "Is that what you want to do?" The answer had disturbed Hannah so much that from that moment on, she never again questioned the convention.

Now, eyeing herself in the mirror, Hannah could see her mother's point. The jeans were a little short but otherwise fit her form perfectly, emphasizing the length of her legs, the smallness of her waist, the roundness of her buttocks. When she stood with her legs together, there was a triangular gap just below her crotch, and two more at the top and bottom of her calves. The gaps seemed almost like invitations.

But. Hannah cocked her head, tasting a new idea. If women's pants were suggestive, men's were equally so, and they revealed a great deal more of what was underneath them. There was almost always a bulge—you couldn't help but notice it—and if the pants were tight, you could see practically everything. And the way men were always drawing attention to it! Touching and scratching themselves with total unselfconsciousness, as if they were alone and not in public. She'd even seen Aidan do it a few times, absentmindedly. And yet no one accused men of being improper or of encouraging sin by reminding women of what hung between their legs. She looked at herself in the mirror, irritated suddenly by the double standard. This was how her body was made. The fact that it was well made and encased in a pair of blue jeans didn't mean she was inviting anything.

"You alive in there?" Kayla called out.

Hannah went and joined her in the kitchen. "Morning."

"Morning," Kayla returned brightly. The cheerfulness was a bit forced, but Hannah was glad to see that the despair of yesterday was gone.

"Where's TJ?"

Kayla shrugged. "He was gone when I got up. Left me a note saying he'd be back by three. I'd like to be out of here before then."

"You mean, for good?"

"Yup." There wasn't an atom of doubt in Kayla's voice.

"Where to?"

They discussed their options over breakfast. Neither of them wanted to stay in Dallas; the associations were too painful. But the idea of going someplace where they knew no one was daunting. "I've got a cousin in Austin," Kayla said. "He's completely mental but he's family, I bet he'd help us get on our feet. And there's Annie, my best friend from college, she's down in Corpus." Kayla looked expectantly at Hannah.

"All my friends and family are here." It struck her then, just how small and contained her life had been: a snow globe, without the snow. "I vote Austin, if your cousin will help. But we'll need a car."

"I've got one. It's parked at my old apartment, assuming it hasn't been towed. My problem's lana. I'm pretty close to broke."

"I've got plenty of money. Enough to last us for a good while." Kayla looked at her curiously but didn't ask, for which Hannah was grateful. "Anyway, before we can go anywhere, I need to get some clothes and some other things from home. Which means I need to call my father. I doubt my mother would let me in the house."

"I hear you. If TJ hadn't gone to my apartment after I was arrested and picked up my port and some other stuff, I'm sure my mama would have thrown it all away."

"Daddy gets off work at six. He could probably meet us somewhere by seven or so." *If he's still speaking to me.*

Hannah used the vid in the bedroom to make the call. To her relief, her father picked up at once.

"Thank God," he said, when he saw her face. "I've been worried sick, and so has Becca. Are you all right?" He looked careworn, anxious—her fault, Hannah knew.

"I'm fine. I'm with a friend in East Dallas."

"I know, I found you on geosat. I was just about to head over there. But Hannah, why did you leave the center? I haven't had time to look for a place for you, I don't have any job leads—"

"It's all right, Daddy. You aren't responsible for me."

"If you had a daughter of your own, you'd know better than that."

His words summoned an image of Pearl as she might have been: lying on her back in her crib, waving her chubby arms and smiling up at Hannah.

"I'm sorry, that was thoughtless of me." Her father sighed, a pained hiss. "We'll figure something out, Hannah. I'll come pick you up as soon as I get off work."

A siren song, to which she longed to surrender. How wonderful it would be, to give herself over to his loving guidance, to let him swoop in, take charge, figure out what to do next. Daddy to the rescue.

No. She wasn't a child anymore, and she'd dragged him deep enough into her troubles, him and Becca both. Hannah shook her head and made her voice firm. "I'm leaving town. I just need you to bring me some things from home."

"Don't be ridiculous. Where will you go? You have no connections, no money."

"My friend has money," she lied. "And my mind's made up. I can't stay here, not after everything that's happened. Surely you can understand that."

"This friend of yours, is she also a . . ." He faltered.

"A criminal? An outcast? Yeah, she's just like me." He flinched at that, but Hannah pushed down her remorse. As much as she hated to hurt him, she knew she'd only cause him more pain if she stayed.

"All right," he said, defeated. "Tell me what you need."

She gave him a list—her port, some clothes, some toiletries— and they agreed to meet at seven in the parking lot of the little shopping center near the house. Hannah hung up and then, unable to resist the impulse, did a search on Aidan. There were over a hundred thousand entries. She looked through the more recent ones and found a news vid of his swearing-in ceremony as secretary of faith. He stood on a dais with Alyssa, his parents, President Morales and some other officials. The president extolled the work Aidan had done so tirelessly on behalf of children and the poor, the hope his ministry had brought to millions across the globe, the power of his vision for an America and a planet united in the love of God. Alyssa held the Bible while he took the oath of office, swearing to support and defend the Constitution against all enemies, foreign and domestic, so help him God. Then, to enthusiastic applause from the assembled guests, Aidan stepped up to the podium. In close-up, his face was drawn, his spirit visibly dimmed. He began with thanks: to God and His blessed Son, Jesus Christ, to the president and vice president, to his predecessor, to this senator and that congresswoman, to his parents and finally, to his wife, whom he credited with making him not just a better minister, but a better man through her loving and compassionate example. This elicited an abashed smile from Alyssa and a chorus of *aww*s from the audience, but to Hannah, his words—all of them—seemed rote, deadened, and she knew it was because he was mourning her. She wondered, had she made him a better man, or a worse man? Had that even been in her power, or had she simply allowed him to be the man he was, good and bad both?

The speech continued, but Hannah turned it off and rejoined Kayla in the kitchen. She'd reached her crazy cousin, who was indeed willing to let them stay with him until they found a place of their own. While she was packing her things, Hannah did the breakfast dishes and made the bed. Fifteen minutes later, they were ready to go.

As they were about to walk out the door, Hannah said, "You're not even going to leave him a note?"

"Nope. Got nothing to say but goodbye."

They headed toward Greenville and the train station. The sidewalk was narrow, so they went in single file, with Hannah in front. They didn't speak, but she could hear the soft slap of Kayla's footsteps behind her, moving at a slightly different cadence from her own. How different she felt from when she'd walked this same sidewalk yesterday, because of that simple, companionable sound. A car turned onto the street and approached them. Hannah reached up to raise her hood but then stopped herself, letting the bright afternoon sun shine down upon her naked red face.

KAYLA'S OLD APARTMENT was in Oak Lawn. They took the train to Lemmon and the bus across to Wycliff. The driver was indifferent to them, but their fellow passengers' eyes were hard and unwelcoming, herding them to the rear. There were two other Chromes back there, one on either side of the aisle, a Red and a Green, both male. The Red was a bum, probably homeless, definitely unbathed for quite some time. Snores smelling of booze and rotting teeth issued from his gaping mouth. The Green, on the other hand, was young and good-looking, with a coiled intensity and manic eyes. Hannah and Kayla exchanged a glance and chose the loud, smelly bum. They took seats two rows behind him, four rows behind the Green, who watched them as they passed. As she had with the Yellow in the train station the day before, Hannah found herself automatically assessing him, mining the information presented by his face and body. Greens were a wide-ranging category. If he was an arsonist or an armed robber, he probably wasn't dangerous, at least not to them. But if he'd been chromed for something like aggravated assault . . .

He turned his head and looked back at them. "I've got TJ's bowie knife," Kayla said under her breath. She opened the duffel bag and showed the knife to Hannah. "I took it from his room this morning."

"Good, we may need it," said Hannah. "But not for this guy." Once again, she marveled at her certainty. Had becoming a Red given her an extra sense, a knowledge of the hidden desires and evil in other hearts? She shook her head as a more likely, less romantic explanation occurred to her: becoming a Red had forced her, for the first time in her life, to really pay attention.

"That bus driver wouldn't lift a finger to help us, I can tell you that," Kayla said. "And neither would any of those other upstanding citizens in front."

"That's all right. We won't need them to." Hannah gestured toward the Green, who was now intent on a hologame he was playing on his port. "Look, he's already lost interest in us."

Kayla gave Hannah an appreciative look. "God seems to be sending some information to you that I'm not receiving on my bandwidth. But all I can say is, praise be."

"God's got nothing to do with it," Hannah said.

"I thought you were a serious Christian."

"I was, once. Are you?"

"Nah, I'm not religious. I mean, not like they taught us in church, anyway. I figure if there is a God, She's good and surged right now about the state of things down here."

That's blasphemy, Hannah thought, with a flare of outrage that was followed, a beat later, by wonder at the vehemence of her reaction. Why, when she no longer believed, would she respond like that? It had been pure reflex, she realized. She had no more control over it than she would over her salivary glands in the presence of freshly baked bread. Was that all her religious beliefs had ever been then, a set of precepts so deeply inculcated in her that they became automatic, even instinctive? Hear the word *God,* think He. See the misery of humankind, blame Eve. Obey your parents, be a good girl, vote Trinity Party, never sit with your legs apart. Don't question, just do as you're told.

"Hey, where are you?" Kayla said. "You're graying out on me."

"The past," Hannah said. "Where else?"

"I hear that. Spent a lot of time there myself lately, and somehow I always come back feeling worse, not better. Figure I'm better off leaving it in the rearview mirror where it belongs."

Watching the lights of the city fly past outside the smudged window of the train, Hannah was gripped by a sudden sadness. When she was a child, it had always seemed to her as though the landscape were moving, hurtling past her while she remained in place. Now, the illusion was gone. It was she who was leaving all this behind.

They reached the apartment complex just after sunset and found Kayla's car. It was a converted Honda Duo so old it had no smartfeatures, but the solar panels had done their job, and there was enough of a charge to start the engine and get them on their way.

"Good girl," Kayla said, patting the car's dusty dash. "This is Ella. She's seen me through a lot."

"Why Ella?" Hannah asked.

"After the First Lady of Song, of course." Hannah gave Kayla a blank look, and she said, "Oh, come on. You telling me you never heard of Ella Fitzgerald?"

"Nope." The only music allowed in the Payne household was the kind her parents considered inspirational: classical, gospel and, when her mother was in a tolerant mood, Christian rock.

Kayla plugged her port into the dock. "Well *that* is a tragedy we're going to rectify right here and right now."

Ella sang for them all the way to Plano. Her voice made Hannah think of satin, lustrous and rippling, with unexpected hues that changed with the angle of the light; yet at the same time, it had the purity and weightlessness of white tulle. "It's like she's never known pain," Hannah said.

"Oh, she knew plenty of it. She was orphaned, sent to reform

school, divorced twice, diabetic. At the end of her life she had to
have both her legs amputated."

"Wow. How do you know all that?"

"We're related, a few generations back," Kayla said, with quiet
pride. "I grew up listening to her music."

The traffic on Central was unusually light, and they arrived
in Plano half an hour early. They stopped at a DuraShell to juice
the car. Hannah paid with her NIC and was astounded all over
again by the six-digit balance in her account—more money than
she'd ever had in her life. She was still spending her own money,
but she knew it wouldn't last long. One day very soon, the balance
would dip below a hundred thousand, and she'd be officially in
Aidan's debt. And the fact that he was wealthy and had given her
the money freely, out of love—or guilt—didn't make the pill go
down her throat any easier.

When they reached the mall, they found the lot packed with cars
and holiday shoppers. Lights in the store windows illuminated a
host of robotic elves, drummer boys and reindeer prancing in bio-
plastic snow. A group of carolers dressed in Dickensian costumes
sang "Good King Wenceslas," while nearby, a Salvation Army volunteer in a Santa suit rang a handbell. The two women observed this
happy pandemonium from a parking spot at the rear of the lot. Ella
kept them company. *"Someday he'll come along, the man I love . . ."*

"Surreal, isn't it?" Hannah said. She felt so remote from the
people hurrying past, absorbed in their mundane errands and
thoughts—*Must find something for Uncle John. Maybe a tie, or
did I give him a tie last year?*—she might as well have been watching them from the moon. She pointed to a young woman in a 3-D
Frosty the Snowman sweater, laden with shopping bags. "That was
me, a year ago. Well, minus the tacky sweater."

"I don't guess we'll ever get back to that place," Kayla said in a clotted voice.

"Hey, you might. Your sentence is only for five years."

"He'll build a little home, just meant for two," Ella sang.

"Well, one thing's for certain, I'm not gonna make it five more minutes if I keep listening to this." Kayla brushed the back of her hand across her eyes and said, "Track nine. Volume high." Ella launched into a more upbeat song, and Kayla sang along. She was wobbly for the first few bars, but her voice grew stronger as the music took her out of herself.

The innocence of the lyrics made Hannah wistful. She was thinking that if people thought the world was mad back then, they should see it now, when suddenly both doors to the car were yanked open, and two figures in dark clothing grabbed hold of her and Kayla.

"Get out of the car," said the man on Hannah's side. She fought him—she and Kayla both did—but their assailants were strong, and they wrestled the women out of the Honda. Hannah started to scream, and the man clamped a hand over her mouth.

"Listen to me," he said. "The Fist is coming for you. They'll be here any minute. If you want to live, be quiet and come with us."

Hannah stopped struggling. The man was behind her, so she couldn't see his face, but his fingers smelled faintly of garlic and basil.

"How do we know you're not Fist yourself?" demanded Kayla.

"Tabarnak! We do not have the time for this," said the tall figure holding her. The voice was a woman's, nasal, with an angry edge and a foreign—French?—accent.

The man holding Hannah let go of her. "You've got five seconds to make up your minds." She risked turning her head to look at him. She saw dark, disheveled hair, olive skin, solemn, intelligent eyes. She couldn't see his companion; Kayla was in the way. She was looking at Hannah: *What do we do?*

"I say we trust them," Hannah said. "The Fist doesn't admit women." And ruthless vigilantes didn't make pesto.

"Hurry," the man said.

They were hustled to a van parked in the next row, facing the Honda. The double doors in back were open, and the four of them clambered into the cargo area.

"Close doors. Privacy mode on," the woman said. The doors swung shut, and the windows darkened ever so slightly. The man scrambled up to the driver's seat but made no move to start the van. The woman remained crouched beside Hannah and Kayla, eyes fixed on her port. It bathed her face in faint bluish light. "They are here," she said.

"Why aren't we moving?" Hannah asked.

"Quiet."

With mounting panic, Hannah said, "We can't stay here, they can track us."

"The van has a jammer. It blocks the nanotransmitters," the man said. He was pointing a small vidcam out the windshield.

"But what if—" Kayla began.

"Ta yeule!" Hannah didn't speak French, but the woman's meaning was unambiguous, and her tone that of someone who absolutely expected to be obeyed. Hannah heard a vehicle approaching, coming fast. Another van jerked to a halt near the Honda. Two masked men jumped out and strode briskly up and down the row, peering through the windows of all the vehicles. As the shorter of the two neared the van, Hannah's limbs quivered with the overpowering urge to run. Fingers dug into her arm. "Be still!" the woman hissed in her ear.

The man outside pressed his masked face against the driver's-side window, inches from the camera, then turned to his partner. "No sign of her. You got anything?"

"Nada," said the other man, looking at his port. "Signal's gone." He shoved it in his pocket and hitched up his jeans. Hannah saw a glint of metal: a belt buckle, as big and round and shiny as a hubcap.

"Looks like we lost another one."

"Shit," said Cole.

As the two men got in their van and pulled away, Hannah leaned weakly against the wall. Her bravado of yesterday now seemed ludicrous. The thought of being at the mercy of her brother-in-law and his friends was terrifying.

"He has not yet killed," said the woman.

"How do you know?"

"Interior lights on." The lights revealed a tall, lean woman in her thirties with an angular face and a shock of cropped, white-blonde hair. Her eyes were disconcertingly pale and fierce. "It is a new Hand. None of them have killed, they are still working up to it. Your Cole is a follower, he will wait for one of the others to go first."

"He isn't *my* Cole," Hannah said disgustedly.

"Hang on a minute," said Kayla. "Cole, as in your brother-in-law Cole? He was one of them?"

"Yes." To the other woman, Hannah said, "How do you know all this? About Cole and the Fist, and me and Kayla? Who are you?"

"Friends of Raphael's."

Kayla looked at Hannah, bewildered. "Who the hell's Raphael?"

"The doctor who did my abortion." Hannah remembered how inexplicably rattled he'd been after he told her why he'd remained in Texas. *Saw myself as a revolutionary, let them talk me into staying here.* Them: these people, whoever they were.

"We've been tracking you since you left the Chrome ward," the man said. "I'm Paul, and that's Simone."

"Why would you be interested in us?" asked Kayla.

"Not you," Simone said. The *you* was more of a *yeu*—like the sound you'd make spitting a piece of gristle into a napkin. "You are not a part of our mission."

"What mission?" asked Hannah.

"Enough!" Simone made a brusque chopping motion with her hand. *"Enwaille."* It was clearly a command, and Paul started the van at once and pulled out of the space.

"Wait, I'm supposed to meet my father here," Hannah said.

"And I need to get my stuff from the car," Kayla said.

"This will not be possible," Simone said.

"But my father's bringing my port and my clothes. And he'll worry if I'm not here."

"You cannot keep your ports," Simone said. "The police can track you through them."

"But we're not wanted by the police."

"You are now," said Paul. "They were alerted when the signals from your transmitters were interrupted."

"But—"

Simone's hand shot out and grabbed Hannah's arm, hard enough that she winced. "Do you want to die, eh?" Her gaze was as pitiless as her grip. "Many Chromes, they want this, but they cannot admit it, or they do not have the *gosses* to kill themselves, so they walk around begging for someone else to do it. Is this what you want, Hannah Payne? If so, I am sure the Fist will be content to oblige you." She let go of Hannah's arm and grasped the handle that opened the back doors. "Well?"

"No. I want to live." Hannah spoke without hesitation, feeling the truth of it sound deep within her. As bleak as her life had become, it was still precious to her.

"Me too," said Kayla.

"*Bon,*" Simone said to Hannah.

They pulled out of the parking lot. Hannah pressed her face against one of the van's small back windows, trying to spot her father. She didn't see him, but she knew he was there somewhere, scanning the lot with anxious eyes, searching in vain for the daughter he had lost.

SIMONE HANDED HANNAH and Kayla black hoods and told them to put them on. They exchanged a wary glance but complied. What choice did they have? Hannah was full of questions, but she didn't ask them. Whatever was in store for them, it was bound to be better than what the Fist had in mind. Her stomach growled, reminding her that she hadn't eaten since breakfast. She hoped there'd be food where they were going.

A port chimed. "*Allô,*" Simone said. A short silence, then, "Yes, but there has been a complication. She was not alone. Another Red. The Fist was too close to leave her." She raised her voice. "*Yeu,* what is your name?"

"Kayla Ray." Her voice was muffled by the hood.

"Spell it."

Kayla did so. There was a pause, then Simone said, "Kayla Mariko Ray, age twenty-two, serving five years for attempted murder. No prior convictions."

Kayla made a little sound of dismay, and Hannah was pierced once again by the utter loss of their privacy.

"Have you had your renewal yet?" Simone asked.

"No. I'm not due till January fifth."

"Less than four weeks," Simone said. "I agree. All right then, until soon."

"Where are you taking us?" Hannah asked.

"To a safe house," Paul said. "It's shielded, like the van."

"Then what?"

"That depends," Simone said.

"On what?"

"On whether we decide you can be trusted."

They rode the rest of the way in tense silence, broken only by the plaintive growling of Hannah's stomach, which apparently didn't know or care that she was a fugitive whose life was in grave danger. She found her body's mundane insistence oddly comforting.

The van slowed, turned, went up a short slope and stopped. The motor cut off and Hannah heard a garage door close. Her hood was jerked off her head. Simone removed Kayla's as well, then opened the back doors to the van and hopped out, gesturing for them to follow. They found themselves in a two-car garage. The walls were festooned with shovels, power tools, barbecue tongs and tennis rackets. Metal shelves held boxes with innocuous labels like SNORKELING GEAR and PHOTO ALBUMS. Paul was waiting for them by the door that led into the house. A welcome mat that said BEWARE: ATTACK CAT was flanked by a pair of muddy garden clogs and a set of golf clubs. Whatever Hannah had expected a safe house to look like, it wasn't this perfect slice of ordinary Americana.

They entered a kitchen with the same homey feel as the garage. A handwritten note pinned to the fridge added to the effect:

GONE TO TARGET, BACK BY 9 LATEST. DINNER
IN OVEN, HELP YOURSELVES! —S & A

Paul and Simone read the note and exchanged a weighted glance, and Hannah wondered if there was another message embedded in the words.

Something rubbed against her calf, and she jumped. She looked down and saw a brindled gray cat. "That's Emmeline," said Paul. Another cat, this one ruddy-colored with large ears, appeared and made a beeline for him, mewing loudly. He picked it up and cradled it on its back like an infant, rubbing its belly. "And this is Sojo."

Hannah leaned down and stroked Emmeline's soft head. The cat purred, and the rumble of its contentment traveled through her fingers, up her arm and to her eyes, which prickled with tears. Whatever taint she bore, this creature couldn't sense it.

"She likes you," Paul said.

"She wants food," Simone retorted.

"Well, that makes two of us," said Kayla. "Is there really dinner in the oven, or is that secret code for something else?"

Simone gave Kayla a sharp look and Hannah smiled, proud of her friend's fearlessness. Paul opened the oven door, and the odor of roast chicken wafted out.

"We might as well eat while we wait," Paul said to Simone.

She shrugged. "Go ahead. I am not hungry."

The dining room table was set for three. Simone took one of the empty places and drank coffee while the rest of them had supper. Their hosts were brimming with the Christmas spirit. The plates were decorated with Christmas trees and the napkins embroidered with poinsettias. A reindeer-antler candelabra dominated the table, and mistletoe hung from the archway leading to the living room. They ate in silence. Hannah's mind was a jumble of unasked questions: What would happen if these people decided she and Kayla weren't trustworthy? Would they actually let them go, knowing the two women could identify them? Paul seemed kind enough, but Simone was another matter. Hannah remembered the strength of the other woman's grip and how fragile her own bones had felt in comparison. There was no doubt in her mind that Simone would do whatever was necessary to protect herself and her "mission."

The sound of a door opening interrupted this disturbing train of thought. "Wait here," Simone told Paul. She got up and went into the kitchen. Hannah couldn't see the newcomers, but she could hear them, a man and a woman, speaking too low for her to make out what they were saying.

Paul rapped his knuckles on the table, drawing Hannah and Kayla's attention to him. "Listen to me, both of you," he said, in a soft voice at odds with the intensity of his expression. "They're going to try to separate you. They'll make it sound attractive, try to convince you it's in your best interest. They may even tell you they *have* to separate you, but don't let them." He looked at Kayla. "If you do, you'll be in danger."

"What do you mean, we'll be in danger?" she said.

"Not Hannah, just you."

"Why just me?"

"You aren't supposed to be here. You're not part of our mission."

"I don't understand," Kayla said.

"Just do as I say. No matter what they promise, you insist on staying together."

"Why are you telling me this?" Kayla asked.

But Hannah knew, even before she saw his eyes drop to his hands. He was warning them in part out of simple humaneness, because that was his nature, but he had another, equally compelling motive, and it had more to do with passion than compassion. Paul raised his eyes to Kayla, and the expression in them gave Hannah a pang of jealousy. She ducked her head, caught off guard. Who or what exactly was she jealous of? But before she could examine her feelings, Simone strode back into the room and ordered Hannah to follow her. To Kayla and Paul, she said, "Stay here."

Hannah complied with reluctance. In the archway, she turned and looked back at her friend. The swift glance they exchanged held an entire conversation:

Don't let them make you afraid.

I won't if you won't.

We survived the Henleys, we can survive this.

If we stick together.

If we stay strong.

And if we can't?

We have to, or they win.

"Come," Simone said, impatiently. Hannah followed her down a hallway to a small, nondescript bedroom. "You will sleep here."

"What about Kayla?"

"What about her?"

"What are you going to do with her?"

"You must be very tired," Simone said. "Go rest yourself. You will have need of it." She left, closing the door firmly behind her.

HANNAH DIDN'T THINK she'd be able to sleep, but she did, almost immediately, falling asleep on top of the covers with the lamp on. She woke in pitch dark, disoriented, and then remembered where she was and why. "Lights on," she said, but nothing happened. They must have disabled the room's smartmode to prevent her from unlocking the door or windows. She fumbled for the lamp and turned it on manually. The windows were tightly shuttered and there was no clock or vid in the room, but she guessed it was still the wee hours; she felt too groggy to have had a full night's sleep. She went to the bathroom, did her business and brushed her teeth. She longed for a shower but settled for washing her face and hands. She wanted to be ready when they came for her.

She tried the door to the hall and found it locked. She pressed her ear up against the wood but was unable to hear any voices or other sounds of human presence. Next she tried the windows. The shutters were metal and mechanized, but there was no switch. She broke two fingernails trying to pry them open and finally gave up.

The too-familiar sense of being pent, confined, took hold of her. It evoked an image, not of the mirrored oubliette of the Chrome ward, nor of the narrow halls and lowering rooms of the Straight Path Center, but of her little workroom over the garage, a place she'd once seen as a haven. She pictured herself there, head bent, deft fingers pushing white thread through white silk and taffeta, the stitches so tiny as to be invisible—as invisible, Hannah now realized, as she herself had been in the small white room in the white stucco house in the middle-class, mostly white suburb where she'd been born and lived her whole life and expected she would always live unless her future husband had a job that took her elsewhere. She saw her fingers making the tiny stitches, thousands upon thousands of them, all alike, while her mind hungered for forbidden things on the other side of the white walls, things so hazy and inchoate she couldn't name them, and then she heard her mother call, "Hannah, come and set the table," and watched herself set aside her needle and her imaginings, her myriad questions and gossamer dreams, and say, "Coming, Mama."

She struck the door with her fist. How long did they mean to keep her here? What if they'd harmed Kayla or taken her away? Hannah beat on the door until her hand was too sore to continue, then leaned back against it and scanned the room, taking in the tan carpet and off-white walls, the cheap colonial-ish furniture, the tasteful floral bedspread and botanical prints: decor that reminded her of every hotel room where she'd ever met Aidan. How she'd grown to hate those rooms—their anonymity and cheerful banality, their imperviousness to the people who passed through them, made love and argued in them, showered and pissed and shit in them, all evidence of their presence wiped away, rinsed down the drain, vacuumed up as if they'd never been there. Hannah prowled the room restlessly, searching for traces of its past inhabitants. She opened the drawers of the dresser and found a motley assortment of clean, nondescript men's and women's clothing: cotton T-shirts, jeans, socks, underwear, all used. Who had last worn these things? Regular people—a category, she was aware, that no longer included her—or fugitives like herself? There was nothing in the closet but a few forlorn-looking jackets and windbreakers, nothing beneath the bed except dust balls, nothing under the mattress. But as she started to get up from the floor, her eyes were drawn to the underside of the bedside table. Something was written there, carved into the faux wood. She couldn't read it—it was upside down—so she lay on her back and maneuvered her head between the narrow legs of the table. Incised in neat, blocky letters was a short poem:

> Ruts of love in the bed—
> This is how Menelaus
> Described the absence of Helen

The words perforated her heart. She didn't know who Menelaus and his Helen were, but what he'd felt for her, and what the man or woman who'd painstakingly carved these letters into the table must have felt for someone, once, was as familiar and inescapable to her as the throbbing of her fingers after hours of needlework or the cramping of her abdomen before her period. *He is gone. And who am I, without him?*

She sat up and was confronted with the bleak expanse of the bed. Unable to bear the thought of getting into it alone, she pulled the pillows from it and curled on the floor with one between her knees and the other hugged to her chest. Her love was gone, and his absence from her bed, from her life, was permanent. The waves pounded her until she cried herself to sleep.

A KNOCK WOKE her, and Simone's head appeared in the doorway. She considered Hannah, her pale eyes missing nothing. "Go wash your face," she said, with unwonted gentleness. "I will wait for you outside." Hannah had the feeling she wasn't the first woman Simone had seen weeping in this room.

In the dining room, Paul was sitting at the table next to a couple in their fifties. Kayla wasn't with them.

"Hello, Hannah," the woman said, with a welcoming smile. "I'm Susan."

"And I'm Anthony," said the man.

They were on the chubby side, both of them, with pleasant, ordinary features. They wore tracksuits that made them seem at once benign and a little ridiculous. Susan's was a throbbing shade of lavender, and her fingernails were painted to match. Anthony was balding, with a double chin and a rueful countenance that seemed to say, *Yes, I'm everything you think I am.* The two of them, Hannah thought, were a perfect match for the house.

"Please, sit down," Susan said, gesturing at the chair across from her. "Would you like a cup of coffee?" If her appearance was conventional and a little silly, her voice was anything but. It seemed to peal within Hannah, mellifluous and powerful, impossible to ignore.

She remained standing. "Where's Kayla?" she asked. It came out thick and nasal; her nose was still clogged from crying.

"Here," Anthony said, holding out a box of tissues. Feeling uncomfortably exposed, Hannah took one and blew her nose.

"Kayla's sleeping now," Susan said. "She was very tired. I'm afraid we kept her up late."

"I want to see her."

"She's fine. All we did was ask her some questions."

Hannah's eyes darted to Paul. He didn't move his head, but he blinked once, slowly and deliberately.

"And now," Susan said, "we have a few we'd like to ask you, and I'm sure you have some for us as well. Won't you join us and have some coffee?" *Trust me,* that beautiful voice said. *I have only your best interests at heart.*

"Who are you people? Why did you help me?"

Susan leaned forward, locking eyes with her. "It's personal," she said.

Hannah shook her head, not understanding, and then she did, and her arms broke out in gooseflesh. "Oh my God, you're Novembrists."

The Novembrists were infamous, a shadow pro-abortion group named after the 11/17 bombers, the militants responsible for blowing up the Missouri state capitol two weeks after the governor signed the SOL laws. The Novembrists rarely resorted to violence, however; intimidation and public humiliation were their preferred weapons. In keeping with their motto, "Abortion is personal," their attacks were always against individuals who were vocal opponents of choice. Hannah's mother had been a volunteer for the Womb Watchers when the Novembrists released shocking holos of Retta Lee Dodd, the Watchers' founder, pole-dancing nude in a strip club as a young woman. More recently, they'd rocked the Trinity Party—and stunned every evangelical in the state of Texas, including Hannah and her family—by exposing the Trinitarian lieutenant governor as a homosexual who was partial to underage male prostitutes. The Novembrists were on the FBI's Most Wanted list, but as far as Hannah knew, none of the group's members had ever been caught.

"That's right. The government calls us terrorists, but we think of ourselves as freedom fighters. Raphael is one of us." Susan cocked her head, appraising Hannah frankly. "You could have betrayed him. Most women tell what they know rather than add three years to their sentence. Why didn't you?"

"Because he was kind. And besides, I doubt I'll be around long enough to serve the extra time. I'm familiar with the survival rate for female Reds." As Hannah said the words she felt a wave of cold pass through her. This wasn't the first time she'd had the thought that she could die, be killed or reach a place so dark she killed herself, but voicing it made it suddenly, horribly real.

"We can help you be one of the exceptions," Anthony said.

"Help me how?"

"That depends on you," Susan said. "On your will and your courage."

"Let's say I'm willful and courageous. Then what?"

"Why don't you sit down, and we'll discuss it."

Her eyes roved over their four faces: Simone's taut and watchful, giving nothing away; Paul's earnest and intense; Anthony's and Susan's amiable, completely at odds with their shrewd, assessing eyes. Except for Paul, she didn't trust any of them, and even he clearly had his own agenda. Still, they were offering her hope. Even if it was only a glimmer, that was more than she'd had five minutes ago.

She pulled out the chair and sat. "I'll take some of that coffee," she said.

THEY ASKED HER TO TELL them about herself, and Hannah obliged, sketching her upbringing, her family, her work. She had the sense that they were less interested in the particulars of her answers than in what they revealed about her beliefs and her character. When the narrative got to her pregnancy, Anthony asked her who the father was. "It's personal," she replied tartly, and he and Susan bobbed their heads as if the answer pleased them. Hannah covered the abortion in one sentence, and they didn't try to excavate further, but they questioned her at length about the police interrogations and her weeks in jail. Susan did most of the asking and was plainly in charge. When Hannah spoke of her time in the Chrome ward—her shame and lethargy, her mental deterioration—Paul got up and started pacing the room restlessly.

All four of them perked up when she began to recount her experiences at the Straight Path Center, and when she described the enlightenment sessions, their expressions turned avid and their questions pointed: Did the Henleys live at the center? How often did they go out? Was Hannah sure she hadn't caught the enlightener's last name, or the names of any of the doctors who'd visited? It dawned on Hannah, with a flash of pure glee, that Bob and the Henleys could be in for a nasty, personal surprise one of these days.

Mindful of Paul's warning, Hannah wove Kayla into the story, emphasizing her generosity and loyalty. Susan and Anthony made no comment, but Hannah could feel their impatience. When she told them of her decision to go to Austin with Kayla, Susan interrupted. "But you've only known her for what, six weeks?"

"That's right," Hannah said. "But believe me, six weeks in that place is like six years anywhere else."

"Did you know she shot her stepfather?"

"Yes, she told me the first day we met, and I don't blame her. He was molesting her little sister."

"So she says."

"She wouldn't lie about a thing like that."

"People lie about all kinds of things," Susan said. "The fact is, there's no way to confirm her story."

"I don't need to. I believe her, and so should you."

Susan looked sidelong at Simone.

"What you do not know is that she killed him," Simone said. "He died of sepsis two days ago. Kayla is wanted for murder now. If we had not picked her up last night, the police soon would have."

The news shocked Hannah to silence. How would Kayla feel when she found out? Remorseful? Pleased? Hannah wondered how she herself would feel, knowing she'd killed someone, even someone evil, and then crashed into hard truth: she already had, and her victim had been innocent.

"What will they do if they catch her?" she asked.

"Resentence her, most likely," Anthony said. "They don't usually send first offenders to prison, especially women. Though they could, if she gets a tough prosecutor."

"You can't let that happen," Hannah protested. "Kayla can't go to one of those places, she wouldn't survive." Conditions in the state and federal prisons were notoriously brutal. There were no live broadcasts from the prisons, no cameras allowed at all.

Susan took back the baton, her tone sympathetic, reasonable. "We understand you've become attached to her, Hannah, but you must see what a liability she'd be. If you were caught with her, they could charge you with being an accessory after the fact."

"And then what, I'd be chromed?" she said sarcastically.

"The point is," Susan said, with an edge of irritation, "the road you're about to take is long and dangerous, and Kayla would just increase your chances of being caught."

Not to mention yours. There'd be one more person who's seen your faces, one more person who could expose you. "Tell me about this road," Hannah said, thinking of the Henleys and their path. "Where does it lead?"

"East and north."

"And what's at the end of it?"

"Redemption," said Anthony. "A new life."

"Right, I've heard that one before." R-O-A-D: RAGGED, OUTCAST, ALONE AND DESPERATE.

"I'll put it another way," said Susan. "Reversal."

Hannah went very still, searching their faces for signs of disingenuousness and finding none. "Of the chroming?"

"Yes."

"But how? It has to be done by a genetic team at a federal Chrome center."

"Not necessarily."

"But they're the only ones with access to the genetic codes and the viral lockouts. If somebody gets it wrong, I'm dead."

With an impatient wave of one plump hand, Susan said, "We can't go into specifics now. All you need to know is, there's a place where the procedure can be reversed safely, and we can help you get there."

"How far north?" Hannah looked at Simone. "Canada?"

The other woman's expression didn't change, but the charged quality of the silence in the room told Hannah she'd guessed right. It made sense. Canada had severed relations with the United States after the Supreme Court upheld the constitutionality of melachroming. Hannah had only been six at the time, but she could still remember her parents' indignation, and the snide references to "backstabber bacon" she'd heard at church. Diplomatic ties had been reestablished out of necessity during the Great Scourge, but relations between the two countries had been strained ever since. Québec in particular was known to be a hotbed of opposition to chroming.

"Well, wherever it is," Hannah said, "I'm not going without Kayla."

"I'm afraid that won't be possible," Susan said. "You have to understand, we have a very specific mission, and we don't go beyond it."

"And yet you monitor the Fist," Hannah pointed out.

"Because they often target women who've had abortions. We can't save everyone, Hannah."

"Not everyone deserves to be saved," Simone said.

"You sound exactly like Cole," Hannah said, not hiding her contempt.

"What do you mean?"

"Two days ago he told me, 'Some things don't deserve to be forgiven.' Maybe you and the Fist should team up, pool your resources."

Simone's nostrils flared. "You dare to speak to me like this? If it was not for us—"

"Our resources are limited," interrupted Anthony, shooting a quelling look at Simone. She sat back, though she continued to glare at Hannah. "We use them for one thing and one thing only: to defend women's reproductive rights. We are feminists, not revolutionaries."

Feminists. The word made Hannah bristle with distaste. In her world, they were viewed as unnatural women who sought to overturn the order laid down by God, sabotage the family, emasculate men and, along with gays, atheists, abortionists, Satanists, pornographers and secular humanists, pervert the American way of life. Many people Hannah knew blamed feminists and their fellow deviants for calling down the wrath of God, in the form of the 9/11 attacks, the LA bombing and natural catastrophes like the Great Scourge and the Hayward quake. Hannah had always found it hard to believe that God would destroy millions of lives out of vindictiveness, despite what the Old Testament said. Still, she'd never questioned much of what she'd been taught, and certainly not the precept that women were meant to submit to the loving guidance of men.

She considered Simone, who looked like the stereotype of a feminist, and Susan, who did not, and then the two men. "*We* are feminists," Anthony had said, without a trace of embarrassment. Did it not feel unnatural to him and Paul to name themselves that, and even more so, to follow Susan and Simone's lead? Why would these men, or any man, willingly surrender their authority to a woman?

Paul's chair scraped loudly against the floor. His somber eyes met Hannah's, reminding her of Kayla somewhere in the house, scared and vulnerable.

"You say you're feminists," Hannah said, meeting each of their eyes in turn. "I don't know what that means exactly, but it seems to me it ought to include helping women who protect young girls from being raped."

"She's right, and you know it," Paul said. He was addressing Simone, not Susan and Anthony, and from his tone Hannah guessed this was an old argument between them. "It's not enough to just fight for choice, or even for women's rights. If we want a truly fair society, we have to go beyond that."

"And how do we do this, eh?" Simone said. "How can we know

who is innocent and who is not, who deserved to be chromed and who did not? We have only their word, the word of convicted criminals."

"No one deserves that." Paul pointed to Hannah's face. "It's fucking barbaric."

Simone shrugged. "I agree. But this is not our concern."

"So," Paul said, "you're willing to risk your life fighting for a woman's right to privacy and control over her own body, but you think it's perfectly fine for the government to do *that* to people?"

"Most of them are scum," Simone said. "Rapists, drug traffickers, pimps."

Simone was exactly like Bridget, Hannah thought, with a burst of antipathy. She wondered whether Simone too had painful secrets underlying her stridency and then decided she didn't care. Hannah's life wasn't exactly a fairy tale either, but it hadn't turned her into a caustic bitch.

"Sure, some of them are," Paul conceded, "but how many are just screwed by a system that's stacked against them from the day they're born? It's no coincidence that seventy-five percent of Chromes come from the lower classes."

"And eighty-five percent of Chromes are men!" Simone said. "Maybe if you would stop raping and shooting your guns and—"

Susan's hand struck the table hard, making Hannah and the others jump. "Enough, both of you! This isn't the time."

Simone gave Susan a curt nod. "You are right."

In the ensuing silence, Hannah considered Paul, disconcerted by what he'd said. Melachroming had been the law of the land since she was four years old, and while the sight of a Chrome sleeping on the street or standing in line at the soup kitchen had often stirred her pity, she'd always accepted its necessity and the justice of it. How else, after the Second Great Depression, to relieve the financially crippled federal and state governments of the prohibitive cost of housing millions of prisoners? And why should precious tax dollars be wasted on criminals when honest citizens were going hungry, schools were failing, roads and bridges were crumbling and Los Angeles was still a heap of radioactive rubble? Besides, the old criminal justice system had been a patent and abject failure. The prisons were disintegrating and filled to bursting, the vast majority of their inmates living in conditions so horrific as to be unconstitutional. Rape, murder, disease and abuse of prisoners by guards were endemic. Meanwhile, recidivism increased with every passing year. Melachroming all but the most violent and incorrigible convicts was not only more cost effective than imprisoning them, it was also more of a deterrent against crime and a more humane means of punishment. So Hannah had been taught by her parents and teachers, and so she'd always believed. Even when they'd injected her, there hadn't been a shred of doubt in her mind that she deserved her punishment. But now, she found herself questioning the system's fairness. Would she have been chromed if she'd had the money to hire a seasoned attorney instead of being represented by a public defender two years out of law school with sixty other cases to juggle? Would Kayla have been convicted if she'd been white?

"There's something else you should know," Susan said, interrupting Hannah's thoughts. "If you decide to take the road, there's no turning back. You'll never be able to return here or have contact with anyone from your previous life, not your family, not anyone. You'll disappear, and eventually, they'll assume you're dead. And if we find out you've been in contact with them, you will be. We won't allow you to jeopardize our mission."

The beloved faces of her parents, Becca and Aidan, sick with worry for her, then grief, then finally, acceptance, passed in succession through Hannah's mind. Aidan, unlike her family, wouldn't be able to mourn her loss openly, but there was no shortage of other causes to which he could attribute his sorrow: *Such a tragedy, all those families left homeless by the wildfires, all those civilians massacred by the insurgents, all those children dying of malaria in Britain.* He'd always felt the suffering of others so keenly; no one who knew him would suspect a thing. Hannah thought back to the last time she was with him. He'd just returned from a grueling cross-country "Nights of Abounding" tour to raise money for the water war refugees in North Africa. His face had been drawn and his eyes redrimmed from lack of sleep, with dark smudges beneath them. When she chided him for pushing himself too hard, he waved off her concern, describing in horrifying detail the camps he'd seen in western Egypt, Libya, Algeria: the bloated stomachs of the children, the desiccated bodies of the dead, the mothers too dehydrated to produce milk or tears. They hadn't made love that night. Hannah had spooned behind him, stroking his arm until he fell asleep, thinking of the life within her and knowing she must extinguish it, not just for his sake, but also for the sake of all those unknown children and mothers whose survival depended on his work. She crept out of the room before he woke. Before she could change her mind.

How, she thought now, could she bear never to hold him in her arms again? *A new life.* Never to sit across a table from her parents again? *Redemption.* Never again to touch her forehead to Becca's? *Reversal.* Her skin would be normal, but she would be alone.

But no more alone than she was now. The truth was, she'd lost them already, all except her father, and if she spent sixteen years as a Red she'd lose him too, because she'd no longer bear any resemblance to the daughter he loved.

"Well?" asked Susan.

"I will take the road," Hannah said, "provided you offer it to Kayla too."

"Even if we allow her to go with you," Susan said, "she may decide the price is too high."

"And if she does?"

"We'll release her, of course." Susan's voice was even, her eyes wide and shining with sincerity. Anthony dipped his head in confirmation. But Hannah had seen, in the instant before they'd answered, how both of their gazes had flickered to Simone, and the almost imperceptible nod she'd given in answer.

"Of course," Hannah said, wondering how Simone did the killings, and where she disposed of the bodies.

SUSAN ANNOUNCED THEY were breaking for the night so everyone could get some sleep. "We'll talk again tomorrow after we've spoken to Kayla," she said.

"I'd like to be there when you do," Hannah said.

"I think it's best if we speak to her alone. She needs to decide this for herself."

"Fine, I won't say a word. But I want to hear her decision from her own lips."

Susan glanced at Simone, looked back at Hannah. Said, "Fine."

Simone escorted her to her room in angry silence. At the door, Hannah said, "Kayla looked out for me when I had nobody else. I owe her, do you understand?"

"And now, you owe us," Simone said. "You owe *me*."

Simone was right, and Hannah acknowledged it with a weary nod. Thinking, *You, and practically every other person I know. And damned if I know how to begin to pay any of you back.*

Enervated from the questioning, she fell asleep almost instantly, waking some hours later to the sound of Simone's knock and brusque announcement that they were meeting in twenty minutes.

Hannah took a quick shower and got dressed. The idea of

putting her dirty clothes back on was distasteful, so she chose clean underwear, socks, khakis and a sweater from the chest of drawers. She looked in the mirror and saw her mother's face: the high cheekbones and voluptuous mouth, the black, catlike eyes and thick, slanting brows. It hit her then, that the mirror was the only place she'd ever see her mother's face again. They'd never been truly close, but now Hannah felt a surge of love and longing for her. Would she search for Hannah in her own mirror from time to time, or would she shun her own likeness, not wanting to be reminded of her daughter's disgrace?

Back in the dining room, Susan and Anthony were already seated and having breakfast. The tracksuits had been replaced by business attire that managed to convey the identical impression of ever-so-slightly humorous bad taste. Susan had a large rhinestone panda pinned to the lapel of her unflattering red suit, and Anthony wore khakis, a blue blazer and a polka-dotted bow tie that was perfectly askew. They looked like a bank teller and a high school math teacher, certainly not terrorists on the FBI's Most Wanted list.

Breakfast was set on the sideboard. As Hannah filled her plate, the gray cat rubbed against her, twining between her legs. "Hello, Emmeline," she said, bending down to stroke the soft head. Paul and Kayla entered the room, the latter still half-asleep. Her posture was slumped, her eyes swollen, her face desolate. Hannah knew that look, that feeling: *He is gone.* The echo of its roar sounded in her own head, and she muted it forcibly. Neither of them could afford to show weakness. She caught Kayla's eye and gave her a look, accompanied by a slight, upward jerk of her chin. Kayla straightened a little and went to fill her plate.

Once everyone was seated, Susan got quickly to the point.

"Well, Kayla, we've decided to offer you the same choice we offered Hannah."

Kayla's eyes flew to Hannah's. "What choice is that?"

With a glance of warning at Hannah, Susan and Anthony launched into their tag-team description of the road, but where with Hannah they'd emphasized its possibilities, with Kayla, they stressed its dangers and the sacrifices it required. Hannah could see her friend becoming more and more dubious, especially when she learned that the road was one-way only.

"I don't know," she said, obviously torn. "Never to see my little sister again, or my aunts and uncles and cousins?" She looked at Hannah. "Did you say yes?"

Hannah nodded, and Kayla turned back to Susan. "You know I'm due for renewal on January fifth. Can we make it to wherever we're going by then?"

"There are no guarantees," Susan replied. "The road is unpredictable. And so is the virus."

"What do you mean?"

"I mean you may not have that long. Some people start fragging out early. Others go two or three weeks before they feel anything. And of course, the ramp-up varies from person to person. If you're one of the sensitive ones, you could be completely fragmented in a matter of a few days."

Kayla bit her lip and stared down at her plate.

"However hard you imagine the road to be," Simone said, "it will be more hard. The feeble and the doubtful do not survive it. You must not take it unless you are certain this is what you want."

Kayla was silent for a long moment. "I don't know," she said, looking at Hannah with an unhappy, sheepish expression. "If I had sixteen years to serve like you do, I wouldn't think twice.

But my sentence is only for five. Maybe I should take my chances here."

Hannah was incredulous. She'd put herself on the line with these people for Kayla's sake, and now she was backing out? *Abandoning me, just like Aidan did.* The thought was unlooked-for, and it released a flood of pent-up rancor that Hannah saw had been there for some time, roiling just beneath the surface of her love for him. *I sacrificed our child's life, and my own, for his sake, and the coward deserted me.* As painful as the realization was, the anger felt good. And it beat the hell out of mourning Saint Aidan.

"If you aren't sure, then you shouldn't go," Anthony was saying to Kayla.

Hannah felt Paul's eyes on her, prodding her: *Don't let them separate you.* She studied her friend, evaluating her with the same dispassion she'd trained on Paul, TJ, the Green on the subway. She saw fear and doubt and vulnerability, intelligence and pluck. What she did not see was cowardice. If she were in Kayla's position, would she not have the same reluctance to give up her whole life? Except Kayla wasn't in the position she thought she was, and Hannah knew that unless she said something, they'd allow her to decide unknowing.

"Your stepfather's dead," Hannah said.

Kayla stared at her for a moment, stunned, and then turned to Susan. "Is it true?"

A grudging nod. "He died of sepsis two days ago."

"That son of a bitch. He would have to up and die." Kayla's voice splintered on the word, and Hannah could see that beneath her bravado, she was deeply shaken. Her expression turned grim as she absorbed the implications. "Murder's what, ten years minimum?" Another nod from Susan. "Son of a *bitch.*"

"At least he'll never touch your sister again," Hannah said.

"Yeah, there's that." Kayla took a deep breath and sighed it out. "Guess it's two for the road."

SUSAN HAD TOLD them they'd be leaving in a few days, but a week and a half later, they were still cooped up in the house, waiting. "There's been a delay," was all the explanation they were given. Susan and Anthony were gone during the days, presumably to their respective, respectable jobs, and either Simone or Paul babysat. Hannah and Kayla felt increasingly caged and irritable. They couldn't go outside and were forbidden to access the net—to keep them from contacting anyone they knew, Hannah supposed—which meant they weren't even allowed to turn on the vid unless one of their minders was in the room with them. There was little to do besides eat, worry and play with the cats. Susan and Anthony's nondigital library, such as it was, consisted mainly of cookbooks, military histories and women's self-help books with wince-inducing titles like *How to Feed Your Inner She-Wolf.* Hannah suspected that all of it—the books, the dubious taste in clothing, the cutesy decor—was an elaborate camouflage. She imagined them leading a totally different life somewhere else: in a sleek condominium, perhaps, where they drank French wine and discussed politics over elegant dinners.

Except at night, Hannah and Kayla were allowed to wander the house freely, but every few days, and always in the early evening when Susan and Anthony were home and Simone was there, the women were locked in their rooms for an hour or two without explanation. After the second time, Hannah saw five used coffee cups on the dining room table. She figured the visitors were other Novembrists, coming to report to and scheme with Susan and Anthony, and she wondered how many members of the group there were and what they did in their other lives. It was disconcerting to think that she might have met one of them, shaken hands at church or made small talk in line at the grocery store, and never known it.

Fortunately, Paul was their daytime minder much more often than Simone. His kindness was a reassuring counterweight to the nerve-wracking state of limbo in which they found themselves; that, and his cooking, which was very good. He prepared sumptuous lunches to distract them and put flesh on their scarecrow figures: chicken parmesan, asparagus risotto, spinach soufflé. Hannah had never had such food in her life—her mother was a conventional cook, and she herself had never been interested enough to learn beyond the basics—and the flavors astonished her, often making her moan out loud. But when Paul served the food, his eyes rested on Kayla, and when she ate with gusto, they lit with pride and pleasure.

She began to bloom under his attention. Her despondency over TJ lifted a little, and her wit and irreverence reasserted themselves. She tried to banter with him, but more often than not, her flirtatious remarks left him tongue-tied. Hannah observed them, trying to suppress her envy. How wonderful it must feel, to be wanted by a man—a decent, attractive, unchromed man—in spite of your red skin. Paul seemed impervious to the fact that Kayla was a Chrome. When he looked at her, it was plain that what he saw was a desirable woman.

Hannah's thoughts returned constantly to her family and Aidan, her mind circling around them like a June bug on a fishing line. Aidan was the most insistent presence of them all. There was no escaping him, even in sleep. He was waiting behind her eyelids, erupting jubilant from the lake, rocking Pearl in his arms, unbuttoning Hannah's dress, his mouth following the path of his fingers. Once, after a particularly erotic dream, she touched herself, pretending it was him, but the pleasure turned bitter afterward, when she opened her eyes and saw the vacant space beside her. She speculated fifty times a day about where he was, what he was doing, whether he thought of her, and then castigated herself for her weakness. She had to let him go. So she told herself, fifty times a day, but it was like letting go of her own lungs, her own beating heart, and she wasn't yet ready for that death.

And then one afternoon, she was sitting with Kayla and Paul in front of the vid searching for something to watch, when suddenly, as though she'd conjured him, there was Aidan.

"Stop search," she said. He was on a stage in a large arena, preaching to a group of teenagers. It was a live show. The camera panned over the crowd, lingering on the rapt, adoring faces of the young women.

"I'm really not in the mood for a sermon tonight," Kayla said crossly. "Continue search."

"Go back," Hannah said. The camera zoomed in on Aidan.

"What is *up* with you?"

"Shh, I want to see this."

"Fine, watch what you want," Kayla snapped. She got up and flounced from the room. Paul swore and went after her.

Hannah stared at Aidan. The last time she'd seen him, on the vid of his swearing-in ceremony in September, he'd looked sad and drained. Now, just three months later, his face was shiny and pink with vitality. His eyes were lit with passion, his movements across the stage powerful and exuberant. And his words! He was afire with the spirit of God. She could see it passing like an electric current from his lips to the ears of his mesmerized listeners, many of whom stood with their arms stretched up to the ceiling, eyes closed, swaying back and forth to the cadence of his voice. Hannah watched, hurt warring with furious incredulity. Here she was, a Chrome, a fugitive, targeted by the Fist, running for her life. And he looked . . . happy.

Her spirit puddled within her, a leaden thing, shapeless and abject. How remote he must be from her, and from the love they'd shared, to look like that. Had it ever been real, or had it just been a vivid dream? She didn't want to believe it, but the evidence before her eyes was damning, irrefutable.

He had let her go.

She had been dead for some time now and not even known it.

FOUR

THE WILDERNESS

HANNAH DID LITTLE BUT SLEEP in the days that followed. The alternative—to stay awake brooding about Aidan, missing her family, worrying about Kayla's looming renewal date and watching the growing attraction between her and Paul—was intolerable. There was nothing to break the monotony of the days, nothing to keep the darkness at bay. Even Christmas failed to lift her spirits, despite the efforts of their minders to make it festive. Susan and Anthony played carols on the vid and gave Hannah and Kayla gifts of warm jackets, gloves and sturdy boots. Simone was absent, but Paul arrived on Christmas morning with bags of groceries and spent the day cooking, with Kayla as his sous chef. Hannah sat listlessly in front of the vid, a prisoner to the memories summoned by the happy sounds and smells emanating from the kitchen. At home, she would have been peeling potatoes while her mother kneaded dough and Becca basted the turkey. Her father would have poked his head in every so often, hoping to steal morsels of food, and her mother would have pretended to be vexed and shooed him theatrically from the kitchen. Aunt Jo would have brought her famous buttermilk pie, and Hannah's cousins would have come bearing homemade pralines, ginger bread and casserole dishes of macaroni and cheese and sweet potatoes studded with marshmallows. The women would have chatted in the kitchen while the men watched football and talked politics in the living room. When dinner was served, they'd have all joined hands while her father led them in prayer.

No prayers were said in Susan and Anthony's household, not that day or any other. Anthony opened a bottle of red wine and poured it round. He raised his glass and said, "Merry Christmas, everyone." Hannah took a cautious sip. She'd only drunk alcohol once before, some pink box wine her boyfriend Seth had procured the night of their high school graduation. If his plan had been to get her tipsy enough to have sex with him, it had backfired; she got sick after two cups of the stuff, and he spent the next hour holding her hair while she retched.

This wine, though, was altogether different. It was lush on her tongue and tasted of cherries, vanilla and, faintly, leather. She downed the first glass more quickly than she'd intended and began to feel a pleasant, floating detachment from herself and the others. The sensation of being unmoored, of drifting outside the present moment and watching it grow vague and unimportant, like something seen in the rearview mirror of a slowly moving car, intensified as she drank the second glass. When she reached for the bottle to pour herself a third, Susan moved it out of her reach.

"Oh, let her have it," Anthony said. "It's Christmas, and she's far from home among strangers. If she wants a little oblivion, who can blame her?"

Hannah stumbled to bed that night and was locked in alone as usual. But when she woke the next morning, her mouth thick with fur and waves of pain pulsing through her head, Emmeline's warm weight was lying across her abdomen and chest, and the cat's paws were kneading her in rhythm with its purring. A kindness, a gift—Hannah couldn't be certain from whom, but she had a strong hunch it had been Anthony. She lay there for a long while, stroking the cat's sleek body, grateful for the brief reprieve from loneliness.

Her bladder and her aching head forced her from the bed eventually. Her face in the mirror looked puffy, especially around the eyes, and she had a deep crease in her left cheek from a wrinkle in the pillow case. A month ago, she reflected, she wouldn't have noticed these details; she would have seen nothing but red and quickly looked away. She realized she was beginning to get used to it. Soon, her scarlet skin would be as unremarkable to her as the mole on her neck or the tiny scar, legacy of a tumble from her bicycle, beneath her lower lip. And say she made it to Canada and the chroming was reversed. Would she ever be able to look at her face and *not* see red?

She felt marginally better after brushing her teeth and showering. When she came out of the bathroom Emmeline was prowling by the door to the hallway, probably wanting breakfast. Hannah gave the knob a perfunctory twist, expecting to find the door locked, but it opened under her hand. The cat darted out into the hall, and Hannah followed more slowly. As she neared the end of the hallway she heard raised voices, coming from the dining room. She crept as close as she dared to listen.

"It's either got to be George, or Betty and Gloria," said Susan.

"Stanton suspects George," said Simone.

"Well, I'd put my money on the ladies," said Paul. "The disappearances didn't start until after we made Erie a way station."

"Coincidence," said Simone emphatically. "It is impossible that Betty and Gloria would do this thing. They are lesbians, feminists."

"So?"

"So, they betray their sisters? They help these Bible-frapping *salauds* to subjugate other women? Never."

Paul made an impatient sound. "Here's a news flash for you, Simone: women are human, just like men, and so are lesbians. You're just as capable of treachery. When you shit, your *merde* stinks just as bad as anyone else's."

Hannah's eyes widened. *You're* just as capable, he'd said. Was Simone a homosexual, then? Hannah only knew one person who was gay, a sweet, fluttering young man who worked at the drugstore near her house. She'd always felt sorry for him, an attitude her father had fostered in her and Becca when their mother was out of earshot. John Payne didn't share the view of his wife and many evangelicals that gays were minions of Satan. Instead, he looked on them as misguided, damaged souls deserving of prayer and pity. Hannah pictured Simone: her fierce gaze, the proud, unyielding set of her mouth. There was certainly nothing pitiable about her. And Hannah seriously doubted she'd appreciate being prayed for.

"We may not even have a traitor," Anthony said. "The road is dangerous. Anything could have happened to those women."

"Three in seven months?" Simone said. "And only the young and pretty ones? I think it smells."

"Me too," Susan said.

"Ben," Simone said. "There is only one way to discover the truth. We use the girl as bait. We take her to Columbus, and when she leaves, we follow and see what happens."

"Wait a minute," Paul interjected. "You said 'the girl.' What about Kayla?" There was a fraught silence. "No," he said, raising his voice. "We offered her the road, and she accepted. We're bound to help her."

"We have lost too much time," said Simone. "She is now a liability we cannot afford."

"You know the code as well as any of us, Paul." Susan's tone was regretful but firm. "No one life is more important than the mission."

"And no life will be sacrificed except as a last resort," Paul said, "and we're not at that point yet."

Hannah felt the hairs on her arms rise. She'd suspected Simone of being ruthless enough to kill, but to hear Paul speak so matter-of-factly of "sacrifice" was chilling.

"That is your opinion," said Simone.

"That is fact. Kayla hasn't done anything to endanger us."

"Yet."

"Paul, surely even you can see the folly in this," said Anthony. "The girl's due in a week, for Christ's sake."

"Ten days. And what do you mean, even me?"

"He means your heart is too soft," Simone said. She spoke like an older sister, exasperated but not unkind. "You attach yourself too easily."

"It's personal, remember? That's the whole point of what we do. I'd think you of all people would understand that."

"Paul!" Susan exclaimed, at the same time Simone said, "What are you talking about?"

He didn't answer.

"Explain yourself," Simone said.

"I know what happened to you," he said. "I've known for a long time."

"You know shit," Simone snapped.

"I know you're willing to die to keep other women from having to go through that."

Meaning an abortion? It had to be; what else could Paul be referring to? And besides, it explained so much. Having something so profoundly personal in common with Simone gave Hannah a queer, unsettled feeling. Except in her case, all she'd had to "go through" was the abortion itself. Nothing had gone wrong, not until afterward. Had the doctor botched Simone's procedure or hurt her in some other way? Had she served time for it? Though abortion was legal again in Canada, it had been a felony offense during the scourge and for several years afterward.

"Yes, I am," Simone said. "But I am not disposed to risk my life and yours for some girl who killed one of her own family."

"Well, I am."

"You think she cares about you, eh?" Simone made a scoffing sound. "She is using you. And if you were not thinking with your other head, you would see it."

"What I see," Paul said, "is a young woman in trouble. Someone we looked in the eye and promised we would help."

"I'm sorry, Paul," Susan said. "I have to agree with Simone. We can't risk her going into fragmentation on the road."

That's it then. Hannah leaned into the wall, mind whirling. She and Kayla would have to escape somehow. Steal a car, leave Dallas. Outrun the Novembrists, the police, the Fist. And if they managed to do all that, what then? Where would they go? Who would take them in?

"On the other hand," Anthony said speculatively, "the girl's young and pretty."

"So?" said Simone.

"Double bait for the hook."

"He has a point," Paul said quickly.

A silence fell, and Hannah knew they were all waiting for Susan to decide.

"Simone?" Susan said finally.

"All right," Simone said. "But if she starts to frag out, or if she compromises the mission . . ."

"You follow the code," Susan said. "Agreed, Paul?"

"Agreed."

Hannah shivered. If he was dissembling, she couldn't detect it.

She was about to steal back to her room when she heard a faint meow coming from the dining room. She froze. She'd forgotten about Emmeline, who was supposed to be locked in with her. If they realized she'd been listening in . . . She ran back to her door and closed it loudly, then strolled to the dining room, praying none of them had noticed the cat's presence until just now.

"Good morning," she said, striving for nonchalance.

They were all startled by her appearance, all except for Anthony, who studied Hannah with a narrowed gaze. "I put Emmeline in her room last night," he said to the others. "I must have forgotten to lock the door."

Four pairs of eyes skewered her, looking for telltale signs that she'd overheard them. With a rueful smile, she raised her hand to her forehead. "I think I had a little too much holiday cheer last night. Have you got some aspirin?"

For long seconds, no one moved. Then Paul said, "I'll get it," and Hannah felt the tension drain from the room. She sat down, wobbly with relief.

"Fetch Kayla while you're at it," Susan said. She turned to Hannah. "You'll be leaving tomorrow."

TWENTY-FOUR HOURS LATER, she and Kayla were back in the van, hooded, on their way to Columbus, Wherever. The only one Hannah was familiar with was in Ohio, but there was probably one in every state.

She had a sense of dislocation, an untethered feeling that grew as the minutes and the miles passed. Here she was again, hurtling forward in the darkness, destination unknown. It seemed an apt metaphor for what her life had become. She pressed her back into the wall of the van, feeling suddenly giddy with loss, attached to nothing and no one. Everything she had was dropping away from her, everything. And then Kayla moved and accidentally kicked Hannah's foot, and she corrected herself. She had a true friend, if nothing else. It was enough, for now, to sustain her and give her life some meaning.

Her life, which was somehow continuing despite the loss of Aidan. She was inexorably in motion, on her way to a fate that would not include him, and though she missed him still, she was conscious that something had shifted inside her since she'd seen him on the vid. Through some unknown agency, the roar of his loss had diminished to a loud rumble, and the waves had spent much of their fury. The hole he'd left inside her was beginning to knit itself closed, and if she squinted, she could see that one day far in the distance, all that would remain of it would be a ragged seam, sensitive to the touch perhaps, but no longer tender.

She and Kayla were walking into grave danger, Hannah had no illusions about that. But still, she felt more hopeful and less afraid than she had two and a half weeks ago, when she'd decided to accept Susan's offer. Part of that was knowing they wouldn't be actively hunted by the police. She fiddled with the ring Susan had given her that morning, tracing the smooth bulge of the stone with her finger—a fake opal concealing a tiny jammer that blocked the nanotransmitters. Kayla had one too, a moonstone.

"What if we get caught with them?" Hannah had asked.

"Say you got them in Chromewood," Susan said. "Black-market jammers aren't hard to come by."

That was news to Hannah. Why, if jammers were so common-place, had she never seen anything about them on the net or the news vids? She could think of only one reason: the government didn't want to advertise the fact that such evasion was possible. If people knew that Chromes were going about unmonitored . . .

"But the good ones don't come cheap," Kayla said, surprising Hannah again. How would she know that? "Where would we get that kind of lana?"

Susan looked her up and down in sly appraisal. "The time-honored way. Say you bartered for them."

Hannah bristled when she took Susan's meaning, but Kayla

merely laughed. "Yeah, I guess if you ain't got money, there's always honey."

When it was time to leave, Susan and Anthony walked them out to the van. Hannah smiled when she saw for the first time the logo painted onto the side of it: NEW LIFE CHURCH. "Is there really such a place?" she asked.

Susan smiled back at her. "You're standing in it."

Hannah had expected to part with handshakes, but the couple hugged both her and Kayla warmly. The feel of Susan's ample, motherly bosom pressing against her brought an unexpected lump to Hannah's throat. She wasn't exactly fond of these people, but they'd sheltered her, risked their lives to help her, shown her a sort of tough kindness. And they were a known quantity, whereas the road, and the people they would encounter along it, were a looming question mark.

"Thank you for this chance," Hannah said. "If you hadn't sent Simone and Paul for us that night—"

"It's personal," Susan replied. "And you earned it. Good luck to you."

Her words came back to Hannah now, as she sat on the cold metal floor of the van. Had she earned it? By not having betrayed Raphael, had she made herself worthy of the gift of a new life, a clean slate? Did she not deserve punishment for what she had done, if not melachroming, then some other sort? The Novembrists would say no, that she'd committed no crime. Simone had tried to convince her of it one day, insisting that a fetus wasn't a life, merely a bundle of cells that had the *potential* for life. Hannah could tell that the other woman truly believed what she was saying, that she wasn't just being kind and trying to make her feel better (though she sensed, with some surprise, that kindness was part of it). Hannah didn't buy it, though. Her own bones told her a different story.

And yet. She *had* paid, and dearly, for the abortion. She'd lost her family, her love, her dignity. She'd truly repented her crime. Was that not enough? The Bible said yes, that God was merciful, that repentance earned His complete forgiveness and His Son's blood cleansed all sins. But if there was no God, or if He was indifferent, where did that leave her? The world was an unforgiving place; she'd seen enough of it to know. A thought bloomed in her mind. She rejected it, but it stole back: *I have to forgive myself.*

The van picked up speed, and Simone told them they could remove their hoods. Hannah did so gratefully, feeling claustrophobic. The sight of the two large wooden crates with which she and Kayla were sharing the cargo area didn't help matters. On them, in big, bold type, was stamped: FOOD DONATIONS. CANNED AND PACKAGED FOOD ONLY. NO PERISHABLES. With two 120-pound exceptions. She and Kayla would have to hide inside them every time they crossed a state line or "frontier," as Simone called them. Clearly, the crates wouldn't withstand a thorough search by the border police, but Paul and Simone didn't seem too concerned. The church logo had an immunizing effect, Paul had explained, and all the police had ever done was take a cursory look inside the van.

Through the windshield Hannah saw a road sign fly past: SHREVEPORT, 170 MILES. She registered belatedly that they were traveling east on I-20, the same route she'd once taken with Aidan on that goldenlit day in October, in that other skin, that other life. How safe she'd felt then, despite the risks they were taking, how happy and carefree—all of it, an illusion.

Kayla drifted off, slumping awkwardly against the wall of the van, and Hannah took her friend by the shoulders and settled her head in her lap. Automatically she began stroking Kayla's hair, just as she and Becca had often done for each other, usually when one of them was upset but sometimes just for the simple pleasure it gave them both. She felt a spasm of longing for her sister, commingled with helplessness. She'd told Cole she'd be watching over Becca, but that had been an all-but-empty promise even then. Now, Hannah was bitterly aware, it was an utter impossibility. Becca's fate and her own hadn't just branched, they'd been severed, irrevocably unjoined; Becca just didn't know it yet. Hannah felt momentarily jealous of her sister's ignorance, but then the feeling vanished. If bitter certainty was terrible, how much worse must it be to be the one who went on hoping and wondering, despairing a little more each day that passed with no word?

Hannah's leg was growing numb from the weight of Kayla's head, but she didn't shift her position. She might not be able to keep Becca safe, but she was determined to do everything in her power to protect Kayla. And so, Hannah reckoned, was Paul, who kept glancing back at them with wistful eyes. She wondered whether they'd made love. Kayla hadn't confided in her, but then the two women had had almost no time alone together since they'd arrived at the safe house. Kayla and Paul certainly could have stolen some private hours during the day, when Susan and Anthony were out and Hannah was sleeping. Imagining them together gave her a pang. To be kissed and enfolded in a man's arms, to feel the warm press of his weight against her and hear his voice murmuring endearments in her ear—would she ever know that again? Looking down at Kayla's sleeping face, Hannah hoped she had known it with Paul. After all she'd lost, and all she was faced with, she deserved some sweetness in her life. On the heels of that thought came another: *And if she does, then just maybe, so do I.*

They'd been traveling for several hours when Simone pulled off the highway and stopped at a juice station. The change in motion woke Kayla. "Where are we?" she asked, sitting up and rubbing the sleep from her eyes.

"Almost to the Louisiana border," Paul said.

"I need to use the restroom," Hannah said.

"Me too," Kayla said. "And I'm getting hungry."

Paul tapped on a cooler sitting on the floor between the two seats. "There are sandwiches and chips in here. Help yourselves."

Kayla reached for the lid, but Simone stopped her with a curt, "Not now. We will eat after we cross the frontier." She told Paul to charge the van while she went to get coffee and the restroom key.

"God, she's a piece of work!" Kayla said, the instant Simone and Paul closed the doors behind them. "I'd bet money she practices that sourpuss expression in the mirror, except it would crack if she did. She—"

Hannah cut her off, aware that they didn't have much time. "We need to talk. You're not having any symptoms, are you?"

"No. But I'm not due for nine days yet. And hopefully there'll be a grace period. If there isn't . . ."

"Listen to me, if you start to feel anything, anything at all, you tell me right away. And don't let on to the others."

"Why not?"

"I heard them talking about it yesterday with Susan and Anthony. They think you're a liability. Simone has orders to kill you if you go into fragmentation."

Kayla's eyes widened. "And what did Vincent say?"

"Who's Vincent?"

Kayla's hand flew to her mouth.

"That's Paul's real name?"

"Yeah. They all take the names of famous feminists. Susan B. Anthony. Simone de Beauvoir. Alice Paul."

With the exception of Susan B. Anthony, the names were unfamiliar, and even she was just a face on an old coin in Hannah's father's collection. Something tugged at her memory. "Rafael," she murmured, making the connection. Not Raphael, the archangel of healing, but Rafael Patiño, the governor of Florida, assassinated soon after he'd vetoed the Sanctity of Life laws passed by the state legislature. Hannah had been twelve. Her parents had had one of their rare arguments that night, when her mother adamantly refused to pray with her father for the governor's soul. Becca, the peacemaker as always, went to soothe her, while Hannah knelt with her father on the living room floor and prayed. Afterward he put his hand on the crown of her head and told her she was his good girl. She could feel it now, a phantom of that warm, approving weight, and it twisted her heart into a tight, dry strand.

"Hannah!" Kayla gave her arm an impatient shake. "What did Vincent say?"

"He argued with them. But in the end, he agreed that you couldn't be allowed to jeopardize the mission."

"Then he was playing them," Kayla said. "He'd never let Simone hurt me."

"I don't know, Kayla. I couldn't see his face, but he sounded like he meant it."

"And I'm telling you, he didn't. He couldn't have."

Kayla's certainty, and the undisguised tenderness that infused it, irritated Hannah. "Just because you're sleeping with him doesn't mean you can trust him," she said.

"I do trust him, completely. I know him, Hannah."

"Like you knew TJ?"

Though the comment must have wounded her, Kayla didn't show it. She just looked at Hannah steadily, with a quiet dignity that filled her with chagrin. *Who's the caustic bitch now?*

"I'm sorry," Hannah said. "I guess I'm jealous. Not because you have Paul—Vincent—but because you have *someone*. Because you're not alone with this." She gestured at her face. "I know it's small of me."

Kayla gave Hannah's leg a forgiving squeeze. "Love's a bitch, isn't it? It spoils you for being on your own."

"Yeah." And for being with anyone else, Hannah reflected. Even after all that had happened, she still couldn't imagine ever loving another man. She wondered, not for the first time, whether loving her had spoiled Aidan for being with Alyssa. Hannah had never asked him about their relationship, whether they were intimate. She'd hoped not. But now that she was out of the picture, he would almost certainly go back to his wife's bed, if he hadn't already. If he'd ever left it in the first place.

Hannah saw Simone leave the mart and stride toward the restroom. They had a few minutes at most.

"Listen," she said, "there's something else I have to tell you. Some of the other women they've sent this way have disappeared. They plan to use us as bait to try and catch whoever's behind it. Simone suspects someone named George, but Paul thinks it's two women named Betty and Gloria."

Kayla's face was troubled but unsurprised. "I know. I was going to tell you. Vincent told me last night. He said to be on our guard, but not to worry, he'll be watching over us." She paused and looked at him out the window. Softly, she said, "He talked about coming to Canada and finding me there. I think he's in love with me."

"Do you love him?"

Kayla sighed. "I don't know. I love the way he looks at me. I love how he touches me, like I'm . . ." She trailed off, searching for the right word.

"Like you're something fine. Something incredibly precious."

Hannah's eyes burned, and she squeezed them shut. She would not cry.

"You still love him, the guy who got you pregnant."

"Yes." *Even if he no longer loves me.* "But it's all jumbled up with anger and hurt. It's not clean anymore."

Kayla let out a short laugh. "Is it ever?"

"I thought it was, in the beginning, but who was I kidding? He was married. Still is."

"That how come you never say his name?"

Hannah didn't answer at first. She hadn't said it aloud in six months and had never spoken it to anyone but him. "Reverend Dale," she'd said, but not his first name, the one she cherished. The one that was forbidden. She'd held it behind her teeth like a coiled snake for two years. Long enough, she decided.

"His name is Aidan. Aidan Dale."

"Whoa! As in Secretary of Faith Aidan Dale? The Right Reverend Holier-Than-Thou?"

"He's not, actually. He's one of the humblest people I've ever known."

"Holy crap! Aidan Dale. He must've been scared shitless you'd talk."

"No. I think he wanted me to name him as the father. He practically begged me to at my sentencing." Hannah heard a *thunk* and looked outside. Paul/Vincent was unhooking the charge cable, and Simone was headed their way.

"Look, I know you think you can trust Paul, and I hope you're right. But promise me you'll talk to me first if you start to feel anything funny." Kayla gave her a halfhearted nod, and Hannah gripped her friend's arm hard. "Promise. And stop calling him Vincent, don't even think of him as Vincent. If that slipped out in front of Simone there's no telling what she'd do."

"*Okay,* Sergeant Payne, I promise." Kayla smiled, and Hannah felt a rush of love and gratitude for her. And to think, if it hadn't been for the horrible Henleys, they wouldn't have found each other.

Paul drove them around to the side of the station where the restroom was. Kayla went first, then Hannah. The room was filthy and rank with the smell of urine. The walls were covered in graffiti: EMILIA ES UNA PUTA; FUCK ALLAH AND THE CAMEL HE RODE IN ON; STOP THE BLOODSHED, KILL MORALES!!! The drawings were even more disturbing: a Blue being lynched, his eyes bulging and his tongue hanging out, above hangman-style letters reading B L U E C O L L A R; a robed Chinese man with a Manchu-style queue holding his penis, peeing on an image of the earth. Six months ago, Hannah would have felt a mix of revulsion and shock that anyone was capable of such ugliness and rage. Not that she'd been oblivious to the violence that existed in the world; she was a city girl, albeit a sheltered one, and her father's near-death in the terrorist attack had disabused her of any notion that she and those she loved were invulnerable. But she'd thought of that as a freak occurrence, something from another, distant reality that had intruded on her own. Now, looking at the sordid scrawls, the revulsion was still there, but the shock was absent. In the world she inhabited now, hatred and violence were commonplace, and she was uncomfortably aware, not just that it seethed in the hearts of people all around her, but of her own capacity for it.

When she returned to the van, Simone was in the passenger seat, and the crates were open in the front. Kayla was already inside hers, sitting with her knees pressed to her chest. Hannah's nervousness must have shown on her face, because Paul said, "The opening is hinged, see? And the crate locks from the inside, not the outside.

To let yourself out, you just flip this latch." He demonstrated. She glanced at Simone. The other woman gave her a hard, assessing look. Hannah took a last breath of fresh air and crawled inside. Paul swung the door closed, and she fumbled for the latch and locked it. Soon afterward, she felt the van moving.

"You okay in there?" Paul asked.

"I'm feeling mighty perishable," Kayla said, "but other than that I'm dandy."

Hannah smiled. "Me too," she said, discovering it was true. The pitch-blackness helped; she couldn't see how confined she was. But the crate also had a pleasant, sawn-wood smell that reminded her of her father's shop in the garage. Carpentry was his hobby, and Hannah had always loved to watch him work. One of her favorite possessions was a dollhouse he'd made for her when she was five. Becca had gotten one too, and every year for their birthdays and Christmas he'd given them one or two pieces of miniature furniture, meticulously crafted to look like the real thing. The tiny dining room chairs were stuffed and upholstered in red velvet, the tiny dresser drawers could be opened and closed, the toilet lid raised and lowered. As she got older Hannah had started to make her own decorations, needlepointing miniature rugs and sewing little curtains and bedspreads. Even after she outgrew the dollhouse, she never packed it away. It held pride of place in her bookshelf, a vivid reminder of her father's love for her.

Another cherished thing that she had lost.

Paul called out a warning as they approached the checkpoint. They slowed, and Hannah held her breath. She could almost feel the eyes of the police scouring the van, deciding whether or not to stop them. Her lungs were beginning to burn when she felt the van accelerating, and Simone said, "We're through. You can get out now." Hannah's breath escaped in a loud whoosh.

Simone passed out the food. Hannah's appetite, which had been nonexistent since she'd seen Aidan on the vid, had returned, and she wolfed down the sandwich. Wordlessly, Simone handed her the other half of her own. As Hannah ate it, she studied the other woman, thinking what a puzzle she was: harsh and ruthless one minute, kind and generous the next.

"Where are we headed?" Kayla ventured to ask, around a mouthful of tortilla chips.

"Eastern Mississippi, close to the Alabama border," Paul replied. "A little town called Columbus."

"Good thing we're going in December," Kayla said.

"Why's that?" Hannah asked.

"Because most of the year it's hotter than a red-assed bee. I visited there when I was applying to colleges. I don't know how anybody can stand to live there. I like to melted during the campus tour."

"Well, Dallas isn't exactly the North Pole."

"No, but we don't have humidity like they do. It's like being in Satan's favorite sauna. I never sweated so much in my whole life."

Paul chuckled, and Simone said, with undisguised impatience, "If the three of you are finished with your chitchat, I am trying to think."

A bruised silence descended on the van. *Some people just can't stand to see other people happy,* Hannah thought. And then she recalled, with a twinge of guilt, her own sour reaction to Kayla's happiness about Paul. *Please, God, don't let me become like that.* The plea was reflexive, and its futility struck Hannah the instant after it was dispatched. God, if He existed, didn't answer the prayers of the faithless or the damned.

• • •

HANNAH HAD NEVER been to Louisiana—in fact, she'd never been anywhere outside her home state—but to her eye, it looked no different from East Texas. The same monotonous green line of pine trees sped past, punctuated every few miles by the falsely cheerful glow of the same dozen holosigns in endless repetition: MCDONALD'S, BKFC, FUJITJUICE, COMFORT INN, MOTEL 6. The effect was surreal, as though the van were traveling in circles, going nowhere.

They got back in the crates near the Mississippi border and passed through the checkpoint without incident. They reached Columbus four hours later, just as the sun was beginning to set. Hannah got to her knees and peered over Simone's shoulder out the windshield. The town's outskirts were a generic string of chain stores and restaurants, but once they were off the highway the tackiness gave way to historic charm. Downtown Main Street was lined with vintage two-story brick buildings, once home to small-town mainstays like the general and feed stores, now housing boutiques and restaurants. An old art deco movie theater advertised a 2-D-era double feature: *The Ten Commandments* and *Ben-Hur*. Hannah tried to remember the last movie she'd seen in an actual theater; something animated, when she was very young.

Simone made a couple of turns onto a tree-lined street, taking them past the imposing redbrick buildings of Mississippi University for Women. The campus was surrounded by lovely old houses with lush green lawns and large flower beds filled mostly with winter stubble, though there were some shrubs in bloom. Hannah was startled to see coiled garden hoses mounted on the side of several homes.

"Don't they have rationing here?" she asked.

"No," Kayla said. "Mississippi's like Georgia, they get plenty of rain. In fact, they get so much they sell their excess to other states."

"Imagine, having so much water you can use it on your *yard*," Hannah said.

"Imagine, selling water to your own countrymen." Simone's tone was contemptuous. "How typically American."

"I suppose you do it differently in Canada?"

"But of course. We are socialists. Even in Québec, where we have much rain, we ration to aid our sister provinces who have little."

The absurdity of it all bubbled up inside of Hannah, erupting in a helpless snort of laughter. Here she was, being rescued by a socialist, feminist, lesbian, baby-killing, foreign terrorist. What would the ladies in the sewing circle say to that?

Simone was glowering at her in the rearview mirror. "You find something funny?"

"You wouldn't understand."

"Put your hoods on."

Hannah and Kayla obeyed. The van made half a dozen more turns and then stopped.

"Speaker on. Call Stanton," Simone said.

A deep, rumbling voice answered on the third ring. "That you, sweet Seemoan?"

Hannah's brows lifted. *Sweet* Simone?

"Yes. Are we green?"

"Green as a drunk on a roller coaster. What's your ETA?" Stanton spoke in a drawl that sounded ever so slightly exaggerated, the vowels thick and round, like he'd just eaten a spoonful of pudding.

"We will arrive to you in five minutes."

"Give me fifteen." He hung up.

"You should leave now," Simone said, and Hannah realized

she was speaking to Paul. Kayla drew in a sharp breath, echoing Hannah's own dismay.

"Yeah, I'd better."

"Thank you, Paul. For everything," Hannah said, extending her hand.

He took it and squeezed it hard. "Good luck. Take care of each other," he said. *Take care of Kayla,* Hannah heard.

"We won't forget what you've done for us," Kayla said. Her voice was strained.

Hannah pictured their goodbye: Kayla's red hand groping for Paul's white one, their bodies fighting the leap of their hearts, trying, in the space of a few seconds, to communicate through their joined hands what they'd meant to each other, in case they never saw each other again. A cruel farewell, but better than what Hannah had had with Aidan, which was none at all.

"Godspeed," Paul said.

The van door opened and closed, and presently Hannah heard another car start up and drive away. *Godspeed to you too, Vincent,* she thought. Trying, and failing, to imagine a God who would bless a mission such as theirs.

The three women waited in silence. It grew hot and close under the hood, and Hannah's lungs ached for fresh air. How had she come to this point, this nadir so absolute that even air, that most basic of things, had become a luxury? Forget chocolate, silk, love—right now, she would have sold her soul for a single clean, unprocessed breath.

"*Ben,* we go now to meet Stanton," Simone announced finally. "He will take you on the next leg of your journey. You will do exactly as he tells you." She started the van, but they didn't move. "Listen to me. You think you have seen the worst from the world because you are Chromes. You think this has made you more tough, more sage. And maybe it has, a little. But you are still all two of you like infants. You give your trust too easily." Her tone held none of its usual derision. What Hannah heard instead was something that sounded remarkably like empathy. "The road will become much more dangerous after you leave Stanton's. You must trust no one but yourselves. No one."

The van accelerated then. They drove a short distance, no more than a couple of miles, and stopped. "Wait here," Simone said. She got out. Hannah heard another door open. She risked lifting her hood up and found Kayla already peering out the windshield. It was too dark to see much, but Hannah could make out Simone's tall, thin form hugging—hugging!—a considerably shorter figure that must be Stanton. Behind them, she saw the faint silhouette of a high bridge and the glint of water below it.

"I recognize this place," Kayla said. "We're down by the river. What did you think of that little speech of Simone's?"

"I think she's been where we are, or someplace a whole lot like it."

"What makes you say that?"

Hannah hesitated, feeling reluctant to divulge what she'd gleaned about Simone's past. She pictured the guard's face at the library, before and after she'd scanned Hannah's NIC and known she'd had an abortion. *It's personal.* Suddenly, the phrase took on a new meaning. Simone's secrets hadn't been freely given. Even knowing them was a trespass, but sharing them would be a violation.

"Just a feeling I have," Hannah said. "Anyway, I think she's right, we shouldn't trust anyone. Including her." Simone and Stanton were approaching the rear of the van. "Here they come." The women hastily drew their hoods over their faces. The back doors were opened, letting in a waft of cool air.

"Come," Simone said, grasping Hannah's arm and helping her past the crates and out of the van. When she tried to stand, her legs buckled, cramped from all the hours of sitting.

"Whoa there," said Stanton. A hand took hold of her other arm, supporting her. "I'll take her from here, Seemoan. You get the other one."

Simone let go, and Stanton led Hannah carefully forward. "Steady now, I've got you." He stopped. "Open trunk," he said, and Hannah heard it release. "I'm afraid that's where you ladies will need to go, but it'll only be for a short while, I promise."

Hannah stiffened as he tried to ease her forward. She felt the hard bumper of a car butt up against the front of her thighs and jerked back from it. "I'm not getting in there," she said, forcing the words out of her rapidly closing throat. This time, there would be no latch on the inside. She and Kayla would be trapped, helpless.

"You will, and you will do it now," Simone said. Her voice was like a whip against bare flesh. Hannah shook her head violently and felt a wave of dizziness. She felt like there were fingers around her throat, choking her. Her hand flew up to rip the hood off, and another hand, gentle but implacable, took it and forced it back to her side.

"She's hyperventilating," Stanton said.

"*Sacrament!* We do not have the time for this." The hood was pushed up above Hannah's nose, and she threw her head back, gulping in air.

"Hannah? Are you all right?" cried Kayla. Hannah heard her struggling to break free of Simone.

"Be still!" Simone hissed. "Each second we remain here puts us at a greater risk. You want the police to come? *Non?* Then you will shut your mouths and obey. I will not allow you to compromise this mission."

The grim words broke through Hannah's hysteria. She'd heard Simone say them before and knew the threat wasn't idle.

"I'm fine, Kayla," she said, but the quaver in her voice said otherwise. She swallowed, willed it steady. "Really, I'm okay now. We'd better do as they say."

"Good girl," said Stanton. He loosened his grip on her wrists, and she felt his hand in the small of her back, guiding her forward and helping her into the trunk. "It's less than ten minutes to the house. I know you're frightened, but just try to relax and think of something pleasant, and I'll have you out of there before you know it."

Hannah curled onto her side and felt Kayla crawl in next to her, wriggling in an effort to find a comfortable position in the confined space. "You can take your hoods off as soon as I've closed the trunk," said Stanton. "That should help a little."

"Goodbye," Simone said. "Good luck to you." She sounded as cold and remote as the stars. But then Hannah felt the soft touch of a hand on her leg. *"Courage,"* Simone murmured.

The hand withdrew, and the trunk lid closed with a *whomph*. Hannah pulled her hood off at once. Her eyes met utter blackness. She heard Kayla removing her own hood and drawing in rasping lungfuls of air. The sound of her breathing calmed Hannah. She could imagine how easy it would be, without the anchor of Kayla's presence beside her, to lose herself, to stop believing in her own existence.

As the car started to move, Kayla's hand fumbled for hers and gripped it tightly. She was trembling, but Hannah actually felt her own fear receding. Her helplessness at this moment was so absolute as to be a kind of release. There was nothing she could do or say that would change what was about to happen to her. The lid would open in ten minutes or ten hours or never. She would find safety on the other side of it, or peril. She would live, or she would die.

She lay in the blackness, stroking her friend's warm hand, waiting to be born.

A SHORT ETERNITY LATER, the trunk opened to reveal a round, white face beaming down at them. "Well, hello there. I'm Stanton. Welcome to Columbus."

He was in his early forties, Hannah judged, but his smile was that of an eight-year-old boy who'd just found a puppy under the Christmas tree.

"Let's get you out of there." With the courtly manner of a footman helping ladies from a carriage, he assisted them out of the trunk. "I assure you, the accommodations in the house are much more commodious," he said, tilting his head back to look at them. He was quite short, no more than five foot two. His deep voice sounded incongruous issuing from such a diminutive frame. "Hannah and Kayla, am I right, or do I have it backwards?"

Hannah wasn't fooled; the mind behind those shrewd eyes knew exactly who was who, and probably every other detail there was to know about them too. But she played along, saying, "Good guess. Pleased to meet you."

Stanton gave her a decorous nod of his head. He was small and round, with a small, round head, a neat mustache perched above a small, round, rosy mouth and a bird's small, round eyes covered by small, round, rose-tinted wire spectacles. He was elegantly dressed in black wool slacks and a black cashmere sweater, neither of which could disguise his small, round, protuberant belly. And yet, Hannah mused, watching him greet Kayla, he wasn't unattractive. He had a gracious, dapper air—the word "dapper" might have been invented to describe this man—that was very beguiling.

She pulled her gaze away from him and took in her surroundings.

They were in an old, slightly dilapidated wooden garage, but with none of the homey clutter of Susan and Anthony's. It was bare of everything except two cars: the nondescript sedan they'd ridden in and a vintage dark-green convertible shaped like a bullet. The sinuous beauty of its lines made her fingers itch to touch it.

"It's a '75 Jaguar XK-E," Stanton said. Languidly, as if he could scent her desire, he trailed a small, neatly manicured hand across the hood. "Still runs on gasoline. It costs the earth to drive it anywhere, but I couldn't bear to have it converted." He looked back at the two women, his black eyes shiny as beads. "I bet y'all are ready for a hot meal and a shower. Get your things and come with me." He gestured at the ground behind them, and Hannah saw the backpacks Anthony had given them that morning leaning against the rear wheel of the sedan. She slipped hers on, comforted by the feel of its weight against her back. Though there was nothing in it of any personal significance, the pack contained the few possessions that she could call hers. Such a small vessel, she reflected, to hold her entire life.

Stanton led them behind the Jaguar to an open trapdoor in the floor. A metal ladder led downward. "Ladies first," he said, waving them ahead. Kayla shot Hannah a *what-the-hell* look and climbed down into the hole. Hannah followed, and then Stanton. The trapdoor closed behind them with a heavy clank. For a moment, the sound filled her with the reflexive panic of a trapped creature, but it also reminded her of something, and finally, she identified what: the sound of the gate closing behind her the day she'd been released from the Chrome ward. She made herself remember that this too was a gateway, to freedom from the red prison that was her body.

They ended up in a narrow, well-lit tunnel lined with some sort of hard gray material. It gave off a dull sheen and was warm to the touch. Stanton jumped the last few feet, landing nimbly beside them. "Kinda makes you feel like you're in a James Bond vid, doesn't it?" He hummed a few bars of the theme song, and Hannah couldn't help but smile at the thought of this natty little bespectacled man as 007.

He led them down the tunnel for perhaps fifty feet and stopped at what appeared to be a dead end. "By valor and arms," he said, and a hidden door slid open. "That's the Mississippi motto." He waved the women through, adding, "This door only responds to my voice, just in case you were wondering."

They entered a windowless bedroom in what had to be the basement. "Voilà, the guest suite," Stanton said, with a sweep of his arm. "I hope you'll be comfortable here."

Hannah looked around and felt some of the tension go out of her. Though the room and what she could see of the adjoining bath were sparsely and simply furnished, it was a refined simplicity. The walls were painted a soft yellow that helped compensate for the absence of natural light. The matching twin beds were wrought-iron, their down comforters drawn back to reveal crisp white sheets. A large orchid arched over the nightstand between the two beds. The white blooms with their throbbing fuchsia centers were so perfectly formed they looked fake, but Hannah knew that if she touched them, they'd feel like skin beneath her fingers, soft and vibrant. The orchid reminded her of the one Aidan had given her, but that wasn't the only reason for the sudden stinging in her eyes, or even the main one; it was the simple fact of the flower's existence, here, in this room that this man had decorated with such care, believing them worthy of this grace, the perfection of this beautiful, living thing.

"I'll leave you ladies to freshen up," Stanton said. "I like to dress for dinner, and I hope you'll oblige me. There are some clean clothes in the closet you can change into." He pointed to a staircase at the other end of the room. "When you're ready, come on upstairs. Supper'll be on the table in about forty-five minutes. I hope you brought your appetites. I'm making my grandmother's crawfish étouffée, which has been known to make grown men fall to their knees and weep in ecstasy, convinced they've ascended to heaven." With a little half-bow, he left them.

The women washed up and got changed. There were a dozen or so outfits in the closet, all surprisingly stylish and feminine. Once again Hannah was moved by Stanton's thoughtfulness. Kayla chose a split-neck tunic of dark gray satin over black leggings, and Hannah a black lace dress with full, draping sleeves. The bodice was a little low, but she didn't care; it felt good to dress like a woman again. The bathroom mirror was brightly lit from above with a row of round bulbs like you'd see in a starlet's dressing room in an old vid. Hannah examined her reflection with a critical eye and found herself wishing for her pearl studs. A chuckle slipped out of her.

"Look at us," she said. "Red as a couple of fire trucks and still trying to gussy ourselves up."

"Well, and why shouldn't we?" Kayla was standing next to Hannah, braiding a section of her long black hair. "We didn't stop being female when they chromed us."

"No, but . . ." Hannah left the thought incomplete, not wanting to sour the moment.

"But what?"

Hannah shrugged. "It's not like anything we do is actually going to make us pretty." And yet, even as she said it, she was thinking how beautiful Kayla was, red skin or not. And if she could see beauty in Kayla, and Paul could, could someone not also see it in her?

"Speak for yourself," Kayla said, with an affronted look. "You go on and be a frump if you want, it'll just make me look better by comparison." She sucked in her cheeks and struck a model's pose, then burst out laughing. Hannah laughed with her, feeling a warm glow inside her.

They headed upstairs. The door at the top was made of the same metal as the tunnel. Hannah opened it and stepped into a large foyer. She was expecting a nice house, but this could only be called a mansion. The floors were of black-and-white-checked marble, polished to a high gloss, and the ceilings were easily twenty feet high. A chandelier hung above the entryway, its hundreds of tiny, faceted crystals as dazzling as diamonds, and stained-glass panels flanked the mahogany front door. A grand staircase carpeted in burgundy led to the second floor. Looking up, Hannah could see a second set of stairs winding to another story above that.

Kayla gave a low whistle. "Nice place. Wonder what our friend Stanton does for a living?"

Four rooms led off the hallway, and the women peeked inside them as they went past. The first was a large parlor, littered harmoniously with antiques and Oriental rugs. A regal woman in a Victorian riding costume regarded them from a painting above the mantel. There wasn't a single object in the room that wasn't exquisite, and yet somehow, the ambience was welcoming rather than intimidating. The plush sofa invited sitting, the logs stacked in the marble fireplace begged to be lit, the rugs urged Hannah to take off her shoes and curl up on them.

The room opposite was a library lined with floor-to-ceiling bookcases. Standing reading lamps cast intimate pools of light over two chocolate-brown leather chairs and a chaise longue upholstered in cream damask. Heavy velvet drapes covered the tall windows, and an enormous dictionary sat open on a carved wooden stand in one corner. Hannah lingered in the doorway, eyeing the shelves and their leather-bound contents longingly.

"If this were my house, I'd never leave this room," she said.

"You kidding? If this were my house, I'd sell it in a heartbeat and move to the French Riviera."

The door to the third room was closed, and the women moved past it with reluctant sidelong glances, but the door to the fourth was cracked a few inches in what could have passed for invitation. As Hannah hesitated, Kayla pushed it open. The hinges squealed, making them jump and look nervously toward the back of the house. When Stanton didn't come charging down the hallway, they peered inside. After the splendor of the parlor and the library, they were unprepared for the shabbiness that greeted their eyes. The room was clearly meant to be a dining room, but a scuffed side table and a couple of three-legged chairs were the only furniture. The plaster medallion in the ceiling was chipped and cracked, its hook empty, and the wallpaper hung down in forlorn strips over the wainscoting. The drapes were moth-eaten, the carpets threadbare and smelling unpleasantly of mildew. Hannah pulled the door closed hastily, feeling uncomfortable, as if she'd glimpsed the holes in Stanton's underwear.

They followed the enticing smell of seafood to an eat-in kitchen that looked like something out of a "Homes & Gardens" vid. Stanton was standing over the gleaming industrial range, stirring the contents of a copper pot with a wooden spoon.

He saw them and did a theatrical double take. "Ah," he said, placing his hand over his heart. "'She walks in beauty, like the night, of cloudless climes and starry skies, and all that's best of dark and bright, meet in her aspect and her eyes.' Ladies, you are a vision of loveliness manifested in my kitchen."

"You must be partial to red," Kayla said drily.

"Indeed, it's my favorite color." He held up a glass of red wine. "May I offer you some of this excellent claret?"

The women accepted. Hannah made herself sip it slowly. She didn't want to get drunk like she had on Christmas.

"I have to tell you," Kayla said, "you have one of the most beautiful homes I've ever seen."

"That's kind of you. It's getting there, little by little." Stanton's tone was light, but his eyes gleamed with possessive pride. "This house has been in my family since it was built in 1885. It was once a showplace, but like a lot of old homes and old families around here, it's fallen on hard times. I've got a long way to go to restore it to its former glory. I haven't even started on the upstairs yet, but I'm already dreading it—all that dust and racket and workers tromping in and out of the house." He took in their bemused expressions. "I gather you've never experienced the living hell known as home renovation? No? Well, I don't recommend it."

Hannah felt a prick of resentment. *Don't talk to me about living hell,* she thought, eyeing his flawless granite countertops and gleaming hardwood cabinetry.

But her irritation melted away once they sat down to eat. The food was as superb as everything else under Stanton's roof, and he was the consummate host. He carried the conversation, entertaining them with stories about Columbus and its distinguished inhabitants, who'd once included Tennessee Williams and Eudora Welty. All Hannah knew about them was that they were both long-dead writers, but they were evidently favorites of Kayla's, because her face lit up, and she plunged into an animated discussion about them with Stanton. Listening to their exchange, Hannah was suffused with bitterness about her own ignorance. If she hadn't had to sneak books into the house and read them in hasty, furtive snatches, if she'd gone to a normal high school and then on to college as Kayla had, she too would have been able to assert that Miss Welty could write circles around Faulkner and have an opinion as to whether *Streetcar* or *The Glass Menagerie* was Williams's masterpiece. She'd always believed that her parents had done right by her, but now, sitting mute at Stanton's table, she found herself seething over their choices. Why had they kept her life so small? Why had they never asked her what *she* wanted? At every possible turn, she saw, they'd chosen the path that would keep her weak and dependent. And the fact that they wouldn't see it that way, that they sincerely believed they'd acted in her best interest, didn't make it any less true, or them any less culpable.

"You're mighty quiet, Hannah," Stanton said. "What do you think?"

"I don't," she snapped. "I was raised not to."

She flushed, embarrassed by her churlishness, but Stanton didn't seem the least bit offended. An approving glint appeared in his eye, and he raised his wineglass to her in salute. "Well, my dear," he said, smiling his beatific child's smile, "welcome to the other side. Something tells me you're going to like it here."

Fleeting images of everyone and everything she'd loved passed swiftly through Hannah's mind and then receded, leaving a vast, white space that, except for Kayla, was completely empty. For a moment, the emptiness was yawning, overwhelming. What in the world would she fill it with? And then the answer dawned on her, and she caught her breath. If she was given the opportunity to furnish that space—if she survived the road and made it to Canada—she could fill it with whatever she wanted. For the first time in her life, there would be no limits to what she could do or who she could be, no one to tell her what she should and shouldn't think about.

She smiled back at Stanton. "Something tells me you're right."

HE CLEARED THE table, sternly refusing their offers
of assistance. "You're not allowed to touch the dishes until you've
eaten three meals at my table. House rules. Now, can I get you a
brandy or a coffee? Or I have chamomile tea if you'd prefer that."

Hannah shuddered, tasting crawfish étouffée in the back of
her throat. From the queasy look on Kayla's face, she too had been
catapulted back to Mrs. Henley's parlor. "Coffee, please," Hannah
said, for both of them.

Stanton served it in a delicate china pot with matching gold-
rimmed cups and saucers, and then poured himself a snifter of
brandy. He swirled the amber liquid around the glass and took an
appreciative whiff, followed by a good-sized swallow.

"Now, to business," he said, looking at Kayla. "Seemoan ap-
prised me of your situation. It's unfortunate that you didn't get
renewed before you left Texas. It would have greatly simplified
matters." His voice held a distinct edge of annoyance.

"Yeah, well," Kayla said, "it wasn't like I had much of a choice."

"No, I don't suppose you did. How are you feeling?" Though the
question was casually posed, his gaze was intent and unblinking.

"Fine. Normal." She shrugged.

"You sure you haven't been a little distracted lately? Or maybe
thinking Hannah's been talking to you when she hasn't been? It's
important that you be honest with me."

Kayla's eyes darted to Hannah's in mock alarm. "Did you just
say something?" Nobody smiled. "I'm telling you, I feel fine," she
insisted.

Stanton studied her for a moment longer and then nodded,
apparently satisfied that she was being truthful. "All right, then.
Here's the plan. Tomorrow at sunset, I'll take you outside of town.
A car will be waiting. I'll give you directions then."

"We're going by ourselves?" Hannah asked.

"Yes. That's normally how it works. I was surprised Seemoan brought you, Susan and Anthony usually don't like to risk her." Stanton waited, bright eyes trained inquisitively on the two women. When they didn't respond, he sat back and took a sip of brandy. "And I'm glad they don't, happy as I was to see her. Seemoan's family." His face lit with amusement at their bemused expressions. "What, you don't see the resemblance?" He laughed. "I don't mean literally, we just go back a long way."

Sensing he wouldn't tell them any more, Hannah asked, "What's our destination?"

"Bowling Green, Kentucky. George will be your host there."

"And where do we go after that?" Kayla asked.

He spread his hands wide, palms up. "Your guess is as good as mine. All any of us knows is one stop ahead and one behind."

It made sense, Hannah thought. People couldn't tell what they didn't know. If someone got caught and interrogated, they couldn't expose the whole network.

But. Betty and Gloria were three stops ahead of Dallas, and all four members of Susan's group had known about them. Which must mean she and the others were higher up than Stanton in the Novembrists' hierarchy. Could Dallas be the headquarters for the whole organization, and Susan its leader? Recalling the persuasive power of the woman's voice, Hannah could well believe it.

"I've never even laid eyes on Susan and Anthony," Stanton continued. "You have the advantage of me there. Just tell me one thing," he said, in a conspiratorial tone. "Does Susan have a face to match that magnificent voice?"

The comment, skirting so close to Hannah's own thoughts, disconcerted her. She hesitated. Susan and Anthony clearly trusted

Stanton, but that trust just as clearly had its limits. If he hadn't met
them, it was because they hadn't wanted him to. "Yes," Hannah
lied, "she's very striking."

"Can I ask you something?" Kayla said.

"You may," he replied, inclining his head graciously.

"Why risk your life for women you don't even know?"

Parentheses appeared in the corners of his mouth, bracketing a
sad little smile. "It's personal. My mother was a flaming feminist,
though you wouldn't have known it to look at her. She was the
quintessential Southern belle, about yay tall," Stanton's hand hovered a few inches under the top of his own head, "partial to pink,
wouldn't dream of setting foot outside the house unless she had on
lipstick. She wanted to go to medical school, but then in her last
semester of college, she met my father, whoever he was, and got
pregnant."

"She never told you?" Hannah asked.

"Nope, and as far as I know she never told him, either. This was
before there was such a thing as paternal rights, you understand."
He sipped his brandy. "She graduated, came home to Columbus,
gave birth to me and enrolled in nursing school. My grandparents
raised me, more or less, while she was pursuing her degree and then
her career. She started as an obstetrics nurse and eventually became
a midwife. It wasn't until they passed the SOL laws that she started
doing abortions. By that time, my grandparents were dead, and I
was thirty years old and at loose ends, so I moved back here to help
her. I'd set up the appointments for her—vet the women and find
a location—and she'd do the procedures."

That was what Rafael had called it: *the procedure.* Hannah remembered how the term, along with the other equally clinical and
dispassionate words he'd used, had calmed her. She saw in retrospect that they had in fact enabled her to go through with it. You

didn't temporize, much less agonize, over a procedure, you proceeded with it. A procedure didn't induce regret or require expiation. But how different the scenario became when you substituted words like "murder" and "abomination." The truth of it, Hannah thought now, lay somewhere in between. She'd ended her pregnancy out of love and fear and necessity. It hadn't been simply a procedure, but neither had it been an atrocity.

"There wasn't much demand for abortions at first, because of the scourge," Stanton was saying. "Back then, women who were clean were *trying* to get pregnant, whether they were married or not. The orphanages were empty, and childless couples were paying fifty-thousand dollars for a baby, and double that if it was white."

Hannah glanced covertly at Kayla. Her friend's face remained politely attentive, but there was a flicker of something in her eye, anger or maybe a weary resentment. How many times, Hannah wondered, would you have to hear comments like that before they ceased to bother you?

"But after they found the cure," Stanton went on, "we started to get more and more calls. There were a whole lot of charlatans and butchers doing abortions then—still are, for that matter—and word of my mother's skill spread." He took a long drink of brandy, and his expression turned pensive and a little wistful. "She was so tender with them, so gentle, especially the young ones."

Like Rafael had been with Hannah, and it had still been awful. It wasn't hard to imagine how much worse it could have been with a different kind of doctor.

"And of course if they were poor, she wouldn't take a dime of their money. We had women coming from as far as Colorado and Virginia. And the more of them that came, the more dangerous it got, but that just made Mama more determined." He paused, lost in memory, and absently removed his spectacles and wiped them with his napkin. Without them, his face looked even more child-like. "Things got even riskier once we joined the Novembrists, but I'd never seen my mother more alive. I honestly believe she felt she'd found her purpose on earth."

Stanton's plaintiveness was naked and painful to hear. Hannah wondered whether his mother had ever shown him that much attention, that much tenderness. Although her own mother would have denied it, Hannah had always known she loved Becca more. She hadn't minded, but then, she'd always had her father.

"When did she pass?" Kayla asked.

"A year ago last September. Pneumonia." His voice hitched, and the two women murmured condolences. "I told her she was working too hard, but she wouldn't listen, just kept running herself ragged. I'd gone down to Jackson for the weekend, and when I came back I found her lying unconscious on the bathroom floor. At the hospital she woke up just long enough to refuse consent for the custom antibiotics that might have saved her. Said she was too far gone and we couldn't afford it anyway." Stanton finished his brandy and poured himself another. "You know the last thing she said to me? 'You use that money to finish the tunnel, son. Promise me.' That was Mama, never thinking of herself."

Or of you either, I bet. Hannah felt a stab of pity for him.

"It must have been a great comfort to her to have a son to carry on her work," Kayla said.

"Frankly, I think she would have disowned me if I hadn't."

There was an awkward silence. "Well," Hannah said, "we're very grateful to both of you."

Stanton stood abruptly. "It's late, and you ladies must be tuckered out. I'll show you back to your room now."

"Don't trouble yourself, we can find it," Kayla said.

"You could try, but I highly doubt you'd succeed."

When they reached the front hallway Hannah saw what he'd meant. She examined the paneled wall where she thought they'd come in, but until Stanton said, "By valor and arms," and the door cracked open, it was invisible.

"For your own safety, I'll have to lock you in for the night," Stanton said. "But when you get up in the morning, or if you need anything, just press this little button here. It sends a signal to my port, and I'll come as soon as I'm able."

Hannah and Kayla exchanged an uneasy glance. "As soon as I'm able" was a far cry from "right away." Stanton could leave them down there for a long time. And if something happened to him, not even Simone would be able to find them. They would slowly, inexorably starve to death.

"Don't fret yourselves on my account," Stanton said, with palpable irony. "I may be a little on the chubby side, but my doctor says I have the heart of a twenty-year-old."

Kayla's eyes were mirrors reflecting Hannah's own thought: *What choice do we have?* Right now, the only way forward was down.

As Stanton was about to shut the door, he stopped and tapped his forehead with a stubby finger. "I almost forgot. What's your favorite breakfast?"

"French toast," Hannah said.

"And bacon and grits," Kayla added.

"Then that's exactly what we'll have," he said, smiling his little boy's smile. "Sleep well, my dears."

BUT HANNAH DIDN'T sleep well, despite her exhaustion. Her claustrophobia reared up, and she jerked awake multiple times in the night, troubled by nightmares of being buried alive. In the morning she woke up disoriented, to the sound of water running. She felt panicky until she turned on the light and saw the two beds, the yellow walls, the orchid. She wasn't at the Straight Path Center; she was at Stanton's, with Kayla.

When Kayla was finished, Hannah took her time showering and dressing, trying to recover the sense of calm she'd felt last night in Stanton's trunk, but it eluded her. They climbed the stairs together, and Hannah pressed the button with a shaking hand. But her fears proved baseless, and a scant two minutes later Stanton was opening the door and wishing them good morning. The promised breakfast was as tasty as supper the night before, and when he pressed seconds on them, they accepted without even a token protest.

"Where'd you learn to cook like this?" Kayla asked.

"My grandmother taught me, behind my grandfather's back. He thought cooking was an unmanly pursuit. He was a tough old bird, lost an eye in Korea. He's buried in Friendship Cemetery. I don't suppose you passed it as you came into town?" The women shook their heads. "It's a military graveyard, over sixteen thousand soldiers are buried there. Columbus was a hospital town during the war. Thousands of casualties, both theirs and ours, were brought here and were laid to rest together in the cemetery." Hannah was puzzled. Why would Korean casualties have been brought to Mississippi? "Then in April of '66, a group of ladies decided to decorate the graves with flowers, and that was the first Memorial Day."

"Ah," Hannah said, "you mean the Civil War."

Kayla laughed. "You're in the Deep South now. There *is* no other war."

"Spoken like a true daughter of the Confederacy," Stanton said, with an approving bob of his head. "And now, I must leave you ladies for the afternoon. I'm one of the Friends of Friendship, and I give volunteer tours of the cemetery every other Friday. I've never once missed my shift, and I wouldn't want to raise any eyebrows by starting today."

Back in the basement, Hannah paced, feeling unaccountably jittery, while Kayla lay contentedly on her bed with a plate of brownies resting on her stomach. "Tell you what," she said, her voice garbled by the food, "for a couple of desperate fugitives, we sure are eating like queens. You've got to try one of these. They're incredible."

Hannah didn't respond. Something was nagging at her, like a finger tapping on her spine. "All right, out with it," Kayla said.

"You don't feel like there's something a little . . . off about Stanton, and this whole situation?"

"Apart from the fact that he didn't give us any milk to go with these brownies, no. But tell me why you do."

Hannah sat down at the end of Kayla's bed. "I was thinking about how much he told us. About himself, his family. If we got caught we could identify him in two seconds flat. I mean, how many tiny middle-aged men can there be in Columbus, Mississippi, who live in a Victorian mansion and had a midwife for a mother? Why would he reveal all that?"

Kayla let out an amused *humph*. "You don't have much experience with alcohol, do you? A person'll tell you all sorts of things after polishing off a bottle and a half of wine and two glasses of brandy."

"Maybe, but he was stone cold sober a few minutes ago when he told us he was a volunteer at the cemetery. I mean, he was pretty darn specific. Think about it. What do we know about Susan and Anthony's real lives, or Simone's? Nothing. Because unlike Stanton, they were careful not to reveal anything in case we were caught."

Kayla shook her head. "But they trust him completely, even

Simone, and she's hardly the trusting type. And if he means us harm, why put a hundred-dollar plant in our room and feed us crawfish étouffée? The fact is, he could've turned us in to the police or killed us ten times already if he'd wanted to. The man had us in the trunk of his car—he could've taken us anywhere. Or locked us in the tunnel and left us to die, or drugged or poisoned these brownies." Kayla popped the last bite into her mouth and offered the plate to Hannah.

"True," Hannah said. Kayla was right; she was being paranoid. She took a brownie and bit into it. "Mmm."

"What did I tell you?"

But after just two bites Hannah set the remainder back on the plate. It was too rich, too sweet. Cloyingly so. "I can't eat any more of this."

Kayla gave her a disbelieving look. "You're crazy, you know that?"

Hannah shrugged. She couldn't disagree.

STANTON CAME FOR them an hour before sunset. They ate a quick supper, and then it was time to go. He led them back through the tunnel to the garage, stowed their packs in the back-seat of the car and opened the trunk.

"We'd best say our goodbyes now," he said. "There won't be time once we get to the car."

Hannah and Kayla thanked him for his kindness, but he brushed their gratitude aside with the now-familiar "It's personal."

"Good luck surviving the renovations," Kayla said.

Stanton smiled. "It's a painful process, but it'll be worth it in the end. And now, I'm afraid it's back in the trunk with you two." With his customary gallantry, he helped them climb in and get settled. He took hold of the lid with one hand and contemplated them. "I *am* sorry about this," he said, with sincere, almost tender regret. "But you won't have to endure it for long." He brought the lid down gently, shutting them in. Hannah heard him get in the car, start the engine and turn on some classical music. They backed out, accelerated. She could feel panic rising, wanting to erupt out of her throat, fists and feet.

Kayla made a scratchy, hissing sound in the back of her throat. "Good evening, this is your pilot speaking," she said, with artificial cordiality. "Welcome to ClaustrophobiAir. We hope you enjoy your confinement. If there's anything we can do to make you feel more cramped and suffocated, please don't hesitate to ask one of the flight attendants."

Hannah smiled, despite her fear. What would she do without Kayla?

Ten or fifteen minutes later, the car stopped. Hannah heard the driver's door open and the crunch of Stanton's footsteps, and then another door was opened and a second set of footsteps approached the car. Suddenly, the lid of the trunk popped open. A flashlight shone into her eyes, blinding her, and then shifted to Kayla. The finger that had been tapping on Hannah's spine earlier became a fist, pummeling her.

"Nice," a male voice said, drawing out the word lasciviously. Before either of the women could move, the lid slammed shut again.

"Hey!" Kayla yelled. She jerked upward, and Hannah heard the *thwack* of her head hitting the lid. "Ow! Shit!" She started kicking the lid of the trunk. "Let us out of here! Stanton!"

"Settle down!" the stranger barked, with a sharp rap on the lid.

Kayla was breathing in loud, harsh gasps. "Shh," Hannah whispered, fighting down her own terror, straining to hear what the two men were saying.

". . . too bad," the stranger said. There was an unintelligible response from Stanton, and then the stranger said, "Bet she woulda fetched triple that if her renewal wasn't up so soon. I never seen the bidding get that fierce over a ticker."

Bidding? Ticker? Hannah's body went cold. She felt a dawning horror as she apprehended what was happening. *No, he can't have, he wouldn't have, he fed us crawfish étouffée and brownies.* Her mind cowered from its own conclusions, casting in all directions for alternatives but finding none.

Stanton had sold them.

She pictured herself and Kayla last night, primping in front of the bathroom mirror in their sexy outfits, lit up by that bright row of bulbs, the kind you'd find in a starlet's dressing room—or on a film set. Dear God, he must have been filming them the whole time. There must have been a camera behind the mirror, streaming their images to his waiting clients, because of course, they'd want to examine the merchandise before putting in their bids. The auction would have taken place later, after she and Kayla went to bed, or this afternoon perhaps, when Stanton was supposedly out playing tour guide. But *ticker* . . . ?

"Oh God, he means me," Kayla moaned. "I'm the ticker."

Bile surged up into Hannah's throat as she grasped the meaning of the term. That was why Stanton had been so annoyed that Kayla hadn't gotten her renewal; it decreased her shelf life, and hence, her value. *Tick, tick, tick.* Kayla would go into fragmentation any day now, and Hannah sometime in February. And when they did, when they became so fragged out that they'd outlived their usefulness to their owners . . . "You won't have to endure it for long," Stanton had promised. They wouldn't be taken for renewal; their captors wouldn't dare risk it. They'd be disposed of like a couple of empty milk cartons.

"Till next time then," the stranger said. Stanton didn't respond. Hannah heard receding footsteps, the sound of a car door closing. "Stuck-up dwarf prick," the stranger said.

He banged on the trunk lid, making the women jump. "Listen up, gals. It's a three-hour drive to where we're going, and you're gonna stay nice and quiet till we get there. If I hear you making a racket, trying to get somebody's attention, you'll get it all right, from me, and believe me, you don't want that."

As the car started to move, an image formed in Hannah's mind, of the naked hook in the ceiling of Stanton's shabby dining room. A hook where a chandelier would hang, casting its radiance over the silk wallpaper and jewel-toned rugs, the antique mahogany table neatly laid with silver, china and lead crystal, all of it sparkling in that dazzling white light.

THEY RODE IN stunned silence at first, each locked in her own thoughts. Hannah's were grim. She was looking at five to six weeks of slavery, and that was if she was lucky; it could take as long as two months before she was totally fragged out. She had no illusions about what kind of slave she'd be. "Only the young and pretty ones," Simone had said. Hannah calmed herself by picturing Simone's face: clenched, furious, resolute. A woman with such a face wouldn't let them be taken by slavers, hadn't let them be taken by the Fist. She would come after them, would kill if necessary to save them, because for her, it was personal. And for Paul, it was even more so. He wouldn't let Kayla be harmed. Surely he wouldn't.

Hannah heard faint music playing, and then their captor started singing along, belting out the song with full-throated sincerity and absolutely no sense of pitch. *"Seen you and him dancin'*

*at the Broken Spoke last night . . . He had his arms around you and
was squeezin' you tight . . ."*

"He *would* have to be a country and western fan," Kayla
murmured.

Hannah felt Kayla shaking with what she thought was laughter,
and then she heard a sniffle and realized her friend was sobbing.

"Hey," Hannah said, "Listen to me, it's going to be all right.
Simone and Paul—Vincent—know where we are. Their plan was
to follow us. Think of him, Kayla. Think of Vincent."

*"I itched to break both his arms and pizzafy his face . . . Wanted
to skin him alive but it ain't my place . . . Cuz he's your husband and
I'm just the other man . . ."*

"They mean to kill us," Kayla said. "Once we're too fragged out
to rape anymore."

"Vincent isn't going to let either one of those things happen. He
cares too much about you."

"What if he can't find us in time? What if they kill him?"

"They won't. He'll find us, he and Simone, and I wouldn't want
to be the guy driving this car when they do. I'm sure they're following us right now, making plans to rescue us. And after they've got
us, you know the first thing they're going to do? Go back and get
that bastard Stanton."

"I'll help them do it," Kayla said. "When I think of all that fucking food he made for us, I want to puke. And we just sat there and
gobbled it up like rabbits in front of a pile of carrots." The image
was familiar, and Hannah tried to recall where she'd seen it. "Remember in *Watership Down,* how the nice farmer kept putting the
food out every day, and the rabbits kept eating it and getting fatter and fatter, and then the one rabbit finally figures out that the
farmer's planning to turn them all into fricassee?"

Hannah suddenly felt her breakfast churning, threatening to come up. "Oh God, I feel sick."

"Take deep breaths," said Kayla. "The only thing worse than being kidnapped and locked in a trunk is being kidnapped and locked in a trunk full of vomit." Fighting her panic, Hannah breathed. In, out, in, out. "On the other hand," Kayla added, "if we puked all over ourselves maybe they'd decide to send us back and ask Stanton for a refund. What do you think? Might be worth a try."

The deep breathing and the humor had the desired effect, and Hannah felt her nausea begin to subside. "The funny thing is," she said, when she could speak again, "unlike the farmer, I think Stanton actually feels bad about what he's doing. I think that's why he cooked for us, as a sort of . . . expiation."

"Huh. Expiation my ass. 'Sorry, ladies, I'm selling y'all into slavery,'" Kayla said, mimicking his accent, "'but here's some nice brownies before you go.' Two-faced son of a bitch." She sounded stronger and less afraid. *Nothing like a little anger to blunt fear and grief,* Hannah thought. "I wonder how many other women he's done this to," Kayla said.

"Simone said there were three who disappeared before us."

"One for the parlor, one for the library, and one for the kitchen. You and me should finance the renovations on the dining room and the master bedroom."

Their captor had reached the grand finale: *"So if she makes eyes at you run as fast as you can . . . Cuz you don't want to be the other man . . . Oh yeah it's hell to be the other man."* He jumped up an octave on the last syllable, delivering it in a screeching falsetto.

When he fell silent Kayla said, in a small voice, "I suppose they're all dead by now, those other women."

"I hope so, for their sakes."

BY UNSPOKEN AGREEMENT, they passed the time by talking of other things—childhood, family and, inevitably, love. Their murmurs wove a soft blanket around them, and they took what comfort they could from its all-too-temporary warmth. Hannah knew they'd probably be separated once they reached their destination. She pushed the thought to the back of her mind and listened to Kayla reminisce about her first love, Brad, "who turned out to be gay, which I guess I always sort of knew, but I was still pretty busted up when he told me," and two subsequent boyfriends: "Shaun was smart and funny and sweet as he could be, but he was the rebound guy, and I just wasn't ready to get serious again so soon. Then there was Martin, he was a rich Englishman twenty years older than me. I met him at the Kimbell in front of a painting of some eighteenth-century lord in a powdered wig, which is kind of what he reminded me of. It would never have worked, even if I hadn't fallen in love with TJ. Martin just wanted to keep me in a box. It was a velvet box, but it was still a box, you know what I mean?" A little laugh. "Stupid question, considering where we are right now."

"Oh, I know, all right," Hannah said bitterly. "I could write a book on the subject." One by one, she conjured all the boxes she'd been put into: The good girl box and the good Christian box. The confines of her sewing room above the garage. The mistress box, played out in the boxes of all those indistinguishable hotel rooms. The sweltering room in apartment 122. The jail cell, the interrogation room, the witness box at her trial. The bad daughter and fallen woman boxes. Her red body in the mirrored cell of the Chrome ward, a box within a box within a box. The enlightenment room, Mrs. Henley's parlor. The locked rooms at the safe house and at Stanton's. The wooden crate. And now, for the second time, the trunk of a car. She saw with a painful blaze of clarity that every one of these boxes had been of her own making, either by consent or lack of resistance. She had no right to bitterness; she had put herself in them. And she would get herself out, she vowed. And once she was out, she'd never willingly climb into another box again.

Kayla nudged her. "Hey, you listening?"

"Sorry. What were you saying?"

"I was asking you if Aidan was your first love."

"Yes, first and only." Hannah told Kayla about how they'd met at the hospital, their long, torturous wait, their first time together and their last, when she'd lain behind him with her belly pressed against his back, knowing it was the closest he would ever be to their child. She'd never spoken of him to anyone, and the more she talked, the wider the breach grew in the dam inside of her and the more furiously the words spilled out. Kayla listened, with periodic murmurs of sympathy, to the whole story, which Hannah ended, dry-eyed, at the moment she'd seen him on the vid, so vibrant and far away, and known that he'd moved on. She fell silent, feeling wrung out but tremendously lighter. If the trunk opened right now, she mused, she'd float up out of it like a big, red balloon.

"You don't see it, do you?" Kayla said.

"See what?"

"How strong you are, to have made the choice you made. That took real guts." Hannah started to protest, but Kayla forestalled her. "*And* to have kept his identity a secret, *and* to have stood up to the Henleys like you did, *and* to have come after me when you thought I'd been kidnapped, and, and, and. Hell, Hannah, you're one of the strongest people I ever met in my life." She paused, added, "And that means you have a serious shot at surviving this."

"What do you mean, *I* have a shot? You're strong too."

"Look," Kayla said. "I'm not kidding myself. It could take Vincent and Simone days or even weeks to figure out a way to free us, and I probably won't have that long. But you've got time—"

"Yeah, lucky me," Hannah interjected. "I've got six or more fabulous, all-expense-paid weeks to enjoy this."

"My point is," Kayla said sharply, "you've got the strength to survive whatever happens until Simone and Vincent come for you. Remember that, no matter how bad it gets."

"I will," Hannah said, perplexed by Kayla's manner. It wasn't like her friend to be so fatalistic. Or so silent. "Kayla?"

A long exhalation. "I'm not positive," Kayla said, "but I think I've started fragging out."

THE BRINY TANG OF THE SEA was the first thing her senses registered when the trunk was opened and the men pulled her out, eyes squinting and watering from the sudden incursion of light. The second thing she registered was shooting pain in her limbs. When she tried to stand, her cramped legs collapsed under her weight, and the man holding her jerked her up roughly, his hand a tight cincture around her upper arm. The third and fourth things were cold, sea-damp wind against her face and a sense of spaciousness that was dizzying after her confinement. She could hear the susurration of the sea now, that was the fifth thing, and see the glittering golden path cast by the moon upon its dark expanse, that was the sixth. The seventh was the size of her captor. He was a colossus, a breathing mountain. The eighth was a jab of pain in her upper arm, the one he wasn't gripping, after which the rest was a kaleidoscopic blur: The world tilting as an arm hooked beneath her knees and another beneath her back. Hungry brown eyes staring down at her from a wide white face, the odor of unbrushed teeth overlaid by coffee, a sprinkling of stars made faint by a fat, gibbous moon. A wooden dock tapering toward a big white blob, feet clomping on wood, Kayla's head limp and bent backward, bobbing down the dock away from Hannah. A hand pawing her breast and pinching the nipple hard, the cough of a motor swallowing her gasp of pain.

The salt smell of the sea was the last thing she registered before she slipped into the void.

FIVE

TRANSFIGURATION

A T FIRST, WHEN THE BLACKNESS began to recede, she was unaware of it. There was no she to have awareness, only infinite nonbeing. She was not in the void, she *was* the void.

She. Was.

The void began to lighten, fading to a not quite black, fading to a deep, sooty gray, fading to slate gray, fading to cloud gray. A glowing pinpoint punctured the darkness. It pulsed—*Hannah!*—and she saw a shining mote suspended there. It pulsed again, and again— *Hannah!*—becoming brighter with each burst of incandescence. It seared her eyes, stabbed her ears, threatened her nonbeing. *Hannah!* The mote blazed like a sun, overwhelming, all-encompassing. She entered into it entered into her. She was the mote.

"Hannah! Wake up!" Her eyelids felt like they were weighed down by bricks, but the command forced her to lift them. The room—she was in a room—swam. She was lying on her side, in a bed. She was naked from the waist down. It stirred a memory: a sweltering room, a table covered in dinosaur-patterned sheets, the glint of medical instruments, the smell of blood. She groaned, suddenly queasy. Her body broke out in a sweat and she retched. A trash can appeared beside her face. She threw up into it. A washcloth wiped her mouth.

"Better now?" The voice, a woman's, was familiar. Hannah shook her head, groaned, vomited again. The washcloth returned, wiped her mouth again. "Better?" She nodded. "Turn onto your back," the voice said. Hannah tried to obey it—she *had* to obey it— but her limbs were too weak. Hands turned her, and a cool, damp towel was pressed against her forehead. A face came into view, a white moon hovering over her. She knew it, combed her mind for the name attached to it.

"You are safe, Hannah. The men who tried to kidnap you are dead."

Hannah remembered another face, leering down at her. A huge hand groping her, hurting her. She whimpered and recoiled, trying to escape it. Hands gripped her shoulders and pushed her down. "Shh, calm yourself, you are safe," the woman—Simone, that was her name—said. At once, Hannah's muscles relaxed, and she let her head fall back against the pillow. "They did not harm you, but they drugged you, the *salauds*. This is why you are sick, from the sedative they gave you."

She remembered a prick in her arm, Kayla being carried away, head lolling. With effort, Hannah turned her own head to the right and then to the left, searching for her friend. There was a second bed in the room but it was unoccupied, still neatly made. A pistol lay on the bedside table. Alarm shot through her, dispelling some of the fog in her brain. Where was Kayla? She tried to ask, but her tongue was inert, immovable. She strained, managed a whispered, "Where?"

Simone misunderstood. "We are still in Mississippi, some place called Palagousta, Pascalula." An impatient wave. "It is on the coast."

Hannah groaned in frustration. "Kay," she said.

"Ah," Simone said. "They had a boat. We were no more than a kilometer behind you, but they were quick. We arrived as they were carrying her on board. They put out to sea during the gunfight."

We. Meaning Simone and Paul. Where was Paul?

"We captured the two who had you, and they talked. That *fils de pute* Stanton sold her to a rich businessman in Havana. Paul has gone after her."

Hannah exhaled, dizzy with relief, but Simone was plainly annoyed. Of course, she'd think it a fool's errand: Paul, being too soft, not following the code.

"You, they were taking by car to a brothel in New Orleans that specializes in Chromes. It caters to foreign businessmen and tourists who are looking for something . . . exotic. Reds are very popular."

Hannah felt another swell of nausea and swallowed, forcing it back. Her mouth tasted foul and her entire body was slick with cooling sweat. She shivered, and Simone lifted the sheet covering her and looked underneath. *"Mon Dieu,* you are soaked, and so is the bed. We must get you into the shower."

Simone moved to lift her up, but Hannah, aware that she was half-naked, shrank away, clutching the sheet against herself. Simone slid an arm beneath her armpits and pulled her up forcibly. "Do not be ridiculous. We are all two women. And in all cases, I have already seen it."

Blood rushed to Hannah's face as she realized that Simone must have undressed her. Why would she have done that, and only from the waist down? Unless . . . Panic seized her. Simone was a lesbian, the two of them were alone, Hannah was drugged, helpless, trapped. "No!" she cried, struggling to free herself.

Simone gripped her harder and gave her a little shake. "Who do you think cleaned the piss off you, eh? Now *come.*"

Fueled by humiliation—*Oh God, I must have wet myself*—Hannah's panic turned to hysteria. She had to get away, now, but her body did the exact opposite, lurching upward, toward rather than away from Simone, straining in its eagerness to obey her.

Simone frowned and looked closely at her. "Be still," she said. Hannah froze. "Shut your eyes." Hannah shut them. "Spread your legs." Beneath the sheet, she spread them. *"Ostie!"* Simone let go of her, jerking away in disgust. Hannah cringed, terrified that she'd displeased the other woman, and forced her legs wider apart until the muscles of her inner thighs burned. "Stop!" Simone exclaimed, and then, more quietly, "Stop, Hannah. Relax." Her muscles went slack. With a gentleness Hannah wouldn't have believed her capable of, Simone took hold of her legs and pushed them back together. "It is all right," she said. "You have done nothing wrong."

Simone sat on the edge of the bed, staring down at Hannah with a haunted expression, as if she were seeing something or someone else. "They did not only sedate you, they gave you thrall. Do you know what this is?" Hannah shook her head. "The chemical name is thralaxomine. It is a drug made for rape. When you are on thrall, you have no will of your own, you must do what they say no matter what. You want to combat them, you want to kick and scream for help, but instead, you beg for more, because they tell you to beg. You are completely conscient the whole time, watching yourself, hating yourself for obeying them. And after . . ." Simone crossed her arms over her chest, hugging herself. "After, you remember everything. Everything." Her voice was low and serrated by pain. The sound of it hurt Hannah's heart.

"This was done to me," Simone said, as Hannah had known she would. "There were three of them, and they take me to a motel much like this and keep me there for two days." Her eyes darted around the room, refurnishing it with different paintings, tables, bedspreads. Repopulating it. "After, my friend finds for me the pill, the pill of the next morning, but it was too late. Two months later I know that I am pregnant. This was in Québec, before we changed back the law. I found a woman who knew a woman who knew a man who made abortions. I met him in a cave, a . . . basement of an abandoned building. It was filthy, and he was a butcher. When he did it," she made a stabbing motion with one hand, "he, he pierced me. After that I was very sick. I almost died from the infection." She paused. "Sometimes, I wanted to die."

The words "I'm sorry" formed on Hannah's lips, but she didn't try to speak them, even though she was, deeply so. This woman wouldn't want her pity, would fling it back at her like a dead snake. Simone may have been victimized, but she was no victim. She hadn't allowed herself to be. Instead, she'd fed her outrage, using it as fuel, first to survive and then to help other women do the same. *It's personal.* Hannah fully grasped, for the first time, the meaning of the words. They weren't just about choice or even the right to privacy; they were a declaration of self-worth, a demand for personal dignity. Their fundamental truth pealed inside of her, clarion bright.

"I'm glad you didn't," she said, discovering that she could speak again. She reached out and touched Simone's leg. "The dead can't fight back. And if we don't fight, they win."

SIMONE HALF WALKED, half carried Hannah to the bathroom and eased her down onto the toilet, where she lolled like a rag doll. Her mind was a little sharper, but her limbs still felt sluggish and uncoordinated, and she was as tired as though she hadn't slept in days.

"I think we had better make it a bath, *non?*" Hannah nodded; not that she could do otherwise, now that Simone had expressed a preference. The other woman started the water running and said, "I will leave you for a little. Knock when you are ready."

"Thank you," Hannah said, grateful for the modicum of privacy. Simone withdrew, closing the door behind her. There was a mirror on the back of it, directly opposite Hannah. A pitiful creature sat there, huddled on the toilet. Its scarlet face was slack, like a half-deflated balloon. Its hair was matted, its sweater torn and filthy. One knee was encrusted with dried blood. The creature was weeping, and who could blame it, as hideous and abject and lonely as it was? But its tears, Hannah perceived suddenly, didn't just spring from wretchedness. They were also tears of relief, because it was alive, because it had survived another day. How could anything be grateful for such an existence? And yet, this creature was, and when it saw itself and knew that it wanted to live in spite of everything, it wept even harder, sobbing inconsolably until it was depleted.

When Hannah knocked on the door, Simone returned with the toothbrush from her pack. She took in Hannah's swollen eyes but made no comment, merely applied the toothpaste, wet the brush and handed it to her. Hannah used it clumsily, still sitting on the toilet, spitting into a plastic cup Simone held out for her, rinsing, spitting again. Afterward, she drank several cups of water and felt better for it.

"Ready?"

Hannah nodded and lifted her arms, and Simone pulled off her sweat-soaked sweater. Her touch was brisk and impersonal, and she averted her eyes from Hannah's body, but Hannah still felt self-conscious and exposed, and she had to resist the urge to cover herself with her hands. Simone helped her up off the toilet and into the tub.

"Do you need help to bathe?"

"I think I can manage," Hannah replied, but then it occurred to her that if she lay back in the tub to wet her hair, she might not have the strength or coordination to get up again. How absurd it would be, after everything she'd survived, to drown in a foot and a half of water! She briefly considered skipping her hair, but her desire to be completely clean outweighed her modesty. "On second thought, I guess I'll need help washing my hair."

Simone shrugged. "It is not a problem." She took the cup Hannah had drunk from and knelt beside the tub. "Move forward." Hannah scooted toward the center of the tub, sloshing water over the side in her haste to comply. "Sorry," Simone said, with a rueful smile. "I will try to stop telling you what to do until the thrall wears off."

Hannah stared at her, startled. The smile had transformed Simone's face, peeling ten hard years off it and making her look surprisingly . . . feminine. She wasn't conventionally pretty, but there was an arresting purity to the sharp, clean planes of her face. She was finely made, Hannah thought, with a sort of dreamy dispassion. Like she'd been chiseled by a master carver.

"It should be completely dissipated by morning." Simone dipped the cup in the water and tipped Hannah's head back. "Please, close your eyes."

Warm water streamed from the crown of Hannah's head down her scalp. *What a strange baptism,* she thought, with that same detachment. Simone poured cupful after cupful over her head, lifting her hair to wet it underneath, and then her fingers worked in the shampoo, slowly massaging Hannah's scalp. It felt sublime, and she started to get drowsy. As Simone began to rinse her hair, Hannah listed to one side.

Simone righted her with a clucking sound. "Almost finished," she said. A wet washcloth moved gently across Hannah's face, around her neck, down her back, under her arms, across and under her breasts. Like a child she let her limbs be raised and lowered, let herself be drawn upward and enfolded in a towel, her hair tousled and combed. Like a child she let Simone lead her to the second bed, turn down the covers, remove the towel, ease her under the cool, clean sheets and tuck them around her. She felt a soft brush of lips against her forehead, heard the other woman murmur, "Sleep now, *chère.*"

Chère, Hannah thought. *Cherished.* It was a good thing to be. She wrapped the word around her and carried it down with her into sleep.

WHEN HANNAH OPENED her eyes, she saw Simone's face inches from her own, illuminated by a vertical filament of sunlight peeking through a gap in the curtains. Confusion turned to panic as the events of yesterday cascaded through her mind, and then to relief. Safe, she was safe. Because of this woman.

Hannah studied Simone, remembering what she'd revealed about her past, her courage and anger and sorrow, her tenderness in the bath. She was lying on her side, as Hannah was. Her mouth was parted slightly, her face softened in sleep, one hand curled beneath her chin. Her eyelashes were the color of honey, and they made a thick, curved fringe against her pale cheeks. A faint line of worry bisected her brows, and Hannah's hand, of its own accord, lifted from the bed and reached out to smooth it, the barest brush of her thumb against the other woman's skin. Simone sighed, and Hannah yanked her hand back.

What am I doing? Her pulse quickened at the thought that Simone might wake up. *And if she did? What would she do? What would I want her to do?* The first two answers her mind supplied— *Nothing,* and then, *I don't know*—came reflexively, one after the other. The third was slower to materialize, a reluctant dawning that gave the lie to them both.

I'd want her to touch me back.

The realization was staggering, inconceivable, and Hannah's immediate response was denial. But it was a weak no, and when it had faded away, the third answer was still there in her mind, waiting, and she knew that it was the true one.

Wickedness, perversion, abomination: here it came, the virulent, all-too-familiar vocabulary of shame. But this time, she halted its onrush and examined it for truth. To her surprise, she found none that she recognized. These once-powerful words from her former life were tired and feeble, harmless unless she gave them teeth by believing them.

Hannah's hand returned to Simone's face, hovering above it. She owed Simone her life, and she knew that gratitude was part of it. She recognized too her own loneliness, how starved she'd been for the loving touch of another human being. But as her hand descended and her fingers traced the blade of Simone's cheekbone, Hannah knew that she needed and wanted to touch as much as to be touched, and not just any human being, but this one. This woman she admired, respected. Was undeniably attracted to.

Simone jerked awake, stilling when she recognized Hannah. The crease between her brows deepened, and Hannah reached up and stroked it with her thumb. "What are you doing?" Simone demanded. "Stop."

Hannah paused for a moment, and then her hand resumed its slow, deliberate odyssey, sketching the divot between Simone's mouth and chin, gliding down and across the angle of her jaw, down the soft, vulnerable column of her neck.

"Stop," Simone said again, but more questioningly. Hannah's eyes followed the path of her hand, so lurid against Simone's pallor, marveling that it should be there, moving across the other woman's bare shoulder, down the length of her lean, corded arm to circle her palm. A quiver ran through Simone's body, and as Hannah's hand traveled back up her arm, she felt the stippling of goosebumps rise beneath her fingers, and within herself, her own desire rising. As if from a great distance, she watched her hand drop down to the hem of Simone's tank top.

Simone pulled away and heaved herself up. "*Non,* this is not a good idea."

"Stop," Hannah said. "Lie down." She lay her hand flat against Simone's chest and pushed.

Simone searched Hannah's face and then relaxed, lying back with a languid surrender that made Hannah's heart pound. Her hand drifted slowly up from Simone's waist to her breast, the landscape less sinuous than her own but still unmistakably feminine. Simone was still, watchful, her lips slightly parted. Hannah's fingers skimmed across the lower one, followed the whorl of an ear and threaded the short-cropped hair, finding it soft as a pelt. A pulse beat visibly in her neck, beckoning Hannah's mouth. She cupped the back of Simone's head and drew her close. Her lips encircled the pulse point, and she felt the insistent throb of life beneath the delicate skin. She breathed in, smelled sea salt and vanilla, a deeper musk. Simone made a sound between a groan and a sigh, and Hannah pulled back to look at her, rubbing her cheek against the other woman's like a cat.

Simone took Hannah's chin in her hand, pressing her fingers into the soft flesh between cheek and jaw. "You are sure?"

Hannah thought back to her first time with Aidan, remembering how utterly certain she'd felt then, how confident that she was carrying out God's will. This feeling was entirely different. She had only her own volition to follow, her own desire to act upon, or not. Whatever decision she made would be hers alone.

"Yes," she said. Her foot found Simone's under the sheet, stroked the warm, tender underside of the arch. She pushed herself up, leaned down to kiss Simone's mouth. "Close your eyes," Hannah murmured. "Spread your legs."

THEY DOZED A little afterward, lying in a tangle of limbs. When Hannah woke for the second time, Simone was regarding her with something like bemusement.

"You are full of surprises."

Hannah looked away, feeling suddenly shy. "So are you."

Simone's lips curved into a sly smile. "It was nice, *non*?"

"Yes," Hannah said, but the fact was, it had been a great deal more than nice. It had been astounding, both physically and emotionally: intimate, intensely erotic, healing in a way she hadn't known she needed. Nothing would ever erase the horrors she'd been through, but Simone's touch and her own response to it had dimmed them, diluting their power over her and pushing them away to a bearable distance. For the first time since she became a Red, Hannah felt fully human.

"We cannot stay much longer," Simone said. Hannah heard the regret in her voice and felt a twinge of it herself, mixed with relief and guilt and other emotions she couldn't even identify. The guilt was mainly for Kayla: because Hannah had been rescued and Kayla had not; because she'd been intimate with the woman who'd been prepared to kill Kayla just three days ago; because while she'd been making love with Simone, she'd put Kayla from her mind. *I'm a terrible person,* she thought.

Simone rolled onto her back and stared at the ceiling. Her expression turned dark, reflecting Hannah's own thoughts. "We will leave as soon as it is dark," she said. "I have business in Columbus."

Hannah smiled grimly. "Guess Stanton won't have to suffer through the living hell of renovations after all."

"What do you mean?"

"That's why he sold us. To pay for restoring his house."

"*This* is for what he betrayed us? For a fucking *house*?" Simone shook her head. "His mother, Claire, was one of the very first to join us. That a son of hers would do such a thing is unimaginable."

"He spoke about her. I got the feeling he resented her for putting your cause first."

"She was a true patriot. She would kill him herself if she were alive."

Instead, Hannah knew, Simone would do it. Hannah pictured the scene: Stanton tied to one of his precious chairs while Simone questioned him. Tortured him, just as she and Paul must have tortured Hannah's would-be abductors yesterday to find out what they knew. Silenced him. Once, this would have troubled her conscience. But now, thinking of the women Stanton had consigned to abuse and death, thinking of Kayla, drugged with thrall, begging her captors to rape her, Hannah was not only undismayed, she felt a deep, primitive pleasure. Cole's words echoed in her head: *Some things don't deserve to be forgiven.* Perhaps the two of them weren't so different after all. It was a disturbing thought.

Simone sat up, bent down and grabbed her pants from the floor, fishing in the pockets for her port. "Go now and shower. I need to make some calls."

"Okay." As Hannah pushed herself up, her stomach growled. "Is there anything to eat? I'm starved."

"Nothing, sorry. We will stop as we leave town and get something. It will have to be fast food, though. We have a nine-hour drive to make, and the sooner I deliver you to George in Bowling Green, the sooner I can come back and take care of that *chien sale de* Stanton."

"No," Hannah said, without thinking, her hand flying up in emphatic denial. "No more."

Simone knitted her brows. "He has to die, surely you must see that."

"I mean no more being at the mercy of strangers. No more huddling inside of crates and trunks and locked rooms, wondering whether the person on the other side is going to let me out or not."
No more boxes.

Simone stroked her arm. "Ah, *chérie,* I understand very well your feelings, but it will not be for much longer. Next you go to George, and then to Betty and Gloria. You can trust them. They will see you safely on."

"Like Stanton did?" Hannah saw Simone flinch a little. "And what about the next person, and the one after that? Can you look me in the eye and tell me you're a hundred percent certain I can trust them all?"

Simone made an exasperated sound. "What in life is a hundred percent certain? But yes, I have confidence in the others. And in all cases, there is no other way."

"Yes, there is. Rent me a car and give me an address in Canada. I'll drive at night and hide during the day."

"Es-tu folle?" Simone exclaimed, circling her forefinger around her temple. "You would never make it past all the frontiers."

"I won't cross the state borders on the major highways, I'll take the back roads. You can't tell me they man every single point. And when I get to the Canadian border, I'll walk across in the woods, if I have to. I'll figure out something."

"And this you call a plan?"

"People do it all the time," Hannah said, with more confidence than she felt. Border security between the United States and Canada wasn't airtight, but advances in thermal scanning, biometrics and robot surveillance had drastically reduced the number of illegal crossings since the days of "Thousands Standing Around." Still, some people made it across. "There are ways, there have to be. And I bet you know what they are."

"*Non.* It is too dangerous."

Hannah knew Simone's objections were well founded, but even so, her high-handedness was galling. "I'm willing to take my chances."

"That may be, but I am not disposed to risk you."

"I'm not yours to risk," Hannah retorted, more angrily than she'd intended. She saw a flash of hurt in Simone's eyes and was briefly sorry for it, but on a deeper level, she wasn't sorry at all. What she'd said was nothing less than the truth. She wasn't Simone's. She wasn't anyone's but her own.

Hannah reached out, touched the other woman's cheek. "Don't you see? I can't go back to being dependent, to being *handled* by other people. I've spent most of my life being that person, and I've had enough. Please, help me do what I need to do."

Simone's jaw tightened. Brusquely, she took Hannah's hand and returned it to her lap. "I cannot permit this, Hannah. You know too much now. If they catch you, they will drug you, and you will tell them everything."

Hannah felt herself quail a little at the idea of being drugged again. But then her gaze fell on the nightstand, and the object lying upon it. "Then give me the gun and show me how to use it. If they come for me I'll use it on myself, I swear it."

"I am sorry, truly," Simone said, "but what you ask is not possible."

The finality in her voice cracked something open inside of Hannah, a hard kernel of tenacity submerged so deep within her she'd never known it existed until now, when she saw her hand reaching out and grabbing the pistol, her fingers curling around the solid steel of its barrel and holding it out, butt first, to Simone. "Then you do it," she said. "Because I'd rather be dead than be anyone's victim again."

A wild exaltation seized her as she realized that she meant it; that she was laying claim to her life as she'd never done before. She had never felt more wholly alive than at this moment, sitting naked with a gun pointed at her chest, in a cheap motel room with a woman she'd just made love to in defiance of everything she'd ever been taught, a woman who was looking at her in shock and consternation, because she could see that Hannah meant it, and empathy, because in Hannah's place, Simone would have felt exactly the same. All this, Hannah read in an instant. She held herself stone-still, watching the war of emotions on Simone's face, and saw the moment when empathy won.

Simone let out a long breath. Carefully, she took the gun from Hannah and set it back on the table. "I do not like this," she said.

Hannah leaned forward and kissed her. *"Merci."*

As she got up and walked to the shower, Hannah allowed the treacherous thought that had been tunneling deep in her mind to wriggle to the surface: Now, she could go to Aidan.

IN THE END Simone decided to rent a car for herself and let Hannah take the van. "You will be much more safe this way," she said. She was rooting through her suitcase, completely and unselfconsciously nude. Hannah was sitting on the bed fully dressed, studying Simone—*my lover,* she thought, with undiminished amazement—covertly; or at least, she hoped she was being covert.

"The logo of the church will dissipate suspicion," Simone said. "And you can sleep in the back without being seen."

Hannah wondered, not for the first time, how the Novembrists were financed. They must have plenty of money, if they could afford to just give her a vehicle. "Won't Susan and Anthony mind you giving away their van?" she asked.

"They will get it back eventually, or another one similar."
Simone shrugged. "In all cases, it is not their place to object to
anything I decide. Susan and Anthony follow my orders."

"Come again?" Hannah said.

Simone regarded Hannah with amusement. "I am their
superior."

Hannah felt flummoxed. "But you all deferred to Susan," she said.

"Did we?"

Hannah thought back to the group's interactions at the safe
house, remembering how Susan's and Anthony's eyes had constantly darted to Simone—to give her instructions, Hannah had
thought at the time, but now she saw that they'd been checking
in with her, getting her approval. And during the last conversation, the one that Hannah had overheard, it had actually been
Simone, not Susan, who'd made the final decision to send them
to Columbus.

"Huh," she said. "Well the four of you sure put on a good act."

"We have had a lot of practice. Susan, Anthony and Paul are
among the very few who know the truth. And now, you."

Why me? Surely not because they'd slept together. Simone was
the last person in the world who'd let sex rule her judgment. But
why else would she have confided in Hannah?

Simone finished dressing and inspected herself briefly in the
mirror. Her pale eyes, now a gray blue, shifted in the glass and
found Hannah's. She saw attraction in them, but they also held
a new respect. For her, Hannah realized. She felt a gust of something, sweeping through her like a powerful, bracing updraft, and
recognized it finally as pride. How long had it been since she'd felt
proud of herself? More than being desired and trusted, more even
than her freedom, this—the return of her self-esteem—was a gift,
infinitely precious because she knew it wasn't lightly given.

Simone put on her jacket and walked over to the bed. "And now, I must go out for a little and get you a cash card and some food for the journey. The less often you have to leave the van, the more safe you will be."

"I have plenty of money," Hannah objected.

"You cannot access it. The moment that you use your NIC, the police will know where you are."

"Right. Of course," Hannah said, feeling foolish and naive.

"Do not be embarrassed, *chérie*. It takes time to learn how to think like a ruthless terrorist."

The comment didn't register for a few seconds, but when it did, Hannah dropped her jaw and widened her eyes in burlesque surprise. "I can't believe it."

"What?"

"You, Simone, actually made a joke."

Simone smiled wryly. "*Ben,* there is a first time for everything." She bent down and gave Hannah a lingering kiss. Hannah felt her lips tingle, an electric thrumming. "I will return in one hour," Simone said. "And then, perhaps . . ." She dragged her thumb across Hannah's lower lip, eliciting a soft, involuntary moan.

Simone chuckled. "Wait for me. I will drive fast."

After she left, Hannah flopped back onto the bed and stared as Simone had at the ceiling, letting the events of the morning—immense, concrete, irrefutable—take shape in her mind. She'd just been intimate with another woman. She'd initiated their intimacy, taken pleasure in it, felt deeply connected to another woman. Did that make her a lesbian then, or a bisexual? Would she be attracted to other women besides Simone, or had this been an anomaly, sparked by her kidnapping, near-rape and rescue? A phrase came to her: "the act of love," and Hannah shook her head, rejecting it. She cared about Simone. What they'd shared had gone beyond sex. But there hadn't been the fever of love between them, the yearning of two souls for union, not like she'd once known with Aidan.

And might again. Her earlier thought about going to him in Washington came winging back. She'd resigned herself to never seeing him again, but now that it was possible, now that she'd been given this unexpected chance to travel on her own, how could she not at least try? She needed to look into his eyes and know the truth of his feelings for her. To ask his forgiveness, to hold him and be held, to weep with him for what they'd lost. But what if he refused to see her? Surely he wouldn't be so cruel, even if he were no longer in love with her; at least, the old Aidan wouldn't. But the one she'd seen on the vid at Susan and Anthony's . . .

There was only one way to find out.

She sat up and turned on the vid. Her first thought was to call him, but she rejected it almost immediately. He could be with someone, and besides, she wasn't ready for him to see her. She'd have to face him eventually, of course, if her plan succeeded, but not today. She knew if she let herself go there now, to that moment, she'd never find the courage to contact him.

She opened her mail account, intending to send him an audio message, and there, waiting for her, were three vidmails from Edward Ferrars, one of them sent just four days ago, on Christmas morning. She felt a feathered rush of hope, mixed with worry. Now that she was a Red, netspeak was riskier than ever. She knew the government randomly monitored the mail accounts of Chromes, and she could only hope that Aidan's messages would get lost among the millions they had to keep watch on.

She opened the first one, sent the evening of December 8—two days after she'd left the Straight Path Center. Aidan's face was drawn and tense, his complexion curd-pale, as if half his blood had been drained from him.

"Hannah, where are you? Ponder Henley called me yesterday. He told me he had to expel you from the center. He said dreadful things about you, things I can hardly believe." Despite his agitation, he kept his voice low. He must have been at home then, calling her after Alyssa had gone to bed. "I don't believe him, Hannah, I know you better than that, but—" he faltered, and she looked at the rumpled sheets that surrounded her, the loaded pistol on the nightstand. She saw herself shouting at the enlightener, threatening Cole, defying Simone, pointing the gun at herself. How little he did know her now, she thought.

"You haven't been answering your port, so finally I called your parents' house. I just hung up with your father. He's out of his mind with worry, and so am I. He said he waited for you all night last night and you never showed up." Hannah pictured her father driving around the parking lot until the lights from the stores were extinguished and the shoppers and then the employees parked in the far reaches of the lot drove off, leaving him alone, growing more and more scared and despondent as the hours passed and she didn't appear. *Oh, Daddy, I'm so sorry.*

"I can't even find you on geosat, because your signal has disappeared. I don't know what to do." Abruptly, he looked away, toward something outside the field of the screen, and she heard a faint female voice—Alyssa, who else could it be?—call out something unintelligible. Aidan pinched the bridge of his nose between his thumb and forefinger and let out a pained breath. "I have to go now. Please, Hannah, call me or send a message as soon as you get this. I need to know that you're all right. If anything happened to you . . ." His voice cracked. "I love you."

The image froze. Hannah sat back, stunned. So, as recently as

December 8, he was still grieving her absence. What could possibly have happened to transform him so dramatically?

She played the second message, dated eight days later. And there he was, the new, improved Aidan, ardent and vibrant, his despondency gone as though it had never existed. "My love, I've spent the last week praying to hear from you, praying that you're alive and safe. I have to believe you are, because if you were gone from this world my soul would know it." He leaned forward. His skin actually seemed to be glowing, as if it were lit from within by an otherworldly radiance. He'd never seemed more beautiful to her, or more remote. "I once told you I could never leave Alyssa, but that was before you disappeared, before I spent the last week thinking I'd lost you forever." He passed a hand over his face. "Hell is a paradise compared to where I've been. You can't imagine."

Hannah recalled the hours, days, weeks she'd spent racked by the pain of the Aidan-shaped hole in her heart. "Oh yes, I can," she whispered.

"I prayed to God for guidance, and then last night, at the moment of my deepest despair, He sent me a vision of us, living together openly as man and wife. We stood side by side in a circle of golden light, and I knew that if I could hold that light in my hand I'd be one, not just with you, but also with God. But as I stretched out my hand to grasp it, it disappeared, and you with it, leaving me alone in the dark. And into that darkness He sent a second vision, showing me the price I'd have to pay for loving you. I'd be cast down, cast out—of the cabinet, of my ministry, of the hearts of all those who've believed in me and looked to me as an example of godliness. I would be a worm and not a man, scorned and despised by all who saw me. But I'd be with you, Hannah, and I'd no longer be living this lie that burns inside of me, this constant red heat that torments me with the difference between what I seem to be and what I am.

"What God was telling me, as plainly as if He'd spoken in my ear, was that the truth alone will save me, and that without it, without you sharing my life, I have no life, only darkness and death." Hannah rocked back and forth on the bed. How could she have doubted him?

"I'm going to ask Alyssa for a divorce," he said. "But before I do, I need to know that you've forgiven me, that you still love me. If you don't . . ." His face sagged, and she saw the same hollow despair she'd seen in the mirror for weeks. He banished it with a shake of his head and said, "No—I can't believe it. However much I've wronged you, I know your forgiving nature, the constancy of your heart. And I can't believe that God would have sent me these visions if it weren't in my power to make them real. So please, my darling, call me and give me the courage to do what I need to do, so that we can begin our life together."

The message ended. Hannah rocked herself, her emotions a welter of love and pain, joy and disbelief. *Our life together.* Whatever she'd expected him to say, it hadn't been that: the very thing she'd always longed to hear from him while knowing she never, ever would. And now, he'd said it—and gotten no reply from her for almost two weeks. What must he be thinking? That she was dead? That she no longer loved him?

Resisting the urge to contact him right away, she played the final message, which he'd sent at five o'clock on Christmas morning. He looked awful: drawn, pallid, manic. His forehead bore a faint sheen of sweat.

"Hannah, I still haven't heard from you, and I can only pray it means you can't forgive me, and not that you're ill or in some sort of trouble. If you've been harmed in some way because of my cowardice, I'll never forgive myself."

He reached up and gripped the cross around his neck so hard that his knuckles turned white. "I wanted to be sure that you were mine, but I see now that this is the final test the Lord has set for me, that I confess the truth to Alyssa without knowing whether you still love me, without knowing where you are or even if you're alive—though I believe you are, I have to believe it. My parents are staying with us through the end of next week, but as soon as they're gone I'm going to tell her. And then I'm coming back to Texas to find you." Aidan's color was alarmingly high now, and beads of sweat dotted his brow. "I won't fail the test this time, my love. I won't fail you or our Savior. I swear it." The message ended.

Hannah scrambled out of bed and over to the vid. "Compose reply, audio only." Her mouth was so dry it came out as a croak. She paced in front of the screen, anxious, confused. What would she say to him? What did she want to say? "Stop recording."

She went to the bathroom, drank from the tap and splashed water on her heated face. She studied her reflection in the mirror, trying to parse her feelings from her expression. She had no doubt that he meant what he said. He would wreck his marriage, his ministry, everything—for her. They would weather the storm somehow, marry, go somewhere and live quietly, grow old together. It was a beguiling vision, and a familiar one. How many times had she lain beside him or in her own lonely bed and fantasized just such an ending to their tale? Except the Hannah in those fantasies had been someone else, and not just because her skin had been white. What she'd told Simone was nothing less than the truth: she couldn't go back to being that person. But could Aidan love the Hannah she'd become?

The faint sound of voices outside reminded her of the minutes passing. She had maybe half an hour before Simone returned. She hurried back to the vid. "Show quickest route from here to Washington DC, avoiding all known checkpoints."

She studied the shimmering red line: a bumpy diagonal leading northeast through Alabama to Atlanta, through North Carolina and into the southwestern corner of Virginia, up I-81 along the line of the Appalachians to northern Virginia and then due east to Washington. The driving time was eighteen hours, plus stops, which she planned to keep few and brief. Two nights, then. She'd hole up tomorrow somewhere in North Carolina. And then, the next day, she would see him. And she would know.

"Resume audio recording." She took a deep breath. "Aidan, it's Hannah. I just now got your messages. I'm safe, and I'm coming to you. There are things you need to know, important things I have to tell you before you speak to Alyssa. I'm in Mississippi now, it'll take me two days to get to Washington. Send me an address, and I'll be there sometime before dawn on Monday. Until then, I beg you not to tell her about us. And whatever you do, don't tell anyone you've heard from me, not even my parents. Please, Aidan. Wait for me." Her face flamed as she registered what she'd just said. She ended the recording abruptly, before she could add, *I will drive fast.*

S HE WAITED TWENTY AGONIZING minutes for his reply, hovering by the window, watching the parking lot with mounting anxiety. When the vid finally informed her she had a new message from Edward Ferrars, her heart leapt into her throat.

There was no picture this time, only audio, sent from his port. She could hear street noise in the background. "Hannah, thank God you're all right." His voice was so pitted with emotion she scarcely recognized it. "But why did you leave Texas? You know if they catch you they'll add years to your sentence. They could even send you to prison. Dear Lord, the thought of you in one of those places—"

She heard someone else speaking, interrupting him. A woman, but not Alyssa; the voice was too low-pitched, too coarse. "I'm sorry, Hannah, just a minute," he said. And more faintly, "Yes, I am, but—" The woman's voice rose, became an excited babble. He cut her off. "Yes, all right. Do you have a pen?"

Hannah groaned in frustration. Aidan was constantly being accosted by people wanting his autograph or his blessing or both. He would pray with them, lay his hand on their foreheads, scrawl his name onto their port screens and the backs of receipts, pages torn from magazines, dollar bills, palms, forearms, whatever they thrust into his hand, while they watched with hungry adulation. Sometimes they wept. He never said no to anyone, never expressed the slightest impatience, but she could hear it in his voice now as he hurriedly asked Jesus to give the woman another child and stop her husband from drinking.

Hannah paced back to the window, just in time to see the van pulling into the motel's parking lot. "Fast forward thirty seconds."

". . . don't know what to do, Hannah," Aidan was saying. "I'd tell you to stay put and wait for me to come to you, but I have no idea if you're somewhere safe or when this will reach you or how you're traveling. One thing's for certain, you can't come to the capital. There are too many checkpoints, and they're constantly moving them around. Let me think a minute." He paused.

"Come *on!*" Hannah exclaimed. Simone was getting out of the van, would soon be climbing the stairs, opening the door. What would she do if she discovered Hannah had been in communication with someone from her former life? Would Simone carry out her threat? Was she capable of that, of killing someone she'd made love to a mere two hours before? Hannah's instincts said yes.

"All right," Aidan said finally, "here's what we'll do. I have a weekend house in Maxon, Virginia, the address is 1105 Chestnut. Go there. I'll drive out tonight and disable all the sensors, and I'll come to you Monday morning as soon as I can get away. The police make regular patrols so if you have a car, don't park it at the house. The train station's about a mile away, you'll have to leave it in the lot and walk from there. I'll leave the back door unlocked. Oh, and if you get to the house before dawn, don't turn the lights on. There's a flashlight on the wall in the mudroom, use that." A long, hard exhalation. "Please, my love, be careful. I—"

Hannah heard footsteps approaching outside. "Log out. Vid off," she said. She remained standing by the window and composed her face into a smiling mask. Simone opened the door and stepped inside, letting in a cool rush of air that smelled of the sea.

"That was quick," Hannah said, a little too brightly.

Simone cocked her head, regarding Hannah with slightly narrowed eyes. "I keep my promises," she said. The unspoken challenge seemed to hang in the air between them: *Do you?*

But the moment passed. While they ate, Simone pulled up a map on the vid and plotted a rough route north for her, through Alabama and Tennessee to Kentucky, West Virginia, Pennsylvania and then up through New York. She highlighted an area on the New York/Canada border. "This is where you will cross the frontier. But first, you will go here, to the town of Champlain. You must cross between midnight and two in the morning. If you are not sure you can arrive to Champlain in time, wait wherever you are until the next day. You must not park the van in town." She switched to satview and zoomed in on a small commercial building. "Go to Main Street and look for this place, Aiken's Animal Clinic. You see the sign? If all the letters are lit, you cross that night. If one letter is dark, you go the next night. If two, the night after. It should not be more than two, but make certain you have enough food with you just in case, because once you arrive to the final point, you will not be able to leave it until it is time to cross."

"And where is the final point exactly?"

Simone refocused the map. "Here. An abandoned farm, I will give you directions. Park in the barn and wait until midnight to cross. When you leave, turn off the jammer of the van—you must not forget to do this, otherwise they will not know you are coming—and walk due north. I will give you a compass with which to navigate. It will be very cold, so wear all the clothing you have. After a half hour, take off the ring and let it fall. Someone will come for you."

Puzzled, Hannah asked, "If I have the ring, why do I need the van's jammer at all?"

"The rings are not nearly as powerful, and they can be unreliable," Simone said. Hannah frowned. Susan hadn't told them that.

What if it failed when she was with Aidan? Would the police arrest him too, for harboring her at his house?

Simone snapped her fingers. "Are you listening? For this and many reasons, leave the van only if you must, and when you do, make it quick."

She continued the list of dos and don'ts: Cross state frontiers on the smallest routes possible. Avoid all tunnels and important bridges, even if you must go miles around. Leave the speed control system of the van on at all times so you will not exceed the limit by accident. Turn on the privacy mode before sleeping but leave it off while driving, it makes the police suspicious. Apply mud to the plates to obscure the word "Texas." Do not carry the gun into stores or restaurants, too many of them have metal sensors. Use only toilets with exterior entrances. If you are attacked, cry "Fire!" not "Help!" You will want to run but you must hold yourself and fight unless you are certain you can escape. Smash the nose first with the heel of your hand and then attack the balls. Do not use your knee, he will be waiting for that, kick them as hard as you can with your foot. Do not stop at truck stops, there are too many lonely men. Do not park in small towns or rich neighborhoods. Never ignore your instincts. If you feel yourself afraid, there is probably good reason for it.

Hannah grew increasingly nervous as she listened to this matter-of-fact recitation. She'd forgotten, during her weeks at the Straight Path Center and the safe house, how hazardous a place the world was for a Chrome. She repeated the instructions after Simone, committing them to memory, knowing she couldn't afford to forget again.

Finally, Simone showed her how to load and fire the pistol. Feeling its cold heft in her hand, Hannah wondered if she was capable of using it. On herself, yes; if she were about to be captured, she was pretty sure she wouldn't hesitate. But could she do as Simone said and shoot someone else, aiming for the chest, for the kill, without stopping even for one second to think about it or trying to reason with her assailant?

Simone took the gun from her and set it back on the table. "We have a little time until sunset," she said. She ran her hand lightly up Hannah's arm to her neck and gave her a knowing smile. "How shall we pass it?"

Hannah stiffened, just barely, but Simone felt it. Her hand dropped to her side and her eyebrows lifted. *"Non?"*

"I, I don't know," Hannah stammered. This morning she'd thought Aidan was lost to her, but now that she knew he wasn't, that she'd be with him in two days, how could she be intimate with Simone again? How could she want to? Because the fact was, a part of her did want to. "This is all just—" she broke off and looked down at her hands.

"Hannah." When she didn't look up, Simone gently lifted her chin. "Listen to me. Do not worry about this . . ." her hand waved rapidly between the two of them, "about what has passed between us. Perhaps you are a lover of women or perhaps not. You cannot possibly know, in the midst of a *crise* of this kind, who and what you are. But I pray to God that you will have the chance to find out one day."

The sincerity in the other woman's voice took Hannah aback. Somehow she'd always assumed Simone was an atheist. "Do you mean that literally? That you pray?"

A Gallic shrug. "But of course. Without God, we have no purpose, no soul. We are just walking sacs of blood and bones."

"But . . . But—you're a lesbian."

"So?"

"So how can you pray to a God who considers you an abomination?"

Simone let out a distinctly impious snort. "I do not believe in this God of theirs, this pissed-off, macho God of the Bible. How can such a being exist? It is impossible."

Hannah found herself envying Simone's certainty, even as she doubted her words. "What makes you say that?"

"If God is the Creator, if God englobes every single thing in the universe, then God is everything, and everything is God. God is the earth and the sky, and the tree planted in the earth under the sky, and the bird in the tree, and the worm in the beak of the bird, and the dirt in the stomach of the worm. God is He and She, straight and gay, black and white and red—yes, even that," Simone said emphatically, in answer to Hannah's skeptical look, "and green and blue and all the rest. And so, to despise me for loving women or you for being a Red who made love with a woman, would be to despise not only His own creations but also to hate Himself. My God is not so stupid as that."

MY God. Hannah shook her head, stunned by the concept. There was only one God, you couldn't just make up your own. Certainly not in the faith she'd been raised in, which was fixed as absolutely as a figure in a painting. The Mona Lisa's hands would always be crossed just so. She would never turn to look at the view behind her, never smooth an errant lock of hair from her face, never yawn or grin from ear to ear. You could observe her, but it certainly wasn't your place to take a brush in your hand and change something you didn't like about her. Even to think of doing so was heresy.

And yet, Hannah's parents had taught her that faith was deeply personal, something between her and God alone. The contradiction struck Hannah now, as she fully appreciated how little volition she'd ever had in her own faith, how little her opinion had ever mattered.

"My God is a God of infinite wisdom and love and compassion," Simone was saying, "not some bully who spends His time in throwing fire and uh . . . rocks of *soufre*—"

"Brimstone," Hannah supplied.

"*Brimstone* at homosexuals."

Could it be true, or was it just wishful thinking on Simone's part—and her own? Because if Simone were right, Hannah might yet find a way back to Him.

"Your God is beautiful," she said.

"But of course," Simone said.

Beautiful, and seductive. Hannah's mother would have said this was Satan whispering in her ear, but it didn't feel that way at all; it felt too clean for that, too numinous. She hesitated, then asked, "Did you ever lose Him?"

"I thought I had, after I was raped, but that was idiotic. How can you lose what is inside of you, what is integrated in each molecule of your body? You cannot lose God any more than you can lose your brain or your soul. Without either of them, there is no you."

"There is only the void," Hannah murmured, and as she said it, her dream from when she was unconscious came back to her. Only the void, cold and black and empty. A place she never wanted to go back to. She shuddered. Simone saw it but made no move to comfort her. The other woman's gaze was steady and compassionate, demanding nothing.

Hannah leaned forward and kissed her softly on the cheek. "Thank you. For everything."

Simone smiled. "It was my pleasure."

And mine, Hannah thought, *and there's no getting around it.*

Simone went to the window, pulling the curtain aside to peer out. "The sun has set," she said. "It is time to go."

As they packed up, Hannah reflected how easy it was, in hotel rooms, to lose track of time. With Aidan, it had always passed too swiftly, and then it was time to steal out, her first and then him, into the night, to their separate lives. She'd never once done as she had this morning with Simone: lain beside him and seen the light of dawn illuminate his face.

In two days, perhaps, she would.

When they got to the van, Simone surprised Hannah by asking her to drive. It had been months, and she was a little jerky at first. Simone gave her directions but was otherwise silent, contemplative. Hannah found herself tensing. Did Simone suspect something? Was she about to change her mind? Hannah kept her eyes on the road, trying not to appear as culpable as she felt.

But when they arrived and parked in the lot, Simone programmed the van to respond to Hannah's biometrics and then pulled a large book from beneath the passenger seat: a battered North American road atlas, ten years out of date. "What's that for?" Hannah asked.

Simone gestured at the dash, and Hannah noticed for the first time that there was no nav. "We do not use navs. They have memories, and the sat companies keep records that the police can access whenever they want. So, we navigate in the old-fashioned way." She handed the atlas, along with a wristwatch that was also a compass, to Hannah, who eyed them dubiously. "In all cases," Simone said, "the jammer blocks the sat signals, so even if there were a nav, it would not work. You will be invisible. Not even we will be able to track you."

Simone was watching her closely, and Hannah nodded, hoping her relief didn't show. She hadn't even considered the possibility that the Novembrists would be able to follow her movements. *Some terrorist I'd make.*

"The most important thing to remember, Hannah, the thing you must do immediately if you think you are at the point of being caught, is to turn off the jammer. That way, we will know, and we can take the necessary steps to protect ourselves." From whatever Hannah told the police, under interrogation. "And if you are caught outside the van, let fall the ring if you possibly can."

"I will," Hannah said, humbled suddenly by the enormity of what Simone was risking in letting her go. This was pure faith on the other woman's part—faith, she was uncomfortably aware, that was partly misplaced. She slid her hands under her thighs to keep from fidgeting.

As if reading her thoughts, Simone locked eyes with her. "I trust that you will keep your word and not contact anyone you know. You do not have a port, but this will not stop you from using a public netlet if you choose, or of calling once you arrive to Canada. When you feel yourself tempted to do this, and you *will* be tempted, if not today then next week or next year, remember, you hold in your hands the lives of many good people."

Hannah waited, expecting a threat, but none came. Somehow, that made her feel even guiltier. "I'll keep my word," she said. *Except in this one thing.* "And I'll keep your secrets." That, at least, she could honestly promise.

"*Bon,*" Simone said. Her expression softened. "And now, we must follow our own roads. There are two ways we say goodbye in Québec. One is *adieu,* which is 'goodbye forever.' The other is *au revoir,* which means 'until we meet again.'" She leaned forward and kissed Hannah lightly, first on the lips and then on the forehead. "*Au revoir, ma belle. Courage.*"

"*Au revoir,*" Hannah replied automatically. It was only as she was pulling out of the lot that she realized she hoped it would prove true.

SHE HEADED DUE northeast, pulling over periodically to consult the atlas, cursing the lack of a nav and the need to leave the interstate every time she crossed a state line. The maps weren't completely accurate, and she burned a good two hours trying to find back roads into Alabama and then Georgia.

She made her first stop outside of LaGrange. The van's charge was getting low, and after six and a half hours behind the wheel, she needed to stretch her legs and use the restroom. She decided to bypass the busy, well-lighted chains just off I-85 and settled instead on a small, dumpy juice station a couple of miles down the road. She chose it because it was poorly lit with no other customers in sight.

She was scanning the cash card Simone had given her when she felt the prickling of eyes on her back and turned to see the clerk watching her from inside the store. She started the charge, locked the van and headed for the restroom at the rear of the building, walking quickly with her head down.

"Hey, lady, where you think you going?" a male voice called out.

Hannah turned and saw the clerk standing in the doorway. He was middle-aged and dark-skinned, with eggplant-colored half-moons under his eyes. His stance was unmistakably aggressive. "To the restroom," she said.

He wagged his finger at her. "No. No Chromes using toilets."

Her bladder was burning. If she didn't go soon, she'd wet herself for the second time in two days. "Oh, come on. I'm paying for a full charge. Surely that entitles me to use your restroom."

As soon as she'd said it, she knew it had been a mistake. The clerk stepped outside and strode toward her. He was a little shorter than her, but his slender body had a wiry strength. Hannah cursed herself for her imprudence. Why had she argued with him? She felt in her coat pocket for the gun and realized she'd left it in the van.

As he neared her, his hostile expression turned speculative. His eyes dropped to her breasts, returned to her face. He smiled, revealing stained, crooked teeth. "Yes, lady, you are right, and Farooq is wrong. Farooq must keep the customer happy, this is the number one rule. Come, he show you where the restroom is." He waved toward the back of the building, sending the reek of unwashed male wafting toward her.

Hannah felt a hot bolt of fear. She glanced quickly at the road, but there were no cars in sight. She was completely alone with him. "Never mind," she said.

She started to edge away from him, toward the van. Still smiling, he mirrored her movement, keeping his body between her and escape. He spread his hands wide. "Why you leaving, eh? Farooq is very sorry, he should not have said no. He have a nice clean toilet, good for lady, you will see." He took a step toward her, and she stepped back instinctively. Another few feet and they'd be behind the building, out of sight of the road.

"I really need to get going." She considered running for the van but knew she'd never make it in time. Her mind raced, trying to remember the moves Simone had shown her. In the motel room, Hannah had felt strong and confident, but here, now, she wondered how she could possibly pull them off. He took another step toward her. This time she held her ground.

"Stay away from me."

His eyes narrowed. She could feel the aggression coming off him in waves, like heat off newly laid tar. She subtly widened her stance, inching her left foot slightly forward and bracing the right one for kicking. All she had to do was disable him long enough to get to the van. He moved a little closer, but not quite close enough. His stench was dizzying. She drew her arm back, bending her hand at the wrist to expose the heel. *Smash the nose first and then attack the balls.*

Just then, she heard a vehicle approaching, a motorcycle from the sound of it. Farooq froze and angled his head in the direction of the sound, but he didn't take his eyes off Hannah. They stood together for long seconds in a tense confederacy, the foggy strands of their breath twining in the chilly air. The motorcycle slowed and its whine lowered to a drone. Farooq scowled and looked over his shoulder as it appeared and turned into the lot. It pulled up to the pump directly behind the van.

Weak-kneed with relief, Hannah stepped out from behind the clerk, and the driver swiveled his head to look at them. She started walking briskly toward the van. She was halfway there when he pulled his visor up, revealing his face.

His bright, lemon yellow face.

As she neared him she saw that he was young, about her age, with African American features, and big. His biceps strained against the leather jacket he wore. His eyes, she saw, were a startling aquamarine, like two exotic fish swimming in a yellow sea. They moved from her to the clerk and then back to her. "You all right, ma'am?" he asked. His voice was unexpectedly soft and genteel.

She stopped in front of him. "Yes, thank you," she said in a quavery voice. "Thank you so much."

The stranger cocked his head and surveyed her. "He didn't lay hands on you or hurt you in any way?" Hannah heard it then, a molten, barely checked rage that she knew was not just directed at Farooq, but at all those who victimized Chromes, taking advantage of their vulnerability, secure in the knowledge that they could do so with relative impunity. She felt that same rage rising in herself, imagined the stranger's yellow fists crashing into the clerk's face again and again, turning it to pulp. She shook her head, dispelling the grisly image. "No, really, I'm fine."

"Well then," he said, raising his voice so Farooq could hear, "I guess it's his lucky day." He looked over her shoulder, leveling a flat, deadly gaze at the clerk. Hannah turned and saw him take a step backward. The stranger revved his engine, and Farooq jumped. He seemed to go berserk then, brandishing his fists at them and bouncing frenziedly from foot to foot.

"Fucking Chromes, you are dogshit! You soil the ground you stand on. Get off my property, or I will call the police!"

With a last, grateful look at her rescuer, Hannah hurried to her vehicle, ignoring the fulminating clerk. The stranger waited while she unhooked the cable with clumsy hands. She got in the van and started it, and he pulled up alongside her. She rolled the window down. "You take care, now," he said.

She searched his yellow face, wondering what crime he'd committed. Whatever it was, she thought, he'd just earned some absolution for it. "You too," she said, and then surprised herself by adding, "God bless you."

"YOU'RE DRIVING ERRATICALLY," the van admonished, adjusting Hannah's steering for the third time in twenty minutes. It was still an hour from dawn, but she was struggling to stay awake. Mindful that she couldn't afford to draw attention to herself, she got off the highway in Greensboro and parked in the lot of a twenty-four-hour dollar store. She slept badly, racked with cold and troubled by nightmares, jerking into wakefulness at every slight noise.

That night, as she was squatting behind a bush somewhere in Virginia, she thought how tired she was of feeling weary and afraid; of never being able to let her guard down. She'd avoided public stops since the incident with Farooq, doing her business in the woods or in the weeds behind deserted barns, surrounded by the chirping of insects, the peeping of frogs and the rustling of branches and dead leaves. She was unused to such sounds, but they didn't frighten her. In fact, they had a calming effect.

She was stirred by the beauty of the increasingly rolling expanses of country—so different from the flat, endless, cookie-cutter suburbs of North Texas—between the cities she traveled through; by the swathes of untamed forest in North Carolina; by the looming grandeur of the Appalachians to the west, dimly and intermittently glimpsed by the light of road signs and the glow of cities. She yearned to see this land by day but knew she never would, now. She imagined the many wild places in Canada, vowing to visit them and perhaps even to settle in one of them. She was sick of people and the stink and noise they made, clustered in large numbers; sick of cement under her feet and the press of buildings with their rows upon rows of windows staring out like blank, lidless eyes; of straight lines and right angles; of starless, yellow-gray nights and sunsets made spectacular by pollution.

When the clock on the dash went from 11:59 to 12:00, she felt a flutter of excitement mingled with nervousness. It was December 31, New Year's Eve. The day she would see Aidan.

Last year, she'd celebrated at home with her family and some friends from church. She'd smiled and refilled people's glasses with sparkling cider, and when midnight arrived, she'd lifted her own glass and kissed her parents, Becca and the others, wishing them a joyous New Year. And all the while she'd been picturing Aidan with Alyssa at the annual black-tie fundraiser for Save the Children, knowing that their images would be plastered all over the net the next day, Aidan looking handsome in his tuxedo, Alyssa smiling up at him; knowing that she would be incapable of not searching for them, of not scrutinizing his features for signs that he was truly enjoying himself with his wife.

Today, she had no reason to be jealous. Today, she would see him. And he would see . . . what? The woman he loved, or a monstrosity? What if he no longer desired her? What if her red skin was a stop sign he simply couldn't go past? How could she bear to look at him and not touch him, kiss him, hold him one last time? The knowledge had crouched in a dark closet of her mind since the moment she'd decided to come to him, and it burst out now, awful and unassailable, into the light.

After tomorrow, she would never see Aidan again.

He couldn't join her in Canada; if he did, the Novembrists would certainly find out and kill them both. Simone might delegate the job to someone else, but she'd see to it that they were silenced. She'd have no other choice, especially given Aidan's celebrity. Even if he and Hannah left North America, there was nowhere in the world they could go where his face wouldn't be recognized. And she wouldn't subject him to this danger and perpetual, gnawing dread.

But. For a day and a night, he would be hers, and she wanted it to be perfect, a shining jewel she could carry with her into the blank expanse that was her future.

It wouldn't be enough. It would have to be enough.

. . .

THE COUNTRYSIDE SURRENDERED to suburban sprawl as she neared the capital. She exited I-66 and headed south, into the residential purlieus of Washington's elite. The farther she got from the highway, the more immaculate the neighborhoods and the larger and more stately the homes.

At last, she reached Maxon. It was impossibly quaint, more of a village than a town, with a single stoplight. As she waited for it to turn green, a light snow began to fall, lending the scene an even more surreal perfection. Hannah could picture Alyssa here, shopping with a wicker basket on her arm at The Gourmet Pantry, having her hair done at the Ritz Salon, sipping on a latte with a friend at the Muddy Cup. She could see Aidan, browsing for a gift for Alyssa at Swope's Fine Jewelry—nothing too ostentatious, a string of pearls, perhaps, or some tasteful diamond studs—and then presenting them to her over crème brûlée at Chez Claude. A dream life, one Hannah tried and failed to imagine herself entering into.

Her hands tightened on the steering wheel as she turned onto Chestnut Street. It was as picturesque as everything else, broad and tree-lined, with large wooded lots and gated manors set well back from the road. Number 1105, from what little Hannah could make out, was a white Colonial farmhouse with a big porch and dark shutters. A pine wreath with a cheery red bow hung from the wrought-iron gate. Alyssa would have hung it herself, Hannah thought. She would have stood back about where Hannah was now to be sure it was perfectly centered, adjusted it a little, smiled with quiet pride at her handiwork. Alyssa would have chosen this house and decorated it, furnishing it to Aidan's taste and her own, adding the feminine touches that made a house a home.

What in the world am I doing here? Hannah had the sudden urge to turn the van around, head back to the highway and keep driving to the Canadian border. But if she did that, she would break his heart. She was going to break it anyway, she knew, but she didn't want it to be out of cowardice.

And so she proceeded down the street, crossing a bridge over a small brook, passing more homes, a darkened church, a public park. It was almost midnight, and the train station was deserted except for a handful of unoccupied, snow-dusted vehicles, most of them foreign, all of them expensive. Feeling stiff and creaky after seven hours behind the wheel, she put on her coat and gingerly slid the gun into the right pocket, then grabbed her backpack and opened the door, bracing herself for the cold. It had been in the mid-fifties when she left Mississippi and in the low forties in Greensboro, but a cold front had swept in, and the numbers on the van's temperature gauge had dropped as she'd gone north. Here, it was seventeen, and within seconds of leaving the van she discovered that there *was* no bracing for this kind of cold. Hastily, with a silent thank-you to Susan and Anthony, she put on the gloves they'd given her and drew her hood up over her head, then set off down the road at the fastest walk she could manage on the slippery pavement. The snow grew heavier, swirling into her face and numbing her cheeks, obscuring her surroundings. Still, she was grateful for it; there was almost no one out braving the storm, and the drivers of the few cars that passed her either couldn't see her or were too intent on getting home safely themselves to be curious about a lone pedestrian.

Halfway to Aidan's house, she came to the church she'd noticed before. Now, she was surprised to see, the stained-glass windows were glowing in jewel-toned splendor, and the cast-iron lamps lining the front walkway were lit, illuminating a sign that read: CHURCH OF THE NATIVITY, FOUNDED 1737. Hanging from it, swinging to and fro on its hinges in the wind, was the familiar

THE EPISCOPAL CHURCH WELCOMES YOU sign. She paused at the foot of the walkway, admiring the church's dramatically peaked roof, its massive bell tower topped by a white clapboard steeple. Hannah had always liked the aesthetics of Episcopal churches, their spareness and grace. Once, driving past the Church of the Incarnation in Dallas with her mother, Hannah had remarked on its beauty.

"Beautiful is as beautiful does," Samantha Payne had retorted, referring of course to the Episcopal Church's notorious liberalism: its early opposition to melachroming and the SOL laws, its sanctioning of divorce and women priests, its tolerance of premarital sex, homosexuality and alcohol consumption, and most damning of all, the willingness of some parishes to be presided over by gay priests and bishops.

Hannah arched her neck and followed the line of the bell tower up to the snow-shrouded spire, a finger pointing to God in longing. She wondered whether this church would indeed welcome her, an adulteress who'd had an abortion, lied to the police, run from justice and had a homosexual affair.

"May I help you?" a man's voice said.

Hannah jumped and dropped her gaze to a strip of golden light on the side of the church. A face stuck out from an open doorway. Hannah knew she should turn away and keep walking, but she was paralyzed, so rattled that all she could do was stare, like a large, red rabbit caught in a pair of headlights.

"You must be freezing," the man said. "Why don't you come in and warm yourself for a few minutes?" His voice was clipped and a little brusque, but also kind. It reminded her of something; she couldn't think what, but the association was a positive one, engendering trust.

Trust no one but yourself. "Thank you, but I'm fine," she replied, snapping out of her stupor. She gave a little wave of thanks, ducked her head and turned away, knowing full well that even with the snow, he had to have seen her upturned red face by the light of the lamps. *Please, I'm harmless, I'll go away. Please don't call the police.*

"There's no one here but me," he called after her. "Are you sure you won't come inside?"

Hannah stopped and looked back at him, and then up at the church's stained-glass windows, wanting more than anything to step over the threshold into that jeweled luminescence, that possibility of grace. It came to her then, where she'd heard his accent before, that same nasal, aristocratic enunciation, and although she wasn't conscious of having made a decision, she suddenly felt her legs carrying her up the walk toward the widening strip of light.

And then, just as suddenly, they weren't, because her feet were slipping on a patch of ice and flying out from beneath her. She landed hard, on her behind. The pain was intense, almost as bad as the time she'd fallen out of a magnolia tree and broken her wrist. Dazedly, she wondered, *Is it possible to break your behind?* She started to laugh and then to cry at the same time, heaving sobs that grew in intensity and volume, building to a near-howl. Though she was aware that she was putting herself in danger—nothing like a hysterical Chrome on your doorstep to make a person call the police—she was helpless to stop herself. The fear, uncertainty and sadness of the last days erupted out of her into the snow-laden air and were absorbed in its whiteness.

A face was bending over her. A hand lightly slapped her cheek, once, twice. Hannah blinked, and her hysteria gradually subsided into hiccups. She registered wrinkles, short gray hair, kind eyes. A black shirt, high-collared, with a white rectangle in the center. A priest. A priest, she realized, who wasn't a man but a woman, a woman who was brushing the snow and tears from Hannah's upturned face with brisk tenderness and saying, in a voice almost identical to President John F. Kennedy's, "Are you all right, dear?"

"I don't know. I fell on my rear end. Hard. *Hic!*"

Her rescuer—yet another rescuer—laughed. "Well, we all do that, from time to time."

The priest hoisted Hannah up, grunting with the effort, and for a woozy moment she was back in the motel room, being lifted from the bed by Simone. Only when she was standing did she register how tiny the woman was, and how inadequately dressed. She wasn't wearing a coat, just a cotton shirt and trousers, and she was trembling from exertion or cold or both. Hannah stood upright, taking all of her own weight, and the priest straightened with a soft grunt.

"Let's get ourselves inside, shall we?" she said. "It's colder than Jack Frost's balls out here."

REVEREND EASTER—"YES, that's the name I was born with, God's not the least bit subtle when He really wants you to do something"—led Hannah down a hallway to a small, cluttered office paneled in dark wood, settled her into an armchair and covered her with a hand-knitted blanket before bustling off to get some refreshments. Hannah sat limp in the chair, her mind shuttered to everything but the small realities of this moment: the throbbing of her tailbone, the tingling of warmth returning to her fingers and toes, the smell of books and old wood and furniture polish, the distant shriek of a stove-top kettle. Reverend Easter returned bearing a tray with a plate of cookies and two steaming mugs of tea. She set it down on her desk, shoving aside a pile of papers, then went to the bookcase and pulled a bottle of amber liquor out from behind a large, leather-bound tome—*The Lives of the Saints,* Hannah saw, with amusement. The priest held up the bottle. "This is from Scotland, the land of my forebears. They were coal miners, most of them: dirt-poor, old by thirty and dead by forty, forty-five if they were lucky. My great-great-great-grandfather indentured himself for seven years to get the money to pay for his passage here. Amazing, isn't it, what people will do in search of a better life."

No, Hannah thought. *Not so amazing.*

Reverend Easter poured a generous amount in one mug and a splash in the other and handed the former to Hannah. The pungent smell of alcohol assaulted her nose, and she held it at arm's length. "You drink every last drop of that. Consider it medicinal," the priest said, with serene authority. Hannah complied, raising it to her lips and taking a tiny sip. She expected it to be acrid and unpleasant, but it was delicious, tasting of honey and lemons and something charred that must be the Scotch. And it did make her feel better, and swiftly, fanning ripples of warmth outward from her belly, relaxing her muscles and soothing her frayed nerves.

Reverend Easter sipped her own in companionable silence, leaving Hannah free do nothing but sit and warm her bones. The older woman—Hannah guessed she was in her late fifties or early sixties—looked at her from time to time, her expression curious but not avid or calculating. Not judging. The priest didn't want anything from her, Hannah realized. Not thanks or contrition or confession, though she had the sense that if she wanted to confess, Reverend Easter would listen with sincere interest and unflappable calm, no matter what came out of Hannah's mouth. She studied her companion for more clues to her nature, wondering what it was like to be a female priest, whether she'd ever been married—she wore no wedding ring—and how much of what the Bible said was true she actually believed. Somehow, Hannah couldn't imagine a woman who kept a secret stash of whiskey and referred to Jack Frost's balls like old friends believing there'd been dinosaurs on Noah's Ark.

"Feel better?" Reverend Easter asked, after a while.

"Much. Thank you."

"Well," the priest said, with a satisfied nod, "that explains it."

"Explains what?"

"You know that nagging feeling you get sometimes, like you've left something undone? Less than an hour ago I was in my nightgown, brushing my teeth, seconds away from crawling into my warm bed, when it reared up and started its poking and prodding. 'Oh, no,' I told it, 'I'm not about to go out in this mess, there aren't a dozen people in this entire city who know how to drive in snow, and though I may be old I'm not ready to die just yet.' But it's stubborn, that feeling, even stubborner than I am. It just kept pestering me until finally I gave in and got dressed and drove back down here. And now, I know why."

"You think it was because of me."

"I'm sure of it."

"Do you believe it was God's doing?" Hannah wanted so badly for the priest to give an equally unequivocal answer: *Yes, absolutely, of course it was.*

"Do you?" the priest asked.

"I'd like to, but . . ." Hannah shook her head.

"But how can God exist, in the face of all the cruelty and injustice in the world, is that it?" the priest supplied.

Hannah nodded, and Reverend Easter said, "A Catholic would tell you that questioning God is your first mistake, that faith must be blind and absolute or it's not faith at all. Of course, if I were a Catholic, I'd be wearing a habit not a collar, and my opinion about such important doctrinal questions wouldn't matter a damn to anyone." She took a sip of her tea and considered Hannah with arched brows. "Something tells me you're familiar with that kind of faith."

"Yes, I am, but I'm not . . . I wasn't Catholic."

Reverend Easter waved her hand dismissively. "It doesn't matter to God what we call ourselves, or even what we call Him. We're the only ones who care about that. But as an Episcopalian and not an evangelical," she said, with a knowing look at Hannah, "I'll answer your question with another question, or rather, with a bunch of them, which is how we tend to do things. How else do you explain the miracle of your beating heart, the compassion of strangers, the existence of Mozart and Rilke and Michelangelo? How do you account for redwoods and hummingbirds, for orchids and nebulas? How can such beauty possibly exist without God? And how can we see it and know it's beautiful and be moved by it, without God?"

Hannah felt a jolt of recognition, of rapport. But then, with a shrug, she refused the offered bait. "Maybe beauty just is," she said. "Maybe it's inexplicable, or beyond explanation."

Reverend Easter beamed with the pride of a teacher whose student had just solved an especially tricky equation. "An apt definition of the Almighty, wouldn't you say?"

Hannah bit her lip and looked down into her nearly empty mug, swirling the remaining liquid around.

"You don't have to stop thinking and asking questions to believe in God, child. If He'd wanted a flock of eight billion sheep, He wouldn't have given us opposable thumbs, much less free will."

Hannah stared at the eddy in her mug, her thoughts an untidy muddle. She'd been taught that free will was an illusion; that God had a plan for her and for everyone, a pre-mapped destiny. But if that were true, then He'd meant for her to get pregnant and have an abortion, to be chromed, to be despised and humiliated, kidnapped and almost raped. She saw suddenly that this was at the core of her loss of faith: a reluctance to believe in a God who was that indifferent or that cruel.

And yet. There had been good things too, gifts of kindness and love: Kayla, Paul, Simone, the messages from Aidan, the stranger on the motorcycle, and now, this compassionate, knowing priest. Hannah had not been tortured by the Fist, had not been raped or captured by the police. God's doing, or the result of her own choices—to become Aidan's lover, to have the abortion, to take the road the Novembrists offered, to make love with Simone? What was all of that, if not an exercise of free will? She squeezed her temples between her thumb and middle finger, feeling confused and utterly spent. How could predetermination and free will both exist?

"It's late, and I can see that you're tired," the priest said kindly. "I'll just ask you one more question. You needn't answer it unless you want to."

Hannah made herself meet the older woman's gaze, prepared to say, *Because I had an abortion.*

"I know why I'm here tonight," the priest said. "Do you?"

"No," Hannah said. A lie, but if she spoke the words—*I came looking for Him*—then she would have to act on them, would have to leave the shelter of her skepticism and hack her way through the tangle of her doubts and fears, failings and longings. What if she lacked the strength? What if she mustered the strength, but there was no grace at the end of the journey? What if she found grace but lost herself again in the process?

"If you want to unburden yourself, I'll listen." Reverend Easter bowed her head slightly and angled her body away from Hannah's— inviting to her to confess, she realized, and to receive absolution.

What a relief it would be to lay down her burdens, to hand them off to Reverend Easter and to God! But as badly as she wanted to, it just felt too easy right now, and too overwhelmingly hard.

"I can't. I'm sorry."

Reverend Easter turned back to her. "There's nothing to apologize for. When you're ready, you'll know it."

They stood, Hannah with a wince. "You should take some aspirin and put some ice on that when you get wherever you're going. Cabbage leaves are good for swelling too."

Hannah smiled at the image of herself walking around with cabbage stuffed down the back of her pants. "Thanks, I will."

When they reached the side door, the priest asked, "Can I drop you somewhere?"

"No, I don't have far to go."

Reverend Easter considered her, head tilted to one side as if she were trying to make out the words to a faraway song. "That may be," she said finally. "Or it may be that you have a greater distance than you think. But either way, you'll get there eventually."

Hannah leaned down and gave her a swift, impetuous kiss on the cheek. The priest stiffened involuntarily, and Hannah knew somehow that she was uncomfortable because she wasn't used to being touched. Was she lonely? Did she ever regret the choices she'd made?

"May I give you a blessing before you go?" the priest asked, her color high.

Hannah took the other woman's hand in both of her own, ignoring the slight resistance, and squeezed it. "It's not necessary, Reverend. You already have."

. . .

SHE ENCOUNTERED NO one else on the way to Aidan's. She was the sole inhabitant of an eerie white universe, silent except for the *squidge* of her boots on the snow.

She had an anxious moment when she came to the gate and another at the back door, but both were unlocked as promised. She stepped into marvelous warmth; wastefully, Aidan had left the heat on for her. When her eyes adjusted to the darkness, she saw the flashlight on the wall. It came on when she pulled it from the socket, revealing a narrow room lined with boots, umbrellas and coats hanging from a row of hooks. One was empty, and she hung her own jacket there, between a large wool overcoat and a smaller light blue one. The irony of the arrangement wasn't lost on her, but she was too weary to care.

She took off her boots and moved through the house in her stocking feet, getting quick glimpses of a large kitchen, a formal living room, a family room. She found the stairs and went up them, feeling like a burglar in an old vid, flinching a little with each protesting groan of the wood. Half a dozen doors opened off the hallway. She hesitated before turning the handle of the first one, hoping it wasn't the master bedroom. She didn't want to see it, didn't want its specificities imprinted on her brain: the antique or modern wood or wrought-iron frame of the queen- or king-sized bed where Aidan and Alyssa slept; the stripes or flowers adorning the cotton or linen of the duvet cover or bedspread or handmade quilt; the pale pink or yellow of the cotton or silk or cashmere robe draped carelessly over the chaise longue or footboard of the bed; the two pairs of satin or leather or boiled-wool slippers on either side of the bed, neatly aligned, waiting for his and her feet.

She opened the first door and found a book-lined office. As she stepped inside Aidan's scent enveloped her, triggering an ache, a hollow pang akin to hunger. The temptation to linger here in his

sanctum, to shut the door, turn off the flashlight and sit breathing in his scent in the chair that had cradled his body countless
times was outweighed, barely, by her need for sleep. She left, closing
the door behind her. The room across the hall, she was relieved to
find, was the one she sought: a smallish guest room with a double
bed and a connecting bath. She dropped her pack gratefully on the
floor and shucked out of her clothes, wrinkling her nose at their
musky odor. It occurred to her that she could give Farooq a serious
run for his money, but she was too done in to do more than run a
wet washcloth over her face and upper body and brush her teeth
before collapsing into the bed.

Her last thought before sleep claimed her was of Reverend
Easter, snug in her nightgown in her own lonely bed. Without
pausing to think about it, Hannah sent off a prayer that the priest
would have a long and happy life, and someone to love her and hold
her in his—or her—arms at the end of it.

THE RHYTHMIC CREAKING of the stairs yanked her
from oblivion into instant, total wakefulness. She waited, holding
her breath, and heard him pause, as she had, at the top of the stairs.

"Hannah!" he called out. His voice was hoarse, urgent. She felt
it enter into her blood and tissue and bones, felt her body incline,
plantlike, toward it, even as her mind quailed. The moment was
here, now.

"Hannah?" he called again, a question this time, colored with
worry.

"I'm here," she said. She heard his step quicken and sat up in
the bed.

"Where?" he cried.

"Here, in the guest room," she said. The windows were heav-
ily curtained, but there was morning light coming in from the

hallway. At the last second her courage failed her, and she shifted position, putting her back to the open door. She heard him stop on the threshold.

"Hannah?"

"Close the door," she said, "and leave the light off."

He made a sound of impatience and longing. "No, my love, please don't be ashamed. I want to see you. I *have* to see you. Do you think it matters to me—me, the man who is to blame for your suffering!—what color your skin is?"

She heard him take a step toward her. "Don't," she said sharply, and he stopped.

An image came to her from "Beauty and the Beast," not the sanitized version she'd grown up with, but an older, darker tale she'd found in an illustrated book at the library, about a maiden who was forced into marriage with the king of the ravens and carried off to his castle. He'd been turned into a raven by an evil sorcerer who'd cursed him to remain a bird for seven more years. Until then, she was allowed to see him only during the day, in his bird form, and was forbidden to see him at night, when he took off his feathers. For six years and 364 days she lay obediently beside him, their bodies separated by a sword. But on that last night, she couldn't bear it anymore and decided to see what he looked like. She lit a candle and found a naked man, beautiful beyond words, lying on the other side of the sword. A drop of wax spilled onto his bare chest, startling him awake. By seeing him in his true form, he told her, she'd cursed him forever. Hannah had never forgotten the engraved image of the young girl, mouth agape in wonder, staring down at the horrified face of her husband in the instant he apprehended his doom.

Hannah knew that Aidan meant what he said. He was a hundred percent sure that if he turned on the light, he would see beauty and not a beast. *But what in life is a hundred percent sure?* He thought he was prepared for the sight of her, but she knew that he wasn't, any more than she had been, in the Chrome ward. He'd be horrified, even if he didn't let his face show it.

"I'm not ready, Aidan," she said. "Please, do as I asked."

She waited. The door shut, plunging them into absolute darkness. He remained standing near the doorway, his breathing loud and uneven. She could feel his uncertainty fighting with his need. She went to him then, navigating by the sound of his breath. Her outstretched hands found his chest, moved to his face. His arms encircled her, and he gasped when his hands discovered her nakedness. He breathed her name, once, and then he was crushing her against him, kissing the top of her head, her brow, her cheek, her lips, her neck. He moaned and fell to his knees, wrapping his arms tightly around her waist, pressing his face into her abdomen. She felt the wetness of his tears against her skin, the wetness of his mouth, descending. But that was not what she wanted now, not what her body was demanding, and so she dropped to her knees and kissed him, drawing his tongue into her mouth, unzipping his pants and pulling him onto her, into the churning, heaving river that was her body. The current swept them up and carried them home.

SOMETIME LATER HANNAH sat up and got to her feet, swallowing her groan of pain so as not to wake him. Making love on a wooden floor had not, in retrospect, been the wisest choice given the tender state of her backside. She tiptoed from the room, closing the door behind her, and headed downstairs in search of a glass of water. It ought to have been unsettling, walking naked through Aidan's house, Alyssa's house, but instead it gave Hannah a sense of power, primitive and deeply satisfying. She felt certain that neither of them had ever walked unclothed in this or any other house they'd ever lived in. Even in the dark, even if they were completely alone, they would put on a robe. Once, Hannah would have too, but she was no longer that person.

According to the clock in the kitchen it was just after eleven in the morning. There was an almost completely brown banana in a bowl on the counter, and she peeled it and gulped it down in three bites. She hadn't eaten since the cookie in Reverend Easter's office, and before that, since the soggy half-sandwich and bag of chips she'd stuffed in her mouth yesterday afternoon, right before she'd left Greensboro. She eyed the fridge and the coffeemaker longingly but settled for the banana and the water and headed back upstairs to shower. She didn't dare linger; Aidan might wake and come seeking her, and she didn't want him to see her, not yet.

And maybe not at all, she thought, studying her garish reflection in the bathroom mirror. Why break the enchantment and sully what they'd shared, and their memories of it? For she had gotten her wish: their union had been perfect, complete. And as with Simone, healing. Hannah had been objectified by men ever since she was chromed, treated as a thing to be used and disposed of. Being with Aidan had offset that ugliness, restoring her balance. Cleansing her of hate.

In the past, she'd experienced their lovemaking as an intimate incursion—a piercing, not just of her body but of her being. She'd welcomed it, even though the puncture wounds never quite healed; even though a small part of her was always left aching and empty. But today had been different. Today, for a few precious minutes, she'd felt that she and Aidan were truly one: that he was inside of her, and she was inside of him. His dream came back to her: *We stood side by side in a circle of golden light, and I knew that if I could hold that light in my hand I'd be united, not just with you, but with*

God. Perhaps that's what mortal love was, she reflected: a faint, fleeting glimpse of what it would be like to be one with God. This morning, with Aidan, she'd felt true exaltation for the first time in her life.

And tonight, she was painfully aware, she would have to leave him.

He was still asleep when she returned to the bedroom. She paused in the doorway, gazing down at him in the light from the bathroom window. Her eyes confirmed what her hands had told her earlier: he'd grown thin, almost gaunt. Even so, he was beautiful. If anything, his fragility made him more so, lending him the potent allure of the ephemeral: a firefly, a rose in full bloom whose beauty sears the heart because it will soon be gone. She shivered, chilled by the thought.

Aidan stirred, and she slipped inside and closed the door before he could see her. "I'm cold," she said, getting into bed. "Come join me."

He got up, stumbled, banged a knee or an elbow against the bedpost. "Ow!" A rueful laugh. "You might have let me get my pants all the way off."

"I was in a hurry."

He slid in beside her and pulled her to him. "Well, you needn't be, my love, not ever again. We have the rest of our lives." She didn't move or make a sound, but Aidan's body went taut. "What's wrong?"

A part of her wanted to lie to him, to give him the gift of this last day together, unburdened by the knowledge that they must part. But in the end she found that she couldn't. She'd crossed into a place where truth, even if it was brutal, was all she had to offer. And so she pulled out of his embrace and told him: about her ordeal at the Straight Path Center, her near-capture by the

Fist of Christ, her deliverance by strangers (she said only that it was a group opposed to the Fist), her flight from Texas and near-enslavement and near-rape by Farooq. She spared him her amorous encounter with Simone but none of her trials, though she knew the telling would wound him. Only the full truth would make him let her go.

He was agitated during her account, moving restlessly in the bed and letting out sporadic exclamations of shock and distress. Hannah stopped with her arrival here, postponing for now the moment when they'd have to speak of the future. Aidan lay silent and still. She reached for his hand and found it ice cold. His entire body was cold and clammy, and she wrapped her own around it to warm him.

He released a ragged breath. "How can you ever forgive me?" he asked.

She'd known this was where he would go, but it exasperated her nonetheless. "There's nothing to forgive, Aidan. I'm not a child that you've wronged or led astray." She felt him tense a little, and she softened her tone. "What I'm trying to say, what I need you to understand, is that at every point along the way I made my own choices, the choices that felt right for me, and that I'm prepared to live with the consequences. What I won't live with ever again are shame and regret, and I hope you won't, either."

"You sound . . . different. Changed." Was that dismay she heard in his voice?

"I am," she said. "More than you know."

"You're so strong, so certain."

She shook her head. "You can't imagine how lost I've felt in the last six months. I doubted everything: you, God. Most of all myself."

"Doubted," he said. "Past tense." The joy in his voice tore at her.

"Yes. Past tense." As Aidan soon would be. Hannah's eyes burned, and she shut them tightly. He hadn't thought ahead, to where her story inevitably led; hadn't yet seen the place where their paths would have to branch. Very soon she'd have to take him there and extinguish his happiness. But not yet. For just a little longer, she'd allow him the bliss of ignorance.

"I'LL HAVE TO leave you in a little while," Aidan said, after they'd made love again. "I need go home and tell Alyssa."

Hannah lay with her head in the nook of his shoulder. It fit there as snugly as if it had been made to, like a ball in its proper socket.

Except it hadn't, and wasn't.

"No," she said quietly. "There's no point."

He sat up abruptly, dislodging her head. "What do you mean?"

She sat up too, facing him in the dark. "These people I told you about, the people who saved me from the Fist and offered me the road . . . they made me swear never to be in contact with anyone from my past life again. Never." She felt him recoil from the enormity of the word, felt it hunkering over them in the dark. *Sundered,* she thought.

"Nonsense. They can't ask you to do that."

"Aidan, if they found out I'd even spoken with you, much less seen you, they'd kill us both. And if you came with me you *would* find out eventually, no matter where we went. There's no place we can hide."

A silence. "Because of who I am," he said finally. Hannah had never heard him sound so bitter. She longed to comfort him but held herself back.

"There has to be somewhere," he insisted. "Some remote island in Asia or Africa where they've never heard of me."

"It's too dangerous," she said. "I won't subject you to that."

But for a moment, she considered it; envisioned them lying in a hammock next to a rustic jungle lodge, ringed by rain forest encircled by a cerulean blue sea. Her head in the nook of his shoulder, her arm draped across his chest, their legs intertwined. Adam and Eve, before the fall. Minus the Tyrannosaurus rex.

"I don't care about the danger," he said.

The vision shimmered and melted away, a last chimera, acknowledged and gone. "But I do," Hannah said. "I can't live like a fugitive forever."

This was the truth, but only a small part of it. The greater truth, which she'd kept at bay for some days now, came to her with quiet certitude: if she and Aidan had ever fit together, they didn't anymore. She'd traveled too far from him, a distance immeasurable in days or miles, and would soon travel even farther. He couldn't follow her where she was going, and she couldn't go back. She didn't *want* to go back, to the world she'd been raised in and the person she'd been in it; the person he'd expect her to be if she stayed with him. Alyssa was his Elinor: mild, virtuous, sensible. Hannah didn't yet know who she was, but she wanted the chance to find out. And if she stayed with Aidan, she never would. She'd just be putting herself into another box.

But Hannah couldn't say that to him; it would just hurt him needlessly, because he wouldn't understand. How could he, being the man he was, leading the life he led? So when he started to object, she found his mouth, put her fingers over it and spoke to him in the language of his world.

"God has important work for you to do, my love." *Your God, who is no longer mine.* "It's why He put you on this earth: to lead people to Him through your faith. 'I will bring the blind by a way that they knew not ... I will make darkness light before them, and crooked things straight. These things I will do unto them, and not forsake them.'"

The Henleys had perverted the meaning of the words, but now, Hannah felt their beauty and their power. There were so many people in the world who were suffering, who needed help, hope, light. And Aidan gave it to them. Whatever his faults, he was a true man of God. "You can't walk away from that, Aidan. Not for me or for anyone."

"No. I gave my word to God, and to you, that I'd reveal the truth. That I'd acknowledge my love for you even if you were lost to me. I owe you that much."

"If you owe me anything at all, it's to fulfill your purpose. If you go through with this, you shatter the hope and faith of thousands of people." *My parents and Becca included.*

Aidan's body was still rigid, resisting. "And you shatter mine," Hannah added. "If the press learned my name I'd be notorious. My picture would be all over the vids. If anyone recognized me, and someone's bound to eventually, they'd report me to the police."

He was silent for a very long time. She waited, stroking his forehead, trying to allay the pain and confusion she knew were roiling beneath her hand. He breathed out, a great gust of air in which she heard exhaustion and surrender.

"You're right of course," he said. "It's liberating, isn't it, when your path becomes clear at last?" His voice was a swan gliding across a lake, the face of Mary looking down on her baby son.

Hannah frowned, hearing echoes of the vidmail he sent her. "So you're saying you won't do it?"

His hand came up and stroked her cheek. "I'll never do anything to put you in danger again."

She wished she could see his face. She didn't trust it, this glassy calm. She took his hand and gripped it hard. "Promise me."

"I won't fail you, my love, I promise. You're my better angel."

He drew her down into his embrace and stroked her back, her hair, her arms. Memorizing her, she knew. Soothed by his touch, she gave in to her weariness and drifted into sleep, much as she had in the car that October day so long ago.

But this time, when she woke, he wasn't there beside her. She listened, felt the emptiness of the house echo in the chambers of her heart. *Gone, gone, gone.* This time, forever.

The door to the bedroom was open, the darkness breached by the faintly throbbing violet light of dusk seeping in from the hallway. She groped for the flashlight, but it wasn't on the bedside table where she'd left it. She risked turning on the lamp and saw it lying by Aidan's pillow. A note was pinned beneath it.

My darling Hannah,
Of everything in God's creation, you are the most beautiful to me. I love you, now and always.
~Aidan

As she read it she began to weep, pressing it with both hands to her breast, where no burning drop of wax had fallen to warn her.

SHE DROVE INTO whiteness: cold, stark, alien, beautiful. The farther north she went, the more the landscape became all of those things. And yet, as strange as it was to her, it didn't feel intimidating. If anything the whiteness seemed to beckon her onward, northward, a tabula rasa promising nothing at all, except a chance to begin again. A new life, empty of Aidan, her parents, Becca.

She mourned their loss as she drove, even as she accepted its necessity. Her family wouldn't recognize her any longer. And if they knew the full truth, they'd be horrified by who she'd become, and she'd resent them for it and chafe under the strictures they'd expect her to live by. Better, she told herself, that they believed her dead. And better that Aidan stayed with his wife in his world, a world that bore no resemblance to the one Hannah hoped to create for herself in Canada. She envisioned the white space she'd seen at Stanton's, the one she intended to furnish according to her own tastes and desires. Aidan would be uneasy and out of place there, and her family wouldn't even cross the threshold.

Kayla, however, would be right at home. If she survived. She *would* survive, Hannah told herself, willing it to be true. Paul would find her—might already have found her—and bring her north, and the two of them would find Hannah. She prayed for that all through the night, uncertain to Whom or what, but with a feeling that almost resembled faith.

She went due north from Maxon, crossing into Maryland and then Pennsylvania on back roads, and finally caught I-81 in Harrisburg. It would have been faster to hug the coast and then take I-87 up, but that would have meant driving across four state borders rather than two, through too many densely populated areas. The heavy snowfall slowed her progress further, but she soon realized it was more of a blessing than a curse. It acted as a cloak for her and a distraction for the state troopers, who were too busy helping the wounded and distraught passengers of wrecked and stranded vehicles to be on the lookout for escaped Chromes. She passed at least a dozen accident sites, illuminated fitfully, like half-remembered nightmares, by the lurid red and blue lights of the police cars and ambulances. She looked straight ahead as she went by, leaving the victims to their tragedies, not wanting their suffering etched in her own memory.

She was unused to driving in such treacherous conditions, but the van was more than equal to the task. Even so, the miles passed with torturous slowness. She'd hoped to drive straight through to Champlain, but as dawn approached she hadn't even made the New York state line. She'd have to sleep another day in the van, and that meant she'd have to stop somewhere and buy a blanket or a sleeping bag. Even wearing every single article of clothing she possessed, she'd nearly frozen to death in Greensboro, and it was a good twenty-five degrees colder here in northeastern Pennsylvania than it had been there. She'd considered taking a blanket from Aidan's house, an act of petty theft that in the end she couldn't bring herself to commit. She had stolen enough from Alyssa Dale.

On the outskirts of Scranton, she saw the familiar holographic bull's-eye of a Target and exited. The snow-encrusted parking lot was nearly deserted, but the lights inside the store were on. She parked, bundled up and hurried to the entrance, worried that they'd refuse her business. But when the rent-a-cop saw her, he brought his hand to his holstered firearm in warning but made no move to stop her, and as she passed the checkout area, she saw that one of the cashiers was a Yellow. The camping section was on the far side of the store. She walked down aisle after aisle crammed with merchandise, wondering that there should be so much stuff, so much of which was unnecessary—though she wouldn't have felt that way a year ago. Then, she couldn't have possibly lived without any number of things: her port, her morning coffee, her good scissors, her Bible. Her sister, her parents, Aidan.

She chose the highest-rated sleeping bag they had, stopped in the food section to pick up some snacks and bottled water, and headed for the checkout stands. The Yellow cashier had a customer, but she waited for him, even though there was no line at the other register. Hannah expected some sort of recognition to pass between them, a kinship similar to what she'd experienced with the motorcyclist, but the Yellow was brusque and hostile. She was

stung at first, but then a kind of empathy kicked in. Why wouldn't
he be surly, this balding middle-aged man who wore no wedding
ring, who worked the graveyard shift at a small-town Target and
had been forced to live as a Chrome for who knew how long? This
could easily have been her own life, if she'd stayed in Dallas and
served out her sentence. She thanked him politely when he thrust
her bags at her, thinking that whatever she'd been through and
whatever she had yet to go through were worth it, to avoid such
a fate.

As she left the store, she saw a sign above the door: HAPPY NEW
YEAR FROM ALL OF US AT TARGET! She paused, registering belatedly that it was after midnight. A new year had begun. Where would
she be, next January 1? In a house or an apartment, in the country or
the city, with a roommate, a boyfriend, a husband, a cat? She audi-
tioned all these scenarios, trying them out one by one in the empty
space in her mind, but none of them lingered or took on any dimen-
sion. Right now, all she could see before her was white.

SHE PARKED IN the lot of a giant outlet mall a few miles
down the road and slept soundly, for nearly twelve hours, bundled
into her sleeping bag on the floor of the van. It was dark again when
she woke, and the snow had stopped. She checked the temperature—
eleven degrees, with a windchill of six—and opted to pee awkwardly into a cup, wrinkling her nose at the smell in the enclosed
space. She poured it out the window, then brushed her teeth,
splashed some water on her face and headed back to the interstate.
On the way she passed a White Castle. Her stomach immediately
started clamoring for a burger, fries and a cup of coffee, but after
a short, ferocious battle between it and her brain, she settled for
another soggy sandwich from the cooler. She ate every last unap-
petizing bite, telling herself wryly that it was the taste of freedom.

The interstate had been sanded, so the driving went faster, and she was hopeful she'd be able to make Champlain by midnight. She stopped at a service center near Syracuse to charge the van. The temperature had dropped to three degrees, and she needed to do more than pee, so she risked going inside to use the restroom. The giant vid in the brightly lit seating area was on, and a large group of people were clustered in front of it, some of them openmouthed. They were so fixated on the screen that they didn't even notice there was a Red in their midst. Hannah paused to watch.

She saw a perky blonde news anchor—the annoying type still trying, at forty, to be adorable—with a shot of the National Cathedral floating behind her. Then the picture cut to Aidan speaking from the pulpit, red-faced and impassioned. Hannah felt a tilting inside of her, a seismic shifting. *No. No, you promised.* She walked toward the vid as if she were walking along the ocean's floor, her limbs slowed by the water's resistance, the sounds that reached her ears warped and nonsensical. She moved into the crowd, straining to hear.

"...New Year's Day service ended in an uproar," the anchor was saying with breathless excitement, "with the collapse of Secretary of Faith Aidan Dale just after he delivered a fiery and unexpected sermon denouncing melachroming as quote ungodly, unconstitutional and inhumane, end quote, and calling upon the Congress and a very surprised President Morales"—quick cutaway to the flabbergasted faces of the president and first lady—"to rescind the practice. He then further shocked the congregation and the world by confessing to having had an extramarital affair with an unnamed woman."

The picture cut back to Aidan. "Behold me now as I truly am," he said, "a sinner who walked among you, hiding behind a mask of godliness while deceit burned in my heart. For over two years,

I broke my marriage vows, in thought and in deed. I betrayed my God and my wife"—cut to a close-up of a stone-faced Alyssa Dale—"and all of you, who believed in me." The picture cut back to Aidan. His complexion was ashen. "But the Lord is merciful! He has shown His mercy by bringing me here, to this holy place, and giving me this precious chance to reveal my shame and hypocrisy in the hope of salvation. Praised be His name! His will be done!" Aidan's face suddenly contorted, and he clutched his chest. He staggered, and then his knees buckled and he fell to the floor.

Part of Hannah fell with him, her own heart spasming, her own breath leaving her body. Was he dead then? She couldn't see him; he was surrounded by a teeming knot of people, Alyssa among them, sobbing now. Someone—the surgeon general—was pumping Aidan's chest. The picture cut to him being wheeled from the cathedral in a stretcher with Alyssa walking beside it, holding his hand. "Doctors at Walter Reed hospital have confirmed that Secretary Dale suffered a mild heart attack. They report that he's conscious, and his vital signs are stable."

Conscious. Stable. The words registered. Hannah's heart resumed beating, her lungs expanded and took in air. *Oh, thank God,* she said, and then she acted on it, falling to her knees on the floor, bowing her head and praying, the same five simple words, over and over: *Thank You for his life.* At some point, she became aware of movement around her, followed by a charged stillness. She looked up and saw that everyone was kneeling in front of the vid, their heads bent in silent prayer. She experienced a moment of incandescent wonder, a sense of being connected, not just to these people, but to everyone and everything alive: every beating heart, every fluttering wing, every green shoot thrusting itself up out of the earth, seeking, as she was, the sun.

Thank You for his life. And for mine.

SHE WALKED INTO whiteness: cold, stark, alien, beautiful. A full moon lit her way, limning the bare branches of the trees in silver and turning the snow into a diamond-spangled carpet gaudy as a magician's cloak. The cold was brutal at first and blade-sharp in her lungs, but after fifteen minutes of wading through foot-deep snow and scrambling out of hidden troughs that swallowed her to the hips, her blood began to warm. The harsh rasp of her breathing was a reassuring counterpoint to the hush of the forest.

When a half hour had passed, she took off the jammer ring and dropped it into the snow without hesitating, well aware that without it she'd be detectable, not just by the Novembrists but also by the border police. She'd left her backpack in the van, following an impulse she hadn't understood at the time, but now, moving forward unencumbered by anything except the watch and the clothes she wore, she grasped why: *You must set foot upon the path with nothing but yourself.* It felt right and necessary, this letting go, this total surrender. She had never in her life been this vulnerable, or felt this powerful.

She walked for another ten minutes, another twenty. Her legs ached, and her jeans were wet and heavy. Was that a flicker of light ahead of her? She stopped and stared in its direction, but it was gone, and when it didn't reappear she decided she must have imagined it. It wouldn't be hard, here in this eldritch place, to see will-o'-the-wisps, fairy lights that would lead her under a snow-covered mound to a hundred years of oblivious slumber. The more she thought about it, the more alluring the idea was: to sleep peacefully for a century and wake to a different world, one with no mela-chroming, no disease, no famine, no violence or hate.

She shivered. How long had she been standing here? She couldn't feel her face or her feet, and her upper body was wet with cooling sweat. She was conscious, distantly, that she was in danger of freezing to death and tried to force her legs into motion, but they were logs, stiff and uncooperative. She looked down at the snow, thinking how lovely it would be to let herself fall into it as she'd let the ring fall, to sink down into that soft, glistening white. A last surrender. A sweet and endless welcoming.

And then she saw the lights, two of them, closer than before. This time they didn't disappear. They grew brighter and sharper, dispelling her lassitude. The Novembrists, or the police? Hannah fumbled for the pistol, but her gloved hand was too clumsy. She pulled the glove off with her teeth and let it fall to the snow. Released the safety, curled her hand around the butt, her finger around the trigger. Turned the gun inward and up, pressing the barrel into the soft hollow at the bottom of her rib cage. She would not go back; only forward, one way or another. She watched the lights come toward her, two lambent eyes, two all-knowing orbs that held her destiny. Freedom, or death?

In the seconds before she learned the answer, she envisioned her life as it might be, furnished the white space with a large, jewel-toned rug, a sofa upholstered in velvet the deep rose of a lover's sigh, a glass coffee table upon which sat a vase of red roses in full bloom. She added music: Ella singing, Kayla and Paul laughing, all three of them sounding as though they'd never known pain. Kayla and Paul were sitting on the sofa, holding glasses of garnet wine. His bare feet were propped on the coffee table, and hers were tucked beneath her legs. His arm encircled her, and his thumb was lightly caressing her bare shoulder, which was the color of light filtered through amber. Kayla said something, and Hannah heard her own laughter, bright and airy, mingle with theirs.

The lights were upon her now, blindingly bright. The forest and the snow and the moon vanished; all she could see were the lights. She put her free hand up to shield her eyes.

"What is your name?" The voice was a man's, with the same French lilt as Simone's.

"Hannah Payne."

"And why are you here?"

The Henleys had asked her that, and she'd answered them truthfully. How different, and how much more rich and vibrant, her truth was now. "Because," she said, "it's personal."

The lights went away, but her eyes were still too dazzled to see. She heard the crunch of feet on snow and finally made out a pale face, white teeth: a man, smiling at her. She let go of the gun, felt herself falling sideways. The man took hold of her shoulders and pulled her upright. Kissed her frozen cheeks, right and then left.

"*Bienvenue,* Hannah. Welcome to Québec. You are safe now, and so is your friend. Simone asked me to tell you that Paul found her and is bringing her here."

Hannah went back then, to the space in her mind that was no longer empty and white. She saw a bedroom with gleaming wood floors and a standing mirror, a bed with a deep violet coverlet, sheer curtains billowing from a breeze scented with the riotous promise of spring. There was a sleeping figure in the bed, lit by a patch of morning sun. Her hair was long and dark, fanned across the pillow, and her skin was a honey-toned pink that would deepen to golden brown in the summertime to come.

She woke, and she was herself.

ACKNOWLEDGMENTS

Writing a novel is an inherently solitary and often crazy-making pursuit. But there are people who see you through it, who inspire and inform and soothe and prod and tolerate and love you, and generous organizations that house and feed you when you're in the throes of creation. I'm especially indebted to the following:

First, my ingenious and opinionated uncle John, who planted the seed for *When She Woke* sometime in the early nineties over a meal and a bottle of wine in Hulls Cove, Maine. We were discussing the drug problem in America, and he said, "I think all drugs should be legal and provided by the government. They just ought to turn you bright blue." The conversation stuck in my mind and eventually bore this dark, strange, red fruit.

James Cañón and Chris Parris-Lamb, my gay and straight angels, without whose encouragement, thoughtful criticism and unwavering faith at every stage of this process *When She Woke* would not exist.

Kathryn Windley, who read *When She Woke* when it was green, and Jennifer Cody Epstein, who read multiple drafts, for giving me invaluable suggestions about its characters and narrative.

Kathy Pories, who followed me willingly into my very un-*Mudbound*-like dystopia and helped me make it believable and good. And the whole amazing Algonquin/Workman team, which I've had to stop talking about to my author friends because they end up feeling jealous and unloved.

Gay and John Stanek, Fundación Valparaiso, Blue Mountain Center, Château de Lavigny, the Corporation of Yaddo, the Djerassi Resident Artists Program, Hawthornden Castle and the MacDowell Colony, for the gift of unfettered time to write in beautiful surroundings. The Barbara Deming Memorial Fund, for the timely grant. And Charlotte Dixon, Carol Chinn, Alice Yurke and Rob, John and Katya Davis, for giving me a place to lay my head when I had none.

Sharon Morris, for allowing me to borrow the lines on p. 199 from her poem "Not Just an Image," which can be found in her marvelous collection *False Spring.*

Dr. Marc Heller, for educating me about abortion and for having the courage to help women in need and to fight for our reproductive freedom, often at risk to his own life. Dr. Eugene Zappi, Dr. Lisa Susswein, Dr. Theresa Raphael-Grimm, Dr. Dan Burnes and Kirk Payne, for helping me create a plausible scientific underpinning for melachroming and fragmentation. Magda Bogin and Barbara Kingsolver, for early enthusiasm. Denise Benou Stires, for lending me her media savvy and her shoulder whenever I needed them. Elizabeth Fout, for her eagle eye. Lisa Dillman, for being naughty with me, and Nora Maynard, for co-founding the TTWWC. Ron Cunningham, for helping me get my heroine across the Canadian border illegally. Michèle Albaret-Maatsch et Julie Talbot, pour m'avoir enseigné à jurer comme un marin en québécois, et Gérard Hernando, pour m'avoir aidé à rendre le dialogue de Simone authentique. Michael Epstein, for the killer photo. And Nathaniel Hawthorne, for giving me such broad shoulders to stand on.

Finally, I wish to thank all my fellow artists, friends and family not mentioned above, whose love and support have sustained me on this long red road of mine.